THE LONE
GLADIO

THE LONE GLADIO

A NOVEL

SIBEL EDMONDS

This book is a work of fiction. Names, characters, businesses, organizations, places, events, and incidents either are the product of the author's imagination or are used fictitiously. Any resemblance to actual persons, living or dead, events, or locales is entirely coincidental.

Published by Sibel Edmonds, Bend, Oregon

ISBN-13: 978-0692213292
ISBN-10: 0692213295

For Ela, light of my life, truth and justice

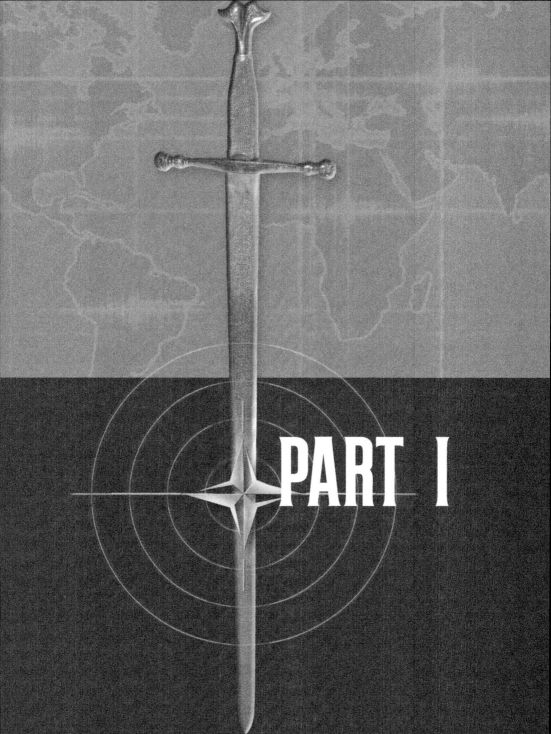

PART I

PROLOGUE

All was quiet but for the lull of small waves and the screech of gulls diving for their breakfast. A body lay crumpled in fetal position between pointy boulders that framed the shorelines of the Mediterranean Sea. This was Northern Cyprus territory.

The lips twitched. No sound but an airless moan. The eyes tried to open: hopelessly crusted; stuck. *Try to move something, anything—* no dice. The pain was so severe he felt himself going into shock.

Some time later. Hours passed . . . *a day?* Jason tried to remember. His wife, Rene—the sonogram—came rushing into focus.

He forced himself. *Think. Remember more.* The image of Nuray flashed before him, her eyes, telling him to . . . then everything went gray. What about Nuray? *That name.* As it started coming back, he lost consciousness again.

The sun was now up. Heat from the boulders revived him. He heard something, or he thought he did—a buzzing vibration like a helicopter. He tried to open at least one eye but only managed to raise his left lid halfway. Despite mucus obscuring his vision like a bloody veil, he was able to make out a group of black objects hovering near his head and neck. At first he took them for monstrous birds, black raptors wheeling high above. Then he saw what they were: bulbous flies, buzzing and landing and sticking to his face.

He felt something thick oozing from his mouth. Though he could taste nothing, it had to be blood.

He remembered now, sitting at a bar; two Russian women coming through the door; and a Range Rover—then driving a considerable distance, pulling off the shoulder to a gravelly beach. As soon as he spotted the other parked car he knew.

A man approached. He came around the passenger side and ordered him to get out. Jason knew him: the one with the scar, loitering at the kiosk. What was that accent, Russian or . . .?

He was told to walk toward the boulders. Both women stayed behind.

The rest was a blur. He remembered a gun pointed at his chest. He tried to say something when the first shot fired. Then three more: two to the legs, one to the stomach. He thought he'd heard a car, the start of two engines then—

Nothing. He could feel it closing in. He tried to fight it. *What was that voice?* Willing himself to stay conscious, he strained his one good eye to see two bodies, standing beside him. They were kids, a boy of six or seven, holding a young girl's hand. His sister? They stood over him, looking with frightened eyes. He wanted to smile, to say something nice so they would be okay. He tried to move his lips, but nothing came out.

He knew it was already too late.

CHAPTER 1

Monday, June 18, 2001
Baku, Azerbaijan

Both alarms—his swatch and the hotel room's clock—beeped in unison at 5:40 A.M. Greg was awake, anticipating them. He walked to the window and raised the shade to watch the street below. Early morning light gave his tall, toned body the quality of marble sculpture. Calm and expressionless, he promptly went over the itinerary.

He went into the windowless bathroom and turned on a harsh fluorescent light. Then he leaned over the vanity to inspect his face. His bleached blond eyebrows absurdly contrasted with his light brown gray-streaked hair. The crow's feet at the corners of his eyes might easily be mistaken for laugh lines; yet three prominent furrows formed a permanent record of a disciplined, mission-driven life. Perfect straight lips betrayed no emotion—none at all.

He stepped out naked and stood in the narrow space between the bed and the L-shaped desk. After two deep breaths, he bent into a crouch and without pause began his daily routine of one hundred rapid knee-bends followed by a hundred push-ups; then a flip to a hundred rapid sit-ups. Breathing and heartbeat held steady during the regiment.

He opened a complimentary bottle of water and emptied it in one long draught. Next, he removed a plastic denture case from his carry-on, took out a tablet in its sealed paper envelope, and then returned the container to the bag.

Grabbing his high-tech swatch, he went into the bathroom, rinsed the porcelain sink, lifted the stopper and filled up the basin halfway with hot water. Then he unwrapped and dropped in the tablet. After a few seconds, once it had dissolved, he set the timer at two minutes and immersed both hands. He waited patiently for the beep as he checked himself once more in the mirror. Six feet two, 186 pounds, 45 years old, and 23 years in the business: Gregory McPhearson—among other names. In fact he had dozens of names and nationalities, different passports, languages, and various job descriptions including engineer, investor, businessman, scientist, techno whiz, both high- and low-level bureaucrat, teacher . . . the list went on. He was an OG Man: OG 68. No one truly knew who he was, if indeed he was truly anyone.

At the beep he removed his hands, pushed down the lever with his right elbow to drain the sink, and rinsed under hot running water. Drying his hands, he examined his shriveled skin: these, no doubt, were his own fingerprints.

Greg checked his swatch. His timing was perfect. Next, a five-minute shower that included vigorous, quick masturbation to optimize and maintain focus.

He dressed quickly in pressed chinos, beige cotton shirt, cream socks and lived-in medium-brown loafers, then carefully placed the sandy-blond hairpiece that matched his bleached Aussie eyebrows.

Dialing room service, he ordered a cup of warm whole milk and one soft-boiled egg. While waiting for his customary mission breakfast, he turned on the TV and played with the remote until the BCB

News came on. He always did that. This was a *company* mission, after all. It felt right.

The breakfast tray was delivered and the waiter received his tip in Australian dollars. Again taking up his carry-on, Greg removed a small-size container of malt powder and poured four carefully measured teaspoons into the warm milk, another set routine.

At exactly 8:30, Greg, wearing Ray-Bans and carrying an Australian-made, burnt-brown leather briefcase, exited the hotel and started toward his first destination.

For this mission he was Luke Garrison, owner of a small computer audio software company, involved in small-scale exports. The front was not for caution dealing with the Azerbaijanis—as they were company friendlies from an ally-controlled, recently taken over territory—but rather to guard against potential Russian agents. Russian spies were always lurking in company-acquired states, especially those *newly* acquired, such as Azerbaijan and Kyrgyzstan; call it a territorial pissing contest.

The older neighborhood changed into a modern landscape where new luxury stores began to pop up, displaying sexy European lingerie, Gucci and Escada leather goods and sunglasses, and cosmetics. He thought of "his" woman—Mai—and tried to picture her in one of the elegant lace and silk robes. He made a mental note to return and purchase the ivory-colored one at the end of the Baku part of his mission.

He crossed the street at the circle, entered the midrise office building, and gave his name to the attractive young Azerbaijani receptionist. She greeted him with a smile, pointed to the black leather seat in the waiting area, and asked whether he cared for some coffee or tea in accented English. He politely declined and took a seat. The office belonged to one of the top global financial investment companies (with headquarters in Fairfax, Virginia) that doubled as a front for the company.

Lawrence Burshaw appeared in the reception area to greet him with a handshake and a Texan howdy. Burshaw was in his late thirties, medium build, with shrewd eyes often found in third-world money grab businessmen.

Greg followed him into a posh office. With the door closed, Lawrence checked his watch. "How're we doing with time?"

"All set."

"So that's it I guess."

"Yes." Greg opened the small coat closet and placed his briefcase on the upper shelf. "I'll retrieve this after I'm done."

Lawrence opened the door. "Follow me." They went down the hall until they reached a door marked EMERGENCY FIRE EXIT in both English and Azeri.

"Take it one floor down and exit through the back alley. Alarms have been disconnected."

Greg nodded and took the exit. Once outside, he turned left in the alley and right into another alley that took him to a main street with a jumble of small shops selling mainly vegetables and fruits, and several teahouses catering solely to Azeri male clientele.

Greg walked another half block before he stopped and entered a large and ornately decorated teahouse. Traditional Persian rugs and kilims hung on the walls and covered wooden backless benches. The entire space was heavy with the aroma of freshly brewed black tea: most distinctly, Darjeeling and Earl Grey; something else—Nilgiri—not so fresh.

The teahouse was half full, a few wooden tables occupied by older men playing backgammon. Younger men in larger groups simultaneously talked, sipped tea, and texted.

At the back was a half-open kitchen with a counter where two dark-mustached men took orders and received payment. In addition to owning and operating the teahouse, the two brothers worked as paid snitches for the Turkish Intelligence—MIT—and facilitated company transit guests, such as now.

All the way back and to the left of the kitchen was a narrow hallway with two doors: one with a WC sign, and the other marked PRIVATE.

Greg approached the men at the counter and greeted them in Turkish, and then added his code—*"Kale uctu. Haziriz."* The younger man nodded.

Greg placed his order for a large tea and proceeded to the back. The brothers promptly ordered staff to move large containers out into the hall, not only to deflect attention but to block the way until all was clear.

Greg slipped into the room marked private and closed the door behind him.

With four quick steps to the back of the windowless room, kneeling down and opening the half wall cabinet, he squeezed inside the tiny space on his knees while his right hand lightly explored the wooden floorboards until it found the four-inch lever. He pulled it up and lifted half of the wooden floor, exposing a ladder leading down into the basement. He went down backward, holding onto the rail with one hand. The brothers would put the floorboard back in place.

At the far end of the windowless basement was a door that opened to a long narrow tunnel, which led to another that branched to the left.

Greg moved through the underground maze until at last he came to wide concrete steps leading up to a shaft blocked by a laminate tile: here was a security access panel with tiny silver numbered and lettered buttons. He entered the lengthy code, looked up at the small lens and waited. At the sound of the beep he pushed up the panel and lifted himself into an empty windowless room with steel walls and one wide steel door. He walked over to it and placed his right hand inside the metal-glass slot. After another set of beeps the automatic door slid open. He was in.

The large underground facility was filled with half a dozen cubicles, some of which were occupied by Western-looking men and

women; it also housed several private offices and a spacious conference room.

Greg checked the latter, a big empty room equipped with high-
tech computers, secure phones, wall-mounted flat-screen monitors,
speakers and microphones. He looked at his swatch. He had minutes
before the session.

Entering an available private office, he inserted a microchip
into one of three large-screen computers. Once his access code was
approved, he was prompted to enter his operation code and date.
He entered the long code starting with *O* and *G*—the company's
macro-operation identity—followed by his ID number, 68, indicating rank; next, two letters and another five digits for the current
micro-operation. To his surprise, instead of *immediate future steps and
details* he received a blinking message: *See OG 52 for changes effective
immediately.*

He removed the chip, leaned back and closed his eyes: time to
conduct a rapid review. He went over the first eight of his twelve-
item checklist. Each had been successfully planned and executed.
That left four final steps: specific target(s), location, execution, and
postexecution publicity and media campaign.

He started with the first two, target and location: sixteen members of the Russian sub–defense ministry, in a conference hall located
in the Hotel Leningrad Europa in St. Petersburg. Execution would
be carried out as per operational directive 02-2001. As to the final
item, postexecution publicity and media campaign, that was not his
area and almost never involved him. So which of the four operation
items was being changed, if only one?

Stop. He would, after all, find out in . . . he checked his swatch . . .
less than ninety minutes. He needed to hydrate. *Never let your brain
get underhydrated during operations.* Spotting the purified water cooler
in the hall, he drank two eight-ounce cups then mentally checked his
heart rate, breathing, and body temperature: all perfect.

Colonel Winston Tanner was already in the conference room, at the head of the twelve-seat table with his steaming cup of Earl Grey when Greg walked in. In his late forties, tall, thin, with the bone structure so commonly found in English men of Celtic origin, the colonel was a good fourteen layers above him in rank and status.

Seated next to the colonel, in a severe pants suit, was a nondescript middle-aged woman who embodied the essence of mediocre. She was medium in every one of her features: height, weight, eye color (medium brown), even the sockets were medium. Greg didn't know her but knew her position in the company: strategic analyst named Maryam, OG 136. The higher the number the lower your ranking—hers indicating bottom level within the company's bottom-tier operatives.

The two men curtly nodded to each other and Greg took his seat.

Across from him, one of the wall-mounted monitors showed the interior of a traditional mosque two floors above them: a large airy room without chairs or tables, decorated with Azeri rugs, kilim-designed floor cushions and intricate turquoise mosaic tiles. This would be where Imams consult with and provide advice to devout Muslim followers.

The colonel was first to break the silence. "I've read the carrier's profile. Good choice as always, Greg. Now, let's see how our Imam performs."

"There shouldn't be any problem or hesitancy," he replied. "Nasrin has been working on her. She was given half the money, and we'll be transporting her daughter to Ankara for the surgery."

He referred to the Chechen woman who would be consulting with the company's Imam any minute. The thirty-two-year-old widow had recently lost her husband, a thirty-nine-year-old Chechen fighter shot and killed by Russians in the last major raid. She had no money and two children, an academically inclined son, fourteen, and a twelve-year-old daughter born with a harelip and no prospect for marriage, thus, survival. The widow's own prospects were slim to none—all of which made her a perfect carrier for the company's coming operation.

"Your Imam has requested a transfer. He says you believe he deserves it . . . and that he is ready," the colonel reported.

"He's done well here for four years," Greg agreed. "I told him to wait until we have his replacement ready. He wants Turkey for his next assignment."

"I bet he does." The colonel chuckled. "He's nowhere near it to ask for a preretirement position. We were thinking more like Kyrgyzstan."

"Yours to do as you wish. He has the language skills, training, and charisma. He'll do well there."

The woman spoke for the first time. "Here he is, our Imam Farajullah."

* * * *

Greg and the colonel turned to look at the screen. The long-bearded Imam, mid to late thirties and traditionally clad, was arranging the extravagant floor cushions. He was good-looking, with dark almond eyes that exuded serenity; even more so his voice and speaking manner, smooth and soft as butter. Innate talent, paired with extensive company training in England and the States, had given him the ability to persuade and even hypnotize people with ease. His followers would do anything for him. They would die for him, and kill many on the way to their deaths. He was a perfect company Imam.

The Imam looked up, confident, into one of the well-concealed miniature cameras. He was ready.

Two women entered the room. The younger was dressed in a modest, long loose dress extending to and covering her ankles; a neat scarf provided full coverage for her hair underneath. This was Nasrin, the company's "facilitator." The older woman wore a traditional veil in the darkest shade of black. She held the two sides together under her chin with one hand, and insisted on looking down at her black rubber clogs. She was their Chechen carrier-to-be.

The Imam greeted the women with a smile and kind eyes. He started off with a few verses from the Quran about life, death and heaven, and about being rewarded for miseries inflicted on you in this life, and that the rewards were contingent upon tests presented by God; he gently went on about partial rewards and punishments issued before death, the larger portion reserved for the afterlife. Then, more somber and serious, he talked about the infidels, the sons of atheists, who killed devout Muslims such as her husband; and the martyrs, and of the special responsibility of those left behind . . . God's test . . .

His thirty minutes of preaching ended with an authoritative question: "Now, are you ready to serve Allah? Are you willful and determined to pass Allah's test?"

The Chechen woman, startled by the abrupt change in the Imam's voice, looked up for the first time. "How can I be sure that I won't be killing any innocent people? How do I know that I will take the lives of the infidel atheists?"

The Imam resumed his velvety tone. "You will know. Within your heart. You will be assured. The answer is already there from Allah. Just listen. You are a chosen one, as was your martyr husband."

The woman was nodding, savoring each word and committing everything to memory.

Nasrin, facing the Imam, held the woman's hand. "The Muslim community has raised money to take care of her son and of her daughter's physical malady. Imam, she wants to know, is this acceptable to God? Will material rewards taint her martyrdom before Allah's eyes?"

The Imam smiled and answered reassuringly, "Of course. Of course it is acceptable. Those generous Muslim donors too are passing a test, making their little sacrifices for your big one—as Allah demands—thus you shall not hesitate to accept their Allah-approved generosity."

Another five minutes of verses, then both women bade farewell to the Imam and proceeded to the praying area above.

The grand mosque doubled as a strategic recruitment and operations center for the company, with full knowledge and cooperation from the country's government. Two sets of tunnels were built to connect the mosque to the Turkish-owned teahouse and the U.S. military attaché building eleven blocks away. The underground operation center coordinated planning and preparation for some of the most elaborately staged terror attacks in Russia, the Caucasus and Central Asia. Many militia-to-be were recruited here, and authentic new passports as well as identity cards and more were produced by operatives in the underground facility.

The colonel removed earpieces that had been transmitting a translation of the upstairs meeting live. "Our man is good."

Greg needed no translation. "I'd say we're good to go. Nasrin will be taking care of medication and preparation, and she'll be ready to deliver on time."

"That reminds me. I'm to give you slight changes on the target and location."

Greg didn't respond, waiting for the colonel to continue.

"Our new target is the day care center of the Russian interior ministry. Moscow."

"Understood. Reason cited?"

"Shock, awe and anger: Children are always best. Young children, the younger the better."

Greg remained expressionless. "As secondary targets, children are one thing; as primary, this will ensure full-scale Russian retaliation against our Chechens. Is that what we're seeking, right at this time?"

The colonel nodded. "Our Chechen base currently is divided.

Those we no longer need will take credit for this attack. Those we keep will run the postexecution show from their HQ in Ankara."

Greg paused. "How do we ensure silence of the other Chechen faction?"

"There won't be any left, at least not with information or ties to us. We're taking out five, three of them in Turkey—blamed on the FSB. We leave a trail of breadcrumbs straight to the Russians. They can blow off steam and throw out allegations, but they won't get far. They don't have our media capabilities."

"We'll have to change the medication and psych prep for our carriers. They can't know or *even suspect* that children are the targets—they won't carry it through, especially the women."

The colonel began packing his briefcase, while the sour woman did the same. "Greg, as far as we know, you don't have a thing for kids. We expect no issues here, correct?"

"That the targets are Russian is all that matters."

The colonel smiled and left without a handshake. The woman followed.

Greg was set. He would leave the way he'd come, then back to his hotel to change, pack, and get to the airport. Just time enough to stop for Mai's gift.

* * * *

Greg did not appreciate the company's last-minute change in plans. Their trademark tactic of *seize, utilize,* and later *divide, abandon or destroy* wasn't the issue; rather, his problem was with the timing. Unless there was more to it—*more*, that is, that he couldn't see—slicing off a faction of their Chechen Jihadis now and feeding them to the Russians could come with a price beyond what they were willing to pay. There could be unanticipated consequences. That would be messy. And messy always bothered him.

With brand-new fingerprints in place, he took up the small wrapped package, opened it, and removed a pair of clear contact lenses, inserting them efficiently. Now the hair, fingerprints and irises were all Luke Garrison's. *No worries mate.*

His itinerary: first to Dubai, a major hub for flights to and from Australia, to throw off any scrutiny; from there he would go to Turkey for three days, then off to Moscow for another three before returning to his home base in Vietnam—and to Mai.

Inside ten minutes he was on his way to the airport, snug in the back of a worn diesel cab.

Greg closed his eyes. He had thirty minutes, more or less— enough time to reflect and rejuvenate his mind.

He visualized the execution stage of this operation, aka What Happens Next.

The Chechen woman, now done up in a poor Russian Babushka outfit, on her way to the four-storey light-gray day care center in Moscow. Hundreds of small children—under age five—their jovial, screaming voices carrying outside. The woman is dazed and glassy-eyed, pumped with hallucinogens and other mind-altering substances, transporting a heavy load: dozens of "bread loaves" for the staff and children's lunch.

Greg's meditation was rudely interrupted by a Nuevo Azeri pop song blasting on the radio. He ordered the driver to turn it off. Irritated, and after no small griping, the cabbie grudgingly complied.

Greg flashed on the janitor's closet on the building's second floor, filled with gallons of igniters hidden inside powdered milk containers, then imagined the undercover operator across the street, ready with her camera. In his mind's eye, he saw the Chechen woman climb the marble steps . . .

*. . . And the company men and women waiting,
listening in anticipation 1,400 miles away . . . the initial
BLAM followed by many more BAMs and BOOMs . . . the
screams . . . the crying. Exploding window glass. Smoke and
the smell of burned flesh. Blood—lots of it—and charred body
parts. Blown-up pieces of people, large and small. A baby's
arm. The operative snapping pictures. Another operative,
less than half a klick away, calling the company overseas. The
sound of the first ambulance and police sirens. Multiple vehicles
converging at once. More sirens. The stench of char and
death . . . of fear . . . of victory—for the company. The stench of
defeat for hope . . .*

He'd had enough.

Back to now. He went over his immediate checklist:

*Short meeting in Dubai inside first-class airport lounge at
the bar. Passport to enter Turkey. Meetings with company men
and sources in Turkey-Ankara and Istanbul. New hair and
eye color, fingerprints, contact lenses, passport and clothes for
Moscow op. Meeting with sources in Hotel Europa. Visiting day
care building: memorize layout. Every curve and alcove, every
nook, every inch.*

When the taxi stopped in front of Baku International Airport,
Greg was here, in present time. He would be Luke Garrison for less
than a day; then Michael Chase for a few days more. After that he'd
be Andrei Volkov. And beneath all, the OG man.

He wasn't sure how this made him feel. And Greg didn't like
that feeling.

CHAPTER 2

Saturday, April 20, 2002
Karsiyaka, Northern Cyprus

At the sound of the doorbell Jason stretched every muscle and willed himself off the sofa where he'd been lazing for the past two hours.

Today was a Saturday in April, with all the windows open. Though ephemeral flowers and vibrant Bougainvillea vines dotted the hilly neighborhood, notorious summer threatened.

Jason crossed the distance between the open living room and the entrance in three long steps.

The petite brunette with hazel eyes was scanning the street behind her and seemed startled when he opened the door.

"Merhaba Nuray. You are not being followed by any scarface, goombahs or mercenaries, I assure you."

Her cheeks slightly colored. "It's not that. Just one of those habits Turkish journalists acquire within the first few months on the job. We call it *survival.*"

"Well come on in," and in strongly accented, newly acquired Turkish he added, "*Hos geldiniz.*"

Quickly, he explained, "No need to remove your shoes—I'm too lazy to give in to that. Besides, I haven't the customary slippers to offer my barefooted Turkish guests."

Nuray stepped into a small living room with tastefully selected furniture. The espresso-brown leather sofa faced two wooden side chairs topped with bright cushions, and in the middle was an impressive antique trunk covered with a laptop, magazines, an English-Turkish dictionary and a pair of Ray-Bans.

Nuray picked the side chair nearest to the open balcony and sat.

"I don't know about you but I'm ready for my cold beer." He pointed to the small yellow retro fridge. "I've got an ice-cold bottle of white wine, Villa Doluca, Efes, and a few bottles of Heineken."

"Efes."

As he went to the kitchen, he saw Nuray stand and nervously begin to pace.

He placed two bottles of Efes on a tray, added two frosty mugs, and carried it to the living room, where Nuray was bent over studying the photo on the side table.

"Our vacation last December on Cat Island in the Bahamas: no cells, no Internet, no TV . . . pure bliss."

Without moving her eyes, she acknowledged the perfect couple: handsome and beautiful, blond and dark, intimate and confident, happy and in love; one, a boyish California surfer, the other, a mixed, mocha beauty with bohemian flair.

"We're expecting. Five months and three days . . ."

Nuray quickly turned, almost knocking the tray. "*Oops*—congratulations! Does this mean you'll be transferring back to D.C.?"

"All settled and confirmed. Back there in September, on leave for two months, D.C. for fifteen months, after that, who knows? Let's have our beer out here, shall we?"

Nuray followed him out to the balcony with its peekaboo view of the not so distant blue of the Mediterranean. A rustic Greek blue wooden table occupied the right side, surrounded by four white wooden chairs with red and blue striped cushions; to the left hung a double wide hammock.

For the first few minutes they sat quietly, nursing and sipping their ice-cold Efes.

Jason flashed back to three weeks ago, to when they first met. His college buddy, Serkan, now in Indonesia working for the IMF, had contacted him about his cousin, a Turkish investigative journalist named Nuray, who accidentally had opened a can of worms—no, make that *poisonous snakes*—involving dark international figures, some highly connected. Two days later, Nuray had called him at the office and they met for lunch in a quiet restaurant run by a local fisherman and his son. They had two more get-togethers since: Hemingway's Bar and the Harbor Tea House.

Jason was first to break the silence. "I've been thinking nonstop about our last conversation. I need to know more. We need documents. I can't take it to anyone until I have something substantial. Did you meet with him yesterday?"

"I did. He's not giving me the actual documents, Jason. Hell, he hasn't even told me everything. But I trust him. Everything so far, one way or another, checks out." She paused. "We have the name of the two banks, several account holders, and enough to trace the money trail. Isn't that enough?"

"When it comes to high-level, well-connected laundering cases, one needs more."

Nuray put down her bottle. "Okay . . . we know they use the heads of states in places like Azerbaijan and Kyrgyzstan to issue government bonds. We know the involved two banks and their connection to high-level Turkish individuals and crime families, including the King of Casinos—you know he also owns ninety percent of the casinos in Azerbaijan, right?"

Jason shook his head.

"Well, he does. Nobody really knows how he got the capital to instantly open them all. Sure, he always had money and access to top underground figures, but nothing like this. What makes it intriguing," she continued, "and also very dangerous, is the connection to the high-level military. One with eyebrow-raising account activities happens to be a Turkish lieutenant general—"

Nuray stopped herself. This was the first time she had mentioned a specific fact.

A Turkish general, Jason acknowledged to himself.

Nuray locked eyes with his. "We know the bonds are being converted to U.S. dollars and being sent to accounts in Dubai with connections to terrorist financiers in several countries including Pakistan . . . oh, and three Russian-sounding—"

Jason stopped her. "Those names may not be real. Highly likely pseudonyms are being used."

"Okay then," she said, exasperated. "Why don't you go ahead and give whatever we have to your FBI—they're all about targeting Arab terrorists, aren't they? Don't they say they are? We're talking men in the upper echelons of the network that brought your nation to its knees less than a year ago!" She brushed aside a curl from her forehead, adding, "They have the means. With what you give them they can take it further and find out the rest."

"It's not just the FBI. State Department also plays a role. I would say this falls more in the area of my agency's work than the FBI. And I'm telling you we need more. You must persuade your source, Nuray. I need documents."

"It's not as if he is one of a hundred in this banking scheme: he happens to be one of *five* management members with direct knowledge. How long do you think it would take them to single him out as a rat—as the leak?" She looked down and said, almost in a whisper, "You know what they do to rats over here . . . in Turkey. This is not like your country. We don't have witness protection. Plus, those with power to grant such immunity happen to be the ones involved in crimes in the first place."

Nuray sighed. She took a long sip from her drink, lost in thought.

Jason could see dark clouds forming in her eyes. "You want another Efes? I can sure use one."

"No." Checking her watch, "I must get going soon."

Jason tried to lighten the mood. "Come on, Nuray, I'm not being difficult; I want this case. But without a significant database here in this dingy little Cyprus division . . . we need more."

Nuray agreed. "Let me think about it and talk with my source. I may be able to get *some* documents without his being jeopardized . . . I have an idea . . . I believe he's holding back. Give me a few more days."

"I *could* try to dig up something from the embassy and facilities we have on the Greek side," he suggested.

"No, no," she quickly dismissed the idea. "The Russians have a major presence with the banks over there: too risky. And frankly, everyone knows that most State Department positions are filled by your own CIA. Why do they even continue using them as fronts?"

Jason sighed.

"We don't want to tip off the wrong people," she insisted. "Just don't do anything yet. Let me see what I can do with my guy first. Okay? Promise me, Jason."

"All right."

* * * *

Sunday, April 28, 2002
Girne, Northern Cyprus

Jason entered the almost empty bar at 11 A.M., walked determinedly to the table and pulled up a chair. Over its back he slung his computer case.

A young waiter appeared and asked in broken English for his drink order. Jason responded in Turkish. The waiter smiled. Like nearly all Cypriots, he loved Americans—unlike Europeans or Russians, Americans always tipped. His draft Efes ordered, Jason returned to his racing thoughts.

He'd finally heard back from Nuray. She had more. "I don't think you're going to like what you see and hear—it goes higher than either of us thought," was the quote. Jason had asked her to meet him right away, but she'd insisted that they meet here, at this peculiar little seaside bar, Hemingway on the Way, the following day. She was adamant.

Before hanging up, she'd said with no small urgency, "Do not approach anyone in your office with this. You understand? *No one.*"

He'd responded with silence—having said nothing about a cryptic phone conversation with his friend Andy, who worked in the U.S. consulate on the other part of the island. He had pressed for access to the department's intel database on Cyprus. Andy, ever curious, was only too willing to help. By the end of their talk, he too had warned Jason to watch his back.

Jason had spent the night tossing and turning, his exhausted mind working various scenarios, a dozen of which were real possibilities. He kept going back and forth.

By 5:30, having given up on sleep, he headed to the shower, and by 7 he'd dressed and downed two cups of coffee.

How would he kill the next four hours? Coming here, to his favorite neighborhood café, seemed the best idea: with feta, olives, honey and eggs. Something, though, made him pause on the way over. A sensation connected to the phrase *watch your back.* He had stopped to scan the street behind him. A boy of six or seven stood in front of a little bakery holding two loaves of Turkish bread.

Up half a block to the left of the boy was a man in his thirties near a kiosk, scanning piles of newspapers and magazines in front.

Here, in this nearly all-Turkish neighborhood, the man stood out as an oddity. He was tall—at least six feet four—well-built and stood erect, with pale Russian–Eastern European coloring and features: blond hair and milky blue eyes. An irregular scar ran from his temple to his left ear.

Jason continued into the alley, paused, and looked behind him before entering the café. All quiet.

Paranoia was as contagious as any plague. He sat with his pint, recalling Nuray's tone. Why was she so keen on pursuing this case without her editor's approval? How had she put it? *Some things are more important than one's career: humanity, justice, the love of one's nation, our family and friends.* It's a nonanswer. At the time, he'd chosen to let it slide.

The question begged an answer. She had gone after this herself—on her own time and her own dime—to what end? Despite growing fear, escalating stakes and increased risk, she was unwilling to let go. Why? Now that she had dragged him into this, he had reason to wonder. Maybe this wasn't such a good idea.

He looked at his watch. It was 11:42 and no sign of Nuray. Their rendezvous was for 11:30. He motioned to the waiter and ordered a plate of fries and another pint of Efes. The waiter eyed his still full glass, and Jason, in broken Turkish, allowed as to how his friend would be joining him any minute. The waiter nodded and smiled, said he'd bring some peanuts to go with his beer while the kitchen fried his potatoes.

It was almost noon. The fries arrived burning hot. As he flagged the waiter for some napkins, he noticed two tall women by the door, scanning the bar area. They looked foreign.

Both, in their mid to late twenties, were stunning—and ice-cold. He guessed them to be Russians. One was naturally blonde, the other, a bottle-induced redhead. The blonde dressed in a skirt suit and heels; the redhead, designer denims, a sleeveless white shirt, and snakeskin cowboy boots with two-inch heels.

The women started to where he was seated. *A Russian hooker duo!* he thought. *Where the hell are you, Nuray?*

The blonde towered over him and in Russian-accented English asked, "Are you Mizter Sullivan?"

Taken aback, Jason nodded.

She bent lower and said, "Our friend asked us to take you to her."

"My friend who?"

"Nuray Akbas. She says she has your present . . . but too dangerous to go around with."

Jason was alarmed. "Where is Nuray?"

"Mizter, that's why we are here," the redhead responded. "We take you to her. She is safe. Don't worry. She is smart girl and knows how to be safe."

Agitated now, Jason stood and motioned for the check. Hurriedly, he placed cash on the table and turned to the women. "Are we walking or taking a taxi?"

The blonde shook her head. Out front, now on the sidewalk, the redhead told her friend, "I go bring round car."

Jason, increasingly distraught, tried with the blonde one more time. "Where is Nuray exactly?"

"She's in a safe place. We'll drive you to her." At that moment, a dark gray Range Rover pulled up to the curb. "We must go. You are coming, no?"

Jason paused. Crazy with worry over Nuray, he was also pissed: she had taken paranoia to a whole new level. He quickly assessed the two women. What could they do to him? On the plus side, they knew his and Nuray's names. They mentioned the evidence, the *present*. Add to that his nationality, his position in the U.S. State Department, being escorted from a populated bar in broad daylight . . . no, he wasn't about to cave to paranoia.

CHAPTER 3

Friday, Late Afternoon, August 29, 2003
Phnom Penh, Cambodia

The beeping of his watch told him it was 4 P.M. On the way to his rendezvous, in that suffocating heat, Lou Brian already had his next move planned out—a frosty mug of that ice-cold golden nectar in an air-conditioned café. Hastily, he turned the corner where the ritzy hotel took up the entire block, making his way into the alley. Halfway in he stopped, glanced at his watch, and took his place near the metal side door. This was to be used by Cambodian staff only.

Lou glimpsed a rat darting in and out of the bins. He looked down and saw a mound of butts. Then he heard the back door open.

A good-looking Cambodian bellhop stepped out and lighted up a smoke. Instantly, he spotted Lou. He gave him the once-over.

Lou could tell what this bellhop was thinking: frayed cargo shorts, camera, phone, sunglasses and water bottle, faded tee with Aussie Outback stencils of smiling kangaroos, open-toed sandals showing hairy toes—milling around the only five-star hotel in Cambodia—*and in a trash-filled service alley! Sure, nobody would notice that.*

Lou nodded. The young man nodded back. After a reserved hello, Lou mentioned a name and handed him a matchbook.

The bellhop read the hastily scribbled two-word code and nodded again. He knew the arrangements. Lou confirmed in simple, monosyllabic English, just in case. The bellhop indicated that he understood.

Now, Lou thought, *here comes the real question.* Sure enough, the young man sheepishly asked for *the money.* Lou explained the deal. They bargained in circles until finally agreeing on half after bugging the room, the remainder to be paid after removing the bugs. Installation was set for noon the next day. Housekeeping would be done by then, with the important American guest expected to arrive around 4 P.M., for one night.

The bellhop checked his watch. "I have to go."

"See you here—right here—at twelve noon tomorrow."

* * * *

Turning into one of Phnom Penh's downtown alleys, Lou found the beer hall he was looking for. Heading straight to the bar, he held his finger up. "One Ganzberg."

It was almost 5. He had time for one more beer, then a quick cold shower back at his hotel, a change into clean clothes and checkout; then, charge his equipment for the following day.

He pulled out his cell, dialed the access code and his girlfriend's number in the States. At the automated sound of her answering service he left an affectionate and slightly X-rated message then put the phone away.

He longed for his girlfriend, Lucy: half-and-half Cambodian American, ultrafeminine, and a beauty. Lucy was the reason he was here on assignment. She worked for two Cambodia-related nongovernmental organizations (NGOs) back in New York City. One dealt with genocide research and the other worked with several international organizations on human trafficking in Southeast Asia. Lucy was the one who had alerted him to credible rumors of powerful, prominent U.S. figures visiting Phnom Penh specifically to engage in sex with children—often boys and girls under the age of six.

Lou had pursued the slippery facts and persistent rumors until he'd established solid leads and contacts. After that, he had pitched his plans—well, more like a proposal—to his boss, haunting the man until at last he relented and assigned Lou the investigation, trip, and, of course, the *documentation* that went with that.

Now here he was, nearing the finish line. This was the final stage, when he would harvest all those months of research, interviews, and more research. Within forty-eight hours he would have provable facts in the form of hard evidence. Add another twenty-four and he'd be in New York with Lucy, job completed—along with the pay and paid vacation. *Jamaica, here we come!*

* * * *

Saturday Noon, August 30, 2003
Phnom Penh, Cambodia

The following day, at 12:07, Lou was inside the lavish presidential suite installing his wireless monitoring devices—in other words, *bugs*. Although not up to intelligence community standards, the devices were by no means old-fashioned; they were in fact the latest in consumer video surveillance and more than adequate for his purpose, with decent resolution and sound quality, motion detection, and wireless to a controller with software and DVD recorder. And finding good spots to hide them was easy.

He had gotten to the hotel ten minutes early, but the bellhop was already waiting. They chatted while they smoked, Lou trying to get the high-profile name out of him; the young man explained, in broken English, how these types of reservations are almost always made through a third party, in this case, a French-sounding company name.

Having strategically placed two devices in the bedroom and one in the private parlor of the presidential suite, Lou exited and took the stairs as instructed by the bellhop: down the hallway, through the employees' canteen on the mezzanine floor and out into the alley where they met at the usual spot.

Lou handed the young man a stack of currency and waited for him to count it. Once he got the nod, he told him, "See you here tomorrow, Sunday, at twelve." The high-profile guest was due to leave by 11 the following morning.

Lou headed to a nearby café where he speed-dialed his boss. After the beep he reported into the machine that phase one was complete.

Then he called Lucy, where he was greeted not with a beep but a soft and sexy kitten voice. He felt good. Things felt right.

* * * *

Saturday Evening, August 30, 2003
Phnom Penh

On the first floor of a residential apartment less than three blocks from the U.S. embassy in Phnom Penh, in a room with curtains drawn, Sander sat in front of three monitors, adjusting volume and zoom control.

One screen showed the suite bedroom with a low California King bed dead center.

The second and third monitors displayed the parlor area where

Donald Keller, clad only in a silk leopard print robe, adjusted a cookie tray on the four-seat dining table. He was a sight: midfifties and balding, with 260 pounds unwholesomely distributed over his five-foot-seven frame. The animal-print silk was translucent enough to show it all, jiggling rolls of middle-aged fat as he delicately arranged the cookies and fruits.

On the other side of the room, two toddler-sized dolls perched on a grand sofa: the one with silky black hair was propped on her stomach with a supersized dildo dangling over her face, her lips just touching the tip; and the other, identical, with her skirt pulled up and panties off, positioned lying down with her smooth plastic legs spread wide. Between them was a second dildo, pointed toward her flat plastic area.

Donald, finished now with the tray, heard the soft knock on the door of the presidential suite.

From his listening cell, Sander yelled, "Bing ba-da boom, it's showtime baby! You comin, Josh?" He heard his partner's footsteps as he turned back to the screens.

Donald now opened the door to Maurice and his Cambodian assistant.

Here was an interesting duo. French-Cambodian Maurice, mid-forties, tall and very thin: he was dressed in creased designer pants and linen buttoned shirt, dark purple—like ripe Italian eggplants. A patterned silk purple neckerchief was carefully arranged around his chicken-thin neck. Small sunken eyes and a wide flat nose gave his face a chilling calm.

As for Maurice's Cambodian assistant, if it weren't for his stoic pose and icy stare, he might pass for a good-looking young man. He wore black leathers and crew-neck top, and pointy red Texan boots with razor-sharp chrome tips.

Behind them were two beautiful Vietnamese girls who appeared to be eleven and thirteen, dressed in traditional white ao dai with turquoise trim.

Donald opened the door wider and let them in.

The two men entered the suite, the little girls following with heads down and eyes on the floor. Neither girl looked up at any point, stationed behind Maurice as though they were hiding.

After a low conversation with Donald, Maurice ordered the girls in broken Vietnamese to go and sit in the parlor. He then turned to Donald. "Mister Keller, sir, enjoy your evening. Phone when you are through and we will pick them up."

Maurice was a legend within this circle of powerful men in need of *extraordinary* subjects. He was discreet, and knew about elegance and finesse. His record was spotless—and he always took care of everything, whether a traceless travel route or an anonymous stay in a luxury hotel. Toddler boy or prepubescent girl, romantic style or kinky and violent preferred, Maurice was the man.

Donald, impatient, dismissed the men with a hastily uttered, "Okayokay, go. At least three hours. I'll let you know. Bye now," then closed the door and locked it.

Sander could feel his own excitement rising. He was new in this part of the world and with this particular target profile. He was the tech geek, and while he'd been on various assignments in other locations, he'd only been a month in Josh's unit. Now here he was, in the thick of it.

Sander didn't like Josh that much; something about his new partner gave him the creeps—a side that repulsed him. Right now, Josh was to his right, drinking in what was happening onscreen.

"The guy's dick hasn't been working," he breathed, "we've got his medical records. Let's see what he has in mind for the two fresh girls."

Fresh? Sander frowned. *Is that what he thinks?* Josh must've noticed, from the puzzled look. "We're going to have him hooked, right?" Sander pressed, eager to retrain the focus.

"Hell yes, if the arrogant bastard doesn't—" Josh quickly turned to the screens. "Hey, the show's about to begin."

Donald moved to where the girls sat squeezed together on the same small chair, quiet, grim. They were trying hard to avert their eyes from the dolls.

Donald grabbed the remote and turned on the music. The opera *Carmen* flooded the room. The girls remained motionless, no reaction.

Donald loosened his robe. Ponderous pendulums of flesh rolled over his minigenitalia. The girls still refused to look, staring emptily at the wall.

Donald called to them lowly. "Girls . . . little girls . . ."; then again, more loudly, authoritative.

Startled, the girls looked up.

Smiling, he pointed to the dolls. "Look at these two girls. They are *good* little girls. I want you to be like them. Can you be good, like them? I think you can."

The girls glanced at the dolls with frightened faces.

Donald untied his robe and let it fall open, exposing two full hairy breasts. He looked like an aging Sumo wrestler, squat and sweating, eager for the prize.

The older girl turned and stared at the cookies and fruit display on the table.

He followed her gaze. "Yes, those are for you, baby. Go on, get yourself a cookie. Soon you'll have my special treat." He laughed. "Go ahead."

The girl looked at Donald, blank.

He pointed to the tray and commanded, "Come get cookie. Cookies are for you."

The girl turned to the younger one, squeezed tight against her side, and signaled something deep, straight into her eyes. Then she stood and moved toward the dining table slowly, elegantly, her face almost serene.

She stopped at the table, her back to Donald and the younger child. In one sweeping motion she lunged for the nearest serrated knife, turned and dropped to her knees.

Sander gasped.

Josh stared, transfixed. "What the fuck is she doing?"

"My-o-my," Donald began, "I like fiery little virgin girls. I am going to give you the honor of—"

Before he could finish his sentence, the girl threw her head back, soundlessly mumbled something in Vietnamese, raised the knife with both her hands and plunged it deep into the crook of her throat.

Blood violently sprayed the upper wall to her right, covering that part of the ceiling. Gurgling now, still kneeling, she stared fiercely at the other child, who appeared to be going into shock. Within moments, blood seeped from the rug to the floor, expanding in every direction. She closed her eyes and fell dead onto her side.

Sander was first to recover his voice. "*Fuck!* What the fuck?" His whole body was trembling.

Without missing a beat or averting his eyes, Josh said simply, "You were right. We really *have* hooked the bastard. He's all ours."

Sander felt another wave—this time of nausea, revulsion, and the sickening release of adrenaline.

Donald went white. The only sound coming out of him now was raspy asthmatic breathing. He looked like a stranded blowfish.

It took long minutes before he could even move. Shakily, he rose and lumbered over to the tiny corpse, muttering. Josh and Sander had to strain to hear until Donald, tottering over the crumpled blood-soaked figure, fairly started shouting, "S-stupid pussy! . . . Crazy *bitch!*"

He paused and swirled around, fixing the younger girl with ferocious eyes. "Do not make a sound," he hissed. "Not a sound. *Quiet.*"

Then he changed direction, heading to the cell phone on a shelf across from the sofa. With his back turned, he dialed Maurice, and at the sound of the automated pickup he dialed again: this time the code for *real bad* emergencies.

As soon as he hit Send, a new sound got his attention. The chair that only a moment ago held a little girl frozen in shock was empty.

Panicked, he scanned the room until his eyes found a silhouette scrambling over the balcony, an ornate French railing. Before he could scream *No!* the shadow had jumped, two storeys—straight down. A muffled *clunk* was followed by the usual street hum of Phnom Penh and motorbike horns' *beep-beep*s.

Sander sprang out of his seat and began pacing. "This is a nightmare—oh my god—this is the worst thing I've ever seen. Shouldn't we do something?"

Josh took out his cell and said over his shoulder, "Yeah. Where the hell is Maurice? We want this guy, and we're not losing him to the goddamned Cam police!"

Donald stared into the abyss, his chest heaving with staccato catching breaths.

A gentle two-beat knock was followed with a louder three knocks at the door.

Donald, still in slow motion, fumbled at the chain. Maurice and the assistant sailed in as Donald quickly closed the door behind them.

Maurice came to a halt. After the second or two it took to regain his composure, he calmly asked, "What have you done, Mister Keller?"

"What have *I* done? You little piece of shit! You bring me two mental, totally defective bitches, who put on a hara-kiri show—and then try to put it on *me*?"

Maurice surveyed the room and hastened to the bedroom, only to return a second later. "Where is the other girl?"

Donald pointed to the balcony with his head. Maurice darted over and scanned the ground below. Then he spewed three terse sentences to his assistant.

The assistant exited without pause.

Donald couldn't contain himself. "Well, what? He's going to get the body?"

"What body, Mister Keller? I see no body there. I sent him for his men to go find her, or her body, whichever; with a fall like that, she can't be too far . . ." Maurice continued, "He also is arranging a new room. We have to move you out of this one before our crew comes in for cleanup."

Donald, now more recovered, emphasized to Maurice, "Do you know who I am? I am WHIP; I am *the* WHIP. This mess needs a pro. We need professionals. How are you going to get—"

Maurice held up his hand. "I have resources, Mister Keller: Intel, men inside the police, whatever I need." After a pause, he continued, "Of course . . ."

Donald gave him a disgusted look. "I don't care what it takes. After the mess you created for me—"

Maurice cut him off. "For the girls you still owe me fifty percent; that's fifteen thousand. With the loss of two investment properties, cleanup and ensuring silence, we are looking at another hundred, at least."

Donald's fish belly face was now turning red, but he decided to hold his tongue.

He looked ridiculous, Maurice thought, this Congressman— *the Whip*—before him in his open robe, angry lobes of quivering fat hiding his shrunken member, so reminiscent of Turkey sticks for toddlers.

"I'll have your suitcases and belongings packed and sent to you in a couple of hours."

Maurice left without waiting for an answer.

Donald put on his creased khaki pants and a crisply ironed powder-blue shirt. In minutes he was dressed; then he exited the suite looking straight ahead, without so much as a single backward glance.

* * * *

Josh grabbed his phone and entered a long string of digits, followed by a code connecting him to his unit's emergency division boss. Then he turned to Sander. "As fucked up as this may seem to you, good sometimes comes from the most deeply fucked situations. Think of it like this: a fuckup for the Whip is a very good thing for us."

"So . . ." Sander hesitated, with a look of agony and disgust. "What next?"

"I don't care what Maurice says," Josh replied. "We need to do our own cleanup. Go ahead and send the encrypted film to the unit. I'll wait by the secure phone for the emergency brief."

Sander nodded and returned to the desk, still trembling.

Keeping an eye on Maurice and his crew, Sander continued to monitor the transmission of the encrypted, time-stamped film, self-consciously labeling the recording *Nightmare on Whip Street (Pasteur)*.

"Talked to the unit," Josh explained. "They're waiting for the big man to come and view the footage himself. They're sending forensics to insure *zero trace* in the room. The guy'll be here by tomorrow noon."

"It takes over twenty hours from the East Coast—"

"He's not Langley: someone from another unit over in Hong Kong." Josh continued, "We still have to do initial cleanup. They want all the transmission units uninstalled. Maurice won't be using the same suite or hotel anytime soon. We don't want to take any chances; this room's served us for . . . what, three years now?" Then he added, "Oh, I instructed Maurice to keep the suite reserved for at least another three days."

Josh looked at his watch. "It's two A.M. We'll leave at two forty-five, and plan to get out of there before five."

Sander closed the bathroom door to shave. That's when he

noticed the freshly used condom in the trashcan next to the sink—another noble testament to Josh. *Typical agency prick*, he thought. *He gets his hard-on from shit like this.*

* * * *

Lou was downing his second croissant when his cell went off at 9:15 A.M. It was his man, the bellhop at Royal. With all the noise he asked the bellhop to repeat himself. "All right . . . say it again. This time slowly."

"Guest check out yesterday. Last night. He now different room to have—you come get stuff out before new guest come. Okay?"

Lou could feel his heart rate accelerating; what could have gone wrong? Had the guest found one of his devices?

He tried to be calm. "Wait a second. What time did the guest change his room? Why, exactly?"

"Mister L, ask again."

This language barrier together with poor cell reception was truly exasperating. "Okay. The guest, what *o'clock* did he move to new room? What time?"

"Night Boy said late. No time. Something happen . . . to room, maybe?"

"Okay, okay. I'm on my way. I meet you in backdoor alley."

Six minutes later, Lou arrived at the hotel's side entrance, in the alley where the bellhop was already waiting.

"How are things?"

"Now the room empty," the bellhop explained. "Housekeeping at eleven. You go finish job?"

"What happened to the guest?"

"He in new suite. Suite three hundred. He check out maybe later . . . today."

"Good. Means now you have a name for me?"

"I have," and with that the bellhop produced a folded page torn from the hotel notepad and handed it over.

Anxious with anticipation, Lou placed the paper in the back pocket of his shorts. "All right. Let's hope I have some good recordings from the few hours before the guest checked out."

Lou worked hard to suppress the urge to take out the paper and read the big name; exactly how big was it? No, he would wait until he was back in his hotel, laptop ready to play the film—assuming it was anything worthwhile.

Once inside the suite, he scanned his surroundings. Everything appeared clean and untouched. It took him less than ten minutes to uninstall and collect his bugs. One last look, to check out the balcony: he opened the double-glazed door and stepped out. Not much of a view; yet something at the bottom of the railing caught his eye. It was white and lacey, tangled at the bottom of the outside railing. On his knees, he carefully stuck his hand through the opening and with two fingers grabbed hold of the object and gave it a gentle tug. It was a white lace hair band with small crochet flowers sewn on both sides. He turned it around and examined it carefully before stashing it in a pocket and heading out the door.

Once back at his hotel, Lou washed off the Cambodian grime with room temperature Cambodia water. Still wet, with a discolored white towel around his waist, he walked to the fridge for a lukewarm beer. Then he went over to his laptop and turned it on.

He inserted the DVD.

He hit Play and hunched forward. As the empty room came into view, he clicked slow-forward until the suite door opened. A beautiful woman in traditional Cambodian dress entered the room with a well-practiced sway. Following her was a bellhop, a few years older than his source, pushing an ornate luggage cart with two large suitcases topped by an oversized, mahogany leather Gucci carry-on.

The bellhop was followed by an older Caucasian man with a

massive girth whose face was partially obscured by a handkerchief. Lou was staring wide-eyed, half mad with anticipation—and then he saw his face.

Startled, he leaned back—then looked again. Yes, it was real. Here was one of the most powerful men in U.S. politics.

Congressman Donald Keller. The Whip himself: who boldly declared his aspiration to one day be president; husband to the prominent environmentalist queen with a famous NGO, and father of two accomplished power players in one of the top world financial institutions. *The* Donald Keller, in the flesh.

And he, Lou, had him, just like that.

* * * *

The plane was late. They were waiting for the agency's clean-up guy from Hong Kong when Josh's cell phone rang.

Josh picked up on the first ring, coded to the unit head. He held one finger up for Sander to see as he walked toward a quieter area, away from the airport's ear-piercing amplifiers.

Minutes later, Josh returned in a rage.

"What's up?"

"That was UB. Major mess. We'll be lucky to get casino security in the Bahamas . . ."

"What mess?" Sander looked confused. "Aren't they happy with what they got? Best Picture of the Year?"

"No, an unexpected extra. When did you start live-monitoring the stream?"

"As soon as they walked into the suite," Sander told him. "Why?"

"There's an actor you missed."

"What are you talking about?"

"Someone, anonymous, went in and bugged the *already-bugged suite.*"

Sander tried for words but no sound came out.

"We have to get to that room and see if his Stone Age bugs are still there," Josh insisted, urging Sander out the door. "Otherwise, he's got *us*."

* * * *

Lou, now soaked in sweat, went to the bathroom to throw up three beers' worth on an empty stomach while the screen continued to display the monotonous clean-up by Maurice's men. He tried some wasabi rice crackers, the only thing on hand. *Bad idea.*

He went to the window and gazed out for what seemed a long time. Then he noticed a change in the voices on the recording: no longer French or Cambodian but American-accented English.

He rushed over to look. Two men, both white, one of whom was clearly in charge: stocky, muscled, late thirties, harsh blue eyes. The other appeared younger and softer—late twenties perhaps, light brown hair worn in a ponytail, triangular face, brown eyes framed by rimless glasses.

"What the hell? And who are you?"

Lou watched as they removed tiny sophisticated receivers from the parlor's flat screen TV, air ducts, and along the tops of picture frames; he listened to them talk about the dirty Whip's penis, his recent threats to the NSA, the agency and their unit boss as they bragged about "slam dunk" successes.

Lou was young but not stupid. He knew what he was looking at. This was CIA, possibly aided by another megaspook agency. Then cold sweat started down his neck. Then fear.

The real-time bugs already were in place—they already knew. They had his face!

He sprang up. Adrenaline and instinct took over. He was thinking fast with his body only a few moves behind. He grabbed his backpack, double-checked his passport and started counting his cash since his credit cards now were useless. Eight hundred sixty-two dollars, combining his currencies. Not much.

He forced himself to think. Laptop—could be used to pinpoint his location; likewise his cell phone. Tossed. What else?

He could not go back home. International airports, his passport—basically, his identity—had to be deep-sixed for the time being; but for how long, and how could he even find out?

He headed out through the hotel back door with the DVD and his backpack, leaving cash on the table to cover his stay. Waving a one-dollar bill, he stopped a scooter and hopped on, telling the guy, "Mekong Ferry Station."

A few blocks before the station he got off. Then he zigzagged through backstreets and narrow alleys until he found a coffeehouse–Internet café. He grabbed the first empty booth and sent short, cryptic e-mails: one to his girlfriend with brief instructions, and one to his boss.

Lou approached the owner and waving a five-dollar bill, asked for the quickest way to duplicate a DVD. The man went to the back, shouted something, and a minute later, a boy about thirteen or fourteen appeared, perhaps the owner's son. The two conferred.

"He know computer electric things," the man told Lou. "He helps you know. You follow."

Lou followed him through more back alleys until they reached a particularly poverty-stricken row. Lou and the boy entered one of the small houses, where they were met by another boy, barely eighteen. This one took them into a hot stuffy room where three PCs were set up side by side.

Less than an hour later, Lou was back on the street heading toward the pier. He had made six digital copies, stuffed four inside his backpack, one in the leg pocket, and the last he gave to the café owner's son, for safekeeping until he came back for it. No questions asked.

* * * *

Josh and Sander had been through that recording three times: specifically, the part where anonymous enters whistling and begins to install his bugs.

Josh could not stop pacing. Sure complications happen; they almost always do—but shit like this? Almost never.

Sander broke the silence. "Maybe there are things we should be doing while waiting for the periodical calls?"

Josh paused, giving it a thought. "Any ideas? You're the brainy one."

"Someone must have given him access. Someone who works for the hotel. When we get the facilitator, we'll have our ID."

"I'll handle the phones," Josh agreed.

"Oh," Sander stopped at the door. "What happened to the second girl? Did Maurice find the body?"

"Doesn't matter," Josh told him plainly. "Even if she did survive the jump."

* * * *

Lou boarded the tiny fishing boat at around 11:30 P.M., congratulating himself for the idea: this would take him straight into Vietnam—*smuggled*, to be more precise. No visa or passport to trace, and all for fifteen dollars.

Among the hundreds of floating villages and inlets along the river, one could remain hidden indefinitely. He would have to find a remote village, until the initial search ended. They'd know by now about his god-uncle in Saigon: let them look there, and everywhere else for that matter; he'd survive out here in the wilderness, long enough at least to outlast their sniffing. He'd have to.

Thus sitting for hours, uncomfortable but preoccupied, with his upper body bent, at last he made it to the other side. They proceeded forward. He had always considered the Mekong mystical and magical. Now, here he was, wanted, by one of the most ruthless, powerful organizations in the world.

Only the night before, he'd thought the mission nearly complete, and everything being *just right. So much for predictability.*

He was about to start feeling good and sorry for himself when he noticed something—*someone?*—standing on the shore. Now that they were past the border control he stood up: there she was again. Surrounded by dozens of anchored wooden boats, looking emptily at the river, was the second girl from the hotel suite. She was still wearing the ao dai, though the dress seemed torn in several spots, no longer white but various shades of brown.

Lou blinked. She was still there, getting smaller and hazier as the boat moved further away. He could not tear his eyes from the image. He kept on looking, long after it fluttered into a slight silhouette, and even after it flickered out.

CHAPTER 4

Wednesday, September 18, 2003
Washington, D.C.

Pushing her way through the morning mob, Elsie Simon ascended the escalator express-style, zigzagging around the motionless stiffs with muttered *excuse me*'s until she hit the top landing mid-stride. Outside she took a breath, as much to shake off the crush of hot bodies as to feel the cool autumn air. Today was the big day.

She checked her watch: 7:36. Good—she would be in Ryan's office early. It would be a big day for their target *Nazim* as well.

First, a pit stop to the ladies' for a little splash of cold to rinse the subway off. Now before the mirror, she took a look at herself. Staring back was a thirty-three-year-old woman in a conservative pants suit, a tired but delicate heart-shaped face and enormous eyes the color of dark honey, overwhelmed by sadness, still. Life had been tumultuous: recently widowed, and with her father—a doctor and political activist—missing for nearly three years now. What had brought her here, to this point, this extremity? What turbulent storm—from without or within? Was it a call to arms? She was a language instructor; how had a short-term patriotic stint—a chance to give something back—ballooned into round-the-clock, exhausting work as a full-blown FBI analyst?

The petite, five-foot-three, 105-pound woman didn't have an answer.

Now, carrying two Styrofoam cups filled with her customary triple espresso topped with a dollop of whipped cream, she entered the Washington Field Office, an imposing buff-colored concrete building that took up the entire block. After passing through security (thankfully without setting off the beep) she proceeded posthaste to the fifth floor, wending her way through a maze of hallways and identical cubicles to the FBI's Counterterrorism unit, housed in its own wing. She stopped before the closed door of Special Agent Ryan Marcello. Knocking softly once, she entered.

Marcello, handsome, in his late thirties, with intelligent brown eyes and chestnut hair, looked up. Even sitting down he was tall.

"Right on time, to the rescue!" Ryan reached for the cup and downed its contents in one long gulp.

"What kind of Italian are you, anyway?" Elsie shook her head. "Sip. It's called *sipping* espresso . . ."

Ryan's expression went from sheepish to one of alarm. "We have a problem," he began. "Major. I've been here since five-thirty this morning—"

"Why? No response from the French?"

"It's not that. They went through all their records and sent me all the manifests. Our guy is not on any of their flights. There's no record of him there; in country or France-bound."

Elsie sat, puzzled. "We've had nothing but solid intel on this. They were specific enough: Nazim was to arrive in D.C. with samples early evening today. They specifically said *AF*; that would be Air Fra—"

"I'm way past that," he interrupted. "I combed through the passenger list, not once, not twice—"

"Did you check the aliases?"

Ryan paused to look at her; then continued, disregarding the question. "I have DEA ready for a bust. I have our end cleared and ready to go. And here we are, with nothing. Zilch."

Elsie checked her watch. "I'm not ready to give up. I'll listen to the tape again. Maybe we missed something." She paused. "We should check the latest transcripts from the CI as well. There may be a few crumbs left on the diplomatic trail—long shot, I know, but let's see if I can find anything."

As a senior analyst, Elsie worked with several divisions at the bureau, including and especially the Counterintelligence unit. For the last eight months, most of her time had been devoted to Ryan's Counterterrorism subunit covering Turkey, Central Asia and the Caucasus, with cases and targets linked to Afghanistan. She remained involved with counterintelligence covering that area—from diplomatic angles and espionage—but not nearly to the same degree.

Fluent in Farsi, Dari, Turkish and many Turkic dialects, Elsie had become something of a prize after September 2001; FBI field offices all over the country vied for her savvy expertise. Not only did she know the region and its politics, but it was knowledge gained painfully, at first hand. She knew the people.

Through doggedness and special pleading with the counterterrorism boss at HQ, Ryan had landed Elsie in his unit for two specific cases. She was his, almost exclusively, for at least two months.

"Fine," Ryan agreed. "Let's see if you find anything." He looked at his watch. "Let's give ourselves till thirteen hundred. If we don't come up with something by then, I'll have to notify the unit and DEA and call it off."

By the time he looked up, she was already out the door.

* * * *

Elsie entered her unit and greeted Rosie, an analyst for South-Central America working exclusively CI. Her other officemate, Meltem, with Turkish Counterintelligence, was out on assignment in New Jersey. Opening the drawer, Elsie retrieved the outmoded headset and in less than five minutes was deep into audiotapes.

After ten minutes, she clicked Stop and took off her headset. What next? Where should she be looking? Thinking better when she moved, Elsie wandered through the labyrinth of cubicles that described the translation unit. The enormous division housed hundreds of specialists in dozens of languages: Russian, Chinese, Hindu, Arabic, Farsi, Spanish . . . The division handled not only Washington, D.C., task forces but nationwide FBI divisions for counterterrorism, counterintelligence, counterespionage and criminal cases.

Abruptly, she doubled back to the Turkic language wing, to stop in on a friend.

"Hello, Emin."

The translator removed his earplugs and greeted her in Turkish. After the acceptable amount of small talk, Elsie checked her watch and asked him a favor. "Listen . . ."

Oh those almond eyes, he thought.

". . . Could you quickly let me have the transcripts for pertinent translations of Embassy and Attaché for . . . hmmm, let's make it for the last three days up till now?"

"Sure," he responded eagerly. "No problem. Give me a few minutes and I'll get them for you. You want to wait here, or you want me to bring them to your office?"

"I'll wait."

Emin began entering code for the appropriate file. He highlighted the requested documents—each arranged by date and time stamped—and hit Print. Moments later, one of four industrial-sized printers nearby began spewing out pages.

She then began the tedious work of scanning the wiretap translations. Mundane details could make or break a case: even the most innocuous-sounding appointment for delivery could be a code for a major deal or operation.

Sitting at a desk and poring over monotonous dialogue can easily make a person drowsy. She wished Ryan would show up soon with coffee—or better, double espresso with real sugar.

She was about to turn a page when something caught her eye: a formal request to the U.S. State Department seeking extra protection for dignitaries arriving at 16:45 on September 18—today. The most significant aspect of the brief instruction had to do with the point of arrival.

She stared at the transcript, realizing she'd been holding her breath; then slowly exhaled. She opened her drawer, retrieved her headset, and clicked on the command to replay the audio, fast-forwarding to the sixteenth-minute segment. She listened carefully then went back over the segment a second time.

Elsie grabbed the phone and dialed Ryan's extension. He picked up right away.

"Sit tight, I'm coming up," Elsie told him. "I believe we found the answer." Bypassing the elevator, she took the stairs two at a time until she reached the fifth floor landing.

Ryan was waiting outside his door.

"Well?"

She stepped in and Ryan followed, closing the door behind them. She laid the page out on his desk, placing her index finger on a line three quarters down. Ryan began reading. *"Forward official request for extra protection for the arrival of our special dignitaries at Andrews Air Force Base, AAF, at sixteen forty-five, on September eighteen, two thousand three."*

"I went over the audio again," Elsie explained. "The target says arrival AF, but with *A* stretched. Accent, speed of speech, sound quality, whatever . . . I think he's saying *AAF*."

The two stood inches apart, for a long minute in silence. Ryan gave out a whistle. "Shit. Let's think about this. If you're right, we're looking at a government-connected target. Not any government, but a major ally and NATO member. And not just anyone but a high-level military and diplomatic figure: Nazim, a *dignitary*?"

"How else would a major target get himself on a plane in Brussels to arrive at an Air Force base in Washington?"

"Do we know whose plane it is?" Ryan wondered. "It can't be commercial; private, military, What?"

Elsie shrugged.

"We need to find out. Also, we need to know who else is on that plane."

She knew what he was thinking; she could follow his pace of thoughts: assuming Nazim—their target—is on that plane, either he's blended in and fooled those people, or he really is a dignitary, connected to high-level officials in Turkey or Brussels or both.

Finally, Elsie spoke. "We're going through with the DEA bust?"

"Hell yes! We've been chasing this guy for over a year. We have the terrorism case on him. We gave DEA the heroin-narcotics crumbs, so they've got that angle going. Nazim will lead us to the money and financing centers, the top command and terror operations . . . Dulles, AAF, what's the difference? A bust is a bust." He paused, expecting agreement.

Instead, Elsie began rubbing her neck, a sign of deep unease. She had a bad feeling about this one. "Let's hope the bosses think so . . ."

That warning in her gut never lied.

* * * *

Elsie was restless. She kept going from half-heartedly working in front of her monitor to pacing her small office. She had been checking her watch every few minutes. It was 5:30 and she had not heard back from Ryan or the team.

She decided to check Ryan's extension one more time. She

dialed then hung up—more like slammed the phone back down. Then she headed upstairs.

Elsie tapped on the door and swung it open. Ryan was in front of the window with his back to the door.

Elsie could feel her own rising anger, mixed with curiosity and deep anxiety.

"Ryan, when did you return? How long have you been back?"

Ryan didn't turn around. "Been a while."

Elsie made an unconscious fist. "I've been calling. I dialed your extension half a dozen times in the last forty-five minutes. You didn't bother to let me know?"

"Not now Elsie. I'm in no shape . . . I'll brief you later . . ."

Elsie had never seen him like this. She was used to him energetic, restless, manic, determined, sometimes arrogant, occasionally angry . . . but never this defeated. She didn't recognize him.

She took two steps in and closed the door. "This is *our* case, *our* project. I work *with* you, Ryan, not *for* you. How could you shut me out like this?"

Ryan grabbed a pen, tore a square from a stack of yellow Post-Its and jotted something down. Without even looking at her, in an exhausted tone he said, "Use past tense, Elsie. This *was* our case. Case no more. There was no *bust*. Operation was *terminated* before even kicking in. As of today, as of an hour ago, our case came to an end."

Elsie stood dumbfounded. What the hell had happened?

Ryan held up the Post-It note facing outward, unreadable from where Elsie stood. She took four quick steps and was able to make out the writing: *Let's not talk here. Wait till we get out.*

Hit by more confusion, she looked at him questioningly.

"I'm sorry," Ryan went on. "It's been a long tough day and I've had enough. Time to get out of here." He regarded her with his usual kind eyes. "Did you take the metro today? If you did, let me give you a ride, it's pissing down out there!"

"Thanks. Let me grab my things. I'll meet you in the garage. P-two?"

"P-two. See you there in five."

* * * *

Wednesday Evening, September 18, 2003
Alexandria, Virginia

Ryan's beat-up black Ford SUV pulled into the small parking area behind the Hot Chili Café. There were only five other cars, three of them in slots designated for restaurant staff.

Despite the rush hour and pouring rain it had taken less than twenty-five minutes to reach the quiet nontouristy section of Old Town Alexandria. Neither had talked much during the drive. Still taken aback by Ryan's rage, Elsie refrained from pressing him with questions.

Ryan opened her door and she stepped out under his jacket held like a minitent.

Once under the refuge of the restaurant awning, Ryan brought down the soaked plastic raincoat, gave it a few shakes and rolled it like a sausage-shaped pillow, holding open the door.

They took their seats in a small corner booth. The waiter materialized and both ordered Coronas.

Ryan leaned across the table. "I am sorry about earlier, Elsie; I'm usually better than that when it comes to handling crap . . ."

"I know. Now tell me about it."

Before Ryan had a chance to respond, the waiter reappeared with their Coronas and two frosty mugs.

Elsie ordered her usual spiked-up Texan chili with raw jalapenos on the side. Ryan asked for the same but with spaghetti and extra corn bread. With the waiter gone, he told Elsie, "I just realized I haven't eaten anything all day."

"Same here, couldn't bring myself to leave the office for lunch . . . Okay, tell me."

Ryan took a long sip from the bottle. "Briefed the DEA guys and then went to Whitman"—at the mention of Michael Whitman, Ryan's boss, Elsie's ears perked up. "He didn't like it a bit, but went to personally brief the deputy at HQ."

He took another long sip and continued, "The big guy was tied up in a lunch meeting, so Whitman had him paged and went to grab a bite. With me bugging him every ten minutes, he said go ahead with the plans and leave the briefing and convincing of the big boss to him."

Elsie could tell his blood pressure was rising.

Ryan went on. "So I got the team ready, and with DEA also ready to go, we headed out around two-thirty. We arrived and waited by the gate, counting the minutes."

He paused to collect himself. "It was around three-ten and suddenly my beeper and cell started buzzing at exactly the same time. Both directly from HQ, so I answered right away—"

"Whitman," Elsie uttered.

Ryan shook his head. "No—the assistant deputy himself, Phil Marshall. He yelled, 'Where are you, Marcello?' I told him, and he said, 'We're calling it off. You immediately tell your guys, turn around, and head back here—to HQ. Now!' Confused by the whole thing, I yelled back, 'What? Why? Where is Whitman, sir? With all due respect, I take orders directly from him."

Ryan made a fist with his left hand and began flexing it. "So Whitman comes on the line and says, 'Marcello, call it off, get your ass and your guys out of there ASAP, and after that get your ass right back here.' At this point I'm pissed; I mean, I'm on fire, so I say to him, 'The reason being? We have all our ducks in order here, Mike. What's going on?' Whitman is now yelling, *'That's enough!* You're not on a secure phone. Not a single word. You get your guys and leave the premises *right now!* We have an emergency situation here. Get over here ASAP.'"

Elsie could feel her own tension rising. "But why?"

"Wait—you haven't even heard yet—so here I am caught off guard and pissed. I get out of the car and tell the team that the operation is terminated. Just like that. They're as shocked and dumbfounded as I am, spewing questions like a damn machine gun. I tell them the little I know, and ask them to go back to their units . . ."

"What happened when you went back to HQ?"

"Well, I didn't; I didn't go there *right away.* With the team gone, I decided to position myself where I could see the vehicles exiting from the base and jot down vehicle numbers. I'm sitting there grinding my teeth and watching the gate, and in about thirty minutes I see a black Ford fly out of the gate with all the bells and whistles, flashing lights and siren. It pulls up behind me and two guys jump out with their badges yelling, *'Get out of the car! Get out of the car now with your hands behind your head!'"*

"Oh my God, Ryan! What the hell . . .?"

Ryan nodded. "Air Force Special Security Unit. They didn't want to listen or acknowledge my FBI badge and government car. They threw me on the ground facedown and patted me over as roughly as possible—including the family jewels. Then they sat me in the backseat of their Ford and stood outside on their cell phones. After a minute, the older, rougher jerk yanks open the car door and says, 'Yo, Marcello. Your bosses at HQ are not happy with your insubordination. According to them you were under direct order to leave here and report back. You didn't. Now you are our pain in the ass until we deliver you to them. Get outta the car.'"

Ryan took a breath. "I got in my car and drove back to HQ with them tailing me as my damned escort."

The waiter showed up with a big tray and a stand then proceeded to place six plates piled high without leaving an inch of space.

Ryan asked for two more Coronas. Elsie was about to object when he told her, "They're both for me."

Ryan continued between bites. "I walked into Marshall's office. I'm told to wait and after twenty minutes or so the door opens and two suits appear followed by Whitman and Marshall. One of the suits gives me this ice-cold stare."

Ryan downed half a beer. "I get summoned into the office . . . I'll spare you the obscenities. The suits are State Department, who supposedly had a fit about a *diplomatic incident*—one of the bosses there ripped into Marshall. Someone clearly was unhappy."

"But who notified State?"

Ryan smiled. "That and a dozen other questions along the same line; according to the suits, everyone on that plane is protected under *diplomatic immunity*. Read my lips: *Untouchable*."

"So Nazim was on that plane, right?"

"Are you kidding me? They would never even entertain the thought of answering *that*. We don't know who was on that plane or how many; we don't know what kind of plane we're talking about; we don't know shit. I don't think Whitman knows either, and as for Marshall . . . who knows? I don't."

"There are only so many people on this case," Elsie reasoned, "and with these new revelations not half a day old, we're looking at less than a handful who could have tipped off the State Department. Think about it!"

"I know, Elsie. I wasn't even willing to talk to you in my office; call me paranoid."

Elsie gave him the look of *You're kidding, right?*

"Then there's the part that concerns you," he continued. "I haven't come to that yet."

Elsie stared. "What?"

"Marshall had a copy of the audiotape on Nazim's guys and the transcript that went with it. He wanted to know how we got AAF and the exact arrival time out of that."

"Oh no! No!"

"I tried to fudge it, Elsie. I said we went back and re-reviewed everything this morning. They're not convinced."

"This could get Emin in major trouble; me as well. You know the protocol: everything on a need-to-know basis and, of course, Thou Shalt Not Dare Mix Up Info from Different Divisions . . . I got the documents from the counterintelligence files and shared those with you, counterterrorism—breaking one of the bureau's top five commandm—"

Ryan stopped her. "I'm going to do everything to shield you, Elsie."

"You can't. It's all traceable. They can easily check the print and audio logs, and then it's putting two and two together."

"That's assuming they want to go that far. Whitman's ass is on the line here too. There's turf to think about."

Elsie was not persuaded. "Yet, you're suspicious of your office being wired?"

Ryan stared at the wall to her left a few moments before responding. "Elsie, I've been doing some extra digging. On my own time. With my own connections. The bureau has declared this case closed—dead—at least unofficially; but for me it's just come to life. I'm going to pursue it to the end . . ."

Elsie straightened up.

She wasn't sure. Oh yes, she knew about criminals with immunity in there, but to put every single one in that bucket? That would be a cynical assumption.

"And I'm wondering," Ryan continued, "would you be willing to take a chance with me? To go all in? Partners?"

Elsie started chewing her bottom lip, a tic when she engaged in deep calculations. What he considered naïve in her, she considered cynical in him. At what point would pursuing targets with diplomatic immunity be seen as an act of sheer futility, and who would make that call?

"Ryan Marcello," she addressed him carefully, "you're not planning to keep anything from me—not a single thing? We are talking *equal* partnership?"

Ryan smiled, his eyes saying, *You bet.*

Sliding out of the booth, Elsie was stopped by Ryan.

"Wait a sec." He reached over and slowly traced his finger over the top of her lips, lingering a moment before removing it. "Chili sauce."

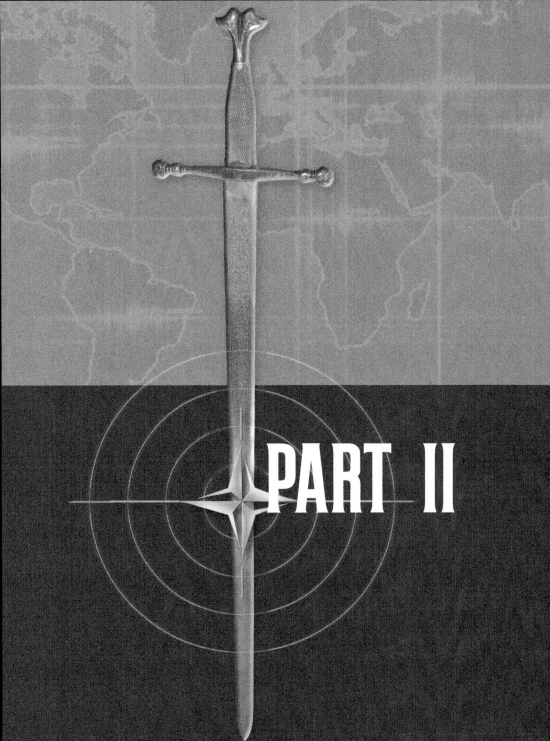

PART II

CHAPTER 5

Monday, September 29, 2003
Alexandria, Virginia

The Chinchilla Persian cat named Simba was half asleep in his usual spot, Ben's wheelchair to the right of the sofa facing the floor-to-ceiling window. During Ben's last five months, this would be the only seat in the house—Ben's lap—where Simba took his naps. Elsie, for her part, would be on the sofa reading a book and frequently looking over, taking mental snapshots of the duo to be forever inscribed in her memory. Until only two months ago, this Benless scene of Simba in the wheelchair left an egg-sized knot in her throat. Now she took it all in and smiled half bitter, half accepting that Ben was gone, forever.

She got on her feet. Time for her twenty-minute run alongside the Potomac River, a quick stop on the sweaty way back for her tall Americano to go followed by five minutes of intense, punching-bag boxing; another few minutes of yoga stretches and a power shower, hair and makeup, e-mails, and fifteen minutes to scan the news.

Today she was taking the car. She had to. The breakfast meeting was at 24 Dim-Sum in Rosslyn. She and Ryan switched off choosing the breakfast spots. Ryan's were the typical pancake house, café or American diner. Elsie was more adventurous: a spicy Korean dive or Mexican for ultrahot bean-filled egg plates or, as today, a Hong Kong–style soup house filled with steamy, exotic aromas. Just the thought of Ryan's likely reaction made her chuckle inside.

On the way to the restaurant she had to make a stop. She pulled into a small strip mall in a mostly Hispanic neighborhood off Wilson Boulevard and Glebe. She passed customer parking and drove to the end, turning right onto a one-lane driveway used by delivery trucks behind the buildings. She pulled in front of one and parked. The store's back door was open, as expected. She let herself in.

The room was divided into eight computer stations and equipped with several printers, three large copiers and two ancient fax machines. Only two of the computers were occupied. This was a minibusiness-Internet office frequented by Hispanic workers, many of whom were without a residency card or work permit. It was safe. No one asked questions. No one ever paid with credit cards or checks.

The man in charge quickly spotted her as she opened her handbag and by the time he came over she had her five dollars rolled and ready for "five minutes or less." The man nodded, took the money and went back into his office, where he turned on the switch for Elsie's computer and went back to watching the door.

Once the green light came on she was in. She entered her password for the second time, clicked on the mailbox and read the text: cryptic as usual, nonconclusive as always. *South of the border to meet with Y. Should have a lead, or nothing, by morning your time.* She blinked, let out a sigh and logged off.

* * * *

Monday, September 29, 2003
Arlington, Virginia

Finding a parking space in Rosslyn proved frustrating as ever. Ryan was tempted to grab one of the three handicap spaces but thought better of it. So he would dish out another eleven dollars for less than an hour!

He entered the smelly cramped restaurant and scanned the room for Elsie, spotting her deep in thought at a corner table next to the fogged-up window. He psyched himself against the nauseating smell, the pathetic glistening ducks hanging upside-down above the kitchen counter, and the suffocating warmth of the steamy room filled with only Asian men. All, that is, except for Elsie and now him. He knew exactly what she was trying to do: repulse him. Get him to object and complain. Well, he wouldn't give her the satisfaction.

He reached the table showcasing his sweetest smile. Make that Ryan one, Elsie zero.

"Good morning." Elsie smiled back. "Don't you love the scent? You're about to discover one of the greatest soups of your life."

Ryan squeezed himself in. "Can't wait. What do you recommend?"

"You can't go wrong ordering pig stomach with ground pork and leek dumplings."

After scanning the menu, Ryan settled on steamed pork buns and chicken shumai.

Elsie poured the Jasmine green tea and now it was time for business. Notes. Updates. Brainstorming. Next moves.

Elsie got right into it. "How was your meeting with Robert?"

"Interesting—but somehow I ended up with more questions than answers." He'd gone to Chicago over the weekend to meet with Special Agent Robert Brown. He and Robert once had been partners and remained friends. This was an off-the-book trip.

"He's not willing to open up . . . share?"

"It's not that," Ryan explained. "He's in the dark as well. The case has been driving him crazy; that and his big boss breathing down his neck."

The food arrived and Ryan shoved the entire pork bun into his mouth, swallowing with a gulp of green tea.

Elsie shot him a half-approving look. The score remained at one-zero.

Ryan, energized, continued. "Nazim's Egyptian partner in Chicago was a dead end, as you know. The guy's business seems legit, and the wire transactions look ordinary. Rob's lead left us empty-handed—until recently."

"What . . .?"

"An informant, from his CI days, connected with the Egyptian consulate. Rob hooks up with the guy out in the Chicago burbs . . . where he is told that he should be looking into the case of one Yousef Mahmoud."

"*Yousef* as in one of the masterminds of the 2001 attack? The one who's been buried in jail for the last two years?"

Ryan nodded. "More like deep sixed—with secret military trials in closed courts and trial transcripts classified even to those of us with the highest clearance. *That* Yousef."

"I know, because the Pentagon took over. It was their case, after all."

Elsie was familiar enough with this mastermind. *Yousef*, as he is known, was well-trained and educated in languages and martial arts; having ascended the ranks of the Egyptian Air Force in record time, he then was stationed here in the States for joint training and "somehow" ended up working for the U.S. Air Force in Nebraska. He certainly pulled the wool over the Pentagon's eyes, having managed high-level international terrorist activities all the while maintaining security clearance as a U.S. Air Force major. At the same time—that is, concurrently—Yousef rose through the ranks of al-Hazar where he earned the title of General Commando. To pull that off takes genius. No wonder the Pentagon buried him alive. Of course, there could be more to it apart from saving face and preventing any further embarrassment. Maybe.

"So are you ready for this?" Ryan was near to bursting. "According to Rob's informant, Yousef hasn't been rotting in solitary at all—far from it. He's been out and about, taking trips abroad, to Egypt."

Elsie leaned over the table, eyes wide. "That's insane. How could that be possible?"

Ryan made a *hold off* motion with his hand. "Wait . . . there's more."

Elsie pushed her bowl aside.

"According to this informant, Yousef is not only linked to Nazim's partner in Egypt but is a frequent traveler, with Turkey as the first hub and center." Ryan paused and pointed to the teapot for a refill. "So of course Rob checks Yousef's status: according to the bureau and joint operation unit, Yousef the mastermind has remained in solitary confinement, sitting in his high-security jail cell since 2001. Now Rob puts in a request for additional information—any tips about or interviews with the guy. Zero. Then he tries to contact Yousef's military attorney, who is stationed *overseas* with location classified."

"So now what?"

Ryan looked skeptical. "Rob's trying to find a contact who works in that Illinois jail. A long shot. His boss got a whiff and told him to back off. He sounded serious."

Ryan could see Elsie's mind racing at quantum speed: processing, sifting, evaluating and reevaluating. It was this quality that made her the best analyst he'd ever encountered at the bureau—that and the fact that she was beautiful.

"Assuming this informant is right," Elsie began, "that could mean the government is using him as a double agent . . . but then he couldn't just show up: the targets well know of his arrest and jailing. So that rules that out."

Elsie took a breath. "So then what are the other plausible alternatives? What else would the government use him for? It makes no sense."

Ryan shrugged. "The information is solid, and no one can prove if Yousef is even alive. I've never seen this level of secrecy. You?"

Elsie bit her lower lip. "Maybe something to do with his Canadian arrest? They notified the bureau and deported him. Our D.C. guys made the arrest here, all on record. Then the Pentagon has hushed it up ever since—like damage control."

Ryan looked expectant. "Your point?"

"What if Yousef has been a double agent all along: one of us posing as one of them?"

Ryan's face soured. "*Bull*. Yousef would have tipped us off, and we would have prevented the 2001 attack!"

Elsie was startled by the defensive rage. "I'm only looking at every possibility, doing what you want me to do: ANALYZE."

Ryan apologized. "Elsie, I'm . . . exasperated. Tired of hitting walls, of pursuing this case outside the bureau in hiding . . ."

Elsie half smiled. "I'll see who brought him in and questioned him at the bureau . . ."

* * * *

Monday, September 29, 2003
Washington, D.C.

On her way into the main building, double espresso in hand, Elsie heard Sami calling, her only close friend at the bureau.

As striking as ever, Sami was an odd combination of unearthly beauty: tall, with violet blue eyes and chin-length honey-col-

ored curly hair, tattoos, no makeup, and wearing almost mascu-
line fatigues, including a bulky sweatshirt, man's swatch and black
lace-up combat boots. Samantha-Sam Bamford, aka Sami to her very
few close friends, was number one in the bureau's Crime Against
Children Unit (CACU). Here was an agent who took no prisoners,
relentless in her pursuit of child-traffickers, and with zero tolerance
of middling bureaucracy or diplomatic games among the FBI's upper
management. She was abrupt, even harsh, yet they couldn't get rid of
her. She was just too good.

Elsie gave her a quick hug. The two stood in stark contrast: one
striking, tough hard beauty; the other, delicate and feminine. Muscular and petite, blond and dark, each in her own way a warrior.

"You got my message?"

"I did," Elsie told her, "and I was going to call you back tod—"

"I know how that goes," Sami interrupted. *"Tomorrow never
comes . . ."*

Elsie started laughing, finishing the line, *"Let's forget about
tomorrow* . . . and get together today: tonight?"

"Okay, before I'm sent on another UC trip. Your place or my
dump?"

Sami was her best when she worked undercover. Unlike most
agents, she loved that part of the job. She loved the escape and
detachment.

"My place. We'll order in Thai, drink vino, and . . . so much to
catch up on."

They boarded the elevator together. Sami got off on two after a
peck on Elsie's cheek. "Seven-thirty. I'll bring the wine."

Elsie headed directly to her office and greeted her coworker
Meltem in Turkish, asking, "How was the assignment? You were
gone, what, three weeks?"

Meltem tilted back her head. "I know. I'll be gone again next
month. So, how have you been?"

Elsie looked puzzled. That really wasn't what she'd asked. "Me? Mostly work. Where're you headed next?"

Meltem turned back to her monitor. "Oh, same. Boston again."

"Boston? I thought it was Patterson and Philly?"

Meltem paused before waving her off. "Right. Those two and Boston." She put in her earplugs and went back to work.

Elsie was about to sit and start up her monitor when she changed her mind, grabbing her notepad and heading out.

She entered the unit's file and archives room where she noticed an Asian translator on her knees methodically filing copies of her printed transcripts. The FBI insisted on keeping with its precomputer methods. Each analyst had to make multiple copies of every translated document or concluding analysis and file them with each corresponding unit. In addition, another copy had to be submitted to the central secretary, who arranged secure hand-delivery to headquarters at the end of each day, and yet another had to be filed here in this enormous archive. Change was despised. Any time-saving resource or innovation was doubly loathed and fought against.

Up until the terror attack, analysts worked at headquarters, where they received hand-delivered translated documents from the language specialists and agents' reports from field offices around the country. Their analyses then were sent to the unit heads, who shared them with the corresponding agents.

Middlemen and redundancies often caused delays and near useless analyses. Raw data without context or a hastily written field report almost never gave the full picture. Analysts and agents need regular briefings and consulting face to face in real time. Stale and dated data produces useless analyses.

Elsie proceeded along the wall opposite to where the translator was finishing up. She opened the first drawer on top, ran through the alphabetized folders until she found the file that corresponded to her unit and current operation numerical code. She removed the file, placed it on top of her legal pad, and quietly closed the drawer. Once she heard the translator exit, she quickly moved near to where the woman had been filing. This was the area for the Arabic division.

Elsie opened the middle drawer for northern Africa–related cases and operations, scanning the folders under Egypt until she reached 2001. Spotting the CT-Counterterrorism section, she pulled the folder rack forward and removed the file labeled MAHMOUD, YOUSEF *CT 119-TSC WFO*.

The file was amazingly thin. She flipped open the jacket. Only two pages: one with a short paragraph summarizing the Canadian unit's memo and deportation date and time; and the other, an itemized list of Yousef's belongings confiscated by Canadian Intelligence, with several items redacted and turned over to the FBI.

According to the list, Yousef carried three international passports, one of which was a diplomatic passport issued in 1997 by the State Department under the name Khalid Ramesh—immediately raising the question of whether or not it was faked. Why would the State Department issue a diplomatic passport to an air force major stationed in Nebraska? If it was real, wouldn't that give credence to her theory that Yousef worked as a double agent? She wondered what Ryan's reaction would be. Still, there was no way for them to verify the passport's authenticity.

Yousef carried a laptop as well, with numerous suspicious files and documents, many of which were encrypted and a few in other languages, including Arabic and Turkic. Notes with regard to this were blacked out; Elsie couldn't help but wonder why.

What was he doing with Turkic documents? She couldn't stop the questions swirling in her head. *The bureau had him for over 72 hours; where is the rest of the usual thick paperwork? Where is the FBI's order for translation and analysis of Yousef's documents? Did they in fact get them translated and analyzed? If so, to whom did they assign those tasks? Where was the insisted-on customary paper trail for that? Why is the file so empty? Who was the arresting agent(s), and where is their mandatory routine report?*

She placed the file back in the folder, closed the drawer and returned to her office. Clearly, she was anxious to share this new finding with Ryan but had to wait. In-house phone or direct discussions of their *outside* case inside the building was verboten. Instead, they used a code to signal each other of the need to meet or talk. She planned to use it now.

For Meltem's sake, she pretended to be working with her headset on while typing and staring at her monitor. After thirty minutes, she grabbed her legal pad and the file she'd removed from the archive room (the current boring case she and Ryan had been working on per their unit boss's order, right after the Nazim fiasco) and took the stairs.

Elsie knocked twice on Ryan's door. No response. She opened it a crack and peeked in. Empty. Going over to his desk, she tore a page from his Post-Its and jotted down a note: *I'll be @ Lunch @ La Luna Pizza, 12 p.m. # 89. 89* stood for fairly important but not urgent. She stuck the note on the center of his desk and went back to her cubicle.

She spent the next couple of hours going over transcripts, one of which instantly caught her eye. It pertained to a State Department request sent to the Turkish embassy on behalf of two employees of US International Education Development (USIED-US) for temporary work visas. According to the document, this was for a "brief education assessment trip" to Diyarbakir, a city near the border of Iraq-Turkey. She took out her personal organizer and wrote down the names, dates of birth, and assignment titles in her coded and abbreviated style, submitting the full versions into her infallible memory database. This case was hers alone and had nothing to do with Ryan's projects or the bureau.

She left her office at 11:45 to give herself time to walk to La Luna. Walking outside like this, by herself, always helped her to think clearly.

She thought about their meeting this morning, and went over everything Ryan had given her. Granted, his intel was almost all fourth hand: from a supposedly reliable informant to Robert, Robert to Ryan and then to her—not ideal sourcing for solid analysis. Much better would be to meet the informant face to face.

Yousef was one of a select few top-tier operatives of the massive terror operation in the United States. He was one of the three who were captured, and one of the two captured alive. How could he be out, roaming freely and traveling internationally?

She had to think. With his education, background, and intimate knowledge of the al-Hazar network he'd be incredibly valuable as an asset-informant-agent. Might the U.S. government, for instance, alter his face and send him out on missions to catch a bigger fish? She supposed so; yet she doubted it. What made Yousef high value also made him risky and unreliable: very hard if not impossible to keep tabs on and control once out. Doing so no doubt would ensure disaster.

Elsie shifted gears, to Yousef's files and history: What happened to them? Did the Pentagon order the bureau to hand over everything, leaving no trace? Again, this was doubtful; not that the Pentagon wouldn't try. Between the two agencies there existed an epic ongoing pissing contest. Besides, someone somewhere in the FBI would always keep a copy, just in case. Even so, knowing that HQ had those files did not help her or Ryan.

Now she was back to the reasoning that had filled Ryan with such rage and adamant denial. What if Yousef had been a government agent from the start? What if his position with the U.S. Air Force and obtaining high-level clearance were by design? What if he was working with and directing al-Hazar as a commando general while being followed and watched by his bosses at the Pentagon? Finally—and horribly—what if his U.S. bosses knew of al-Hazar's plans all along? Who knew, precisely? How many knew, and for how long? Even more, what if al-Hazar had moles in key positions within the government? What if they operated a major network within our government agencies? Could it be? Perhaps. They certainly have the money and backing, and when it comes to high-level U.S. officials, everything is up for sale. Or was this scenario too far-fetched?

She stopped when she realized she'd overshot the pizza joint by two blocks. Turning around, she double-timed it back, making sure to be there at twelve on the dot.

The place was packed. Elsie ordered a slice and tall lemonade and stepped aside. Every time the door opened, she'd glance to see if it was Ryan; so far, no sign of him.

She took her slice to a little wooden table and sat there alone, picking at it. Fifteen minutes later, still no sign. She took one last sip of her too-sweet drink, tossed the oily plate and cup and left. Lunchtime over.

* * * *

At 11:25 A.M., the Irish pub was pretty much quiet except for the sound of clattering silverware coming from the two middle-aged waiters setting up for the noontime crowd. The place was always dark, with its heavy wood paneling and dark walnut floor, and reeked with the stale yeasty after-morning smell of nightlong drunken spills. The pub was a favorite of D.C. cops and veterans. Not Ryan's ideal choice but a comfortable one for his expected source.

John Pulaski, military down to his polished shoes, arrived at exactly 11:30. While his thinning gray hair and weather-hardened face showcased his five decades, his posture and overall fitness could easily allow him to pass for three and some. He had retired a year ago, one year after the 2001 attack. He was Ryan's uncle's brother-in-law, which made him the uncle of Ryan's late cousin David, on the mother's side. His nephew David's murder was Pulaski's main reason for retiring early, and Ryan didn't blame him.

Ryan rose to greet the major, who patted Ryan twice on the back before each sat down.

"Let me guess: you picked the place just for me."

Ryan looked busted. "Convenient location, Irish, beer, meat and potatoes; what more can you ask?"

After brief small talk, John got right down to it. "I tell ya, what you asked me for gave me quite a run . . . it's like a code within a code."

"So you couldn't pin it down? Oh well—"

John held up his hands. "Not necessarily. I got stuff—*some* stuff—whether it'll be any help will depend on you." He continued. "All right, here's what we've got: your plane's departure is shown as NATO, Chièvres Air Base–Belgium with arrival at Andrew's. It was a Gulfstream C-20G VIP-Passenger Cargo aircraft . . ." He reached for his wallet and removed a folded paper. "Write this down: Aircraft ID number XZ-973."

Ryan entered the information into his BlackBerry.

John went on. "The plane, in addition to the pilot and copilot, carried five passengers and three cargo containers, each two hundred pounds. Are you with me?"

Ryan nodded.

"Here comes the mystery, son. The passengers and pilots are identified by code, not unusual. However, the ID codes do not match our military codes. That's unusual. I also checked our NATO personnel ID code system. No match either."

"That leaves us with one other possibility," Ryan guessed. "You're thinking what I'm thinking?"

"Yeah. The agency. I couldn't go any further. After 2001, they put in place several new units for special operations and with that, all new protocols, codes and some such. I'm out of the loop when it comes to all that. But yeah, if I were you, that'd be the lead to chase."

Ryan reflected; NATO airbase, military VIP plane, secret identification codes, State Department reining in the bureau, and Nazim in the middle of it all. What a load of shit this was. Hitting wall after wall, each thicker and more impenetrable than the last. His head throbbed.

The waiter brought two bowls of beef stew, Ryan's iced tea and John's half pint Guinness.

"Okay. I don't know how to thank you, John . . ."

John waved that off. "It's good to be of use now and then. Life can't be all about golfing, you know."

"Well, if that's the case, I have something else to pick your brain on."

John took a spoonful of steaming stew and spoke with his mouth half full. "Shoot."

"Yousef Mahmoud." Ryan paused.

John almost dropped his spoon. "Damn!"

"I understand if you don't want to go there. I know it was one of the military's darkest shames . . . It put you guys in a really bad position . . ."

"Not that," John corrected him, "*damn* as in *damn* I'm glad the case hasn't been forgotten and dropped into one of those famous black holes."

Ryan waited for him to continue.

"First . . . tell me how and why you're interested in Yousef."

Ryan had to hold back. He couldn't share Rob's intel with John, at least not yet. "One of our targets appears to be connected to a man who in turn had connections to Mahmoud."

John seemed comfortable with that answer. "Let me tell you something. What you've got, what the media's got, is not what Yousef's case is about; not at all." He stopped himself and took a draft of foamy stout. "I'm not saying I know all there is when it comes to Yousef. In fact, what has been eating me up on this case is that I don't have any answers . . . but I've got a thing or two, enough, to tell me . . . tell me that what we've been given is a load of shit—a ton of it!"

"Like what? A cover-up to cover air force asses?"

"See, that's the thing. I don't think the AF had anything to do with it. They were not the players. They were played *with*."

Ryan pressed further. "Played by their bosses? Pentagon?"

"I'm not sure. You know the part with Yousef working for Nebraska AF base, right?"

Ryan nodded.

"Well, he never did. He never lived in Nebraska, and there is no record or witness putting him in the facility: as in *ever*."

Ryan had no reason to doubt him. John was the air force major in charge of personnel security whose area included airbases and airfields around the country.

"I chased that as far as I could," John continued, "and all I got was this: the guy's permanent residence was right here in the D.C. area, Falls Church. The house was listed under Victoria Lawson, who worked for some international development company—make that a *megacompany*. Her title: chief of security. I ran a background check on my own and got a fairly ordinary but limited CV: certified fluent in Arabic, master's degree from Georgetown on International Affairs, two years at Defense Language Institute—"

Ryan broke in. "What's her connection to Yousef?"

"He was her tenant; nothing else on paper that connects the two except for the house."

"So where is she now?"

"That's just it. Vaporized. Vanished. She no longer exists."

"The house?"

"New owner. Purchased it through some intermediaries and real estate agents without ever meeting her. Wire transfer . . . Oh yeah, to an account in Cyprus. The account holder is not an individual but a company with some gibberish foreign name."

Ryan rubbed his temples, squinting.

"That's what I mean. Who is this guy? Who's behind him? It's mind-boggling. One of the world's biggest terrorist commandos gets residency here, security clearance, a U.S. military title . . . all the while, trotting the globe to execute terror operations. Add to that secret closed-court trials; everything forever classified."

"And no one has seen him since his arrest."

"That too." John took a swig. "You guys arrested and brought him in. So what else did you get besides his hunk o' muscle self?"

"That's next. The bureau *loves* paper trails. I'll see what I can get from the guys who brought him in. Then there's Canadian Intel."

"Do that, Ryan. Somebody's got to. Two years now, and so many initial answers are proven loads of lies and shit. And let me know what I can do from my end. I've still got sources and know a few tricks. Don't wait."

* * * *

Monday, Early Evening, September 29, 2003
Alexandria, Virginia

Elsie left work earlier than usual. By 6:30 she was already in faded jeans and a tee, preparing cold cuts and crackers and cheese while Simba took a postdinner nap in the wheelchair.

She and Sami had switched tasks. She put herself in charge of the wine and Sami in charge of picking up their food from one of the best and most authentic Thai restaurants near Old Town.

She was rinsing her sticky cheesy hands under the kitchen tap when the doorbell rang—an hour early. She glanced at the microwave clock. Maybe Sami was done early?

Elsie looked through the peephole, ready to twist the doorknob. It was Ryan. What in the world was he doing here? Had something urgent come up?

She opened the door and took a quick step outside. Barefoot, her toes nearly curled on the cold concrete.

"Ryan!"

Here was an Elsie he'd never seen. He took a moment to look at her.

"Oh . . . hi. Sorry to drop in like this. I tried your cell twice but didn't get an answer."

"I left it in the bedroom. Everything Okay?"

Ryan smiled. "May I come in? It's getting nippy . . ."

Embarrassed, Elsie swung the door wide. "I'm sorry, this is *me* surprised. Come in." She went in and headed up the stairs with Ryan two steps behind her.

Elsie pointed to the sofa. "Have a seat. In fact, why don't you join me in a glass of wine? I just opened a bottle."

"That'd be nice."

Elsie headed into the kitchen. Ryan watched the cat who'd been eyeing him before he decided to follow.

He spied the plates and cheeses. "I'm sorry Elsie, you're expecting someone? Don't tell me I walked in on your date?"

Elsie laughed. "No. At least not a *date* date. Sami is coming over for takeout and wine. But she won't be here till seven-thirty."

"Sam Bamford?"

Elsie nodded.

"I didn't know you two were that close. I mean . . . huh."

Elsie knew the kind of impression Sami made on men, especially her coworkers. It was exactly the kind Sami wanted to make. But she was so much more.

Elsie handed him a glass of Pinot Noir.

They stood close to each other in the tiny kitchen. There was so much he didn't know about her. She was complicated, he knew, and with a secret or two. More important, he felt bewildered to stand so close yet need to control his urge to touch her.

As if she'd read his mind, Elsie asked, "So what brought you to my doorstep this evening, Marcello?"

Ryan took a step back into the living room. "Why don't we start with you? I saw your note. Sorry I missed the pizza. I had to meet someone for lunch," then added, "a source and a meeting for info."

"This morning I went in to Archives to check on Yousef's file," she told him.

"You know that room is monitored, right?"

"I didn't take out anything from his folder, I just looked at it."

"And?"

"Zip. The protocol requires forensic examination of his laptop, decryption, translation and analyses of his documents . . . yet, nothing. The bureau either didn't do it or handed over all evidence and translation analyses and then destroyed the copies, which leaves me asking why."

"No arresting agents' names? Not even the interrogator?"

Elsie shook her head. "Something interesting, though: three passports, one of them a diplomatic passport issued in 1997 by the State Department with Yousef's picture under the name Khalid Ramesh."

Elsie noticed him clenching his fist.

"Very interesting . . . and most likely fake. I'll check from my side and see if our database has anything."

"And what about you?" she asked. "Have you gotten anyth—"

"Oh," he interrupted, "you used to work for DLI: Have you ever heard of a Victoria or Vicky Lawson?"

Elsie paused. "I don't think so. Not that I recall. Why?"

"Probably nothing. It came up when I was checking something."

Elsie didn't buy it. She made a mental note to follow up, but for now she'd let it slide. "Okay. Anything besides this *Lawson* woman?"

"Maybe. Here is something: Yousef's primary residence address was listed as the D.C. area. Falls Church, Virginia, to be exact. He never worked or lived in Nebraska."

"So how did the military go along with it? Unless he was a part of our operations, and the AF cover was provided by the Pentagon . . ." remembering Ryan's rage, she paused. "How else do you make sense of this, Ryan? It was the Pentagon that confirmed his position, title, rank, clearance level, and job location in the first place. He didn't forge these. And if we assume the passport is authentic . . . then why would the Pentagon create a cover? What did they use him for?"

Ryan felt the tension go into his head. It was his stress point. "I agree," he answered slowly. "We're on the same side . . . I'm not being biased. This could be a case of a covert operative gone bad. Maybe it is, maybe it isn't. We're still missing facts."

Ryan debated whether to share the rest of John's information. Part of him was afraid Elsie might get cold feet from the likely CIA involvement and decide to back out. He knew how she felt: she hated them. He didn't blame her.

Part of him too felt guilty for not sharing every fact. He also sensed danger and risk to them both. He would not endanger this woman if he could help it. And he could not stay away. It was a mess.

Elsie sensed his struggle. "You're not holding back on me?"

Ryan rushed to a decision. "No . . . but we're wandering in a maze. We need flashlights."

Elsie's eyebrows tied in a frown. "What is it that I'm not getting from you?"

Ryan took a step toward her until they were inches apart. With his index finger he gently traced Elsie's frown lines. "Maybe . . ." he began almost in a whisper.

Elsie didn't move. She held her breath, holding Ryan's gaze.

Ryan dropped his hand and took three steps back. "I better go."

CHAPTER 6

Saturday, October 4, 2003
Saigon, Vietnam

Lou asked the waitress for a second cup of drip and popped the last slice of French bread in his mouth. The small dining room of the mini hotel in Saigon's backpacker district was always full at 8 A.M. At nearly every table were rugged Australian twentysomethings with their maps and brochures spread out, taking full advantage of the hotel's free breakfast.

Lou blended in perfectly with his leathery tan, streaked and dyed honey brown semi-Mohawk, "full sleeve" tattoos on one arm and half sleeve on the other, faded taupe cargo shorts, T-shirt and sandals, all screaming Land Down Under. He'd gone from Lou to Lucas, even eating yeasty sour Vegemite for breakfast.

For the last few days he'd been on a stakeout: monitoring from a safe distance the comings and goings at his god-uncle's bar, the attached noodle shack run by his industrious Vietnamese wife, and the two-storey house behind.

His uncle ran the bar with the help of a boy in his teens. His twenty-three-year-old cousin pitched in; but it was the Vietnamese wife who ran everything, hustling nonstop.

Lou believed the time was right and circumstances safe enough to make contact. It'd been over a month since the hotel and almost two weeks since he'd left the tiny village in the Mekong Delta. Since then he'd been living the backpacker's life at the little hostel-style hotel, monitoring and spying on his uncle.

He finished his second condensed milk–sweetened coffee in two big gulps and got to his feet. Soon he was on his Vespa, zipping and swiveling through the lunatic traffic of Saigon's hectic District One on his way to District Three.

Lou parked in the alley next to the house and approached the front. He tapped on the open door and stepped into the entry where half a dozen shoes were scattered over the marble tiles.

His lean cousin Luan lazily approached, dragging his bare feet. He looked more Vietnamese than Caucasian: small with straight dark brown hair down to his lower neck, slightly slanted eyes, heart-shaped face and odd-looking mustache.

Lou hadn't seen his cousin in a long while. He removed his helmet and stood quietly. Luan took his time examining the face until his expression went from cold curiosity to slightly warm.

"You're here, finally. We've been expecting you, Lou. Come in. He's in the TV room having breakfast."

After the two shook hands, Lou followed his cousin to the second floor. His uncle was watching CNN with his back to the door.

"Uncle Mitch, hi."

"I knew you were going to make it," Mitch began, "but still, Jesus, I'm relieved, boy." He gave Lou one of his bone-crushing hugs. In his late fifties and with a still-full shock of gray hair in a ponytail, Lou's Uncle Mitch held on affectionately, his thick ropy arms displaying an array of military and motorcycle tats.

"Wait . . ." Mitch stepped to the door and yelled, "Hung! Lou's here—and bring some coffee with you!"

"No worries. I've had tons of coffee already."

"You didn't have Hung's coffee. She gets hers directly from the source in Da Lat. Wait until you taste it, just wait."

Luan, a bit intimidated by this affection for Lou, told his father, "I better go. I'm meeting the guys for the project. I'll be back before noon."

"Ya, ya, ya. Don't get carried away with that. Remember the last one, son. Let history teach us."

Luan left without a word.

"Come sit. I like your new look, Lou. And who're you supposed to be, eh?"

"An outlaw from Down Under, Uncle Mitch."

"I'd say you pull it off. Maybe you'll keep it for good . . . at least for a while."

"I can't go on hiding on the run like this anymore. I'm sick of it."

Mitch held up a finger. "Let's not talk about it now. Not here. We'll have our coffee then head out somewhere nice . . . by the river, and you'll tell me everything, how you got yourself tangled up in some big shit. I'd say big shit all right, since they came asking for you. Not the kind you ever wanna get tangled up with, son—ever."

Lou solemnly nodded as Hung entered with three drip-topped coffee cups in a tray. The woman never aged. She seemed as thin, agile and kind-faced as ever. She smiled at Lou and set one cup on the side table next to him before handing Mitch his coffee, and then sat on the bare tiled floor with hers.

It was time for niceties, to catch up on family affairs; for small normal talk. Time to forget about frightening circumstances and life-threatening situations, at least for now. For an hour or so.

* * * *

Lou felt exhausted by the time he finished telling Mitch the entire story and chronology of events. He wanted to provide as much detail as possible: partly for the relief that came with having at least one person in on this story; and partly—cynical person that he was—for insurance to keep his story alive even if he no longer was.

They'd been sitting in an outdoor café on the river in District Two. The constant parade of loud-engine riverboats in front, combined with the buzzing cars and beeping motorbikes behind provided a safe and comfortable zone for their meeting and conversation.

Uncle Mitch had not interrupted him once during the entire narrative, which had taken at least thirty minutes. Every so often he averted his eyes and stared emptily at the passing boats and water taxis or looked down as he sipped his cold coconut water, but otherwise he'd been all attention.

Lou leaned back and let out a breath. "There you have it, from beginning to end." He picked up the green coconut shell to drain whatever was left over.

Mitch signaled the waiter. "I'd say we deserve our beer now, no?" He ordered two Saigon beers, a double platter of fried spring rolls and a plate of lemongrass squid.

"Of all the people and entities in the world, you found the worst and most vicious to mess with, son."

"I didn't *pick* them!" Lou protested. "I stumbled and fell into this shit! It was supposed to be a report on a scandal involving dirty U.S. politicians. Who could have guessed? The CIA has been doing its own stories on these scumbags—for blackmail! I—"

Mitch held up his hand. 'Hey, hey. I know. All I meant was, I can't think of any bigger shit."

"Where do I go? What do I do? They know that I know, and they can't have that. So there's only one choice left: to kill me, and destroy every copy. So far I've scattered around as many copies as possible . . . just for some level of insurance. Well, kinda."

"You think they haven't already figured that out? That one is easy: it is what anyone would do for *insurance*, and that takes out the insurance part."

"So . . . you're saying they'd kill me and not worry about how many people have digital copies?"

"I suspect yes. Think about it. Who in the world would be suicidal enough to take your DVD and publicize it once you're dead?"

Lou smiled slyly. "You would." He produced a DVD from his pants and slid it across the table. "There, Uncle Mitch, consider yourself served!"

Mitch refused to touch it. "I'm serious. You have to think rationally. As far as I can see, you have two options—"

"What about the Internet?" Lou interrupted. "Once the shit goes viral, I go back home and get my life back, no? What would be the point?"

Mitch sadly shook his head. "You could never count on that to protect you. The death warrant already has been issued. You're marked."

The waiter brought their food and set it up in front of them.

Mitch continued. "Option one: you go living like this, on the run and in hiding for as long as you live or as long as they let you live. Option two: you find an intermediary then try to negotiate with them."

"Negotiate how?"

"That's what the intermediary is for: someone who knows the bastards and how they think or bargain. You must find a way to assure them that you're mum for life and help them to retrieve every copy."

"And they'll take my word for it, just like that!"

"Don't be too quick to dismiss that possibility, Lou. They'd know *you* know your life is dependent on keeping your word. What better guarantee to secure every copy? Including *this*." He slid the disk back toward Lou.

Lou had to admit, his uncle had been around the block more than once. He'd survived.

"You said an intermediary, someone who knows the other side. Do you have someone in mind?"

Mitch nodded slowly. "Yes, I believe I do."

* * * *

Monday Evening, October 6, 2003
Mui Ne, Vietnam

On the upper terrace of the four-storey house perched on one of Mui Ne's tallest hills, Greg sat with a cup of dried artichoke tea. Mai, in subtle style, had succeeded in getting him to try it. He almost never deviated from his habits or routines. If he did, it would be at the insistence of Mai: Mai and Mai alone.

The sun had set, his usual time for evaluating, and sometimes reevaluating. The sunrise was for thinking and planning, always here in this spot.

Greg was not retired per se, but neither was he working for the company; he was not completely out or really in: thus the thinking and planning, and reevaluations.

Greg knew that once he was out—completely out—he'd be prey. He'd go from hunter to hunted, meaning that someone *else* would be doing all the thinking, planning, devising and executing of plans. He'd be one step behind. That would not be a good position to be in. At all.

Greg would not allow that to happen. He was always the hunter and was determined to remain that way—so he had to stay at least two steps ahead. And that's exactly what he was doing: *before* hunting season began.

First order of business was his list of sources, cultivated through-out twenty years in the field: those who *owed* him one or two. Next were his strategically placed money accounts—untraceable—around the globe. He also had created several alter egos, each meticulously formed, polished and expertly tucked away. His technological access and gadgets were preserved, in duplicates, and ready for use. Of course, he had taken care of Mai's needs as well. The equation had begun to change when she entered his life three years ago, and over the last two years, significantly. When he opened the door to her, despite himself, he opened what soul he had left.

His last *real* work was the one he'd successfully executed in 2001, in Moscow. At the time he didn't know that mission would be his last true one. Despite his annoyance with last-minute changes in targets and location, he had carried it out to perfection.

What changed his path—or more accurately, his *thinking* of his path—was what took place a couple of months after that last mission. It was the terrorist attack inside the United States, the one that killed thousands and changed the world and all its previous games and rules. At the time, he was in the Lufthansa business lounge in Frankfurt Airport. Despite two decades as one of his country's top operatives, he found out along with the rest of the world—aka the prey—via *BCB*. It was a first, when a tool of the company, say NCN or BCB, had knowledge before he did—a top elite global operative.

This irony carried into the period even *following* the attack: when they announced al-Hazar as the culprit, for instance, the terror group behind the attack; and when the names of culprit operatives were publicized; and when all-out war on al-Hazar was declared. That's right. He was getting all that from lowly little tentacles: BCB, NCN, New York Corp and the rest.

The entire thing was a supreme cosmic joke. Yes, he was deliberately placed outside the loop: before, during, and after the attack. And why? They knew he'd know, of course; it was Greg and the rest of the company who had created al-Hazar in the first place. They created a brand and coined it with a name that started as a joke among company men, and somehow it had stuck.

They were al-Hazar: Greg, aka OG 68, OG 59, OG 42; all of them, from OG 1 to 158. He knew that he didn't do it, nor had he heard anything about it. That left 157 more OGs. He doubted any number higher than his own (which translated to any operative below him in rank), knew of or took any part in it. Could it be possible that the top tier had created a separate branch within the OGs to carry this out? Quite possible.

For an operation within the company's own territory, the top tier would have to go through the profile of each OG and eliminate those not suited or undetermined. What then was he, unsuited or undetermined? They knew him to have no conscience, no attachments in country; they also know his major objective is to attack, destroy and obliterate everything Russian. So which part of unsuited or undetermined does that make him?

The attack on home soil and all the questions it engendered made Greg rethink his position within the company, the risks that entailed, and what was in his future. That they doubted his commitment and questioned his status with regard to the 2001 operation was clear. Surely he would have to be eliminated. Odds were that it would be later than sooner, and that had provided him with time and opportunity to get ready.

Mai appeared promptly at 8:30 to check the temperature of the tea. She picked up the pot and said in the softest voice, "I bring fresh tea for us," gracefully exiting.

They sat with their tea in a comfortable quiet. They'd watch the stars. He'd ask of her plans for the following day. She'd reply simply, about everyday chores and life. She was his dream. He loved the soft, quiet, predictable life with utterly beautiful Mai. He'd had more than his share of scary growing up, with a hooker for a mother who'd guaranteed a life of unpredictability. To never know what's coming next is frightful. Yes. This was the life for him, this woman. No second-guessing that.

* * * *

Tuesday, October 7, 2003
Mui Ne, Vietnam

Lou was getting frustrated and impatient, two things his uncle had cautioned him not to be. For the past two days he'd been watching the posh seafront bar, waiting for his man to arrive. Where was he? A middle-aged Kiwi guy ran the bar; and there were two waitresses, a young man who cleaned, and another who served as some sort of security when he wasn't doing errands.

Lou also had spied a young woman who visited the bar during early morning hours. She always went in the back door and spent less than half an hour inside. Who was she? She was exquisite, dressed simply but elegantly, and glided when she walked, like a weightless fairy. Was she the man's wife, mistress? Uncle Mitch had described her briefly with two words: *very beautiful*. She certainly was that.

Today he decided to follow the young woman instead. He showed up at his usual stakeout and waited. He could see himself living in a place like this: palm and coconut trees, stretches of white sandy beaches, constant breeze and uncharacteristic resorts, everything calm and quiet. He even imagined writing a book, a novel about a no-name journalist who got royally fucked when he tried his hand at real journalism . . .

His reverie was interrupted when Mai appeared, approaching the bar's back door. Abruptly she stopped and turned to stare at the spot behind which Lou was hiding. He held his breath and didn't move. Was she one of those people who could inexplicably sense things?

No sooner had he finished that thought than Mai slipped through the bar's back door.

Lou took out a pack and shook one out, a habit he'd acquired to keep sane on the run and in hiding. He took a drag and held it, then let the smoke out in slow hypnotic ringlets.

Today Mai kept her visit short, under thirty minutes. Sticking with his plan, he followed her on his Vespa down the boulevardlike street. While tricky, it was better than to tail her on foot in broad daylight, which would have been noticed. With his helmet to cover his Mohawk, Lou blended right in.

After stopping for fruits and vegetables, Mai crossed two lanes and began climbing the hilly street opposite the shore. Lou waited at the corner and watched her steady ascent to the top. He saw her open the wrought iron gate; then she was out of sight. He waited a full minute before he drove up the street to check out the house: it was grand, by Vietnamese standards, with two terraces on the upper floor facing back toward the sea. Slowly Lou began his descent. He'd be back up here later this evening, when he'd knock on the door and ask to see the man. He'd tell him about the story, his case, and his fight for his life. He'd show him the DVD—and then what? What would happen next? One step at a time, according to Uncle Mitch: do so carefully and surely. Tonight.

* * * *

Tuesday Night, October 7, 2003
Mui Ne, Vietnam

Mai was in the kitchen boiling water for Greg's tea when she heard the knock. That was unusual. They almost never had visitors. Everyone around them, here and at work, knew that their residence was never to be disturbed. Who then could be knocking at 8 P.M.?

Greg stopped by the kitchen with a fully loaded gun. "You stay here." He and his Bobcat, a Beretta 21A, had been through a lot together. Tonight they were going down to the door.

Lou looked up at the imposing man and instantly forgot his lines.

"Yes?" Greg demanded.

"I-I was sent by Mitch O'Connor. He referred you . . . I-I'm his nephew."

"Don't know any Mitch O'Connor."

"He said to tell you that he owed you one . . . once."

Greg checked out the young New York punk. O'Connor would know better than to send anyone to his door—unless it was life or death. Either way, Greg didn't give a damn. He made a quick calculation. "Follow me." Over his shoulder he calmly instructed, "Remove your shoes and leave them down here."

They climbed the two floors, Lou following six steps behind.

Once inside the ornate half study, Greg pointed to a leather club chair. "Sit. I'll be back."

Greg left the room to put the Bobcat away, back into the nightstand drawer. The punk was harmless.

He returned to find Lou pacing in circles. "I expect adherence to clear instructions." Greg pointed again. "Now *sit*."

Lou sat. Then he started tapping his foot. What was it with this guy? He exuded danger. What if Uncle Mitch was wrong? What if the stupid in him just walked into the agency's trap? His thoughts were interrupted by Greg's no-bullshit voice.

"I'm giving you thirty minutes, no more, no less. Tell me what you came here for. Show me whatever you've got. Get my answer, leave promptly, and never come back. The clock starts now."

Lou swallowed. WTF! Everything about the guy was stone cold creep. Should he just get up and run? No, his uncle was right. This was his only hope to stay alive. Before he knew it, he was halfway through the story.

He finished with a condensed version of his monthlong crouch in the Mekong Delta and final meeting with his uncle. Lou checked his watch: 13 minutes. Not bad. Then he reached into his pocket and pulled out the DVD. "If you would, please play this and hand me your remote. I'll make sure you see only the pertinent parts. I've got seventeen minutes left."

Greg accepted the DVD and turned it over. No labels or ID. He inserted it into the player, grabbed the remote, turned on the TV, and tossed the remote at the punk who snatched it midair. Good reflexes. Okay, not a junkie or regular addict.

Lou hit fast-forward to where Keller enters the suite. "I assume you know who this guy is." Greg didn't respond. "That's the Whip; Congressman Donald Keller."

Lou let the scene play uninterruptedly, right up to the suicide and balcony leap. Maurice and his assistant arrive, the scene is fast-forwarded to the cleanup, and Josh and Sander then debug the room—when Lou and Greg were startled by a shriek.

Both men turned to see Mai at the door, frozen in shock, her hand at her mouth to muffle her scream.

Greg quickly went over. "Mai. You should not have come up. You should not have seen this. This has nothing to do with you. Or your sister."

Mai raised her hand in protest. "That girl . . . she looks like my lost sister. Did they do the same thing to my sister? Tell me Greg, please tell me. Tell me now."

"Mai. That was *not* your sister. Some other girl. Not your sister. We don't know what happened to her. Not yet. You must go now to your room. You need to lie down and rest."

"You promised you find my sister," Mai told him. "Who are these Americans? They talk American. I can tell they are. Why do they do this to our children? Someone must stop them. Greg, why don't you help to stop? Help this man here so he can stop all this . . ."

Greg placed his hands on her shoulders and gently turned her around. "Go now. I will be with you shortly. Go and rest. Now, Mai."

Mai moved off as though in a trance. Greg closed the door. "Two minutes, and I want you out of here for good."

"That's not my fault. You said thirty minutes. I have"—he glanced at his watch—"nine minutes."

"Four minutes and counting," Greg declared.

"They're after me," Lou began in haste. "The CIA, and god knows who else. They want me dead. I'm stuck. I can't go back to the States like this. I can't keep running and hiding. I need your help. Mitch said you'd know a way out, how to resolve this with those bastards in the agency. I need your help. I'm . . . I'll do anything, anything in return."

"There is nothing you can do for me and nothing I need from you." He continued in the same level tone. "Your case is none of my business."

"That's it then? You're saying go to hell, die or whatever? Is that what you're saying?"

Greg looked at his watch. "Your time is up. You must go."

Lou stood up. "Does that mean you'll think about it further? Yes?"

"Leave now." The punk had already caused enough pain, for Mai. Mitch now owed him more than *one*.

"May I have my DVD back? I'll leave as soon as you give me my DVD."

"No. Your DVD stays. You go without it."

"That's not the only copy. I have dozens, tucked away safely in trustworthy hands. If you think it'll help cut a deal, I can get the other cop—"

"Go," Greg commanded.

Lou left without even bothering to put on his sandals. He didn't want to break down in front of his last hope. How long could he go on like this? How long could he last? He had two thousand in cash from his uncle. Where to next? Now his face was covered with tears

and he was shaking. Right now he hated everything and everyone—
including and especially himself. He would get drunk tonight. That
was a plan.

Greg closed the door behind him and went up to check on Mai.
She was wide awake, staring at the ceiling, naked.

"Mai? You okay?"

"Greg. I need to be alone, to be sad. Please go."

Greg understood. He gently closed the door and went down to
brew his artichoke tea. It was way past reflection and evaluation time.
That window was closed. Instead he would drink his tea and think.
He had one new item in his preparatory list: the punk's incriminating
DVD. One day, perhaps, it could have its use.

* * * *

She didn't even blink. It was not the dark ceiling she was staring up
into, but her past and painful loss. It was her little sister, Chan.

> *The morning. Washed down. Then our nicest clothes—
> even shoes that day, plastic slip-ons. Mother, me and Chan on
> the neighbor's motorbike, husband driving. Maybe get some-
> thing to eat? We were hungry, and Chan, only four, crying. No
> money. Never any money . . .*
>
> *Orphanage life. Phan Thiet. Not too bad. In fact, more
> to eat. No beatings or other. We help, younger children. And
> school, half a day. Even bikes to ride, to get to it . . .*
>
> *Sixteen now, officially adult . . . not leaving here without
> Chan. My only family. Like her mother, her only guardian . . .*
>
> *We leave together, government agrees. My care. One bag,
> a change of clothes, two best books, and Chan's only prize:
> her raggedy blond doll, given by French visitor—to buy off a
> terrible conscience . . .*

Job. Good at changing beds at resorts, and scrubbing tiles and fixtures clean. Clean until they gleam. And everyone so beautiful, ever and always elegant . . .

Need someone to look after Chan . . . then a deal with Phung: when not in school Chan would help her carry things, wash and sort the vegetables, and Phung would keep an eye on her. It seemed to work out—for a while . . .

Then . . . that day, called to staff office. Phung, waiting anxiously . . . details all blurry . . . little sister gone . . . disappeared . . . just like that . . .

Weeks looking everywhere . . . anyplace I could think. Police station daily. Even after shooing away, kept on going there. Questioning everyone, every vendor in the market . . . no one saw a thing. Then rumors. Things people heard and whispered back. Hushed talk of powerful white men who like little girls and sometimes little boys, and take them away . . . do bad things to them . . . the poorer the better. Like Chan, who don't mean much . . .

Every minute every day thinking of Chan, every hour outside work looking . . .

Chan . . . who put Greg in my life . . . a man to be afraid of; powerful quiet white man. With extraordinary powers. Who knew many things. A man no one knew but everyone knew of. A strange white man. An American . . .

Greg remembered well. For days, she'd turn up looking to see him. They'd shoo her off. She wouldn't give up. She'd return that same night and next morning. Until, finally, he'd agreed to see her. She'd hopped on the back of the security man's bike without a question or trace of doubt.

When he opened the door she'd held his gaze without a blink and they stayed like that for a lengthy minute—until Greg ordered the security man to go back, without Mai.

Greg had taken her to the second-floor terrace where they sat for a while, neither of them speaking. It had been Mai who'd broken the silence. In halting English and using her hands she told him all about Chan, mixed up with Vietnamese. She presented to him her clumsily made flyer with Chan's picture.

He had listened intently, holding her gaze. He did not interrupt even once. When she finished, after a moment of quiet, he began speaking very calmly and slowly in near-perfect Vietnamese. Mai, he could see, found that somewhat disconcerting.

You speak Vietnam language?

Not really. I know Vietnamese language, but I almost never speak it.

But why?

Because I don't want to. And I don't want them to know.

You mean Vietnamese people?

I mean anyone. Everyone. No one.

Mai had nodded, although she couldn't understand the reasoning. That was the last time he'd spoken to her in Vietnamese. He told her he'd look into her sister's disappearance but that he couldn't make any promises. He would try and continue trying. He knew of some people doing things like that . . . some white men . . .

He had only asked for one thing: He would send her to Saigon to a good English language school, taking care of her expenses for eighteen months. She would also study bookkeeping and computers, followed by a three-month culinary course.

When Mai asked *Why?* he'd answered simply, *When you are done, and eighteen, you will move into this house and manage my domestic affairs, including help with the bar.*

And that was that. Within a week she was sent to Saigon. She would ask about Chan, and he would say he was looking for answers.

The day she returned, that very same day, Mai moved into his house and his life. They'd begun their quiet partnership with a very quiet way of life. She observed and understood his routines, including those involving constricted meals of nuts, rare fish, seared vegetables and malty milk. He too grasped her way, and they became a pair.

A few months later they made love—quietly and calmly, of course; very naturally—and again the next evening, and the evening after that. In almost every way, he thought, they were a perfectly fitted couple.

Mai continued to stare at the ceiling, reliving the loss of Chan.

> *That man with tattoo and his DVD, the real movie of children ... what happened to them ... And Chan? Had she committed suicide like that little girl? Had they molested, raped and tortured her to death? Had she jumped, like the other little girl? Was she hiding somewhere ... in Vietnam, Cambodia, Laos or Thailand?*
> *And what of Greg—why hadn't he found her? Three years? Did he find out and then decide not to share? Why wasn't he helping that man with tattoos? He seemed to be on their side ... Was Greg working with some of those terrible men?*

She thought and thought and questioned, until she drifted off exhausted, lying naked on top of the unmade bed. And she dreamed of Chan.

* * * *

Wednesday Morning, October 8, 2003
Mui Ne, Vietnam

Despite the cold shower and three cups of strong coffee without the usual sweetened milk, Lou's head was a balloon about to break. His neck was a pike and stomach filled with acid. He didn't feel at all optimistic.

Lou sat on his bike at the bottom of Greg's hilly street. No, he would not go back up to try to wangle with the creep. He was waiting for Mai. His one and only chance—no, make that his one and only *possibility*—to obtain Greg's help: beautiful young Mai.

The poor woman had looked so desperate and vulnerable. They had mentioned a sister, Mai's sister: possibly a victim of Maurice or some other pimp? Highly likely. If so, Mai had a stake in this deal, and therefore Greg, by default. He had to speak with Mai. He had to convince her, so that she would persuade her man. He had to, for his survival.

There she was now, walking down the hill. Jesus she was beautiful—and young. The creep must have twenty-five years on her.

Mai wasn't headed toward the bar. Instead she turned right, crossed the street, and took a path along the shore.

Lou pulled into the first dirt lot he could find. He parked, removed his helmet, and followed the woman on foot. In a last-minute decision he decided to run and catch up with her.

"Mai . . . Mai," he called to her, breathless.

Mai stopped and turned around. "You following me every day. Why? Why you follow every day?"

So much for Lou's catlike ability. He sucked. "I followed you," he told her, blushing now, "so that I could find Greg. I'm sorry. I didn't know how else to find him. No one would tell me his address."

Mai smiled. "Long time ago I did that too. Greg doesn't like to be found. He is a *private* man. Very private."

"I know that now. I need his help, Mai. I need him badly. He can stop some dangerous men from killing me. And I need you . . . your help too."

"Why me?"

"Can we . . . just go somewhere and sit, to talk? I don't want to do this out in the open, so exposed. Not good for you, not good for me. How about coffee?"

Mai considered. "I know a place. Down the road, in the alley."

Together they walked to the small shop that served banh mi, made with that morning's baguettes, and drip coffee. They chose one of three low wooden tables and sat facing each other. Mai called to the young girl and ordered two coffees in Vietnamese.

"I want to apologize," Lou began, "for making you frightened and sad last night. I wish you hadn't seen that."

Mai didn't respond, but Lou could see sad dark clouds collecting in her eyes.

"Do you want to tell me about your sister?" he gently prodded. "Did Maurice take her as well?"

"Maurice? Tall white man who brought the girls?"

Lou nodded.

Mai waved her hands. "No. I don't know. Maybe. My sister maybe dead. Maybe she alive and with men like that; maybe."

Lou now understood. "So your sister disappeared and you're looking for her. How old?"

"Twelve," Mai responded quickly then paused. "Now almost sixteen. Her name Chan."

Lou felt a genuine pang of sadness for Mai and for the sister.

"Maybe you help me find Chan. Greg promise to find her. Nothing yet. We don't know. Maybe you do?"

Lou pondered the request. "I don't know, Mai. These guys are very dangerous. Very powerful. Like police, like Government. You understand?"

"I do. But Greg powerful too. Very powerful."

"Well, I am *not* powerful. And I need Greg's help. He might be the only one who can save me."

Mai took this information in. "He can help you if he wants. You make him want first."

"See, that's the problem," Lou began, when a large Honda bike pulled in front of the shack. Two men, one of them very tall, hopped off and approached the shack. Both wore helmets, neither one took them off.

Lou felt panic, followed by churning in his gut. Mai followed his eyes. No one said a word.

The tall one strode to their table. Smoothly he pulled his gun from his leather jacket.

"Bye-bye shithead." Three muffled bangs back to back.

Mai half stood to run but she couldn't move her legs or any other parts. She couldn't even scream.

The man looked at her with cold milky eyes. Mai held his hateful glare. She felt the first bullet hitting near her heart, the second one in her stomach. She crumpled to her knees but her eyes refused to leave his. She thought of Chan.

The man stepped forward while she was still kneeling, aimed between her shoulder blades and fired one more time. She collapsed on her face. For Mai, the search was over. From an early age, she'd prayed hard to Buddha, and later on to Jesus. She had even found a powerful white man to help guide her through this life and protect her. Yet none of that mattered now. No one could help her escape her karma; her fate was sealed at birth.

The tall man hopped on the waiting bike, the shorter man started the engine. Last night they'd taken care of Fat Uncle & Son and gotten the DVD. Now back to Saigon and from there, Phnom Penh. Maurice had a client coming in.

CHAPTER 7

Thursday, Noon, October 9, 2003
Markham, Virginia

Ryan waited for the valet to bring around his car. The meeting had gone entirely differently from what he'd expected. He now was at a fork with less than a week to decide which road to take.

Handing the valet a dollar bill and ignoring the irritating smirk—he still was a government man, for chrissakes, not one of their usual billionaires—Ryan squeezed into the car and readjusted the seat, pulled too far forward by the short valet.

It was justice that had formed his original fantasies: of joining the bureau and pursuing this career. This same sense of justice, which allowed him to put up with bureaucratic insanity for fifteen-plus years, was now driving him to obtain it for others. Those others deserving of justice.

Now, he was considering an out for that reason: justice. He had come to a point where to reach it he had to get out of the FBI. He could no longer help to shield those on the opposite side.

Ryan's cell began to ring with Dean Martin's "Mambo Italiano." He slowed the car and reached for his phone while steering with one hand. "Yeah?"

"Rob Brown here. You have a few minutes?"

"Hold on." He pulled onto the shoulder, next to a manicured horse-grazing field. "Shoot."

The line remained quiet for seconds.

"They're after me. I think I'm fucked."

"Okay, calm down first. What's going on?"

"I guess they were sniffing me while I was sniffing around the Yousef case . . . I was called into the office on Tuesday. They said I had to submit to an immediate mental and physical eval—immediate as in *right now*."

"When was your last evaluation?"

"That's the thing. Less than six months ago. The whole nine yards! Mental, physical, financial . . . everything!"

"And? You took it?"

"Hell yes. Let me tell you something, I've never taken anything like this . . . Some weird shit like *Do I ever think sex when I look at my prepubescent daughter?*! Can you believe shit like that? Sick!"

"And then what?"

"So they keep bombarding me with all these sick insinuations . . . and I kept asking why they were being creeps . . . basically, I was answering each question with a question of my own."

"Calm down, Rob. What happened next?"

"Stop telling me to calm down. I'd like to see how calm you'd be under these circumstances. I'll tell you what: I was asked to turn in my gun and badge, my clearance is put on hold, and they tell me I suffer from delusional paranoia. That's what!"

"Just like that? In one day?" Ryan sounded shaken. "It's not the fucking flu you can catch!"

"I'm to receive treatment, therapy, whatever, for my paranoid delusional tendencies—medication and all. After six months, if I have a clean report, I'm to submit to another eval and then *they'll see* if I can get my job back. I've put seventeen years into this fuckhole. I've got three kids under sixteen. My wife has been out of a job since last year. They may as well have signed my death warrant!"

"Have you considered an attorney? You have legal rights. It's not that easy to fuck a senior agent, you know."

"Let me tell you something, there aren't many attorneys out there who're willing to take on the bureau as an adversary. And the few who do are extortionists."

Ryan could tell he was almost in tears.

"If I were you," Rob continued, "I'd stop digging this shit up. Right away. They'll come after you, Ryan. They'll drop two tons of brick on you. They'll hit you when you least expect it, where it hurts the most . . . Close that Yousef chapter and keep your head down. The bastards are sadists once they see you as the enemy. Let it go."

"I'll beat them to it," Ryan assured him. "I'll dump them before they screw with me. Don't worry about me. I'll call you tomorrow."

"No, no. Don't call, I'll call you: and use more throwaways, the bastards catch up fast. I'll get in touch when I'm ready."

"Okay." Ryan ended the call. His thinking was done. Call it a sign or karma, it was decided. That was *it*.

* * * *

Thursday, Early Evening, October 9, 2003
Arlington, Virginia

Elsie was stuck in the notorious and infuriating D.C. traffic at rush hour. She had left the office at 4:45 P.M., and here she was at 5:30, nowhere near where she wanted to go. She tried the radio: commercial. She pressed button number two: commercial. She gave up and put on her Fados CD. Soon the car was flooded with the mournful, heavenly voice of Dulce Pontes.

Her first destination was an Internet café on a street behind

Ballston Mall, this one in the back room of a Hispanic bakery. She went through the usual steps and the only free PC station was at the entrance, with the least amount of privacy. She brought up her secret e-mail box: two messages.

The first was sent four days ago and consisted of two cryptic sentences: *Looked everywhere but no find. Was told target moved to border neighbor-east.* "Border neighbor-east" would put the target somewhere around the Iran-Turkey border. Not good.

The second e-mail was even shorter: *Check M.box.*

Elsie logged off and exited. She walked briskly to the mall two blocks away and took the elevator down to P3 for her car.

Within five minutes she was on Wilson Boulevard heading north. Less than a mile later, she was in the parking lot of a nondescript strip mall. The post office was closed but the P.O. boxes were accessible round the clock. Elsie retrieved a key from the glove compartment and headed to box 365. Wedged into the box were envelopes, flyers, catalogues and brochures crammed and rolled so tightly that it took muscle and effort to pry them out. Quickly, she shuffled through the pile, simultaneously tossing one envelope after another into a trash-recyclables bin until she stopped at a plain envelope with Paris, France, as the return address.

Without wasting a moment she opened it, removed the folded single white sheet, tucked it inside her coat pocket and meticulously shredded the envelope, scattering the pieces into the trash.

Once back in the car, after locking all the doors, she retrieved the paper and slowly unfolded it. On it was a detailed pencil sketch of an older than middle-aged man's face.

Elsie held her breath. She shut her eyes and opened them. She looked down. Could it be? The face in the sketch had hairlines receding at the temples. The forehead was strong and deeply lined; the cheekbones bony and pronounced. The eyes were intense and almond-shaped, framed with very thick eyebrows. The nose was a boxer's nose, slightly crooked. She couldn't make out the shape of the lips because the lower face was covered by a mustache and beard.

She sat and stared at the drawing. Could this be her father? Definitely the forehead and cheekbones; why was this in black and white, damn it! While the intense almond eyes could be her dad's, she couldn't be sure. Yet, if it were in color, there would be no mistaking those distinctive and unusual olive green eyes. She couldn't check for the cleft chin, either—the one passed on to her. Damn it again!

She knew the rough sketch had to have been mailed from a dusty village on the Iraq-Turkey border, where it changed envelopes in Paris and was mailed to the States. Elsie knew he'd looked for her dad and talked to as many as he could cautiously do, and that her father wasn't in the border area. Now, she guessed from interviews and rumors that he was looking at a different country; perhaps different dusty and mountainous border villages. They'd been going in circles like this for two years.

She would not cry. Not yet.

* * * *

Thursday Evening, October 9, 2003
Alexandria, Virginia

Ryan, feeling a bit like a fool, had been sitting on Elsie's front-door steps since six with a bottle of wine. Pinot Noir, in fact, Elsie's favorite. Though the temperature was falling, he was determined to see her, to be with her, and for that he was willing to wait.

They locked eyes as she pulled up in front of the townhouse. If she was surprised, she didn't show it. As Ryan stood his right leg cramped from sitting in the cold. He smiled as Elsie walked toward him. Seeing her, especially tonight, felt good.

"I thought this was supposed to be your *needed break*; some kinda vacation?"

Ryan helped her with a bag and held up his. "Pinot."

Elsie opened the door. "And I bought food. Not fancy, but your kind: meat, bread and potatoes . . . put together slightly differently than your ordinary stew."

"Ordinary and you? Never."

They climbed the stairs and headed to the kitchen. Ryan set the bag and bottle on the counter.

"Okay. Here are your instructions, Agent Marcello: tray in the oven at three twenty-five and time it for fifteen minutes. Open the wine and let it breathe—no arguments. And see if you can get a fire going. I'll be right down. Think you can handle that?"

Ryan listened as though in a trance. "Yes, I believe I can handle . . . I mean, yes, all that."

Elsie could feel the electricity running through her, and with it, a dark shade of rising pink. "Right. I better go and start."

After Ryan had the fire roaring, he noticed the cat perched in Ben's wheelchair, staring at him. Frankly, it felt disconcerting.

He was lost in his thought when Elsie walked in.

"What do you think? Roaring enough?"

Elsie gave him her distinct approval.

"I was thinking," Ryan added, "how about if we sit and eat at that small cozy table in the kitchen . . . Simba seems to enjoy his territory here and—"

Elsie shot the wheelchair—or was it the cat?—a glance, interrupting, "Don't tell me he's already won? You give him an inch and he'll take several miles. Be warned," and with that she left for the kitchen.

Ryan, still not sure what just happened, looked at the wheelchair and then at the cat, in the eye. "With all due respect, I tried." The cat seemed only to glare; then he opened his wide pink mouth and yawned.

Elsie came back with two full glasses and a stack of paper napkins.

Ryan took his and raised the glass. "Salute!"

Elsie raised hers. "Cheers," and took a sip. "How's your vacation so far?"

"It's been giving me . . . some time to take care of things," Ryan answered evasively. "How about you? How's it going at work?"

Elsie considered. "Nothing significant, based on what I'm digging up. On the other hand, I've found several important leads just through my Internet and library database searches . . . State Department announcements and PR turned up tons on al-Hazar funding and now-blacklisted financial entities in Malta, Cyprus and Turkey. That brings us closer to Nazim's territory . . ."

Ryan didn't want to talk about Nazim or Turkey or al-Hazar. Not tonight. Yet Cyprus got his attention. "Greek Cypriot banks or the Turks?"

"Almost all Turkish—well, as far as I could tell; I'm not done yet."

"Anything else, at work?"

"Not really. Nothing new. Oh, here is something but maybe nothing. A bit annoying and maybe totally innocuous: You know Meltem in my office? The DOD Turkish analyst on loan to us since January?"

"Yep." Ryan nodded. "The cold quiet woman who wears only ugly navy suits."

Elsie smirked. "You're a snob. Well, she was on this rather lengthy trip, about two weeks or so. I was told—we all were—it was for a joint Counterterrorism–White Collar Crime operation in Patterson and Philly. I even asked her about it. When she told me last week she was 'heading back to Boston' it bugged me—and even worse, that she seemed not to care. She was being evasive"—Elsie took a long sip, bypassing the savor—"so today I called Tony in Philly to check, and I asked him how things were going with Meltem. He said he hadn't worked with her or seen her since June; that she hasn't been to the Philly office since then."

"Maybe she's mixed up?"

Elsie shook her head. "It was *not* a mix-up. She's on some kind of hush-hush assignment . . . and it doesn't sound like the bureau. We don't operate that way. And if she's working for the Department of Defense, according to our protocol, she'd be off our roster as a contract analyst-linguist. Yet she remains on the roster. Do I make sense?"

Ryan was not in the mood. She began to pour another glass and he stopped her. Elsie, a bit startled, looked up to see his eyes now fixed on her.

She held his gaze as Ryan walked over to her, reaching for her hands and gently pulling her up next to him. "Let me tell you something . . ."

Excited and with a wild heart, she felt the heat rising—from between her legs and just a breath below her belly to immediately above her womanhood, all up her chest, to her throat, face, and inside her head. She felt lightheaded and strangely lightfooted, as if she'd fall if he let go. She inhaled and breathed in his scent.

He kissed the top of her head; tens of little kisses. He moved down until he reached her left ear. He began kissing the top; then his lips moved down to her delicate earlobe. He paused and took half a step back. "If you're going to stop me," he whispered in her ear, "stop me now . . . you want me . . . to stop?"

She forced her brain to process his question. She raised her head, looked into his eyes, his always warm eyes, fiery now. "No . . . don't stop . . . make love to me . . ."

Ryan completely covered her lips with his and kissed her for the longest minute. He wanted to devour her; lips, her tongue, every inch.

He bit her lips. No longer able to carry her lithe weight, she leaned against him, letting him carry her. His tongue explored her mouth. Moans escaped her, in sounds completely strange. She knew about hormones, chemistry, pheromones but what was this? A fierce combination . . . and more?

Ryan lifted her up and carried her upstairs. He pushed open the first door on the landing—the right one. Her bedroom. *The one she had shared with Ben* . . . until now. He pushed away the thought. He would not let it stop him. Not tonight. Not ever.

Their first lovemaking was mutually urgent and rushed, as if they only had a short window of opportunity. Entering her was like joining with his long sought other half—one he'd kept in shadow for most of his life. Their next round was slow, tender, and spoke of things that could never be expressed in words. She was burning hot. Her body glistened. While clutching her hands with his, he rolled with her and placed himself on top of her possessively, primitively possessive.

They'd always been connected, in so many odd ways; eerily so; uncannily. Now, Ryan felt, the connection was complete. This *was* a complete connection. Few were lucky to find it.

Later, when he was lying on his back and she on her stomach, her head perched close to the crook of his arm, Ryan felt a pang of guilt. Guilt at holding back: Pulaski, Rob, his decision, his new job . . . she'd made him promise, and he'd broken that promise in more than one way. This, tonight, magnified that betrayal. As the guilt intensified, he told himself it was only temporary, he would tell her everything soon. He would explain too his holding back. Very soon.

Ryan caressed the space between Elsie's thin shoulder blades. "Promise me something," he began in his defense. "That you won't try to analyze this, us, what we have here this second, the way you analyze everything."

Elsie, though her eyes were closed, considered what he'd said.

It mildly provoked her, like a gentle reprimand. She thought a little more. It took minutes before she answered in a whisper, "Work. Work is what brought us together. It can also do the opposite: tear us apart."

Ryan thought this might be the perfect moment to tell her about his new job. To confess and let her in on what he was about to do: quit what had been his life for more than fifteen years. Then just like that, he decided against it. He was not about to ruin tonight, what they had here right now, with work and the ugliness that filled the case.

"Shhhhh." Ryan stroked her back with his fingers. "We'll deal with that later; but I can certainly promise you this: work won't ever get between us."

Elsie chose to take him at his word—at least for now. She too wanted to hold onto this moment, which is all any of us ever has.

* * * *

Friday Morning, October 10, 2003
Washington, D.C.

Elsie almost knocked over her espresso as she pushed back her chair and slid out. Meltem had gone to the ladies' room and left her organizer next to her keyboard. Elsie snatched it up and leafed through to September, scanning messy handwritten notes in the boxes. Three words jumped out: *Ankara*, as in Turkey, *Tbilisi*, as in Georgia, and *Baku*, as in Azerbaijan.

She closed and placed it precisely where it had been and nearly ran to her desk to sit, heart pounding. God, how she hated spying. She reached for her coffee as Meltem reentered. Elsie forced a smile. "So you're off this weekend. I can't believe it's already Friday."

"I know. It's Philly then Boston. I'm picking up all the boring slack. How's your assignment going?"

Elsie shrugged. "We've been put on a different assignment. The other one didn't get us anywhere. Like most of our cases."

"My contract ends this coming May. I have to say, I won't miss this windowless place, nor the travel."

You're an unskilled liar, Elsie thought. She pretended to work; she looked at the script on the screen without seeing it. Even the adrenaline rush from spying hadn't helped. She couldn't stop thinking about last night.

Ryan had woken before her. He'd made coffee—weak—and even made toast for her, as though he'd been doing it for years. It was all very domestic, Ryan with his laptop open on the kitchen table; Elsie babbling about pieces of a puzzle, connecting actors and dates that were seemingly unrelated. She'd extracted key communications pertaining to their targets and connected them, by whatever degree, to questionable events in Turkey, Caucasus, Central Asia and Afghanistan—with Nazim a constant presence.

Ryan was only half listening, she could tell. His ears perked up when she casually, albeit intentionally, mentioned Victoria Lawson.

"What about Lawson?" he asked from his computer. "What does she have to do with any of that?"

"Nothing," Elsie replied nonchalantly. "Just that you'd mentioned her the other night . . . so I checked her out." In this line of work, she knew, no detail was too small—that and the fact that Ryan had said the name as if *in passing.*

"And . . .?"

"You first. Why did you drop her name the other night?"

"This is what I mean by your tendency to overanalyze everything." He paused. "Yousef had lived in this area, remember? Lawson was the owner who rented the house to him, that's all. Now you."

"And that was not important? Just some cosmic coincidence that a woman who worked for DOD, DLI, and had clearance from RNT

Corporation doing Pentagon-related whatever, happened to be the landlord of one of the most notorious terrorists in the world!"

"I thought of that as well; but Lawson left those jobs for an ordinary position with some private company. For all we know, her real estate agent could've been the one who found Yousef . . ."

Elsie walked over to where he sat with both hands on her waist. "Okay then. I guess her current job overseas is of no importance."

Ryan, as always, felt himself losing the battle of logic. "Maybe, maybe not. I couldn't trace her current job, not since she left the firm here in Fairfax."

"Aha. You'd like her address?"

Ryan always hated being in this position. "Yes?" he managed to choke out.

Elsie smiled. She got her satisfaction. "I don't know her exact address." Ryan's face fell. "But I have the vicinity. Her last known whereabouts was—or is—Baku."

"Azerbaijan! Huh. Okay. I'll see if I can get more."

Later, Ryan had dropped her off at her usual place a block from the Washington Field Office. She'd asked if he would be back at work today and he'd answered *Maybe*. They'd made plans for later that evening: he was to pick her up at 4:45. Pizza and a movie . . . or *maybe* back to her place. She had no doubt about their choice. None whatsoever.

＊ ＊ ＊ ＊

Friday Noon, October 10, 2003
Washington, D.C.

Elsie checked her watch: 11:45. Time to meet Sami for lunch. Since Sami was coming from headquarters, they'd settled on The Tea House in the middle of Chinatown, halfway between HQ and the Washington Field Office.

When Elsie arrived, Sami was already there sipping tea, talking on her cell. Elsie pulled up a chair and began studying the menu while Sami made a *wait* gesture and mouthed, *Almost done.*

She was lost in her thoughts with her eyes fixed on no particular line in the menu when Sami began to apologize.

"Sorry for the phone thing. It's this peculiar situation, a young woman I met two years ago on a stint in New York. We were chasing this child porn ring with ties to a notorious network in Southeast Asia. Anyhow, the woman, Lucy, was working with this NGO who dealt with human trafficking cases in Cambodia, Thailand and Vietnam . . . and that's where our paths crossed. She called me this morning about her boyfriend missing and, well . . . that was what that call was about."

"Missing as in how?"

"He went to Cambodia on a story. He was supposed to be there for less than two weeks and never made it back."

Elsie's antennae went up. "A reporter?"

Sami drained her teacup and refilled it. "Yeah. An investigative reporter with a small online publication. He was chasing this story on some child sex ring with heavyweight Western clients. He was supposed to be back almost two months ago."

Elsie was intrigued. "So what does the report say? Search results?"

"That's the thing. Lucy has not reported it. She says there's more but she wants to meet face-to-face."

"That's stupid. She should have notified the State Department to contact the embassy there."

"I know, but she's not telling me everything. She sounds freaked out. I'm going to meet with her during the coming trip . . . next month. Patterson is only a short train ride to NYC. I'll find out more."

* * * *

Ryan boarded the elevator and pressed 5. He was here to meet with Mike, his boss, to call it a wrap after sixteen years of service to the bureau. He went through his spiel one more time in his head. It had only been twenty-four hours.

Ryan knocked once and entered. He'd called Mike at noon with a heads up. After a minute of small talk, he launched into his spiel, ending with the decision to take the higher-paying job. He gave all his reasons and more.

Mike told Ryan he understood, how sorry he was to see him leave, et cetera. Mike was good at this. He had a knack. He knew how to handle bureaucratic crap and dirty office politics day after day. Mike knew how to kiss ass and get his ass kissed in return. He'd be up there, Ryan figured, among high-level executives in HQ in no time; five years, tops.

Now for Elsie: how brilliant and hardworking she'd been on all their cases, her unfettered commitment and the difficulty of having to break the news—

Mike cut him off. "Don't worry, Ryan, been there, done that. I'll take care of it. In fact, why don't we call her in and break it to her together?" He picked up the phone and dialed the extension. "Yes, hi, Mike here. Could you come to my office . . . yeah, right now . . . okay . . ."

Shit! Ryan thought. This wasn't part of the plan. He wanted first to help maintain her access and position with the unit's cases. Then later tonight, he would tell her everything and explain. *Not this way! Shit!*

Elsie softly knocked twice and entered. She was good at keeping her cool at the sight of Ryan in the office. She maintained her poise and carriage, though Ryan could see her stiffening.

"Hi. Come on in, have a seat."

Elsie sat next to Ryan, facing Mike. She half smiled and nodded by way of greeting. Ryan returned it with his trying-too-hard-to-be-assuring smile.

"You two have been such a great team, a dynamo working duo. Seeing you together like this makes this that much harder, I tell ya."

Ryan could see her knuckles turning white. *Shit! This was going all wrong!*

Mike continued. "Ryan has been the definition of a perfect special agent, and in many ways: his dedication, passion, sometimes doggedness, loyalty, and his drive. He's given this bureau sixteen years of his life, all of it." He picked up his bulky pen and began twisting it. "Elsie, I'm sure you know about all the hardship Ryan has been going through what with his divorce, his kids and all . . ."

Elsie didn't respond. Mike must have taken that as a yes because he plowed ahead without pause. "Sometimes we have to make tough, *really* tough choices. That's life. Ryan here is in the middle of one of those situations. Having to make a choi—"

Elsie interrupted. "Listen, Mike, why don't you cut to the chase and tell us what this is really about? Are we being fired? What?"

"Well, no!" He sounded surprised. "Firing you? No . . ."

This time Ryan inserted himself. "Elsie, I'm resigning today. I will no longer be working for the bureau . . . unfortunately. Due to circumsta—"

Elsie turned. "You *what*?!"

"It's a really tough choice, Elsie," Mike cut in. "The divorce, and having to handle all the crises, financially, Ryan had to make a hard decision. He's been offered a job, and he's taking it."

"You already have a job lined up?" Everything inside her froze. "Well, Agent Marcello. Forgive my initial shock. Congratulations."

"Elsie, you will stay on the cases," Mike explained. "Tony will be taking over Ryan's CT files, and I'm sure you'll help him catch up. We're all good?"

Elsie forced an icy smile. "Sure we're good, Mike. I'm sorry to see Ryan go, and so quickly . . . and unexpectedly, I have to say. But life goes on. If you don't mind . . ." and she stood up to leave.

Mike nodded. "Thanks, Elsie. We'll go over the transfer stuff next week."

Elsie, feeling dead, headed out.

Ryan followed. "Mike, I'll stop by and turn in the paperwork."

"Fine. That'll be fine."

Ryan caught up with her. "Elsie. Wait a second."

She didn't.

"*Wait a second!*"

This time she stopped, and hissed in a low voice, "I've got work to do. Obviously you don't."

"I'm going to explain all this to you. All I need is thirty minutes to explain everything."

Elsie narrowed her eyes. "You don't owe me any explanation. I don't want it. You made sure I was hit as hard and unexpectedly as possible. I get it. Well done. Sitting there not knowing what the hell was happening . . . thinking we were caught for one goddamn night . . ."

Ryan checked his surroundings to make sure they didn't have an audience. "Listen, I'll pick you up at four forty-five, as we discussed. We'll go to dinner, your choice, anywhere. And I'll tell you everything. Explain it all."

Elsie smiled sardonically. "I am not going anywhere with you. I am not riding with you. Just leave, Ryan."

Ryan sighed. "All I ask is thirty minutes. You don't want to ride with me, fine. You don't want to dine with me, fine. But give me thirty minutes. Today. Tonight. That's all!"

Elsie took a deep breath. "All right. You'll have your thirty minutes. My house, at seven tonight. Now go, get out of here."

"I'll be there."

* * * *

Friday Evening, October 10, 2003
Alexandria, Virginia

Elsie spent fifteen intense minutes working out with the punching bag in her tiny garage. Designed to park a small car, the area was used for storage and as a workout space. Despite the half-raised door to let in cold air, she was soaked in sweat. She needed this.

Exhausted, she threw herself down on the mat and lay still until her breathing returned to normal. Then she went inside to her bedroom, stripped off her clothes, and got ready for a bath. That's when it struck her: Ryan's scent, left over from the previous evening. She felt the anger rising inside, so she rushed into the bathroom, got into the tub and turned on the shower to hottest. She stood under the scalding spray for fifteen burning minutes.

After her shower she headed downstairs into the kitchen. Though she didn't feel the least bit hungry, she would force herself to eat, to try to feed her battered mind and feelings; in vain.

She was halfway through her fruit-yogurt bowl when she heard the knock. She glanced at the clock: 6:30. Downstairs, Ex-Agent Ryan Marcello was waiting when she opened the door.

"Guess I'm early."

"We said seven," she told him blankly.

"Okay, so you want me to come back in"—he checked his watch—"in like seventeen minutes?"

Elsie, sighing, opened the door wider. "No. That's fine. Just come in, have your thirty minutes and then leave." Ryan followed her up.

Elsie pointed toward the living room. "There. Let's get this over with."

Ryan felt unnerved. How to start, and with what? Rob Brown? His new boss? Ret. Major Pulaski from Pentagon security and Nazim in an agency plane? He didn't know where to begin.

Elsie could tell he was nervous. *Good*, she thought. *Suffer!*

"Oh . . . has the clock started running?" No response. He could tell she was holding back tears. Had he fucked this up with her already? Instinctively, he started to apologize. "I'm . . . I'm so very sorry . . . what happened in Mike's office was *not* what I had planned for us . . . totally unexpected . . . I . . ." his mouth went dry. "Roller coaster I've been on, since yesterday . . ." He started to cough. "Before that, can we have something to drink? Glass of water, anything."

Elsie shrugged. "You know where the fridge is."

Ryan went into the kitchen, opened the fridge and scanned its contents: everything neatly arranged in its place, and all mostly healthful. There was a bottle of fancy Belgian Ale. He grabbed it and brought two glasses. He deftly uncorked the bottle and poured.

"That was the last bottle of ale Ben bought," Elsie told him, her voice a whisper. "Before his stroke. I've been keeping it there, not knowing what to do with it. Preserve it somehow? Save it for a toast on the deathiversary?"

Ryan's hand froze. "Oh shit. I'm sorry. I know I keep saying it, then I continue screwing everything up . . ."

"No. That's okay. It's as good a time as any. Maybe it's fortuitous that decision was made for me . . . made even more memorable by the circumstance."

Ryan handed her a glass and waited for her before he took a sip. Then he began, this time cogently.

He started with Major Pulaski, the CIA plane, and the cover-up on Yousef. He told her what happened three days ago, about being approached for a job that would allow him to continue with his case, his earlier meeting with the prospect boss, Rob's call and how that affected him. What the bureau was doing to Rob . . . He'd had to rehearse his spiel for Mike Whitman, and use his divorce as a reason. He'd tried to make sure that she'd stay with the unit, how vital that was . . .

Then, he was done. He was exhausted but relieved. He felt light. Whether she'd forgive him or not, it felt good and right to share that with her.

Elsie sat long in silence. "I still can't figure out . . . why you didn't tell me all this in the first place? Why hold back? I just don't get it."

"I had no idea how deep things went. Once I began to see, it all started happening so quick! Then my concern for you, your job, your safety . . . things snowball."

"Rob. What is he doing? Does he have an attorney?"

"Well, I tried there. After all the warnings about phones, I finally managed to contact his wife, and you know what she said? 'Leave us alone, Ryan. Haven't you caused enough grief?' She mentioned treatment as the bureau insisted . . . and then she hung up on me!"

Elsie felt sorrow and concern for Rob, but even more, she was outraged by the bureau's viciousness. "I'm sorry too," she offered.

Ryan nodded.

"So what's this new job—the private firm that will let you pursue your case? What kind of firm is that?"

Ryan closed his eyes. "Elsie. Listen. I'm going to do you one better. I've set up an appointment—for you to meet my boss, see my workplace, for you to be briefed—personally; directly. Tomorrow at ten."

Ryan began to drift. Was he passing out?

Elsie tiptoed over and stood next to him. His legs were wide apart and stretched forward. His eyes were two thirds closed and his breathing now a soft gentle snoring. The empty glass dangled from his hand. Ryan Marcello had crashed.

Elsie went upstairs and retrieved an extra pillow and a fleece blanket from the closet, reserved for extremely rare overnight guests. She went back into the living room, fixed up the sofa, and kneeled next to Ryan, tapping his shoulder. No response. She carefully pulled him to his feet. His body complied. She walked him to the sofa and lowered him onto it. She pushed him into a prone position with his head resting on the pillow and draped the blanket over him. She patted Simba, who was already asleep, on her way out of the room, and switched off the light before heading upstairs to her now once again lonely bedroom.

* * * *

Saturday Morning, October 11, 2003
Markham, Virginia

They rode toward Markham in silence.

The entire morning had been silent. Elsie woke at 6:30 to find Ryan gone, his car still on the street where he'd parked. He had folded the blanket, topped it with the pillow and placed it neatly on one end of the sofa. She went back upstairs and took a quick shower. Her eyes in the mirror told of a night anything but restful. After a brief session of crying in her bed, holding the sketch of the bearded man, she'd tossed and turned for hours.

Ryan had left explicit directions for their arranged meeting—the one set up specifically for her, at a posh country club in the hilly area near Markham, Virginia. Elsie dressed accordingly: her formal-ish dark-washed jeans, cream cashmere turtleneck sweater topped with her camel sport jacket, and her almost decade-old dark brown cowboy boots. She pulled her hair into a neat ponytail and lightly applied her makeup.

She thought she heard a noise and was startled to find Ryan in the kitchen, setting up bagels and various pastries in plastic containers.

"Hi. I went to King Street and got us breakfast, and your coffee the way you like it."

"Hi. Good. Thanks." She squeezed by and reached for the coffee, what she needed the most while ignoring the mini-electric sparks from the proximity of his body. She opened a jar and added half a teaspoon of brown sugar to the steamy dark brown liquid and stirred.

"We need to get going in fifteen minutes. It'll take us two hours . . . ah . . . you look great, by the way."

Elsie took a bite of her cinnamon bagel. "I'm set. Ready when you are."

They decided to take his car. Traveling in silence, they'd already passed the junction in Fairfax when Ryan finally spoke. "I want to tell you about him and the arrangement, but things being as they are, I . . . well, I'll let him do it and you can decide on your own."

Elsie, looking passive-aggressively out her side window, responded to the passing foliage. "Fine. I can wait another hour to hear all about your mystery job."

Ryan wasn't about to let her get under his skin. Not today. "This is more—it's about you and me, and our case. Our work."

That caught her attention and she turned to face him. "I've got to hand it to you Ryan. You're persistent. What work or case? There is no case. Not anymore. You are no longer with the bureau. *I am*—only with a new partner and different cases. What part of this don't you understand?"

Ryan had to let this go. *For now.* He kept his eyes on the road, unaware of his clenching jaw or the stand-out veins in his neck.

They pulled into the circular driveway, handed the car to the valet, and entered the posh facility. Ryan knew where he was going, with Elsie half a step behind.

They entered the mahogany-paneled library, at the opposite end of which stood guard a tall man in a gray suit before a closed door.

Ryan approached. "Ryan Marcello and Elsie Simon for the ten o'clock meeting."

The man nodded, slipped inside, and returned immediately, holding the door for them.

Inside the opulent room, a distinguished man in his early sixties sat at the far end of an ornate conference table. Impeccably dressed, the man oozed power and influence. Elsie had seen his face more than once. His bright blue eyes were intense.

To his left with her chair pushed out sat a woman who could only be described as arched and slightly whorish. An icy beauty, Elsie thought, and tall—enhanced no doubt by four-inch spike heels. Short cropped platinum-blond hair with black eyebrows and lashes that showcased blue-green eyes made her dangerous. The fire engine lips were a signal touch.

The elegant man rose to greet them while the giant woman stayed seated.

"Hello Ryan. Ms. Simon, pleasure to meet you. I'm Andrew Sullivan."

Now she remembered. This was *the* Andrew Sullivan, Jr., one of the richest men in the States—no, the world—known for a ruthless business style that carried his name forward in even the most far-flung places. Everyone knew what this man was capable of; *ruthless* in fact didn't do him justice. Elsie shook his hand and stepped back.

Sullivan motioned. "This is my assistant, Tatiana Schuliskova. Well, I should say my assistant *for this particular project*."

"And what is this particular project?" Elsie couldn't help asking; it just popped out. Tatiana gave Elsie a frozen smile.

"Ah . . . would you care for coffee or tea?" Sullivan offered. "Or perhaps something else?"

"No thank you."

Ryan shook his head. "Not just yet; and no to coffee or tea."

Sullivan smiled. "Well then, shall we begin?"

Tatiana moved her chair closer to Sullivan.

"I'm not sure how much Ryan has told you, about the job and overall picture. Ryan?"

"I haven't told her anything. We're starting from scratch."

Sullivan moved his eyes to Elsie. "Ms. Simon, do you know much about me? I don't mean about Andrew Sullivan the billionaire mogul."

Elsie reflected. Wasn't there something personal? A scandal? Something major about this guy a year or two back . . . what was it? She drew a blank. "I'm afraid I don't."

Sullivan continued. "A year and a half ago, on twenty-eight April, 2002, my son, my only son, was viciously murdered. He was with the State Department and was serving a yearlong assignment in Northern Cyprus, the Turkish side."

She recalled it now: Sullivan's bullet-riddled body, found on some beach. After preliminary leads and investigations, the case just died. She remembered something about a hooker and maybe drugs; that's all.

"They—the U.S. government—investigated my son's murder for . . . for exactly forty-seven days. They never found an answer. Then they closed the case. *Finito.*"

"You mean they didn't find anything?" Elsie probed. "Not a single lead? No witnesses? Nothing?"

He answered without a pause. "Not a single *fact.* Or even one real witness. So the theories they offered are useless. They put my son's last hours in the company of two hookers, both Russian. They mentioned Russian mafia foul play and potential prostitution and drugs. None of this *fact-based*, nothing substantiated, yet they closed the case—*permanently.*" Elsie noticed a tremor in his hand. He then added, "That's why I started my own investigation—for real facts. And that's why I hired Ryan. To put him in charge of investigating my son's murder."

Elsie took it all in. "With due respect, couldn't you simply have bought some influence and kept this case alive?"

Sullivan liked her bluntness. "You'd think so, wouldn't you?

This is what makes this that much more a mystery. Did I try? Most definitely. There seem to be higher powers—interests, objectives—way above my reach. That no amount of money, clout, or even blackmail has been able to move us forward, well, that should tell you something."

"Why then would an ex-agent or two, even with a few assistants, bring you any results?"

"Oh . . . I've got more than a few. I've put together a fairly sophisticated team: agents, investigators, analysts, informants, operatives, hackers, translators . . ." after a well-timed beat, looking straight into Elsie's eyes, "and we were hoping to add you to our team as well."

Elsie turned directly to Ryan. "Please correct me if I'm wrong. You are now a mercenary, Ryan? An operative agent for hire?"

He held her glare. "No, not right, Elsie. Mister Sullivan's mission and our case have certain leads and players in common. This is a mutually beneficial joint operation. It's more of a partnership."

"Our case as in what? Yousef? Nazim? What?"

"Some . . . or maybe all. We tried, we tried our damnedest at the bureau. Not only were they not on our side, they took a position against us. I lived and breathed my job, my position, my cases with the bureau; I had unquestioning faith in them. I was wrong. They are not on the side of the good guys seeking justice; at least not in this case."

Elsie turned to Sullivan. "Well, Mister Sullivan, I appreciate your offer, but I already have a job. I am not about to quit my work and become some kind of mercenary."

Ryan was about to speak but Sullivan held his hand up. "Ms. Simon, no one is asking you to quit your job. In fact, we want you to keep your job and your access. You'll be far more useful inside the bureau."

"You want me to become your snitch? Your spy?" Then she

turned back to Ryan. "You really thought I'd snitch for your new mercenary operation? Wow, Ryan, you sure know me!"

She stood up. "I believe I've had enough briefing. I must leave. Now. Another word would put me in a *compromised* position."

Sullivan rose as well. "Ms. Simon, may I? Just the two of us." He looked at Tatiana, who crept off like a cat. Ryan hadn't moved.

"You too, Ryan, I'd like to speak with her privately, briefly."

Ryan reluctantly followed Tatiana outside.

Sullivan gestured to Elsie. "Please sit. Only for a few minutes."

Elsie did as requested, ready to spring.

Sullivan retrieved from his sport coat a small stack of what looked to be five-by-seven photos. He shuffled them, picked one, and slid it across the table.

Elsie looked without touching. It appeared to be a picture of Sullivan's son, Jason, taken during graduation. He was flashing a wholesome smile, full of the confidence and spark that spoke of wealthy breeding. She didn't say anything.

Next, Sullivan slid another picture over.

She picked up and studied the photo. It was of Jason with his wife and reeked of love and intimacy, unquestionable happiness oozing from both. Jason's wife was his physical opposite: petite, half black, frizzy brown-black hair, and luscious light brown skin.

This time, Sullivan hesitated before sliding the next one over. Studying the photo intently, he turned it with the white side facing up then handed it to Elsie.

Elsie flipped it to see a sonogram of a fetus. She guessed it to have been taken around the end of the first trimester, at twelve to fourteen weeks.

Sullivan was behind her, close enough for her to smell his woodsy aftershave.

"This is—*was*—my grandchild to be. The doctor said it was a girl. When they delivered the news of Jason's murder to his wife, they killed my grandchild as well. She miscarried. So, you see, that leaves me with two murders, my only child and grandchild." He took a breath. "They were in love. He loved her madly. The hooker story doesn't add up. He didn't do drugs. Their story doesn't hold, Elsie."

This was the first time he'd used *Elsie*; was he trying to appeal to her personal side?

"Justice takes on a different hue when it's personal," Sullivan continued. "It's personal to me, and, I suspect, to Ryan as well with the murder of his nephew. And it's personal as far as the years with the bureau: they destroyed his faith and trust."

He took a step closer. "I'm not sharing this with you for pity or sorrow. I am trying to make you understand. Sooner or later, whether you pay a personal cost or not, you will be touched and affected by it. Disillusionment will come."

"I won't spy for you. I am not a snitch, nor am I planning to become one. I won't steal for you, I won't kill for you. Under no circumstances would I ever consider committing those acts. Frankly, once you take them out of the equation, I don't see how I could be of any use to you or even Ryan."

Seeming satisfied, which struck her as odd, Sullivan sat back down. "Okay, here's the deal," he tried again, "a temporary one, to start with. We'll have a trial period. All we need from you will be your analytical capabilities, your knowledge of various contexts and players. No spying, no snitching, no stealing, no killing. Just you lending us your thoughts, takes, analyses on what we're doing. How does that sound?"

Elsie considered it. Not a bad deal. *Not at all*. She wouldn't be screwing the bureau in any way. Nor would she be compromising anything classified or any ongoing sensitive investigations and ops. Not only that, this would give her an opportunity to find out what *they* had, who *they* were chasing, and how far *they* were going with their investigation. In return, she'd provide them with her take, interpretations of data or consequences of any planned actions.

Sullivan could read her partial acceptance. He didn't waste any time. "Let's invite them back in and conclude this meeting, shall we?"

CHAPTER 8

Sunday, October 12, 2003
Phnom Penh, Cambodia

Tonight was the night. He'd been watching for three days and two nights. He had the schedule, rituals and movements down pat. This fish was little—more like a sand crab. Tiny.

Greg had taken a night boat from Saigon through the Mekong Delta, straight to Phnom Penh. This was stop number one on the first operation of his mission. He had done all his thinking, evaluating and reevaluating, and he was prepared, despite being hit by the changes less than a week ago. They almost had him as prey. Almost.

He had left Mui Ne and spent a day in Saigon to regroup, rethink and replan. He had at his disposal all the necessary resources: the finances, the backup, and the backup for the backup. The rest was taken care of in advance: sources, informants, whoever would be needed. Already he was thinking many steps ahead, meticulous to the nth degree; anything less would be fatal.

Take his coming targets, for example. He knew not only their addresses, schedules, routines, online passwords, bank accounts, mistresses, boyfriends, but also their quirky habits, their brand of soap, their favorite underwear; what soup they liked and whether they ate meat. Some might call it overkill. Few would understand the value. This was not about not taking chances, but rather taking the right ones when you had to.

The agency guy, Josh—his target—was scheduled to leave the following day, Monday, for the United States, with a long layover in Bangkok. The partner, Sander, was on leave in the States with some kind of nervous breakdown. This evening would be Josh's time to have dinner, pack, have one last sex treat, sleep late, and eat breakfast in the business class lounge at the airport. He was that predictable. Not unusual for the agency's scavenger-grade operatives.

Greg instructed his assistant-driver, who could also double as an accomplice-hit man, where exactly to park the car. He scanned the street, cross street and apartment building. He knew that the units above and below Josh's were vacant. The only other tenant, two floors above, was an old Cambodian merchant who spent every weekend with his daughter fifteen kilometers outside the city—meaning Josh had the entire building to himself. So did Greg for his operation.

He observed three passengers pull up in front on a deluxe Harley-Davidson. The driver didn't switch off the engine but the helmeted man in back and the child in the middle hopped off. The man walked straight into the building, the boy following several steps behind.

The man came out a few minutes later—without the boy—said something to his companion, hopped on the bike and off they went with a roar.

Greg waited two minutes before he got out without saying a word to his driver. Then the driver took off after the bike for his stakeout. Greg had three hours. He knew of the arrangement between Josh and Maurice: delivery of a fresh boy under age nine at 7 P.M. for pickup at 10. He had two hours and fifty-six minutes to spend with Josh. Good.

He entered and went to the second floor, where he took up a position to the side of the door. Leaning against the wall with his ear almost touching the door, he closed his eyes and listened.

When he heard the one deep voice accompanied by small footsteps moving from the front room to the back, that was his cue. With a specialized tool Greg let himself in, entering soundlessly.

Josh and the boy were in the bedroom with the door ajar. Greg calmly approached, pushed the door open gently, and from where he stood, ten or so feet away, aimed his Taser straight at Josh's chest. Josh was on the bed, naked from the waist down. The boy, sitting on the corner of one of the twin beds, was the first to notice Greg. He didn't make a sound. Josh looked up. Their eyes locked for one short second before Greg fired two soundless shots, throwing Josh on his back while his legs dangled lifelessly.

There was no blood. There wouldn't be. This was a custom cartridge that combined a muscle paralyzer with a medium-grade electric shock. Josh wouldn't be able to walk, talk, or even move a finger for a hundred twenty minutes or more.

The boy sat frozen, mute. Greg went over and helped him to his feet, then walked him out of there and into the next room, a darkened office. A laptop on one of two desks had a webpage open from Josh's last session: *Of Men and Boys*, featuring real boys in real settings. *How predictable.* Greg exited the page and brought up a search engine. He found what he was looking for: a Pink Panther cartoon. He clicked Play and increased the volume to maximum, then settled the boy in front of the screen. He demonstrated how to operate the mouse and click on additional Pink Panther episodes. On his way out Greg made sure the office was secure, before returning to Josh.

Josh was where he had left him. The paralyzed man was mentally alert—fully alert—the way he was supposed to be for what Greg had in mind. Removing handcuffs from the inside pocket of his field jacket, Greg bent over and cuffed Josh's wrists and ankles together.

Leaving him for the moment, Greg moved into the bathroom, turned on the garish fluorescent light and opened the door to the cramped shower cubicle. There was a handheld showerhead hanging on a hook on the wall. Perfect.

He went back to the bedroom, grabbed Josh by his legs and dragged him into the bathroom. "Josh, are you ready for some water splashing?" He didn't expect an answer. All the man's muscles from his legs to his jaw were totally out of commission. Greg knew, though, that he had been heard and understood. "No quick death for you, Josh. No, no, no. Not for you."

Greg had efficiently and smoothly completed his setup in less than eight minutes. He looked at his watch. Two hours and six minutes. *More than enough.* Josh was on his back inside the stall with his legs propped up against the wall. A hand towel was draped over his eyes, extending midway over the bridge of his nose.

"Are you ready, Josh? Because I am. I am going to kill you slow." He was hovering over Josh just outside the stall. Lifting the showerhead from its cradle, he turned on the water and set the temperature to coldest and the pressure to weakest. He let the water slowly soak the towel over Josh's upper face; then he unfolded and lowered the fully soaked towel until it covered both Josh's nose and mouth. He continued watering, holding the showerhead eighteen inches above Josh's head. His watch beeped: 36 seconds. Time to break. He turned off the water and lifted up the towel. From the color of Josh's lips and skin, he could tell the man was really getting it. His pupils expressed a level of fear rarely reached in the life of the average man. This is precisely what Greg wanted and intended to get—at this stage.

Greg sat on the commode next to the stall and watched Josh. "I suspect you're familiar with our water splash party. How do they teach it to you guys nowadays? CIA Semi-Enhanced Interrogation Techniques, CSEIT 101. A prerequisite to CIA Enhanced Interrogation Techniques, CEIT 200; and what is it after that? I don't think they offer that to guys in lower levels, like you. Because with guys like me, and there aren't too many, we go through Souped-Up Interrogation Techniques—and beyond. Then we top that with the Pentagon's own version of enhanced techniques and . . . well, we become the best in the business at pain and kill. The best in the world. Okay, are you ready for another round? Time to splash."

Greg repeated the same steps all over again. This time he set his timer at 42 seconds: two seconds beyond the sequence limit set by agency guidelines for effective waterboarding techniques. When he lifted the soaked towel the second time he could see Josh regaining some muscle response: he was shivering. *Involuntary muscle response to cold water and splash.* Good.

Greg sat on the commode and gave Josh a few seconds of recovery time. "I have two theories, Josh. One, you killed *my woman* by design and per your bosses' order. Two, you killed my woman because she was in the wrong place at the wrong time, and that—ironically— is coming back to haunt you since she happened to belong to a very wrong man. I'm leaning toward number two. The outcome, what happens to you, isn't going to change. Whether one or two, one fact remains the same: You killed *my woman.*"

Greg grabbed another towel and applied the semi-enhanced technique once more, this time for 48 seconds. By the end of the third session, Josh was shaking violently. His lips were turning dark blue-black.

With 1 hour 43 minutes remaining, Greg decided to move to the next procedure. Not as bad as Souped-Up but definitely above Semi-Enhanced. He plugged an extension cord into the wall socket above the sink and connected his open-end copper wire. "Josh, we're going from cold to hot. Hot as in burning hot. In Spanish, they call it *muy caliente*; in Russian, *ochen' goryachiy*; in German, *sehr heiß* . . ."

By the time he finished the first round of his enhanced procedure, Josh was beginning to recover some movement in his facial muscles and partially his voice. The bathroom smelled a bit like a barbecue joint. A mix of burnt hair, fat and meat not easily distinguishable as human; it could be pork or even a fatty Kobe burger.

Josh whimpered. He kind of howled. Mucus was running down his nose, out of his mouth, and dripping down his chin. His eyes were askew and out of focus, sometimes even crossed. Pathetic, true, but he was not yet out of it. Greg knew. He was not about to let him go so soon.

Greg, now towering over the man, began to free associate. "Unlike you, I don't enjoy this. I did these things for no other reason than that they were in my line of work: mainly, to the Russians. Some people . . . *deluded* people . . . would call this, what I'm doing here, justice. I never use that word. I hear it a lot. I read it all the time but I don't have a use for it. It's a dumb word. It's abstract. It's a phantom— no, a *gremlin*—that affects what people say and what they do to one another, a right to let themselves off the hook, to evade culpability by invoking some codified rule or law . . . are you with me Josh? Am I getting to you?"

He paused and watched him. "Guys like you are a mistake for the agency. Granted, we all get in based on our unique qualifications, our *special* backgrounds. You know. Deviancy, sadism, extreme childhood trauma . . . Some of us, a few of us, can channel those traits in our jobs constructively. The rest, the ones like you, cannot. You end up using the missions—and especially the missions on the side, like this—to satisfy your impulses, compulsions and sickness. You're out of control. I bet you jerked off during Keller's session. The boy in the room back there is proof of your wrongness for the job." He unrolled the wire and approached Josh's limp body. "All right. Let's barbecue some more."

The second round of electrocution knocked Josh unconscious for a full minute or so. The blisters were already forming on his penis, buttocks and lower abdomen. Greg waited for him to come back. He did. Now moaning. Snot all over his face. Time for a break and talk.

"The other day I was thinking. What would happen if agencies like the CIA shut their doors for whatever reason? Consider this, Josh. Men and women just like you, thousands of you, with your inborn apathy, psychopathy, sociopathy, *fuck-all*pathy, paired with your expert agency training, out in the world running amok. Can you imagine, Josh? Think about the spike in murders, serial killings, serial rapes, pedophile rings, theft, hacking, cons and scams . . . one reason to let agencies like that stay operational. Somebody up there must know this. He or she must be watching out for the population at large."

Greg checked his watch. Forty-five minutes before Maurice came to pick up the boy. "We need to wrap this up, Josh. Are you ready? You are going to die. I know you already know that. If there is such a thing as an afterlife, well, you better pray there isn't. Because you and I will be meeting—in hell, that is. I have made peace with that, yet I wonder: Is hell a big open space? Are we all thrown together, all in one place, with no hierarchical division? That would make it a real hell for me, thus, for *you*. A better arrangement would be *compartmentalized hell*. If the delusionals are right about justice, we should be placed in different compartments quite a distance away from each other. Just because you and I worked for the same kind of people—the same bosses—you, Josh, and I are not the *same*."

Greg stared at Josh's hands: they were coming back to life. "Ready for your departure? Maurice will not be far behind. I am going to send him off with you . . . specifically, right on top of you, in a very connected way." He rolled Josh over on his stomach, pulled out his gun and attached the silencer, brought it down to Josh's neck and fired. "This one for Mai." Next, he put the muzzle on the agent's hairy ass, moved it down the middle of his crack and fired another round. "This one for her sister and the boy in the other room."

Greg checked his reflection in the mirror. Except for a few blood spatters, he looked collected as always. Time to check on the boy.

* * * *

His assistant buzzed his cell with the code: Maurice was about to enter the apartment. Greg had left the door ajar and was behind it, waiting for Maurice. He hit him in his neck and the scrawny pimp flopped to the floor like a rag doll.

Greg handcuffed Maurice's wrists behind his back and left his legs free. Maurice, after all, was not a trained operative. No need for ankle cuffs.

He dragged the pimp onto the bathroom floor then sat on the commode to wait.

Maurice half opened his eyes and stared at Greg in a daze. It took him more than a minute to focus; then where he was came rushing back: but why was he cuffed on the bathroom floor, and who was this man in front of him? Then he spotted Josh's bloody corpse in the stall.

Greg noticed at once that his eyes didn't widen. He had to grant him that: here was someone who didn't wince at the sight of a mutilated corpse. *A sign of cold-bloodedness*, Greg supposed. *Guess he's used to it.*

"Monsieur Maurice," Greg addressed him, "most excellent pimp of Southeast Asia. Before we begin, a little small talk, to get us better acquainted. How long have you been on the agency payroll, sucking such prestigious tit?"

Maurice ignored him. "Who are you?"

Greg shrugged. "No one in particular. Or should I say no *body*, since yours is the subject of investigation now? Mine is here, yours is right there. Back to my question. How long have you been on the roll?"

Maurice decided to answer. He would gain time by cooperating. His assistant would be looking for him, and that man was armed. "Going on three years. And you?"

Greg flashed a jaded smile. "Well, Maurice . . . I'm not what you would call an agency man. Let me put it this way, the agency is—was—one of my three main employers. I don't suspect you're truly interested. Are you, Maurice? Are you truly interested?"

Maurice, with dead eyes, slowly shook his head no.

"I appreciate your honesty. Now back to you. I am sure you've been keeping your own private list of our more famous power players: the ones who like little boys and little girls. I would like to have that list."

Maurice nodded agreeably. "I can arrange that quite easily." He glanced at the corpse. "Can we continue our discussion in the other room? Oh, and where is my boy?"

"*Your* boy? Are you his father, Maurice? If you are, you're not a very good one, bringing him here like this. I somehow doubt you're his father . . ."

"I am not the boy's father."

"I didn't think so, and what's more, I find your sudden concern disconcerting. After all, you're the reason he's here, correct?"

Maurice stared at the wall in front of him.

"What? I . . . I'm afraid I didn't hear you. Or are you the type of person who speaks by *not* speaking? I find that type of person hard to understand. We're not mind readers, Maurice. To make your feelings known you have to find the right words, and that's what I'm trying to do with you now, right here. Do I make myself clear?"

"Quite clear."

"That's good! That's progress . . . and progress is key. So tell me about the list. Where do you keep it?"

"One of my assistants keeps it for me. In a safe place. Not here. Not in Cambodia."

"I think you can do better than that. I *know* you can do better. Look at Josh. What used to be Josh. *He* couldn't tell me . . . or maybe he could? I forgot to ask. I'm getting off topic; it's very distracting, you refusing to cooperate. I ask you one little thing . . . and believe you me I can make you tell me. Or you can give me what I'm asking for now. Your choice."

Maurice knew this guy meant what he said. He was head and shoulders above other U.S. spooks in the frightening department. "It is in a lockbox in Bangkok."

"Better, but not good enough. Once more . . ."

"Check my pocket," Maurice implored him. "You'll see a little brass key on a ring. That key opens my safe deposit box in Thailand's Royal Bank, the main branch in downtown Bangkok."

"*That's* what I wanted. Very good. Now I want you to recall a girl, a Vietnamese girl from way back when, four and a half years ago, exactly. Name: Chan, thirteen years old. One of yours, I assume?"

Maurice squinted, searching his memory. He vaguely remembered. Good-looking one. He had purchased her for five hundred dollars, a hefty price for a true virgin. Once done with virginity, he'd sold her to a brothel in Phnom Penh. "I have no idea where she is now. Her last address was La Rouge in the alley on Street Fifty-one."

Greg nodded. While appreciative, he was done with this pimp. "I understand you are quite a man when it comes to screwing things. People talk. And what they say is that you do women, little girls, men, little boys, and even dogs and goats now and then. Is that true?"

Maurice answered matter-of-factly. "I am bisexual, and yes, I do have to test my merchandise and get firsthand knowledge of my clients' taste and preferences. They like me, and I've been successful, because I'm hands-on that way. Virgins being the exception, of course."

"Of course. A virgin would have to be the exception—otherwise, what are they paying top dollar for, right? To have you fuck the six year old first? What kind of fun is that?"

"I am happy with the money. I haven't been asking for anything more. My clients are A-list clients. In a way, I am protecting the children and women of your country. Your powerful strange business-men, elected and appointed government officials, operatives, you name it, can use me to satisfy whatever their needs here, rather than back at home. In *your* country."

"A noble sacrifice. So noble, in fact, you deserve some kind of honor. 'Sacrificing children, for the privileged ones back home.' What would we call it—the Peddy? The Kiddy? Can you think of a name? Maybe we should name it after you: The Maury, as in *more is never enough*. Too bad you won't live to see it presented. Make a nice epi-taph."

Maurice's eyes widened for the first time. "I-I thought we had an arrangement? I give you information, you let me go."

"That is *your* interpretation, not mine, Maurice. I never used those words. Remember what I said about speaking your mind? Like I said, I'm not a mind reader. But tell you what: I *will* give you one last opportunity to screw. Let me ask you, have you ever screwed a corpse?"

Maurice swallowed. "I-I don't understand."

"I'll be clear: I am going to take off your pants, get you inside that stall, get you right up on top of your client and have you screw him—in his cold dead ass. You said you tried to get a feel for your clients' tastes. Some people like having intercourse with corpses. It's time, Maurice, for you to give it a try. The longer you fuck him, the longer you live. Ready Teddy?"

Maurice began to crawl toward the bathroom door, like a worm. Greg put one foot on his leg. "You're not going anywhere, Maurice, but into that stall, to fuck that man—or what used to be one, two hours ago. This way. Don't be stupid now. You are not a stupid man." He pulled Maurice up on his feet and unbuttoned and unzipped his expensive pants, yanking down his silk underwear.

Deadpan now, Greg watched the horrified, frightened pimp will-ing himself into an erection on top of Josh's corpse—unsuccessfully.

The harder he tried, the more shrinking his penis. The pimp closed his eyes and tried imagery. That helped. With a semifirm penis he lowered himself on top of the body, averting his eyes from the ripped and bloody anus. He was in.

Greg slowly walked over to the humping pimp, took out his gun and shot him in the head. He shot him for Mai, he shot him for Chan, for the boy in the other room, and all the child victims of Maurice the Super Pimp.

* * * *

The driver pulled up in front of the alley on Street 51 and double-parked. Greg and the boy sat quietly in the back, the driver with his hands on the wheel up front.

Greg reflected on the boy, who sat staring straight ahead. Here he was, another white man, another big predator, taking him to another torture chamber. Well, this time the boy was wrong.

Greg got out and walked down the alley, with instructions to the driver to wait. Red door, red curtains, red lampshades scattered about, the place was a mishmash of styles: part wood-paneled English pub, part cheesy strip joint, part Latin Quarter French cabaret.

Half the tables were occupied. Except for one middle-aged Japanese man and less than a handful of Chinese, the clients were white, over forty, and ugly for young. The action began usually after 11:30.

Greg went over to what passed for security and handed the man a crisp fifty. Then he asked him to take him to his boss.

The man checked out the bill then went outside without a word. Greg waited. He should have accomplished this three years ago. In all their too-brief time it was the only thing Mai ever asked him to do; but the timing couldn't have been worse. He was still working for the company then, and pursuing Chan would have compromised him. Later, he was in the midst of setting up his own survival plan:

gaining the upper hand to counter the inevitable company mission to eliminate him, OG 68. When doing that, you make sure not to step on your enemy's toes. Again, pursuing Chan would have done just that.

Now, that period had come to an end. The company had acted first by stepping on his toes—no, make that his testicles. Whether they did so or not on purpose didn't matter. Family blood had been shed.

"Security" returned and beckoned him to follow. They went around the building and reentered, this time through a weathered brown door. The second floor was occupied by half a dozen spaces partitioned off with red velvetlike curtains: the fucking rooms. The man led Greg through one of two doors at the other end of the room.

In this chamber sat a tall, bald Asian man, midthirties, behind a gray metal desk. Two large notebooks were open before him showing numbers in columns and short words in Cambodian. These were the expense accounts and records for the brothel, along with possible sideline business: hash, guns, pirated cigarettes. Typical. Greg liked dealing with such businessmen. Everything was rational and predictable. No complications, unlike the so-called legit business world, which would just as soon cut your throat. At least with Kojak, Greg knows where he stands. This would be a simple transaction.

The deal took less than ten minutes. Greg showed him Chan's picture and explained what he wanted, then they quickly negotiated a price. Things done this way made sense.

Greg waited in the office while the boss stepped out to instruct the security man. When that was done they sat, neither making any attempt to fill the silence with words.

Soon they heard a gentle knock. When the office door opened, there stood an imitation Japanese Geisha, made to look like a whore. The makeup was garish, with eyes painted black, a ghostly white face and gray eye shadow. Her lips were too-bright red, and matched her lacquered fingernails, echoing the long red see-through silk ao dai. Her tacky high-heel open-toe sandals were a cheap metallic gold. The hair, so lovely in its natural state, was teased in a bun and secured with imitation jewel-stoned pins. She looked like a lifeless doll, despite the vivid colors. There was no trace of spirit in her face. She seemed tranquilized, as though she'd just stepped out of her coffin.

"Chan?" Greg whispered. It could have been Mai, only smaller, shorter, thinner; lost.

The boss gave Chan a cryptic explanation: this was her new man, a new boss who would take care of her. She was to serve him as would any appreciative mistress. It was time to leave the brothel. She was too old for their clients and so this was a godsent charity.

Yes, thought Greg, *she'll be seventeen next month—too old for the pedophile rapists.* He interrupted the man. "Enough. We go." Then he reached in his pocket and pulled out a neat stack of fifty dollar bills. He threw the twelve hundred dollars on the desk, strode toward Chan with security beside her, walked right past and exited the building, Chan following behind.

Once they reached the car, Greg told Chan, in Vietnamese, to go and sit in the front. She walked around and got in. Greg took his seat next to the boy in back, who was watching Chan intently. He then told the assistant driver, "Time to go. Mekong."

* * * *

The midnight sky was unusually clear for the area known for humidity, haze and smog. Seeing stars brightly was rare in Southeast Asia's flatlands. Yet tonight, there they were, and the air felt light.

Greg & Co. were inside the luxury boat moving on the Mekong's muddy waters toward Chau Doc, where Greg's driver would be waiting. The other two were the competent quiet Vietnamese captain and his young assistant.

Chan was down in the lower cabin. The boy was perched on the side bench next to the captain. Greg stood on the top deck watching the fishermen hustle in their tiny boats. Hundreds, with little lanterns, like a colony of darting fireflies. Greg liked it here. It suited him; but the place he once called home was no more. You're not supposed to shit where you eat, yet the shit was all over, tainting everything in sight.

Something to his right caught his attention. There, among the fishing boats. Something? Someone? He scanned each boat. His eyes moved from one to the next, until they came to rest on a particular boat.

This one was being tended to by a man who looked to be in his seventies; but age is deceptive in this part of the world. He could just as easily have been in his forties.

In the backend of the boat, a young girl was preparing her net by untangling all the jumbled knots.

Greg's sixth sense alerted him. He stared at the boat. Then at the girl, who appeared to be eleven or twelve. When recognition hit, Greg's boat already passed them by.

Of course! The girl who jumped from the balcony that night—the missing girl—but how had she survived? That she did hardly mattered; but things happen for a reason, he reminded himself, and here she was, tonight.

Everything lately seemed tied together. He couldn't shake the uncanny feeling.

He tried in vain to spot her again. All he could see was a vast colony of fishing boats dotting almost every inch of water. His keen eyes flitted from boat to boat but he was never able to find her.

* * * *

Greg didn't wait for the valet. He opened the door for Chan, instructed the boy to remain in the car and told the driver he would be back shortly.

He entered the luxury high-rise with Chan following three steps behind. They rode up fourteen floors to his apartment, sparse but expensively furnished. Chan stayed in the living room while Greg disappeared into one of the bedrooms.

A moment later, he reappeared holding a medium-sized brown cardboard box. Handing it over, he told the girl, "This now belongs to you."

Chan peered into the box. At once she recognized her own picture, and under that the smeared black-and-white copy of that same photo on a paper with her information and a request for help with a number to find her. She lifted the paper and saw the next photo. She looked up brightly at Greg. "My sister Mai! Where is my sister?"

Greg looked at the floor. "Mai died. She died last week."

Chan looked stunned. Her whole face fell; then softly she began to cry. She kissed the photograph. Not once, not twice, but at least a dozen times. The box also held Chan's favorite doll from the orphanage, some clothing that belonged to Mai and a small box of jewelry with Mai's little treasures given to her by Greg through the years.

"She looked for you. All the time. Every day. She never stopped looking for you, Chan."

* * * *

The driver opened the car door for Greg. This time he took the passenger seat. Chan sat in back still holding the box.

"Ham Tanh. Phu-Thai Church," he instructed the driver. "Once we pass Saigon, we stop for children to eat pho and go to bathroom. Let's go."

The drive, including the break, took nearly four hours. The boy had fallen asleep in the back with his head on Chan's lap. Chan, unblinking, stared out the window, cradling her box on the seat.

The main building stood in the center of the compound with

all the bells and whistles of a Catholic church. To the left was the orphanage, a three-storey structure that housed approximately one hundred children from infants to age ten. The building to the right housed older children, young unwed expecting mothers and other troubled runaway girls. The square concrete ground in the middle was more courtyard than garden. Without greenery or flowers or a playground, the place looked grim and sad; but it was safer than the streets—*and safer than any brothel*, thought Greg as he got out of the car.

A woman clad in a light-gray uniform with a loosely placed dark gray veil appeared. Greg had called ahead. Sister Lei smiled and motioned them inside.

He asked the duo to sit on the bench.

"You and I can talk in your office, Sister Lei."

Inside her office, Greg began. "Sister, I have brought you two children who need your help and the safety of your place. They need you."

"They are related to you?"

"Yes and no. I made them my mission."

"I see; your mission. And their story?"

"*They* will tell you their stories when they're ready." He paused. "The little boy doesn't talk. I don't even know if he can. I think he can talk but he doesn't want to, at least not yet. And Chan . . . she was stolen . . ."

"We cannot force them to accept the house of God, the love and the shelter," the sister explained. "Especially the older girl. She has to want it."

"She will."

They came back into the hall together. Sister Lei kneeled and, one by one, held each child's hands in her own. "Don't you be scared anymore. You have come to the right place. Now I will take you and show you around. You will see your sleeping quarters, and after that, you'll bathe and be given clean clothes, and then we shall eat and drink tea . . . and talk, and maybe even smile a little."

Greg cleared his throat. "I must go. I will visit if I can. Someday." And with that he turned and left the main building. He was going back to Saigon. His new mission had already begun. OG 68 was dead; this was now his mission alone. No agency or company. Only one lone Gladio against the rest.

* * * *

Friday, Late Morning, October 17, 2003
Ordu, Turkey

Greg drove up the street in a silver-gray rental Ford sedan, entered the lot and parked halfway between the main entrance and ticket desk. Locking his car remotely gave him a chance to scan his surroundings once more. No one following, no one else had entered the lot. At the counter he purchased a onetime round-trip ticket and proceeded toward the eight-passenger chairlift.

He had the lift all to himself, enjoying the view as the gondola ascended the 300 meters toward Boztepe. With the port to its north as a focal point and cascading hills on the opposite side, the Black Sea city sprawled densely from East to West.

When he reached the top Greg made his way toward the building that resembled a large glass house: surrounded on three sides with floor-to-ceiling windows to provide an optimum view. The panels were movable and could join the interior with the outdoor seating area when weather permitted. The place served as a restaurant-café by day, and by night, a happening bar.

Greg picked a table outdoors, furthest from the building. A watery breeze blew in from the sea; a bit too cool for locals, so he was the only one there.

He sat and took out a French magazine then a pair of small binoculars and laid them on top. Around his neck was a professional-use Canon: another prop. From his angry-looking birthmark to a trimmed goatee to carefully chosen clothes and French mien, he could easily be taken for a tourist exploring the little-known Black Sea region of Turkey.

A sullen waiter came and took his order: plain croissant and café au lait; then disappeared inside. Greg fixed on the sea, the port and the large ship laded with bulk cargo about to depart; it sounded its horn at one-minute intervals.

He'd arrived in Istanbul the previous morning. This quick but intricate mission would be squeezed into less than seventy-two hours. The plan: to terminate Mehmet Turkel and dispose of his body; take the late-afternoon flight to Ordu and check in to the hotel under a French alias; determine the target cargo ship's ID and return after midnight to plant the devices; come to this place and monitor; and afterward, drive straight to Istanbul to catch his late-night flight to Amsterdam.

Terminating Turkel would be easy. The man was in his midsixties, a bit overweight and with some minor heart problems. He was no longer the tough Turkish lieutenant general who had joined the CIA-Pentagon-NATO operation in the eighties. That was the original operation: Operation A, which had lasted till a few years after the collapse of the Soviet Union. Turkel's main task was to handle the *original* heroin route and assist with the training of a small Turkish paramilitary unit that was used to carry out prestaged attacks in Turkey and a few other Turkic countries. The attacks, with their media partners' help, were always blamed on the Communists. Turkel's record wasn't bad; but that didn't help him when it came to coping with the drastic change: *Operation B*, with altered targets, altered tactics, and a *slightly* modified endgame.

In the beginning, the company had given Turkel a semiretirement position: assessing various extremist and religious groups and their members in Turkey; then recruiting selected ones for fragmented yet strategically connected operations in the Balkans, Central Asia and the Caucasus. Also, when needed, Turkel traveled to the States to handle the old-time narcotics players in New Jersey and Chicago, a dying breed. The general was fine with that until the list of operatives began to include non-Turkish actors. It would have been one thing to have groups from such places as Azerbaijan, Uyghuristan or Chechnya—after all, they were all Turkic-rooted— but to venture beyond and bring in actors from Saudi Arabia, Egypt, Pakistan, and even Yemen? Well, that was not acceptable to a proud and loyal nationalist Turk such as Turkel. So, recently, he'd decided to semiretire; albeit not very quietly.

In the last couple of years the company was alerted to the possibility of Turkel going to the Russians. They let him continue his Turkey-U.S. heroin deals while they kept close watch. He would be worth quite a lot to the Russians. Yet his loss—loss as in dead— would mean nothing to the company in its now substantially altered mode of operation.

Greg knew all that. He also knew that he needed solid cover and a patsy for this small operation: someone they'd suspect, from whom they'd expect this kind of blow. He knew too that Turkel's routines were periodically monitored and analyzed by the company, and that the man was under their suspicious eye. With the lieutenant general's fingerprints in his private database, Greg had everything he needed. In a way, he was doing the company a favor.

He had done the same thing with the Josh-Maurice takeout. For that operation he'd used Jack Rodman, a disgruntled former low-level CIA operative who'd ended up leaving the agency. The guy had a reason: his wife, who also worked for the agency, was not only fucking his boss's boss, but actually had been promoted two levels up—in less than three years—while he had been left in the dust.

Fuming and bitter, Rodman resigned and moved to Thailand—a former base of operations. Jack in fact used to work with Josh, doing what Josh loved best. That, along with his trip down alcohol lane, caused him to be seen as "risky." Greg seized on that. As of now, as Greg watched the Black Sea and the port, Rodman was the prime suspect in the atrocious murder of Josh and Maurice. With Rodman's fingerprints everywhere, his computing activities linked to the hacking of Josh's laptop and his proximity to the scene of the crime, there were no other suspects on the agency's list.

Once this particular operation was concluded, the company similarly would see Mehmet Turkel as their number-one suspect: the man who blew up their lucrative cargo for his Russian handlers. It made perfect sense.

The fake French tourist sipped the milky coffee. Greg himself avoided coffee or anything with caffeine. He didn't consume alcohol. He carefully abstained from anything inducing dependency—anything that might alter his mental acuity, even slightly. This would be an exception. He didn't want to raise suspicion or leave any kind of memorable impression: the French tourist, for instance, who ordered a café au lait but didn't even take a sip. Little things mattered. He was anything if not meticulous. One reason he was still alive.

He traced the ship's progress over the vast dark water. He looked at his watch. *Any time now.* He nibbled on the soggy croissant, damp from the salty air.

The company had access to enormous sums of money and resources for its global operations. With worldwide bases and its own wide range of global transportation systems—and with sources and minihubs intricately connected—narcotics trafficking as a major commodity and income source was a given.

The company's main cash cow was Afghanistan, which produced over 90 percent of the world's heroin. Until a few years ago this invaluable commodity had to be shared, reluctantly and resentfully, with the Russians. All that had changed. Now they were competitor-free when it came to Afghan heroin. With official and unofficial bases in Azerbaijan, Georgia, Kyrgyzstan, Romania and Turkey, the company controlled the original source, including the poppy fields and production facilities in Afghanistan. They also controlled the centers in Azerbaijan and Georgia, almost all the transits and routes, and most of the transportation vehicles. They shipped smaller quantities by company planes, with stops in Kyrgyzstan, Azerbaijan and Turkey. From there, transfers were made to Belgium, England and the United States.

The company recently had moved the logistics center and headquarters for their heroin operation to Romania. For very large shipments they used container trucks from Afghanistan to Turkmenistan, where cargo was loaded onto ships and sent to Baku. There, the containers were loaded into trucks and sent to Georgia's Port Poti, where they were transferred into a cargo ship and sent to Romania, and from there to distribution hubs all over Europe and the Americas.

Sometimes it went the other way: large quantities of precursors and secondary chemicals needed for heroin production would be shipped from Germany and Belgium to Romania, then from Romania to Turkey or Georgia, and from there to Azerbaijan, Turkmenistan or Afghanistan.

The same basic operation and logistics applied to other commodities as well. Be it weapons (heavy or light) or even nuclear weapons components. The center also handled the receiving and rerouting of South and Central American–origin cocaine and synthetic drugs. They had a fairly large market in the Middle and Near East for that stuff.

At this moment, Greg was looking at a ship laded with 750 kilograms of pure-grade heroin. The previous day, the cargo ship from Georgia had docked in Ordu port per last-minute company instructions. Sometimes that happened: the company would change the route or the carrier itself. Sometimes they did it to vary the pattern, to create unpredictability. Sometimes additional loading was required along the way. Of course, Greg had been intercepting company instructions and all other communications between HQ in Romania and the carrier operators.

The company also had advised operators of the need to change the carrier ship—that is, to transfer the cargo onto a different cargo ship, a Turkish vessel. As Greg had anticipated, that ship's ID was not sent until the last possible minute as a precaution. He'd spent several hours staking out the dock until the transfer began around midnight. He'd gone back to his hotel and played the tourist ready for a nightcap at the bar, then exited through the hotel's back door, returning to the dock to install and set the explosives.

Greg began counting: less than a minute to go . . . and finally, the distant muffled *Bam*. Vivid orange flames were followed by thick black smoke. He heard the restaurant staff and clients, the *ooohs* and *aaahs*, and more *aaahs*. Several people rushed out and were right there beside him, looking on in horror. The big ship had exploded *just like that . . . Would there be any survivors?* they kept asking one another.

Under the circumstances, Greg didn't bother asking for the check. Instead, he left a few bills on the table, weighting them down with the sugar rack. Tonight the sea breeze was strong; the better to spread a ship fire.

He slipped out of the restaurant and walked quietly to the station platform to wait for the lift. In less than ten minutes he'd be on the road heading to Istanbul. In eight hours, give or take, he'd be at the airport. A few hours after that, in Amsterdam: safe routing for his next trip and for a day of rest. Then Brussels—the company's European HQ.

* * * *

Wednesday Morning, October 22, 2003
Brussels, Belgium

Colonel Winston Tanner was a man of routines as well. It was 6:45 A.M. when he walked out of his house dressed in his starched blue uniform. Before he opened the door to his car, he gave a quick wave to his wife, who was watching, as always, from their bedroom window clad in her floral nightgown.

He placed his black leather briefcase and service cap in the passenger seat, per usual. Then, after fastening his seatbelt, Tanner started the engine, pulled out from the curb, and headed toward the intersection. No other traffic in the neighborhood; still early for morning commuters.

As soon as the colonel turned right at the intersection, Greg straightened up from his position on the floor of the Mercedes, introducing himself with his gun.

If he was startled, the colonel didn't let on; he was, after all, a well-trained company man. He looked blankly at Greg in the rearview mirror, acknowledging the gun that was aimed at his head.

"Good morning, colonel. Please take a left at the next intersection and proceed north until I give you the next direction change."

Eyes on the road, the colonel replied, "And the purpose?"

Greg ignored this question. "The meeting is at eight-thirty. We have enough time."

Tanner glanced at him once more in the mirror. Greg was dressed impeccably, in a uniform matching the colonel's own, yet wearing his service cap. "Are you planning to join us?"

"Yes. I will be joining in a certain fashion," and then continued, "turn left at the next one."

Making the turn, the colonel said, "I didn't know. Was it a last-minute add?"

"I don't do anything last minute, not if I can help it," he

explained. "Just like you, I like my routines, and plan all my actions well in advance. Turn right here, and circle the building. We're entering through the garage."

The colonel did as instructed. This was a new fourteen-storey complex with two-level underground parking. This time of the day, the building was deserted.

Greg pressed the button on the small remote in his pocket. "Keep going. We're going down to B-Two, parking slot number fifty-two . . . to match your G number."

Slot number 52 was a double-wide space halfway between the elevator hall and the entry turn. The colonel pulled into the slot but didn't turn off the engine. "So what is this about? What do you want?"

"Turn off the engine, colonel. And remain seated. And do not remove your seatbelt."

The colonel did as he was told.

"Very good. Now let's talk about the meeting. Four people: you, Number Forty-nine and Forty-six, and the State Department guy. What's his name?"

Tanner kept his eyes on the wall in front. "I don't know. I was not given specifics."

"You can do better than that. Both of us are intelligent, experienced and *well-trained*. So please don't try that line."

The colonel slowly moved his eyes to the mirror. "I don't know. All I have is the meeting agenda. I suspect the same man as in the previous one. But I don't know his name."

Greg nodded. "Okay. Then let's talk about agenda items. Kvarlika: the police station. Suicide bombers?"

Tanner shook his head no. "Assassination. Multiple. Simultaneous."

"Mission date?"

"Undetermined. Eight weeks minimum."

"Then why the State Department? The meeting?"

The colonel did not respond.

"I would very much like us to keep this conversation fluid. No pauses, colonel. Please."

The colonel took in a breath. "Because Kvarlika must be coordinated with a parallel mission . . . you know the reason. We want Dagestan. We are moving inward and forward, from Azerbaijan and Georgia. That's been the plan all along."

"Parallel mission? Where?"

"Need-to-know basis. I don't have details. It's Unit Eleven's territory. That's all I know."

Greg thought about this last bit of information. Unit 11 dealt solely with Western Europe and the States, coined *home front operations*. And this plan—Operation Plan A—had become a rarity since they'd switched to Operation Plan B in the mid-1990s. Clearly, things had changed. The major attack in the United States, two smaller-scale incidents in England, and one in the Netherlands . . . obviously, the *home front* had lost its short-lived sanctity.

"When?" Greg demanded. "What is the date for the parallel mission?"

The colonel shrugged. "Need-to-know basis. We don't know; I don't. I would date it back from the second one in Georgia. Within the next six weeks."

"The 2001 operation, were you in on that or out?"

The colonel hesitated. "What do you mean by *in*? If you mean completely in, as in a direct participant operative, then, no . . ." He stopped himself.

"Go on."

"I'm not included in the core tier. Come on, you must know that! But I'm not blind or deaf. Why else would they round up our al-Hazar cell members and funnel them to the States? So yes, I had some idea of where all those activities were leading: *home front*. But that's all."

"How about OG Forty-nine and Forty-six?"

Again, Tanner shook his head. "Definitely not Forty-nine. He is solely Georgia and Azerbaijan. And I don't think Forty-six . . . I doubt it . . . but the State Department man? Well, surely."

Greg checked his watch. He had almost sixty minutes: time to say good-bye here, a quick stop at his condo on the way, and then his last stop for this particular mission.

He removed the syringe from his pocket. "Colonel, time to go. Please place your hands on your lap." Then he plunged the syringe into the back of Tanner's neck, firmly grasping the man's twitching shoulder. He remained that way for 120 seconds. Then he stepped out, opened the driver's door, pulled the colonel's body out and walked it to the trunk, carrying the deadweight over his shoulder.

After placing the corpse in the capacious trunk of the stretch sedan, Greg slid into the driver's seat, readjusted both seat and mirrors, and checked his image as he rearranged his cap. Time to go.

The highway now had come to life with the weekday morning commuters. Even with the traffic it took him less than twenty minutes to make a pit stop at his apartment to check for any new messages and addendums destined to the colonel's account. There were no updates or changes to the morning's meeting. Good.

He pulled up in front of the base's security gate. While cameras read his license plate, the security officer walked to the driver's side carrying his portable fingerprint scanner. Greg lowered his window, flashed his ID, inserted both hands into the unit's slot and kept them there until the green light came on. The officer saluted as the gate opened up.

Though the compound was massive, Greg knew his way around. He parked in the lot in front of the main building, entered, and took the escalator up two floors. This building was connected to four others—North, South, East and West—via skywalks. He took the left skywalk to Building 5; then the elevator to the fourth floor.

The meeting was set up in VIP Conference Room No. 2 at the

end of the hall to the right. As with the four other conference rooms on this floor, this room was also built as a Sensitive Compartmented Information Facility (SCIF), with several physical security protection features intended to prevent and detect visual, acoustical, technical and physical access by unauthorized persons. The room's built-in aluminum barriers provided solid soundproofing: perfect for Greg's plan.

He consulted his watch: 8:37. He was going to be late by precisely eight minutes, just as he'd intended. He placed his hands in the scanner and got the green light. He pulled out his gun—more accurately, the colonel's gun—as he opened the door and moved into the room like a panther, in long quick strides.

Three men were seated at the eight-seat table. The one at the head wearing glasses had to be State Department: early forties, short and wiry with dark hair and medium olive complexion, Jewish or Middle-Eastern origin. The other two sat side by side, one in uniform, the other in a suit. Greg knew the suit to be OG 49, three years his senior in operation time, one year his junior in age. He knew of OG 46—the man in uniform—by reputation only, supplemented by thorough research.

Forty-six was conversing with OG 49 while State Department read something on his laptop. No one looked up when Greg entered the room, giving him time to position himself. When they saw him it was already too late.

"Good morning, gentlemen! It is eight thirty-nine. Time to say good-bye to Earth." He then fired three times, moving his outstretched arms only slightly after each smooth shot. Then he fired one more round into each of them, starting from the last and moving to the first. Using a silencer in a soundproof SCIF eliminated any risk of outside interference.

He took his time going from one to the other to ensure a *no pulse* status.

Greg methodically removed the drive from the laptop, went

through State Department's pockets and took his wallet and keys, along with some pieces of paper, and placed them all inside the colonel's briefcase. The other two did not have laptops. Greg emptied their pockets as well.

He proceeded next to the computer connected to the large wall-mounted monitor. He removed the CD and pocketed it.

Everything took less than eight minutes. It was now 8:47. Greg allowed himself another five minutes. He sat directly across from OG 46 and closely observed the dead. He studied their bodies, what positions they were in, and the final expressions on their faces. He checked their ring fingers: two were wearing wedding bands. Odd sorts of families, these OGs had; he'd check their wallets later.

At 8:52 he walked out of the room and shut the door behind him. He retraced his entry and was in Tanner's car by 8:59 exactly. He adjusted his mirror and checked his cap. Perfect. As he exited through the gate and entered the six-lane highway, he mentally went over the finishing steps: remove the colonel's identifiable features (this will mean crushing his teeth and eyes, slicing off the face, fingertips and every toe, along with any special markings on the body, to be safe); package the body and then place it in a steel shipping container; ship the container via the Port of Antwerp to Dakar (Senegal) where it would be received and taken to a remote storage facility used by the military and never found; clean the colonel's car and leave it in front of the airport; then take the early evening flight to Reykjavik, Iceland, where he was scheduled to spend two full days with his computer genius source.

* * * *

Saturday Evening, October 25, 2003
British Airways Flight from London to Dulles Airport,
Washington, D.C.

Greg raised the shade on the window panel and watched crimson rays pierce through the clouds. He couldn't help thinking of *justice*; a fitting symbol, these rays of blood. The clouds were just that: cumulus. He thought about accruing, of all that had piled up; of unwitting players, of wolves and prey; and of the rivers of reckoning, each originating from a single point.

His plane had taken off from London's Heathrow Airport at 6:40 P.M. Estimated arrival at Washington's Dulles Airport, 8:25 P.M. With the agreeable wind and on-time takeoff, they would beat that by 25 minutes, Greg thought.

So far everything had gone smoothly: Thailand, Maurice's book and setting up Rodman; Turkey, turning Turkel into a viable target and making him disappear, blowing up the company's carrier and costing them at minimum $75 million in lost drug revenues; Belgium, shipping off Tanner's unearthly remains to an anonymous hole in Africa—and thence to the group execution of three Gladios, including State Department (who turns out to have been the vicious David Perleman, international gangster and traitorous thief, should his crimes ever come to light). All this, along with the retrieval of valuable intel on the Gladios' next operation targets through his dependable source in Iceland. Everything had gone according to his plans, without a single glitch.

Now he was on his way to the far less predictable and much more challenging operation zone: the heart and power center of the global operation called *Gladio*—the real headquarters of the most powerful, dangerous, secretive and destructive paramilitary unit in the world. This was where all ideas and objectives were formed. This was the hub, the nexus.

Here is where the richest moguls and oligarchs set up a colony whose existence depends on synthetic wars, calculated terrorism, implanted third world dictatorships and coup d'états—everything within the realm of bloodshed, destruction and ultimate domination, dependably. It goes by several names, this beast; some call it the Deep State. Once upon a time it was known as the war industry, which formed an indelible partnership with the energy industry, aided and abetted by the global financial industry. This trio determines every nation's destiny: who wins, who falls from power (whether by dethronement, assassination or "election"), who gets to rule, and who gets to take out the rulers. These are the ones who set the stages and pick who goes to war with whom, where the guaranteed outcome is always the same: everyone else loses, the colony wins. Simple.

And how did *he* fit into all of this? If the old saw is right, that "my enemy's enemy is my friend," well, he and the colony shared one objective: fuck everything Russian, and fuck Russia every chance you get. From this he would never be swayed.

Then things changed.

It wasn't that Russia became any less of an enemy. Rather, it was a change in the means to the ends. The mode of operation altered; there was a shift in tactics. These changes were taking place before his eyes: the choices of operation targets; replacing certain types of Gladios; violating the home front sanctity; the unquestioning willingness to sacrifice all to quench the insatiable greed of the few. And of course, the senseless murder of Mai. The enemy of his enemy was now *his* enemy. The old saw stood on its head.

Greg opened his carry-on and removed a plastic box containing several small brown paper pouches. He took out the pouches and lined them up on top of his fold-up tray. Then he set to eating his dinner: unsalted and uncured walnuts, cashews, almonds, peanuts, and sunflower seeds.

The greatest things in life always come in their simplest form. Overprocessing degrades beauty, taste, scent and sound, and robs most substances of pleasure. This too is true about overall health. Greg would know; his mind, body and spirit were living proof.

He repacked his nutcase and returned it to the carry-on, then rested his eyes. In less than thirty minutes they would be ready for landing; in less than an hour, he would be entering the belly of the beast.

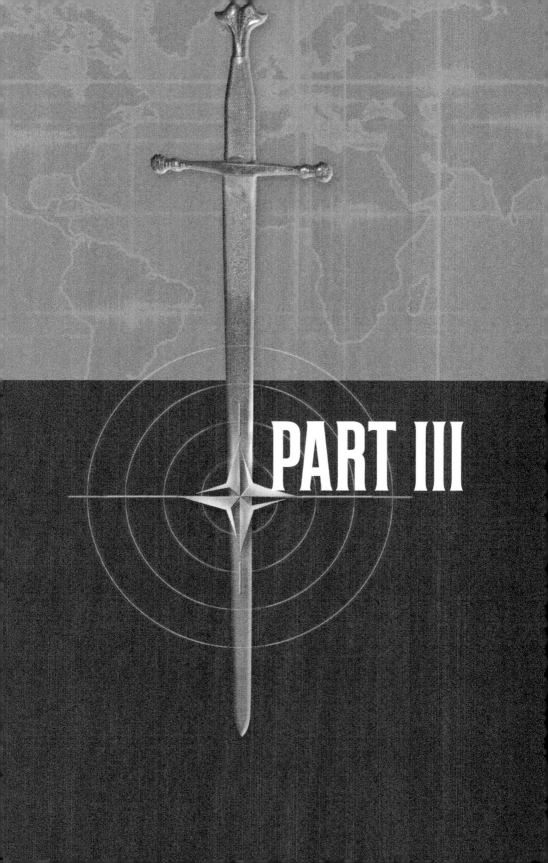

PART III

CHAPTER 9

Sunday Morning, October 26, 2003
Fairfax, Virginia

Tatiana smiled. After clearing her throat, she leaned forward on the conference table and began.

"I think by now I have pushed the FSB angle as far as I could push."

She was referring to the Federal Security Service of the Russian Federation (FSB), the principal security agency in Russia and successor to the Soviet KGB.

Tatiana continued. "Based on my sources—multiple sources, some of them pretty high level—there were *no* hit operations in Northern Cyprus issued by FSB, either officially or off the record, period. They *have*, however, been monitoring the other side's activities, all the usual stuff . . ."

This would be competing Western intelligence operations; those initiated and carried out for the most part by the States either directly or via proxies, mainly Turkey.

Tatiana went on with her briefing. "This may be interesting: they have been closely following several bank accounts, some owned by former Soviet State heads and quite a few operatives connected to the heroin network with Russian markets." She paused; then added, "My sources tell me we shouldn't rule out rogue Russian mafia as a possibility."

Ryan jumped in. "So . . . what, we're back to the starting point, our own government's conclusion? They believe this was a mafia and drug-related hit?"

Elsie looked at Sullivan. She searched his face for any reaction. So far he had none.

Tatiana addressed Ryan directly. "Regardless, we have to check out the mafia angle, even if only to rule it out. One of my contacts is connected to a retired FSB guy, old-time KGB, who now works for one of the top Russian mafia head's security network. His name is Mikhail Alexov. My contact is going to explore that angle in Cyprus. For that we need to provide Alexov with incentives to cooperate."

"How?" Ryan wondered.

Tatiana teasingly pursed her lips then tilted her head sideways. "I was getting there. I can think of two approaches. One: A top Russian mafia man—one of Alexov's—was detained by Russian security a few months back and is now in jail. We get the Russians to release him in return for information. Two: If we are lucky and if it is not Alexov who is involved but one of his competitors with connections to Northern Cyprus operations, then we can get him to talk easily; he'll give us the information, and we'll get Russia to make life difficult for whoever is the competing mafia head."

Elsie, who'd been quiet, could no longer contain herself. "Wait a minute. I have a question. I understand all your *intimate* and *dependable* contacts in Russia, but what makes you so confident of getting the government's cooperation on this?" (Read: *Who the hell do you think you are to make and promise deals on behalf of the Russian government?*)

Tatiana didn't respond directly. Instead, she looked over to Sullivan.

Sullivan, seeing his cue, took over. "My companies have four-teen billion dollars' worth of business and investments in Russia, Elsie. The government there is smart. They know my value . . . and, let's say, they appreciate my economic influence over there. I'm good at dangling that carrot when needed—and for justice for my son I'll be willing to dangle carrots, celery, whatever it takes."

Tatiana gave Elsie a smart-ass smirk.

"Tati," Ryan asked, "I assume that you and your sources will be pursuing this as your next target?"

Tati. His pet name made Elsie cringe.

"Right. I may have to take a short trip and do a face-to-face. Let's see how the preliminaries go . . . I should have that part con-cluded by our next session, next week."

"What have you got for us?" Sullivan asked Ryan.

"My new Pentagon contact, thanks to your *resources*, has been able to dig up some buried TDY records for Yousef covering some of his U.S. government–backed trips overseas. He had at least three trips to Turkey and several to Azerbaijan, Bosnia, Romania, Ger-many, and—catch this—one long trip to Beijing, some bogus assign-ment with the U.S. embassy there. What I'm trying to figure out here is the precise reason for sending him to those locations. During one of his trips to Turkey, Yousef flew over to Cyprus and spent two nights in a hotel called Casino Med. That would be late 2000. Now, remember his landlord, Victoria Lawson? Turns out, she sold the house through some third parties, yet the money was wired to an account in Cyprus. I'm going to check out Nazim's Egyptian partner from Chicago, Imad al-Rauf, and see what his exits and entries for that period show. I suspect we'll have further Cyprus connections on his side as well."

Ryan knew that as long as he found connections—*any* connec-tions—between targets Yousef and Nazim and Sullivan's case and Cyprus, he'd have a world of resources and backing. He knew too that Sullivan cared nothing about these men or even the 2001 attack; he was a man possessed, obsessed with the murder of his son and revenge. It would be up to him, Ryan, to drag this operation out as long as possible; until the inevitable answer got through to Sullivan.

He took a big gulp of coffee. "Also, I'm trying to find an in with Canadian security: we need the details of Yousef's arrest. So far I've gotten zilch. The Canadians adamantly refuse to provide them. I've set up a meeting with a reporter, however, who spent months investigating Yousef's case—until, that is, his editor told him either to shut up or get out. That was Nebraska. He resigned and went to Chicago, where he worked part-time for one of the dying papers there. The guy hasn't given up on Yousef; he's still chasing the story on his own. I was thinking of going out to Chicago to have a chat, see what he's got. While I'm there I'll try to see Robert too . . . if I find a way to get past his wife . . ."

Sullivan raised his hand. "I have another trip in mind. You need to meet face-to-face with Nuray's brother. He's in Jakarta, still with the IMF."

Nuray was the Turkish reporter who had contacted his son Jason about a story that involved the Turkish government and mafia-criminal banking operations in Cyprus. Nuray disappeared the day before Jason was hit; still considered "missing."

"I thought we'd gotten everything we could from the brother?" Ryan objected. "So did the U.S. investigators, which is pretty much nothing. All governments in that part of the world are involved in mafia-crime partnerships."

Sullivan was firm. "It's been two years. Maybe he's more willing now. Less scared or intimidated. I want you to go there, sit with him; keep pushing." He turned to Elsie. "Elsie, what have you got for us? Any comments?"

Elsie felt the eyes of everyone in the room. She could tell Ryan was beyond annoyed: he was seething. During the entire last session she'd said almost nothing, only listened and taken notes.

"Not really, at least not yet," she began. Then after a pause, "Okay, here's the thing: the bureau has an electronic archiving policy for each database accessed by translators and analysts. The communications of each wiretap target go into this database, and the authorized translator logs in, listens or reads, and translates the communication. The archiving policy keeps each communication alive in this database and accessible for five years. After five years, they move the communication into a separate database for archives only. At this point the translator or analyst cannot directly access the file: that person must put in a request for the database center to retrieve the needed file. Either that or do it the hard way, spending hours if not days inside the archive room and searching through thousands and thousands of print files—"

Ryan impatiently interrupted. "Where are you going with this?"

Elsie took a breath. "Last Thursday I decided to check certain target files that could possibly be connected to Nazim and again, perhaps, to Yousef: to go back to the period from 1998 to 2001 and also check for Cyprus as a common theme. So I gave the list of target names–file numbers to the corresponding translator, and he couldn't retrieve any of them. The database gave a message saying *Archived. No longer accessible.* As you can see, that goes against the five-year rule."

Sullivan now seemed interested. "What's your theory? Possible explanation."

"I don't know. I will follow up this week. First, put in a request to the database center; then see if I can physically dig them out of archives."

Mark, the shy techie notetaker with a laptop, raised his hand. "It could be a simple technical glitch. Or may be a screwup during file entry, when they put in the expiration date: in this case, the date when the five-year period ends. Maybe they entered the expiration date wrong?"

Elsie briefly considered it. "If we were talking about only one target or file, then yes, I could see that being possible. But four targets and two different case files? Four out of four not being *accessible?*"

Mark had to agree. Odds were slim to none.

"Or possibly," Ryan added, "you may be right on target with your picks. Knowing how you go about pinpointing leads . . . you may be on to something. We know they made Yousef's file disappear: *Poof!* Gone. As though he were never here."

"Let's wait and see. I should have some kind of explanation by the time we next meet."

"That's good," Sullivan told Elsie, "but you failed to provide us with even one clue as to your four *possible* targets. I assume this is intentional?"

Elsie looked him in the eye. "Ryan may be highly confident when it comes to my hunches and targeting, but I am not. I'm an analyst. I start with leads and then I narrow them down, check them out, test and evaluate, and see if I have an answer. As just explained, I was stopped, cut short. My process got stuck at the earliest stage."

She realized her tone was perhaps too sharp, almost snappy. Sullivan was keen. Yes, she *was* holding back. She had more, and had gone beyond her preliminaries. Still, she remained suspicious of Sullivan. Moreover, she believed this case went well beyond Nazim or even Yousef, their foremost target.

Elsie collected herself and added, more softly, "I understand you're looking at specific leads, characters and potential targets. That's fine. I, though, need to look at the broader picture here, *the macro view*: the forest *and* the trees. I may need to back up, to at least get a glimpse."

She scanned Sullivan's face. "Let me give you an example. I've been researching open-source materials on the net. Believe it or not, sometimes you get far more information that way. A week ago, I discovered a website, a Turkish blog, run by an anonymous user with the screen name Tövbe, a Turkish word that means "repent." Whoever he is, he seems to know a lot; I'd say a former insider. He's been exposing some secret operations by Turkish Intel and NATO that happened in the eighties. One of the characters constantly referred to, a lieutenant general, fits Nazim's profile. And the stuff pouring out fits well with our old case, the botched narco sting op at Andrews Air Force Base—"

Ryan broke in. "You think Nazim is a high-level active Turkish military guy?"

"I didn't say that. I said he fits this guy's description; that, and what you got: Belgium, agency plane and, of course, the State Department stepping in."

Sullivan smiled, rare these days. "I like your approach. Elsie, we'll put you in charge of *the forest*." He checked his watch. "A lunch meeting I must attend. If you'll excuse me," and with that he briskly walked out, escorted by Tatiana, as always.

* * * *

Tuesday, October 28, 2003
Washington, D.C.

Elsie sat across from Special Agent Tony, the new Ryan in counter-intelligence ops targeting Turkic nations. She tried hard to stop her feet from tapping. She was impatient, bored and frustrated.

With Ryan gone and the Nazim operation shut down, she was assigned to a dull procedural case involving some charity opera-tors with offices in Washington, D.C., and Detroit. The nonprofit organization, it was suspected, was a front for a bigger operation in funneling money to two Palestinian organizations now on the State Department's Terror Watch List. Another phony cause, everyone knew, sucking up the agency's time and resources—when major cases and leads were being shut down one by one.

"What do you suppose we should follow up on next?" Tony asked.

"I got the report from the White Collar division," Elsie fumed. "They've got nothing suspicious. I know the feeling of wrong. This is a no-case case . . . it's BS!"

Tony sighed. "I know. I'm going to prepare a report saying exactly that. Of course, HQ won't be happy about it; they want to link this to the terror front. They want it badly."

"Well too bad for them. They can go hire some Hollywood scriptwriters and have them make up stories. Obviously, I won't." She collected her notepad and file and stood up to leave. "When are you going to file that report and the assessment?"

"Most likely by the end of the day tomorrow; as you said, what's there to report?"

When she went back to her unit, Elsie was surprised to see Meltem. "You're back early!"

Meltem closed the file she was holding. "It wrapped up much faster than expected. Well, glad to get that over with."

She seemed neither glad nor elated; in fact, Elsie thought, Meltem looked tense, and judging from the circles under her eyes, sleep-deprived and agitated. *Operation gone bad in Tbilisi?*

"What's next for you? Another assignment? Because I've got one I'd love to pass on to you."

Meltem gave a medium shrug. "There are a couple of old cases I have to finalize. After that, I think I'll use my leave time for some rest and recuperation."

"Sounds good. Maybe a vacation? Somewhere overseas?"

Meltem faced her computer monitor. "Who knows. Maybe. Why not."

Elsie noticed her desk phone blinking as she pulled up her chair. She had two voicemails. The first was from Sami asking her out for a bout of after-work drinking. The second was from the computer database center downstairs: *"Ms. Simon, this is Jeremy. The request you filed with us . . . we were not able to retrieve the requested files. I put in a request memo with HQ for the database. We'll let you know once they respond."*

Elsie was surprised. This thing was getting odder by the second. The files she was after were taken out of Emin's database, despite the expiration rule. Now she was being told that the subject files no longer resided in the FBI's WFO database. This was even more than strange—it bordered on something deeper.

She dialed the database center's extension, asked for Jeremy and was put on hold. She used to know the head of that center fairly well; this guy, Jeremy, she didn't know from Adam.

"Jeremy here."

"Hi Jeremy. This is Elsie Simon from the translation and analysis unit. I got your message, and I am a bit confused—"

Jeremy interrupted. "Well that makes two of us. Granted, I'm new, but it seems confusing. When I submitted the request for retrieval, the system came back with a blinking Red Alert that said, *The file you have requested is no longer accessible. Please report to Division A-Thirty-six.*"

"That's HQ, right?"

"Yes. Further, it's a subdivision accessible only by designated and authorized personnel via the director's office."

"That would be *the* FBI director?"

"Yes. Further, you and I have TS [Top Secret] clearance. For Division A-Thirty-six you need SCI [Sensitive Compartmented Information] clearance, specifically authorized and signed by the director."

"Ah, hold on. *Don't* send the request to HQ until I get back to you. I want to go check a few physical files."

"Too late, Ms. Simon. I already sent them the memo. Also, just my requesting the files sends an automatic alert to HQ anyway."

Shit! Shit shit shit! Elsie thought. "Okay, I understand. And, thank you, Jeremy."

"Sure thing."

Elsie hung up and closed her eyes to recover from this latest.

"What was that about?" Meltem suddenly sounded curious.

Ugh! Elsie thought. She'd forgotten all about the spy sitting next to her. "Database problem. Access to some files has been kind of sketchy. FBI and updated technology, a major oxymoron."

"Any specific division or files?"

Elsie waved her off. "Oh, no. All over the map. Some CI, some CT . . ."

"Good luck with HQ. They never respond in a timely way. If I were you, I'd get up and go there . . . instead of playing phone tag for weeks at a stretch."

"In fact, I may just do that." With that, Elsie got up and headed toward the archives room.

When she entered the coast was clear. She went directly to the Turkic cabinets; this was her division. Her presence here, sifting through the files, was expected. She opened the large cabinet and had to stoop to access the drawer for the years 1996 to 2000. Archiving was organized first by time period, then by file number, and finally, by each target ID number.

Working quickly, she pulled back one file after another until she reached the thick file for the Military Attaché-Azerbaijan. She ran her finger over thick folders until she found it. Straightening up, she expertly balanced the open folder in one hand, rifling through its pages with the other, scanning for the ID number. Nothing. The folder contained not a single page on one of the most active target IDs; nothing whatsoever.

She replaced the folder and repeated the process. This time she looked for a specific ID: Turkey-NATO Cooperation and Coordination Division. She found the file and pulled out the folder for the target lieutenant colonel, bypassing the standard summary translations for routine communications pertaining to him. She reached the end of the folder. Not a single pertinent or verbatim translation or report. Once again, nothing.

Elsie knew there was no more point in searching; she would not find anything here. The files had been combed and sanitized. She returned the folder to its slot inside the drawer. Her heart was pounding. Her mouth was dry. Her palms were sweaty and damp. Whatever information these files contained had been disappeared by FBI higher-ups—possibly, per order of other U.S. agencies, likely the CIA and perhaps in conjunction with the State Department; and quite possibly the Pentagon. Maybe all three.

She left Archives and headed back to her office, cursing herself for her hasty request put through the field office's database center. By doing so, she had alerted the FBI higher-ups. What had Jeremy said? *Blinking Red Alert!*

As she neared her desk she changed her mind, turned around and migrated toward the unit's translation cubicles, over to Emin's desk.

Emin looked up and removed his earphones. "Hi. Need something?"

Elsie scanned the nearby cubicles. Everyone seemed busy, typing away. "Actually, yes. I need *you*."

Emin raised his thick eyebrows and muttered something in Turkish.

Elsie easily switched to Turkish as well. "I really need to speak with you; not here. It's almost twelve. Have lunch with me?"

"You mean right now?"

Elsie nodded.

"Let's go. What are we eating?"

"Let's not leave together. Meet me at the Tea House in . . . fifteen minutes," she told him. "See you there."

* * * *

Elsie wasn't the least bit hungry. She was jittery. The lightweight table was vibrating from her twitchy legs. She needed sugar. She emptied three packets into her tiny teacup.

"You are one of those lucky ones who can eat tons and consume all the sugar you want yet remain thin and fit!"

"This is *not* my usual. Today my body is screaming for sugar," she confessed, then quickly changed the topic. "I would like you to tell me about the translator who left right before I started with the bureau. What was her name? Sarah?" She thought she'd seen that name and signature on some of the older reports.

"Sema," Emin corrected her. "Sema Kaddisi. Why?"

"I'll get to that in a minute. You worked with her, and you took over her translation targets. Please tell me about her."

Emin looked into his tea to reflect. "She was an excellent language specialist. Everyone said she was the best the bureau ever had in its Turkic division. Educated, hardworking . . ."

"Then why did she leave?"

"It's complicated. I'm not sure I even know. Things were twisted."

"Okay. Tell me then what you do know."

"Won't you tell me why?"

"It may be something, it may be nothing."

"Okay . . . you already know the lines and targets she was monitoring and translating; hers was all counterintelligence. She rarely worked crime. She loved her work, maybe too passionately . . ."

"Then why did she leave?"

"Because of what happened in 2001, the attack. Two days after, when we came to work, she was beside herself. She requested a meeting with the Special Agent in Charge—"

"Whitman?"

"No. Whitman took over a few weeks *after* September 2001. Back then it was Marshall."

"Assistant Deputy Director Phil Marshall?"

"Right. He got promoted shortly after the attack. Until then he was the man in charge of our CI unit for Turkic nations. Anyhow," he continued, "she went into several meetings with him, and every time she'd take a bunch of files with her. She believed there were explosive links between al-Hazar, what happened in 2001, and some of her CI targets."

Elsie held her breath. "Which ones? Which CI targets?"

"I . . . I don't know. By the time she left, and by the time I took over her lines, those files were gone. Maybe sent to HQ. Who knows?"

"Did she tell you anything about those targets and the links?"

"Not really. As I said, she was no longer working on any files or targets. She spent all her time requesting meetings—no, *demanding* meetings—going in, coming out even more frustrated, round and round."

"Who else did she meet with?"

"The special agent in charge. The guy who ran the entire field office back then. Then, it was HQ. I think she went up as high as the director."

"What did they tell her? What did they do?"

"Well, at first they said they'd look into it; but later, as she kept insisting, they began to really get annoyed. They removed her access to those files and assigned her to a different target ID. That didn't work. This time she went to the Inspector General. That really pissed off the HQ guys. I mean *really pissed them off.*"

"What did they do?"

"Took away her clearance and asked—no, *forced*—her to get a mental health eval. There may have been an ultimatum. They claimed she exhibited symptoms of PTSD. From the terror attack."

"Of course. Then what?"

"Then . . . I'm out of the loop. Her clearance was removed and she was placed on leave, so I didn't get to see her in the office anymore."

"How about outside the office?" Emin began to squirm. He was one of those make-no-waves people.

"Emin, this—everything here—will stay between us."

Emin sighed. "Okay. Yes. She called my house and asked to meet. We hooked up in a restaurant near her house in McLean . . . she told me she'd taken her case to the congressional offices involved in investigating that attack, and further, to the Independent Commission appointed by the president. The bureau then went after her husband, a nice Lebanese guy, trying to get dirt on him. They were even audited by the IRS. Talk about harassment! Poor thing lost so much weight, she looked dead."

"What did she want from you?"

Emin looked around, nervous. "She said some of these offices—Congress and IG and others—wanted to interview all witnesses, and they'd be contacting me. I said I knew nothing . . . that I had no idea what all these files contained!"

"What then did she ask you to provide?"

"To go on record that those files had been removed. That was it."

"Did anyone contact you? From those offices?"

Emin stirred his tea. "Investigators from the Senate Intelligence Committee contacted me and set up a meeting. Then they called me back and canceled it. They said I would be providing the info to the Inspector General's Office—the Justice Department's IG—and they would share their info with the Senate people."

"And? Did you go?"

"I did . . . but they didn't want to ask me anything about the files or the case. Even when I voluntarily brought it up, for Sema's sake, they ignored me. All they wanted to know was whether Sema looked crazy, or acted crazy around the office. Did she seem paranoid? They asked about her eating patterns when she worked. Did she ever fall asleep during work? All sorts of dumb, irrelevant questions."

Elsie leaned back to check her breathing. It wasn't the sugar. This was outrageous. Sadistic. Maybe even criminal. "Where is she? I need her contact information."

Emin pulled out his cell, pressed a button, and handed her his phone. "It's the last number I had for her."

She copied the number into her phone. This call couldn't wait.

* * * *

Tuesday Evening, October 28, 2003
Arlington, Virginia

Sami finally got the waitress's attention. With her hand up high, she waggled two fingers: another round of margaritas on the rocks with salt.

Elsie was already tipsy. She knew she shouldn't have another.

"Oh, where was I? Oh yeah, the HQ SES guys." Sami was referring to the bureau's managers, senior executive agents turned bureaucrats. "Dickheads. Every one of them."

Elsie laughed. She'd called Sami back earlier that day and accepted her invite for happy hour. Here were the best margaritas in town; and she needed Sami and the talk. No details, of course. All she'd spoken of was her frustration with the bureau screwing up big investigations and shutting them down per higher-ups at the State Department or the CIA or both. Sami had more than one similar story.

"Anyhow," Sami pressed on with her tale, "we bust the sicko bastard with his pants down, literally, in front of this little girl. And guess what? The State guys step in and tell us, *No no no no no, the guy has diplomatic immunity.* D'ya know what *kind* of diplomatic immunity?"

Elsie took a long cold sip and waited.

"Catch this: the guy is the brother-in-law of a diplomat's *cousin.* That makes him, what, four or five degrees of separation? I'm closer to Kevin Bacon! Yes, State Department got him off the hook; like the immunity thingy for Saudis: if you've got that oil, you're golden. Terrorism, child rape, no problem . . . hell, you can even be a serial killer, in fact, we even have a special job for you, with your name on it."

"Still," Elsie mused out loud, "I'm tempted to take this to Congress."

Sami gave her the look. "Weren't we just talking about dicks? Smaller ones, I grant you."

"I said *tempted.* Also, they can't *all* be dicks. Are you saying that there isn't one nondick there? What about the females?"

"You mean the female dicks? They're worse. They're dicks *without* dicks—more dangerous. Dickless dicks are unpredictable, liable to say or do anything."

Elsie shook her head. "Matt, Ben's son from the first marriage, used to work for Keller, way back when. He swore by him being tough: especially when it came to intel and law enforcement agencies and their screwups. The guy is now the Whip."

"*Way back when.*" Sami pushed her straw around the bottom of her drink, jiggling the ice. "Sooner or later they master the art of compromise. They sell out. You're going to him to do what? Blow the whistle?"

"I didn't say that. All I meant was . . ."

"I know you're not telling me everything," Sami said, now serious. "Watch your back. The bureau can be a nasty place . . . if and when you choose to go against it."

Elsie thought about Rob. What did they screw him over for? *Conducting a real investigation.* She was still badly shaken from Emin's story and what they'd done to Sema. Earlier, right after their lunch, she'd called Ryan in Chicago, where he was meeting with Rob and that Nebraska reporter. She'd given him the short version and proposed an emergency meeting for tomorrow. Concerned, he said he'd call Sullivan's team and set up the meeting for 9:30 A.M.

"Hello?"

"Oh! Ah . . ."

"Somebody thinking of someone?"

Color rushed into Elsie's cheeks. "When are you leaving for your next assignment?"

"I thought so. The answer is, tomorrow evening," Sami told her. "Remember that woman with the missing boyfriend in Cambodia? I'll be meeting with her, either before or right after the assignment in New Jersey. Patterson."

Elsie did remember: her name was Lucy. "Any new developments there?"

"Nah . . ." Sami sounded frustrated. "She's a piece of work. It's either face-to-face or nothing! Fine, let's do it, face-to-face, and see what she's got. I'll meet her as soon as I get there." She looked at Elsie, taking all of her in. "I'm concerned about you, girl. I believe you've gotten into some kinda trouble. I don't like being away with you in *any* kinda trouble . . . after all, y'ain't experienced like me . . ."

Elsie put down her glass, still a quarter full. It was definitely time to go. "Don't worry about me, Sami. Take care of yourself: watch your back with all those pervs in Patterson—especially the ones with *immunity*."

* * * *

Wednesday, October 29, 2003
Fairfax, Virginia

It was only 10 A.M., but by the time Elsie finished presenting the summary version of what had taken place, she felt utterly drained, ready to climb back under the covers and sleep for eight hours straight. She hadn't gotten any rest; thinking, analyzing, thinking again in one great loop, all night. Add to that a hangover and, well, she was exhausted.

This morning she'd called in sick. Then the emergency meeting with the Sullivan team. Later she planned to meet with Sema, the Turkish translator. They were to meet at 2:30 P.M. in McLean, in a playground a few blocks from Sema's house.

Now, around Sullivan's conference table, Elsie could sense Ryan's concern and alarm. She could see it in his face, the pulsing in his neck, his fists. Tatiana, to Sullivan's right, like an appendage, was observing her closely, almost studying her. And Sullivan . . . he seemed buried in thoughts, but which ones Elsie couldn't tell.

Ryan was first to speak. "As I said last night, I agree with you, Elsie. Once they find out you've been digging in sacred grounds, they'll come after you—as they did with Rob, and with this Turkish translator. You should preempt it. Get out before hell is inflicted on you. My suggestion is, hand in your resignation tomorrow."

"I believe that to be premature," Sullivan said. "The retaliation, assuming it is inevitable, may come in weeks or months; bureaucracies do not act quickly. A couple of months, even two weeks, with access inside the bureau could be extremely valuable."

Elsie turned to Ryan. "I see your point, but I don't think the time is right. For one thing, I'm scheduled to meet Sema later today. Based on what I get from her I'll be searching and researching further, and for that I have to be inside, with my access."

Ryan was not convinced, she could tell; she would talk with him later, in private.

"Elsie," Tatiana said icily, "there is another issue we would like to talk to you about. Mister Sullivan?"

Elsie didn't like the tone. She turned to face the man.

"Elsie," Sullivan began, "I understand the pressure you're under. This level of stress may cause some to act hastily and thus irrationally. I want to be sure you know at this stage that decisions you make not only impact you but what we are doing as a team as well . . ."

"Mister Sullivan, what are you implying here? Let's speak without the layers. Tell me bluntly."

"I select my people very carefully," he replied. "I hand-picked this team even more cautiously. Yes, to be blunt: I am concerned you are considering other venues on certain aspects of your cases; specifically, the U.S. Congress. My question is, have you been informing or consulting with congressional bodies on some of your issues with the bureau?"

"Before I answer that, which I don't believe is any of your business, please answer my question first. What makes you think I've been communicating with Congress? Where does this come from?"

"We understand you've been frequenting various Internet cafés in select odd locations, in a clandestine way."

Elsie sprang to her feet with white-hot rage. "You've been spying on me? You've had me followed?" Disgusted, she grabbed her handbag. "I have nothing further to say to you. I have nothing further to do with you. I am done with your mercenary operations." She threw Tatiana a look of contempt and added, "And your mercenaries."

Before she walked out Elsie narrowed her eyes at Ryan. "Were you in on this? Answer me, Ryan."

Sullivan stood between them. "I told you, I select my people with care. How do you think I found out about Ryan and his division? I have a contact or two in the bureau, and once I got his name, I had him followed to make sure he was clean; only then did I approach him directly. Same with you. I do my own homework, no matter who vouches for you. I had to check you out independently."

Now inches from his face, Elsie glared. "And who checks *you* out in this deal? Who vouches for you, Mister Sullivan—if that even is your name? I have no idea who you are: how clean or how dirty. I don't even believe in what you present as *your case* . . ." midsentence, she couldn't finish. She shook her head sadly. "I have nothing more to do with you, or this nonsense operation. I want you to cease invading my privacy, immediately."

She strode out fuming. Ryan ran after and caught her at the elevator.

"I didn't know. I had no idea. Do you believe me?"

Elsie didn't respond.

"I did know that he'd checked me out, whether by—"

"What have you done?" she interrupted. "What's your excuse for this level of insanity?"

"I've already answered that, Elsie, you know it. *Justice.* Not only for . . ." he trailed off. What was the point?

They rode the elevator and walked to her car in silence. When they reached it, Elsie stopped. "This is much bigger than what you think. This is not about two or three rogue agents penetrating certain agencies within the government complex. I've been researching and chasing this. The further in I go, the higher the level and bigger the culprit target network gets. Think about it, Ryan: Who is protecting Nazim and Yousef? The State Department is involved. And the agency. And the Pentagon. And NATO. Are you blind? Look at what this ring includes so far!"

"No. Not blind. To expose the ring, we first go after the little guys. In this case, guys like Yousef. This is no different than any other law enforcement operation."

"Law enforcement! Well, guess what? You are no longer law enforcement, and neither is Sullivan."

"What would you have me do? Forget about this whole deal, just drop everything and go work for some big corporation running personnel security?" Ryan sounded angry, tired of fending off her blows but afraid of losing her. He had to fight to change her mind, to convince her to stay somehow; their work on this case was all he had left. "Elsie, I need you with me on this . . ."

There was that word: *need.* Couldn't he desire her for her own sake? Why must everything be on Sullivan's terms—including being spied on, and acting as his mole? What makes that okay? "I'm not interested in working for the bureau that way. Nor am I suggesting just dropping it. I am, though, willing to look around and consider other possibilities: other channels to collaborate and join forces with; because I know this is bigger than anything we can do, or even Sullivan with his clout and his mercenaries."

"Please stop repeating that like a parrot! *Mercenary* I am not! Marriage of convenience, maybe."

Elsie's shoulders sagged with exhaustion. "All right then. How about this: you pursue our case with Sullivan and his resources. I'll pursue it on my own, my way. Let's hope one of us gets there, accomplishes something, and stays alive."

Ryan tried one last time, for himself. "Elsie . . . might you give Sullivan another chance? We're meant to work togeth—"

"I'm done with Sullivan," she cut him short.

"All right. How about this instead: we give ourselves two weeks. You do what you believe you must do, and I'll push from this side for two more weeks. Let's see where we get. Then we'll have a genuine talk, we'll make some real decisions. At least I will: to stay or not to stay with Sullivan. Elsie? Whaddya say?"

Elsie ducked into her car. "I'm not sure what you think may be achievable in just two weeks, but right now I'm too tired, I can't think straight. Can we finish this conversation later?"

"I'm leaving for Jakarta tonight. My flight takes off at eleven forty-five. Can I stop by your place at five, on the way to the airport?"

"I'm meeting Sema, the translator, at two-thirty," she explained. "I should be home by five. See you then."

* * * *

Wednesday, 2:30 P.M., October 29, 2003
McLean, Virginia

Elsie, ten minutes early, watched the playground from inside her car. Two days before Halloween, the leaf-strewn ground appeared melancholy. Maybe it was all that flaming red turning brown, the blanket of leaves stirred by the wind; or perhaps it was the unruly state of her emotions. The toddlers' squeals were no match for coming winter; even thinking about it made her feel cold.

She recalled her earlier self: idealistic, determined, Type A, treating her life as a checklist. She'd planned to have children but life had taken over, asserted and inserted itself in ways she couldn't know; this, for instance. Now.

She blinked away tears and switched her thoughts. What was she trying to accomplish here? Obtain information, hopefully, a key to the bigger picture; the truth. Then what? Was there a plan? What, precisely, would she do?

She spotted Sema walking to the park with her daughter, holding the little one's hand and synchronizing their steps. Both mother and daughter had curly dark hair, big eyes framed by long dark lashes and the same Mediterranean golden-olive skin. They headed for the nearest bench.

Zipping up her trench coat, Elsie briskly walked over and sat next to them.

"Hi, Sema, thank you for accepting this meeting. Hi!" She waved at the little girl.

"This is Zara."

"Hi, Zara."

"Hi." She clutched her mother's coat.

"Hi, *Elsie*," Sema said, for both of them. "Elsie . . . hmm . . . not a Turkish name."

"I'm half Turkish. The other half is a mix: Azerbaijani, Irani and Kurdish."

Sema swiveled sideways to examine Elsie's face then turned back to her daughter. "She will be four next month."

"You're very lucky."

Sema agreed.

"I spoke with Emin," Elsie started right in. "He gave me the generals on how you left the bureau. I'm very sorry you had to go through all that."

"It seems like a long time ago," Sema mused. "You know how some things happen for the best? Well, all that is behind me. Happy to raise Zara and enjoy the precious, the wonderful."

"I understand . . . I don't want to bring up bad memories, but I'd like some information from you. Specifically, what those files contained. They're gone: gone from Emin's computer archives, from the WFO database and from the archives room."

"I'm not at all surprised. I expected this. As far as they are concerned, the files never existed."

"But why?"

Sema swiveled again. "First, you. You tell me. Why are you here? Why are you looking? How do I know you are not sent here to check on me . . . make sure I have no documents or that I'm keeping my mouth shut?"

"My CI agent and I were working on a specific counterintelligence case with a drug angle. We were very close—"

"Let me guess," Sema cut in. "Shut down. Case closed."

Elsie nodded.

"And you're looking for a couple of Azerbaijan attaché IDs . . . and specific meetings in Turkey and Central Asia coordinated by the Turkish-NATO center. Am I right?"

Elsie was not expecting this degree of exactness. "Did you cover a guy with the pseudonym Nazim, aka General Turk?"

"Yes."

"And?"

"Not the biggest fish; somewhere between bottom and mid-level. He used to be a lieutenant general in the Turkish army."

Her hunch based on the anonymous blogger's info was right. "His real name?"

Sema shook her head. "You could be wired, Elsie. Or we could be being monitored. I am not the timid little mouse the FBI wanted me to be but I *am* cautious. I have to be." Her eyes rested on her daughter.

"You can check me out: here, feel." Elsie opened her jacket. "I am not here to set you up or trap you. Without the info, without those files, I have nothing. I won't be able to do a thing."

"And with those files you think you can? Look, this is big. If you're checking Nazim, that means you're at or near the bottom level—which tells me you have no idea how big this really is."

"Okay, then how about Yousef . . . Mahmoud?"

Sema closed her eyes. "That's a little higher. You're on the right track."

"Are we going to play Cold, Warmer, Hot?"

Sema stood up, signaling the end of the discussion. "Tell me this: Let's say you get those files. What do you plan to do?"

"First, *I* get to know. Then my task would be to find the most appropriate channel to—"

"I did all that: FBI, DOJ, House, Senate, the Independent Joint Investigative Commission; even the White House chief counsel. Did I miss anyone?"

"How about the press?"

Sema looked her dead in the eye. "You're kidding, right? They will take your evidence, turn you in, and never dare to publish the story. If you ever see the files, then you'll know how they're managed: how they have the media—the ones that count—on their side." She paused. "You know they'll come after you if you keep on digging, right? You won't last if you pursue this."

Elsie held her ground. "Let me worry about that. Right now, I need to get the picture. The entire picture, and that won't happen if you don't tell me more."

"I don't have to tell you anyth—"

"Okay. I understand you washing your hands of this."

"You didn't let me finish, Elsie. What I am trying to say is, you can get all that info without me *telling you* anything."

Elsie raised her brows. "You mean copies?"

Sema smiled. "Technically, no; but I can tell you how to get some of the most important documents." She took a step toward Elsie and mentioned, leaning in, "Legally, I could not take any of those top secret documents outside the bureau. However . . . nothing prohibited me from making copies and tucking them away inside the building."

Genius, Elsie thought. "Where?"

Sema leaned in closer. "Fifty pages in a folder tagged Tu-Op-Ninety-six dash Zero one. North Africa cabinet, hard archives."

"Got it; and the rest?"

"That's a starting point. It'll give you the outlines of the bigger picture. Others—some of that my own insurance—will have to wait for now."

✳ ✳ ✳ ✳

From the passenger seat of the silver gray BMW Tatiana watched Elsie enter her car and start the engine.

"What do you think, Sergei? No documents changed hands."

The pale blond man took off his sun visor and responded in Russian. "They chatted for a long time. I don't think it was about who's fucking who in the suburbs."

"You should pay Sema's house a visit, see if you can find anything. Long shot, I know. I'll contact FSB with the field report. They need those documents. Badly."

"If the house search yields nothing, then maybe the woman?"

"No. No need for that. We'll get whatever she has through Simon."

"I thought she split. No longer with Sullivan?"

"Right." Tatiana smiled. "But still with our hunky agent."

Ever the helpful assistant, Tatiana had given Ryan a high-end company phone—with a high-end bug inside.

* * * *

Thursday, October 30, 2003
Washington, D.C.

Elsie was late.

It was bad enough slamming the alarm clock to shut it up after last night's session of love with Ryan; now it was 9:05 A.M., and she didn't even have time for her double. Instead, she had to smell the espresso from the sidewalk on the fly. *No justice!*

She went through the usual security checks and searched her handbag for a piece of gum. Chewing always helped her focus and keep her calm. Today was the day.

When she entered her office her computer was on and the monitor lit. Meltem was crossing the room—from Elsie's desk.

"Morning . . . What were you doing with my computer?"

"Oh, someone from the database was here before to check or do something to your machine. Maybe some glitch or update? I don't know."

Elsie scrutinized her face and carefully looked over the desk. "I'll find out." She pulled up her chair but then saw the blinking light. Two voicemails. The first was from SAC Mike Whitman. *"Elsie, I need to see you in my office. ASAP. Thanks, Mike."*

The second was Mike again. *"Elsie, come into my office as soon as you get this message. It is urgent."*

She felt a knot in her gut. She sat and typed the command to retrieve her latest file. After thirty or so seconds, a blinking red message appeared onscreen: *Access temporarily on hold. Contact computer security, extension #801.*

The knot was now fist-sized. She had been expecting some sort of warning response from HQ after the database center inquiry but not so soon, and not like this.

With shaky fingers she typed another command to retrieve another active file. Same stall, same alert. She had to think and act quickly. *Find Sema's file and read it. Now. Before they come.*

She picked up her handbag and without taking off her coat headed to the archives.

She entered and went straight to the North African files. Two thirds of the way through, a yellow file caught her attention. This one didn't have the laminated tag with a typed file number ID. Instead, the raised cardboard tab showed a hastily handwritten ID: *Tu-Op 96-01.*

Ignoring her pounding heart, she pulled out the file, closed the cabinet, and moved to the Turkic Division, where she opened the cabinet and pulled out a drawer at random. Anyone entering would assume she was precisely where she was supposed to be.

She opened the jacket and picked up the fifty-page stapled stack with TS-Classified stamped at the top and the target ID name and number printed boldly below. Then she began to read.

> *Date: June 18, 1998*
> *Subject: A coordinated meeting, U.S. Military Attaché, Baku, Azerbaijan*
> *Participants: Mark Schumer (State Department), David Perleman (State Department), Theodore Kline (Pentagon), Alastair Brown (NATO, UK), Prince Rahman al-Baradar (Intelligence Chief, Saudi Arabia), Amin al-Zakiri (Mujahi-*

deen, Operation Level 2), Masoud Rezai (Party C, Afghani-
stan)

> *Meeting Memo: Phase 2 Training, Mujahideen Cadre in Azerbaijan and Kyrgyzstan camps, genuine Turkish government–issued passports, new transfer route via Georgia, countering Russian heroin operation's new route—Ukraine*

Here it was. Amin al-Zakiri—leader of al-Hazar—the person who had executed the 2001 terror attack in addition to several other attacks in England and Sudan. And this document places him in a high-level meeting with top officials from the United States, UK, NATO, and Saudi Arabia—in the U.S. Military Attaché office in Baku, no less. According to history, this meeting took place when the United States was chasing al-Hazar and its leader around the world and hitting their centers and camps with cluster bombs. At the time it was no secret that certain religious extremists from Saudi Arabia, Egypt and Pakistan had joined the Balkan conflict on the Muslim's side. Yet how many times had the Western governments, NATO, declared these groups to be independent rogue participants with no ties or relations to U.S.-NATO operations? And countering Russian operators' heroin market share?

She flipped the page and continued reading.

> *Date: September 21, 1998*
> *Location: U.S. Military Attaché, Ankara-Turkey*
> *Subject: Heroin Labs & Casinos in Azerbaijan, Operation Banks*
> *Participants: Mark Schumer (State Department), Douglas Frommer (Pentagon), Alastair Brown (NATO, UK), Lieutenant General Mehmet Turkel (Turkish Army, NATO), Ihlas Alevi (Interior Minister, Azerbaijan)*
> *Meeting Memo: Relocation of the remaining Turkish*

*Heroin Labs to Azerbaijan, Casino chain establishment Phase
1 in Azerbaijan, Dubai Bank Accounts Closure & Transfer to
New Turkish Republic Cyprus Branches, Status of Turkmenistan Route, New Pressure Points for Georgia takeover*

She leafed through the stack and stopped at the following, fifteen or so pages in.

*Date: July 23, 1999
Location: Turkish Consulate, Chicago, USA
Subject: Joint Chechen Operation in Mainland Russia
Participants: Stephen Fein (State Department), Matthew
Abriza (State Department), David Perleman (State Department), Yousef Mahmoud (Pentagon), Ali Yuksel (Turkish
Consul), Dogu Gundes (Turkish General, NATO)
    Meeting Memo: Three new passports for Yousef Mah-
moud—with one diplomatic passport issued via Ankara, Suicide Mission, Payoff channels and delivery via Ankara-Turkey
for participating Chechen's family members, setting up two
additional training camps with recruitments from Dagestan,
Baku Operation Mosque via Saudi Arabia Investment Fund,
transferring additional training commandos from Afghanistan
to Azerbaijan and Georgia*

Elsie was shaking. She recalled the headlines of a Chechen terrorist attack that year in mainland Russia with forty-one dead and
many more injured. And here was Yousef Mahmoud: one of the
2001 attack's main culprits. Were they all in this together? The State
Department—which usually means the CIA, Pentagon, Turkish government, NATO—and also, with its knowledge and attempt to cover
it all up, the FBI? How could that be?

She would have to move faster. Elsie thought about placing

the entire stack in her handbag but decided against it. Instead, she went back to the second page and began to read chronologically and methodically. She was nauseated.

Elsie was on page eight when the door to the archives room flew open. The rest was in slow motion: two men—SAS Mike Whitman and SAS George Session, head of FBI personnel security for the Washington Field Office—staring at her. Directly behind them was a massive security guard.

"Elsie, didn't you get my messages? You were supposed to report to my office ASAP! You are not supposed to be in this room or any other top secret facility."

Elsie found her voice, and to her surprise it was calm. "I work here, Mike. What do you mean I'm not supposed to be in TS facilities? My entire office is a TS facility!"

"That's why I asked you to report to my office immediately. Your security clearance has been placed on hold, and under investigation as of this morning. You are not allowed in this room. Now let's go to my office to continue this, instead of creating a scene here, in front of everyone."

Elsie nonchalantly placed the folder in the middle of the drawer, pushed it back in and closed the cabinet door. "All right. Shall we?"

Session and the security guard stepped aside to let Whitman and Elsie pass, then followed them to Whitman's office through the corridor and past the beehive of cubicles and observing eyes.

Whitman entered first, followed by Elsie and Session, who closed the door. The uniformed guard was posted outside.

Whitman pointed to one of two chairs. Elsie took her seat and flashed on this same scene, only with Ryan instead of Session, less than a month ago.

Whitman cleared his throat. "You've been with the bureau for now, what, two plus years? You should know better than this, Elsie. We operate on a need-to-know basis when it comes to accessing information. You've been going around asking for files that have nothing to do with your current assignments . . . first within your unit, and then through our database center downstairs."

Elsie jumped in. "I must disagree, Mike. The files I was requesting had to do with the Turkic Division. That's my division. When I work on my analyses everything becomes relevant—even historic files from other parallel divisions."

"Currently you and Tony have that Palestinian NGO with terrorist ties. How does that relate to Turkey–Central Asia files from the nineties?"

Elsie had to think quickly. "We already had the recent records on the target's communication with the cultural attaché. All innocuous. I wanted to go back and see if he had other contacts or connections in the past. I decided to start with 1998."

"Turkey-NATO coordination office? Come on, Elsie, gimme a break."

Elsie shrugged. "You'd be surprised how unlikely places can produce some pertinent leads. Take it from my experience, and of course, my spotless record, Mike."

Whitman and Session exchanged looks. Whitman nodded to Session.

"I re-reviewed your personnel file and application forms," Session told her, "including your clearance questionnaire, Ms. Simon. I found some missing, thus, falsified information. You want to explain that?"

Elsie gave him a daring stare. "Could you be more specific? Those forms were submitted over three years ago. You checked out my background for almost a year. And you were the ones who cleared me and granted my TS clearance in the first place."

"The section that deals with your family," Session replied. "For your father, you failed to provide any specifics. You have a note saying, *Missing, neither deceased nor alive.* And that's pretty much it."

"Indeed I did answer this same question three years ago, during your background investigations," she vehemently protested. "My father was a doctor; a surgeon. In 2000, a series of assassinations targeted several doctors in Turkey. During that period my father disappeared. He went missing. They never found the culprits behind those assassinations. We never heard back from my father. To this date, we don't know whether he is alive and a captive somewhere or dead. As long as there is no body, there is no conclusive death. You know how that works, no?"

Session's face turned red. He didn't like to be challenged. "Back then, we took you at your word. Since, however, new information came to our attention. Information related to your father."

"Care to share? That is, if you would like some explanation from me."

"We have received information indicating that your father was active with a Kurdish group designated terrorist by our State Department," Whitman said.

"The Kurdish Freedom and Rights Organization," Session added.

"He may have associated with some in that group but he was never an official member. Further, they were not designated terrorists until recently, in early to mid 2002. That would be one year after I filled out your forms, and after you had finalized my clearance."

"So you were aware of the new designation. Yet you failed to contact my office and bring this to our attention," Session pressed.

"Actually, from the bureaucratic standpoint, you were the ones who failed: you failed to check the new designation and contact me to inform and question me at that time. Isn't that right, George?"

Whitman stepped in. "All right. We can chalk this up to human error." He paused. "Elsie, we know you have been going through a rough period; actually, periods."

Aha, here comes the PTSD tactic, so predictable, Elsie thought.

"Your husband passed away about a year ago," Whitman stated out loud, as though for the record, "after a severe stroke and a year of being paralyzed and wheelchair-ridden. To top that, Marcello left and we know how close you were—as partners . . . I could see how shocked and shaken you were when we broke the news a few weeks back . . . All of which, back-to-back, takes a toll. It's normal. It's expected. And in a way it does explain your obsessive behavior."

"Obsessive how, exactly? Where are you getting that?"

"Your disregard for compartmentalized information outside your scope of work," Whitman answered. "Your frequent trips to the archives room with an unreasonable amount of time spent there. The way you've been treating your officemates—"

"What officemate?" she interrupted. "Who?"

"Earlier this morning we had a brief chat with Meltem Drake. She told us about the recent severe behavioral changes in you. She cares about you, Elsie."

"Drake has been on TDY assignments for the last few months," Elsie snapped. "She hasn't spent more than five or six full days here in the office in the last four months. Give *me* a break, Mike. That's BS and easily provable as a load of shit."

Whitman's face became stern. "I see you are irritable. Even more reason to take some time out for yourself. Maybe go and see a counselor, get some rest. You are not mentally or emotionally fit to continue your work. That and the fact that we have to reinvestigate your clearance status. Without your clearance you cannot work here. You know that, Elsie."

"You are forcing me to take leave? For how long?"

"At least four weeks. I'll check with HQ and see if they require a mandatory counseling report before we reissue your clearance."

"I see," she said tersely. "In other words, maybe it would be wise for me to hand in my resignation. Right, Mike? You're forcing me to resign. To go away, disappear, and to make sure I keep my mouth shut."

Whitman exchanged another look with Session and made a few

notes on his pad. "Now you're acting paranoid, Elsie. We love and respect your work here. There is no conspiracy to fire you or force you to resign. We are all concerned about your well-being; your mental health. That affects everything you do here, for the bureau. Now, take a few weeks off. Go chill out and put yourself back together." He turned to Session. "We're done here, right?"

Elsie stood. "I have to go back to my office and collect my things."

Whitman agreed. "George and the guard will escort you. After all, the entire unit is considered TS-Compartmentalized, and we can't let you in there without your clearance."

Elsie swallowed back another wave of rage.

"Ms. Simon, before we leave, please hand me your badge and ID, and all keys," Session demanded.

Elsie gave him a disgusted look before unzipping her handbag. She handed him the requested items. "No need for the *escort*. I know the way. I'll see myself out."

Session held the door for her. She walked out of the office and heard Session instructing the guard, "Please walk Ms. Simon out of the building, Earl."

And that was it. She was leaving the unit, most likely for good, escorted by an armed uniformed guard. *Some two-year career. Quite the finale!* she thought, irate.

She walked out of the FBI building, leaving the guard behind. Cold wind hit her face, and that felt good. She walked briskly in the direction of coffee. Now the cold wind burned. Not only that, it was razor sharp, combined with fresh hot tears—not sad but humiliated, angry tears. She dragged a sleeve across her cheeks before she entered the coffeehouse.

Her Ethiopian barista friend Abdi gave her a look of concern. "Good morning, Ms. Elsie."

She summoned a smile. "And to you, Abdi. My usual please . . . actually, no, make that a tall cappuccino triple shot, whole milk."

Ryan's favorite coffee beverage. She needed the comfort of the creamy hot concoction. It was that kind of a day.

As he steamed the milk with the spout, Abdi asked, "You okay, Ms. Elsie?"

Elsie thought before she answered. "No, but I'm trying to be okay. Does that make sense?"

Abdi thought yes, and handed her the steaming cup. She took it to the counter and filled it with brown sugar, three packs. Her body was about to appreciate it.

Outside, she walked half a block, turned left, and sat on a deserted bus stop bench. She put her cup down next to her and dialed Ryan's cell. She got his voicemail. She checked her watch: 10:30 A.M. Ryan was still in the air. At least another two hours before he landed in South Korea for a two-hour layover before taking off for Jakarta. She really needed him. Damn the timing.

She flipped the phone shut, picked up her triple, and took a couple of sips of the scalding liquid. What next? What was the best plan of action? She had read ten of Sema's fifty pages, and that alone was explosive enough. She had the findings on Yousef through Ryan and his sources: combined with what she'd gotten from Sema, doubly explosive. Yet, it would be all her word; allegations only. Without the document, she would be portrayed as a disgruntled ex-worker for the FBI, someone made bitter and paranoid, likely with an axe to grind. She well knew what happens to anyone who dares expose the official lie, no matter the scope or size, or whose lives are at risk at whatever time. What do they call them? *Whistleblowers.* She would be tagged. She didn't like what went with that, not at all. What happens to them is never anything good.

She had an idea she'd been toying with. Risky? Possibly. Better than doing nothing? Who knows, but she had to do something, take some action.

She flipped open her phone and dialed Matt, Ben's son. Since he was a year older, she didn't feel right calling him her stepson. So she called him Matt and introduced him as Ben's son. While getting his masters degree at law, Matt used to work for Congressman Keller as a researcher and sometime investigator. He admired the congressman, now the Whip, one of the most powerful men in D.C. Keller made his name exposing official corruption, "wrongdoing" and incompetence, especially when it came to the intelligence agencies and their failures. He was known for holding public hearings, making bold statements to the press and even standing up for underdog whistleblowers.

Matt had since moved to San Diego with his wife and infant son. He'd been working as a partner in a small successful law firm.

Matt answered the call.

"Hi Matt . . . Elsie here."

"Hey. Good to hear your voice. How are you?"

"Good . . ." she paused and tried to regain control. "Actually, not so good, Matt."

"You're okay? Something happened?" Matt sounded alarmed.

Elsie took a breath, cold air burning her lungs. "I'm in the middle of a major shit storm involving the FBI. I need to see and talk with Keller. You think you could arrange that, Matt?"

"Of course . . . You want to talk about it?"

"I think not. Not over the phone. It's a long story; a long *scary* story."

"When do you want to see him?"

"Right away. Now. This moment, if I can. It needs to be inside a SCIF—short for Sensitive Compartmented Information Facility. We are talking top security stuff."

"Understood. Where are you now?"

"Um, a couple of blocks from the Washington Field Office. Why?"

"That's good. Let me call his office. I'll call you back right away. You should hear from me in five, ten minutes, tops. Okay?"

"Thank you, Matt. I won't move. I'll be waiting for your call." With that she hung up but kept the phone in her hand.

She thought about her father; love of her life. Her life coach, role model, only family, her best friend . . . maybe running into extreme and frightening situations was karma, some sort of family destiny.

Her father was more than an eminent surgeon; he was an activist in a country of oppression, an avid human rights advocate. He was a doctor who took his oath very seriously.

He also was unafraid to take risks. He and two other physician-activists had spent years treating Kurdish victims of their own government: those who'd been detained, jailed, and severely tortured for advocating basic human rights. Their nonviolent protests were met with a degree of brutality entirely unknown to outsiders; her father knew what measures were used—what uncommon savagery—because he and his friends had been treating these victims in secret. These were crimes against humanity: moral crimes to which all three doctors bore witness, committed behind an official wall of denial and outright lies. A face was presented to the outside world while reality and truth were shrouded in darkness, strangled in a pit and thrown down a well. The doctors had to act. They documented these heinous acts and labeled the evidence with detailed written reports, interviews, photographs and films.

After compiling more than a hundred such cases, they packaged their findings and passed it on to two organizations: Doctors United for Justice, a D.C.-based nonprofit organization, and the United Nations' Office on Human Rights. Less than a month after the information was sent, one of the doctors was assassinated at his home, as he was kissing his wife before going to work. That same evening, at around 5:30, another of the doctors with his assistant both were assassinated by two gunmen who stormed their office. That night her father didn't come home. He was last seen at one of his two private practices. The pharmacist next door was the last known link to her father; he told Elsie that her father had gotten the news about the assassination of the first doctor.

They never recovered his body and he never was declared dead. And Elsie had been looking for him ever since. She was the only one actively searching.

As to those responsible for his disappearance, it had to be one of the two organizations. Elsie had an idea which one. The D.C.-based nonprofit was known to be used now and then as cover for the CIA's clandestine overseas operations. When it came to the CIA and such countries as Turkey, whistleblowers like her father were always fair game. They'd be served up on a platter to despotic governments in return for certain positions in international affairs. Somebody had done this to her father.

She was lost in thoughts when her cell began to ring.

"Elsie, I spoke with Keller's chief investigator. They'll see you at three-thirty today. They'll have the SCIF ready for you by then. Good?"

"Yes. Thank you, Matt."

"Listen, please call me. Call when you get there, and call me when you're done, before you leave the office. Okay?"

"Sure. *Promise.* I'll call you. Bye."

Elsie looked at her watch. She had more than three hours to kill. She got up and headed toward Capitol Hill.

CHAPTER 10

Thursday Morning, October 30, 2003
Washington, D.C.

Greg placed his third laptop next to the other two on the dining table. One was connected to the feeds from Keller's office, cell phone, and the direct landline in his office. The other was for his first CIA target, Marty Watterson, head of the CIA Congressional Liaison & Coordination Division, a fancy name for its political blackmail unit. No "coordination" was involved, apart from the simple terms of blackmailing elected officials, for the most part, members of Congress.

Watterson was the guy who directed parasites like Josh and Maurice in Cambodia and Jack Rodman in Thailand, who would set up and record big name politicians. These goodies then were sent to Watterson, who in turn extracted the highlights and presented them to his boss. The top bosses determined when to use what against whom. The president's office might or might not have a say in the matter, depending on whom or what is being leveraged; as often as not the inner circle itself is a target—in which case the president's hands are tied.

Watterson was a piece of work. He had to be. Petty operations needed petty men. Conventional fronts too were necessary: married, children; for the topmost pick by the president. The top-down approach served appearances well when it came to promoting and bringing up his unit's men: pick psychopathic sadists with conventional resumes to give the illusion of normalcy.

Behind that front, Watterson still fulfilled unconventional needs—carefully, of course. He didn't stray outside the agency. His partners and targets were chosen from inside, those who understood and matched his tastes, and did so with discretion. When it came to psychos, sadists and masochists, there was an awfully large pool to choose from.

Watterson's latest pick was CIA Agent Linda Rodman; still Jack Rodman's wife, sort of. She gave him unusual sexual gratification, so he promoted her and demoted her husband by sending him back to Thailand. That Jack had a breakdown, no one seemed to mind.

After determining Watterson's fixed schedule and the location of his escapades with Rodman, Greg installed his real-time camera in Rodman's Arlington apartment. Within a week he had everything he wanted: at least two hours of debauched sex featuring Watterson, Rodman and a high-priced male hooker; *debauched* to some would be an understatement.

He'd sent the Watterson video to his contact in Iceland. This morning, Greg had his contact send a three-minute clip to Watterson using Rodman's e-mail address with the subject line *Promotion* and the short text *When?*

He had a simple plan. Simple sufficed for this type of bureaucrat. Initially, he'd envisioned a lengthy execution for Watterson, the man who'd sent Josh on the mission that ended Mai. Instead, he decided to make his life bewildering and miserable for a long, long time.

From the kitchen, Greg returned to the dining room where his laptops were set up. The floor-to-ceiling windows of the ultramodern split-floor D.C. penthouse brought in plenty of light and offered sweeping vistas of the Potomac. He sat back and checked his monitors. He didn't expect much from Watterson, who was meeting with the head of his division and another operative fresh from Cambodia to report on the investigations of the murder of Josh and Maurice. The agency had another duo searching for Jack Rodman, their one and only suspect. It was amusing to watch them chase their own tails. Today, Greg had added more complexity to their case: mysterious e-mails with clips of Watterson, the male hooker, and Jack Rodman's wife doing the three-way nasty up, down and sideways. Of course, Watterson could never share that with his boss. Naturally, he assumed it had to be Linda, toying with and pressuring him for more favors. Later on, the two would suspect husband Jack of playing games and seeking revenge.

Greg turned his attention to the monitor covering Donald Keller. Bugging his office had been piece of cake. Security for the dirtballs on Capitol Hill was a joke. He wondered if it was by design—to emphasize their meager status in the hierarchy. All that was needed, aside from the hardware, was a janitor's uniform. The rest was simple: enter the wing with the night cleaning crew, wait for them to clear, go into Keller's office and in less than three minutes install a microdevice in the landline, slip his recording pen into the cylinder-shaped penholder on Keller's desk and then out. His contact in Iceland had taken care of Keller's e-mail and BlackBerry. The house was irrelevant: with his wife and son under the same roof, Keller's extracurriculars would be strictly off limits anywhere in or near the residence. The house was left untouched.

Rapidly moving frequency bars indicated activity in Keller's office. Greg turned up the volume.

"I have the summary report you wanted: the request for increase in funds for the Kyrgyzstan and Turkmenistan Education Grant. It's a joint project. Half of the funds will come from The Global Democracy and Education Fund. State Department is picking up the other half . . ."

"Bullocks. [Keller] *Education my ass. Last time I checked, the money was going to building more mosques and madrassas. They spent less than a hundred thousand for a goofy little science center, and over four million to build five mosques with built-in madrassas. Saudis are already pouring millions into those mosque projects . . . Let them pay for it, for Christ's sake!"*

"I assume you won't approve it? We'll block it?"

[Pause] *"I didn't say that, did I? They think I'm that stupid . . . Put it on my desk, I'll go over it later. Anything else?"*

"Crawfort guys want you to speed up things . . . wanted to know if you were free for din—"

[Ringing phone] *"Donald Keller."*

[Caller on speakerphone] *"Hi Donald, it's Matt. Matt Simon. How are you?"*

"Matt! Long time. Where have you been? Ready to come back? 'Cause I need you here . . . the election's nearing fast."

"I wish. Wife loves it here. I tell you, it's the weather. Listen, I have a favor, an urgent request."

"You're not in trouble, are you? Shoot."

"Not me. Someone I know. Actually, technically my stepmother, Elsie Simon. She needs to brief your cleared investigators urgently. Inside the SCIF. Urgently as in right away; now."

"What's it about?"

"I don't have details. She's an analyst with the FBI, Washington Field Office. Her division deals with Turkic nations: Turkey, Azerbaijan and all the 'stans. She's come across some explosive boo-boos and the bureau wants to see it all go away. Right up your alley, Donald."

"Hold for a second. Let me check . . ."

Greg sat riveted. Here was something he hadn't planned. *Elsie Simon.*

After some back and forth with his chief of staff, Keller came back on the line.

"Matt, are you there?"

"Yeah."

"You remember Chris, right? He's now my chief investigator and has all the necessary clearance and credentials. He's available after two-thirty. I'm waiting to hear back on the SCIF availability."

"I really appreciate it, Donald."

Greg noticed how Keller didn't respond. That man was clearly worried. The bastards surely had gotten to him by now; and from Keller's point of view, no doubt, this business with the SCIF could only make things worse. *What more do they want?* he likely was asking right about now. Greg relished this little extra; he loved to watch the bad men squirm.

[Keller] *"You . . . you think it has something to do with the attack?"*

"Maybe . . . I dunno . . . she couldn't really talk about it over the phone."

[Chief of staff] *"The SCIF is available after three. To be safe, make it three-thirty."*

"Matt, tell her to come over at three-thirty."

"Will you attend the briefing?"

"I don't think so. I've got shit on my plate today . . . you know how it is."

"Right . . ."

"But I'll make sure I get a full briefing. And I'll call you back with that. Alright?"

"Thanks, Donald. You're the best."

Greg reflected on the woman. What kind of explosive discovery? Any decisions to *make it all go away* were never done by the FBI—this was the exclusive domain of the company, done via the agency and typically executed through State Department channels. Had she stepped on the agency's toes? Then there was the region. *His* region.

This was exactly the kind of unplanned development that complicated operations. If this Elsie Simon's case was connected, even marginally, to his side of things, then certain other actors and entities and even the media could be dragged in. That couldn't happen. He had to eliminate that possibility. Greg guessed Keller's office was not her first move; she must've taken her discovery to someone, in secret . . .

He had no other choice.

He had to neutralize this woman.

* * * *

Thursday Afternoon, October 30, 2003
Washington, D.C.

Greg recognized her right away. Despite the distance and her oversize Jackie O–style sunglasses, he'd spotted her sitting on a bench near the side door of the Longworth House Office Building. With the chiseled jaw line, high cheekbones and prep school posture holding the petite frame erect, she was hard to miss. He had gone through photos, from driver's license to graduation to those taken at a grand opening of a technology firm her husband consulted for to the one taken graveside at his funeral.

In a matter of hours, Greg had learned a great deal about her. She had graduated at the top of her class and traveled extensively around the globe, donated regularly to three orphanages in the Middle East and liked ethnic food, particularly Thai and Vietnamese. She had scored 142 on the IQ test taken voluntarily during undergraduate work in criminal psychology. She preferred classic styles when it came to clothes: elegant and understated. She loved going to the opera.

She'd come from a broken family. Her parents divorced when she was eight, and she was raised by her physician father. *Her father.* A story in itself. One that had wounded hardest, Greg suspected.

At 3:10 P.M. she sat lost in thought, waiting for the briefing. Was she optimistic? Did she hold the scumbags in high regard? How in the world had she chosen this office, Donald Keller, among the hundreds of others? Had it been pure coincidence, or was it karma, as Mai would have believed?

Now she started toward the building's main entrance. She stopped and removed her sunglasses then looked in his direction, where he was hiding in plain sight with his cell propped against his ear pretending to be talking. Did she see him? Was she looking? Because Greg was able to see her eyes clearly, eyes the most unusual shade of brown and green and yellow that screamed intelligence, depth and pain.

Elsie turned back and continued through the entry doors. Greg followed her with his eyes as she proceeded toward security, peeling off her camel cashmere coat and placing it on the belt. Then she disappeared from sight.

He had an hour, more or less, before she finished with the briefing. Not enough time to check out her house and plant his devices; that would have to wait. *Maybe later, when she was asleep.* Instead, he would head back to his apartment until the meeting was concluded. He suspected Keller would be making a call: to his blackmailing masters, to alert them. Especially now, after having received his special e-mail, thinking it was sent by the agency to remind him of his duties.

* * * *

Elsie tapped her feet and waited. She had an intense dislike of SCIFs. Being in a windowless room inside an ultrasecured windowless facility always gave her that suffocating feeling. Today she felt even more oppressed than usual. Having been frog-marched through her own department out of the building and onto the sidewalk by uniformed security hadn't helped. And where was Ryan? She'd tried three times to reach him.

Since then, all she had thought about was this meeting. What would she tell them? How much information did she intend to provide? How much to hold back? She considered various ways to give enough information to get their attention and help, yet withhold enough to protect Ryan and his ridiculous operation with Sullivan. She calculated the risk of further retaliation by the FBI and even more so by the CIA and Pentagon, once they found out about her disclosure to Congress. She devised insurance for herself, for her safety: documents *out there* that could be made public very quickly if something were to happen to her. Would that work? It might; or perhaps it would boomerang. Disclosing sensitive classified documents certainly would give them ammunition to go after her legally. It was a crime, after all, to remove them from the premises. So how would she play that?

She wondered about the bureau's possible next steps. Then she countered them with her own. She calculated and evaluated each move's viability and how each plan of action might be vulnerable. Her objectivity, though, was difficult to assess; without it, one is open to doubt, no matter how good the analyst.

What's more, she couldn't shake the feeling of being watched, the mark of true paranoia; that, and of being followed. It was eerie. She could almost feel the weight of her watcher's eyes.

The door to the SCIF opened. A tall, wiry blond man walked in, late thirties, followed by a scrawny twentysomething.

"Ms. Simon, I am Chris Rojack, Congressman Keller's chief investigator. This is Madeleine Mowberry, my assistant."

Elsie shook his hand. "Will Congressman Keller be joining us?"

Chris shook his head. "He wanted to, but he had another engagement. We'll brief him later. Why don't we begin? Let's start with you. Please tell us a bit about yourself and your position and work with the FBI."

And that was how it began. Elsie provided them with a brief biography, her position with the bureau, and the general outlines of some of the operations in which she worked. After that, they moved on to the actual case, what she wanted to report. She told them about Nazim's case and how the operation was sabotaged and later shut down by the State Department. She briefly talked about Nazim's connection to another FBI case in Chicago, and how those seem related to the 2001 attack. Next, she told them about the investigation pre-2001, and pointed to several communications and operations that were directly connected to that attack. She did so without naming Sema or mentioning specific documents or their whereabouts. Elsie had no intention of putting Sema at risk for further retaliation. She described the general outlines of the buried transcripts, including the meetings and working relationship among high-level figures in the Pentagon-State Department-CIA and top-level al-Hazar leaders and commandos. She talked about Azerbaijan, Georgia and Kyrgyzstan operations. She told them about NATO.

Elsie held back on Yousef, partly to protect Ryan's work and partly due to a feeling in her gut. She withheld the names and positions of high-level officials, both the Americans and the FBI's primary foreign targets: diplomatic and military figures. She did not mention Sema's own insurance plan regarding the explosive documents, or how she, Elsie, was able to obtain and read any of those.

Rojack seemed a bit overwhelmed and nervous. It was not overt but Elsie could tell. Anybody would, when confronted by such doings. It's enough to make even the most jaded insider's blood run cold—members of Congress and the media no exception.

He followed up with a couple of questions while the woman took notes. His were fair, yet Elsie knew he was careful not to ask any *real* questions. She went ahead and answered. She described the events and circumstances surrounding her departure from work, including the last few days and the traumatic way she was placed on leave.

What would happen next? she asked. Chris answered vaguely. He would present this to Keller, his boss. They then would decide on a course of action, including requests for documents and summoning key people from the FBI for questioning; also, possibly contacting appropriate people at the State Department. He neglected to mention the CIA. Nor did he bring up the Pentagon.

By the time she left, it was past 5:30 P.M. Before heading into the subway, she stopped to check her messages: two voicemails from Ryan, the second one frantic. She tried calling back but couldn't get through. *The customer you are trying to reach is out of . . .* She left another brief message. She sounded almost defeated. "I'll try calling again tomorrow morning my time. I'm too beat . . . heading home."

* * * *

Greg already had changed into his all-black outfit by 5:30 P.M.: black speedwork spandex running tights, black spandex all-weather top with attached hood, and black Nike running shoes. He also had applied a dark bronzer to his face. He would blend in perfectly with the yuppie night runners in Old Town, Alexandria, where Elsie lived, to say nothing of blending in with the night. He had several hours before that operation; time now to eat a light evening meal and check Keller's communications.

After sautéing a small piece of Wild Alaskan Salmon with a bit of steamed broccoli and asparagus, he poured a small amount of raw cashews and walnuts in a bowl, grabbed a new bottle of Maestro mineral water, placed everything on top of a sleek tray, and moved into the dining room.

He placed the linen dinner napkin neatly on his lap, pulled forward and tilted his Keller-designated laptop, and began. He was halfway through his meal when the frequency bars indicated voice activity. He turned up the volume and recognized Keller.

"Okay, what was that all about? Make it brief."

[Rojack] *"Not good. I wish we hadn't given her the opening. Now our neck is on the line . . . damned if we do something, damned if we don't."*

"That bad, huh?"

"Yes, it is. CIA is written all over this, and of course the Pentagon's Special Operations via DIA. FBI has some documents linking 2001 to our black ops in Central Asia and the Caucasus. And they've got tons on Turkey's role aiding us . . ."

Keller's chief of staff summarized Simon's talking points: FBI's narcotics sting on Nazim, the company plane, State Department, the meetings in Azerbaijan and Georgia, and more.

Greg had to process this further. In any case, she had to be silenced. Being vocal undermined his plans—and if she continued to dig, his operation would be compromised. That was unacceptable.

As soon as Rojack left the room, Keller dialed Warren Shelby, head of the CIA's Office of Congressional Liaison. He told the secretary it was *very urgent.* Shelby was already out for the day, so he waited on hold while being transferred direct to Shelby's cell.

"Congressman Keller. Always good to hear from you."

"Not this time, Warren. I'm about to report trouble headed your way."

"What kind?"

"We were contacted today about an FBI analyst, Turkic regions. She made some discoveries and was told to shut up and back off. Now she's blowing the whistle. I'm thinking her bombshells have more to do with you guys and your shit operations than with the bureau."

"Hold on . . . not through your phone. We'll contact you later for a session. Meanwhile, we'll pursue it through our guys at the bureau . . . oh, and good work. Thanks for the heads up, Congressman."

Greg swore he could hear Keller clench his teeth.

"One more thing . . . and this has nothing to do with the whistleblower."

"Yes?"

"I'm aware of my situation. I got your message loud and clear . . . no need to keep sending me video clips. You hear me?"

Silence crackled. *"Understood, Congressman. I'll make sure of that."*

Greg could picture Shelby's face. He could almost hear him wondering, *What the fuck was that? What clips?* A shallow man presented with such dark spectacle might get giddy and lose his head; but Greg was not that man. This was an operation, just like any other. Yes, he had a personal stake, but that didn't make it any less professional. This one was all on him, to be carried out solo. As a lone Gladio.

* * * *

Elsie got in her car, started the engine, and jacked up the heat. She was shivering. She'd gone all day with no real food and walked for miles in a blustery wind. She was exhausted.

She remembered her *to do* for this evening. Today was Internet café and they would be expecting to hear from her. She was supposed to send them the next IDs. That's how they had partnered up. They looked and searched for her father and, in return, she supplied them with what they needed. Now that they had produced the sketch and given the general new whereabouts, she was supposed to give them the next set of IDs; only then would they pursue the next steps from their end. This was the most important thing in her life, ever since the moment of her dad's disappearance. She *never* missed dates and deadlines. Yet, she couldn't handle that tonight.

In addition, she had to notify them of her access being temporarily on hold, and that she would not be able to supply IDs for some indeterminate while. How temporarily, exactly? And how long is a *while?* She had serious doubts; but she would not let them know—at least for now. One more reason to skip tonight. She needed food. She needed to recover. So she put the car in gear, pulled out of the garage and drove home.

As she entered the dark townhouse she felt Ben's absence more than ever. Walking into an empty house was never any good. She had no one to kiss, no one to talk with, no one to hold on to. Climbing the stairs, she heard Simba's meow. Okay, she kind of had someone; a vocal capricious cat who solely depended on her, Elsie, for her very life. That was something. Better than nothing!

"It's okay, boy. I'm home. Give me a few minutes and I'll have your dinner ready."

She went straight to the kitchen without taking off her coat or high-heel knee-high boots. She opened the pantry and grabbed a can, quickly assembling the fancy canned plus the fancy dried and a bowl of fresh filtered water. That's right. Her cat wouldn't drink from the tap. He was that kind of spoiled.

She placed dinner on a tray and took it to the breakfast nook off the kitchen. She petted Simba and stroked his belly. Right now the cat's attention was fixed on the tray.

"All right . . . tonight we're not going to have our usual quality socialization. I'm too beat. I feel broken. You understand? Okay. You eat, poop, do whatever you want to do. I'm heading upstairs. I need a long hot bath and I need my bed . . . alone. Hope you understand, Simba."

She went back to the kitchen, got a carton of yogurt smoothie out of the fridge, poured some into a glass and drank it all down at once. Then she placed the glass in the sink and ran the tap water. *No.* She couldn't let it sit there; by tomorrow morning, there'd be a crust. She was that rigid, at times.

With compulsions on her mind, she headed out of the kitchen failing to notice the blinking light on her landline phone on the counter. She climbed the stairs and began stripping along the way to her bathroom. Leaving clothes in a trail, she stepped into the bathtub and turned the knob for hot and let it get to scalding. Sliding in, submerged in heat, Elsie closed her eyes.

* * * *

Greg entered through the garage. He checked the alarm but found it had not been activated. The door leading into the house from the garage was unlocked. Elsie Simon was easy when it came to penetrating, breaking and entering. Granted, she was a fairly complex, sharp and educated woman, but not when it came to her safety.

He didn't need the goggles. His night vision was beyond excellent. Also, this city was brightly lit, from the streets to the bridge and headlights from cars against all the tightly packed houses.

He climbed the stairs to the second floor: another fairly tight space with a kitchen, nook, and living room. *Wheelchair. What, she still held on? Sentimental. Mai was that way too.*

The cat gave him a stare. He returned it with his own. Unblinking, Simba was first to turn away, no doubt sensing danger.

Greg checked out her small neat kitchen, including the pantry and refrigerator: organic and fancy label only. Yet he knew all this; her credit card statements had told him as much.

He noticed the blinking red light. She had three unplayed messages. He lifted the phone, turned it over and opened the battery slot; then he planted his microdevice and closed it up. A small magnetic transmitter went right behind the fridge. That would take care of this floor.

He moved upstairs where the door to her bedroom was ajar. With featherlight steps he entered. She was sleeping with the covers piled up and pushed aside at the other end of the bed. All she had on were white cotton panties and a matching tank top, her shiny dark hair fanned out around her. He examined her profile. True, something attractive, almost beautiful as a whole; yet individual features were ordinary. All together, they held a person's gaze. She looked so much younger in her sleep, Greg thought. Furrows and creases relaxed; awake, in public, her intense personality and vibrant expressions wore grooves: the lines on her forehead and around the eyes gave her a careworn look. Here was someone who'd seen her share of life, for the most part hard and unforgiving.

He noticed the trail of clothes on the floor leading to the bathroom. Inside-out labels revealed her size: Petite 4. The tall brown leather boots could be size 6; *make it 6.5*. He had a good eye in determining size. His mental notes of people, whether targets or not, stayed in his mind forever. He decided it was a gift.

Greg silently moved past the bed and placed a device behind the armoire. Then he spied the paper with the pencil sketch face. *Middle-aged, bearded. Piercing eagle eyes. Prominent cheekbones. Father? Most probable.*

He stopped and examined her one more time before exiting. Yes, unconventional; unusually attractive.

He next went into the office and checked out the photos on the bookshelves: little Elsie with her father, age six or seven, making a V for Victory sign with two fingers; Elsie with her father in an orphanage in Baku, Azerbaijan; Elsie with her father and other doctors in earthquake-struck Turkey in 1999; and several more framed pictures of the two. There was only one photo with her husband, Ben: the background looked to be Africa.

In less than three minutes he took care of her laptop and desktop PC. Then he left, quietly and cautiously.

He raised the garage door enough to slide under and used his remote to close it. Like a phantom, he appeared in the street midjog, accelerating his pace into a full-out run as he turned the corner of the cul-de-sac toward his car, parked four and a half blocks away.

* * * *

Friday Morning, October 31, 2003
Alexandria, Virginia

Elsie woke and checked the alarm clock: 6:53 A.M. She'd slept for almost eleven hours! Her body must have gone into recovery mode, putting her into comalike sleep as soon as she hit the pillows. Every muscle ached. Part of her wanted to stay in bed, curl up, and stave off what she couldn't bear to face. The other part, her rational side, told her to jump into the shower, eat a power breakfast, and bravely counter whatever the hell it was.

She made herself get out of bed and in less than thirty minutes was already downstairs brewing a strong pot of coffee. After feeding Simba and filling the water bowl, she reached for a mug when she noticed the blinking light. Three new messages. She debated whether to play them now or drink her coffee first. She decided on the latter. Her body and brain demanded it.

She drank half the mug while watching Simba cleaning out his bowl. Then she topped her cup with the remaining coffee, walked over to the phone and hit Play.

The first message was from Ryan. *Elsie, where the Christ are you? I got your messages. Call me right away. Oh, this cell service overseas is a joke . . . here is my hotel number . . .*

The second was from Ryan again. *My God, where are you? I left messages on your cell. Call me ASAP!* Oops. Completely exhausted, yesterday she'd turned off the ringer on the landline and switched her cell to Flight Mode. Now, she switched everything back.

The third message was from Sami. *Elsie . . . hey, I tried your cell. Listen, remember the conversation we had about dickheads? The one you mentioned, the major dickhead, well, take him off your list. Compromised. Compromised big time and dangerous. I met with Lucy . . . I'll tell you all about it when I get back. It's massive . . . huge. We're looking at a major mui grande scand—*

She was cut off. Voicemail only allowed 120 seconds max per message.

Elsie froze. She reconstructed her conversation with Sami at the bar. They'd talked about the FBI mess . . . the State Department screwing up their cases . . . her temptation to go to Congress—and Matt's connection to Keller! Oh God! Had she gone to the worst possible office? She said *major scandal* and specifically used the word *compromised*. Compromised how?

She ran upstairs and grabbed her cell then dialed Sami on her way back down. Her call went to voicemail. "Hi, Sami. This is urgent. Call me ASAP. I mean ASAP, Sami. I'm in deep shit."

As she hung up, her landline rang. She picked up in a shaky voice. "H-Hello?"

It was Joan, Sami's ex-girlfriend. She was sobbing, hysterical. "Elsie, Sami . . . Sami's gone . . . Oh my God Elsie . . . she's gone . . ."

She tried to process what the woman was saying. "Joan? Calm down, Joan! What do you mean *gone*?"

Joan continued to sob.

Elsie wanted to shake her. She tried this time with more restraint. "Joan, I want you to take a deep breath. Can you do that for me? Take a nice deep breath."

She could hear the inhale and waited.

The words came out choppy, in a nasal, breathless voice. "They called a few minutes ago. The FBI. They said Sami's car exploded last night . . . she was in it . . . driving to her motel late . . . late at night . . . and somehow . . . her car *exploded*. Everything—gone. She is gone. Dead. Burned to death . . . all burned up . . ."

This was beyond Elsie's comprehension. She was experiencing something close to out of body. "What did they mean by explosion? *How* did it explode?"

Joan was back to uncontrollable sobbing. ". . . don't know . . . didn't say . . . just . . . *Bam*, her car exploded and . . . and that she died . . ."

Elsie's chest was tightening. She needed air as well. "Where is she now?"

"Some morgue . . . somewhere in New Jersey. They said they were investigating . . . her car . . . mechanical failure . . . and the body . . . They . . . they said they couldn't send it until they were done . . . a few days maybe . . . oh, Elsie, I don't know what to do . . ."

"Listen to me, Joan. Let me make a few calls. I will call you back. And later, I will come over. Okay?"

Elsie would call the FBI's Patterson office; then find and contact that woman Lucy—the one whom Sami was meeting last night. Was Elsie the last person Sami had called? She didn't know Lucy's last name or address; but she remembered Sami mentioning a Cambodia-related NGO in New York City. How many could there be?

After hanging up with Joan, she dropped to the floor. She sat there, staring into space. She sat like that for who knows how long, until her phone began to ring. When she heard Ryan's voice starting to leave a message she reached up and grabbed the receiver.

"Hello? Elsie? Are you there?"

Then he heard sobbing. She sobbed, and sobbed some more. Ryan, bewildered and worried, talked to her soothingly. "Sweet," he began, with the name he'd grown fond of using lately, "please listen to me now: I'm going to take the first plane and get back there . . . okay, sweet? Please listen . . . again . . ."

It seemed to take many minutes before she could regain herself. Then she began to talk. At first, it was incoherent, with a lot of little breaks in her sentences; but after a few sobering breaths she reverted back to her articulate self. She started from the beginning, her conversation with Sami in that bar, what took place at work the previous morning . . . being kicked out of—no, *escorted* by a guard out the building, her call to Ben's son . . . her meeting with Keller, her sense of being followed, Joan's call, right on the heels of Sami's message . . . Sami dead, burned to a crisp . . .

"Listen to me, sweet. I should be there by tomorrow afternoon *latest.* Okay? Now, until I get there, I don't want you alone, by your-self. Let me call and arrange something through Sullivan—"

"No!" Elsie cried out. "Absolutely not, no way. I don't want a single goddamn word going to Sullivan. Not a word."

"You're sounding irrational, Elsie. Sullivan has the means. He can get the best protection . . . that's what you need right now."

"NO as in *N O*. I will manage. Promise you won't say a word to that man. Come on, Ryan. Say you promise. I want your word."

Ryan sighed. "Fine. You're wrong. But . . . fine. How about this? Go somewhere else. Somewhere away from D.C., someplace safe. At least until I get there. Sweet? Could you do that much? For me?"

Elsie considered it. "Like where? A hotel?"

"No. I have an idea. My folks have a cabin out in West Virginia. Out in the boonies. In the woods. Running water, electricity, electric stove and a fireplace . . . but no phone lines. It's three and a half hours away. Go there, stay put until I get there. Deal?"

"I don't know, Ryan. I'm not good with the boonies . . ."

Ryan didn't let her finish. "You don't have to be good; for Chris-sakes, sweet, it's only for twenty-four hours!"

"Does it have good cell reception? Internet connection?"

"I said twenty-four hours," he repeated, strained. "You'll sur-vive it. No. No good cell reception, and definitely no Internet. Now, write down the address . . ."

She found a pen and wrote it down.

"Go, pack quickly, stop at the market and get some water and readymade food, and drive there. Oh . . . do you have a gun?"

"Gun? Are you kidding? Who am I supposed to shoot?"

"No one. I don't know. But I want you to take one. You can humor me later. Do you have anything?"

"There's Ben's gun. I think it's a thirty-eight revolver."

"Take that and ammunition. Also, a couple of flashlights and extra batteries." He paused. "Get on it now. Right now."

"But . . . okay . . . fine." She wanted to put Ryan at ease; at the same time, she had urgent business: the Patterson office, Lucy, Joan, Sema. No way would she be ready to leave before noon or one at the earliest. Yet she had to tell this voice on the phone what it so desperately needed to hear. The person on the other end left her no other choice; that was Ryan. She was Elsie. She would get there when she got there, but first she had certain things to do, then she had to pack, and . . . something else, something important. Oh! Remember to bring Ben's gun.

* * * *

Sergei, speaking with Tatiana, forwarded Ryan's latest communication with Elsie. With Ryan in Jakarta, the transmission first had to go through Russia's HQ then forwarded to him. That accounted for the time lag. "All right," he told her over the phone, "listen to it and let me know how you want me to proceed."

"Got it. I'll call you back in fifteen minutes."

He had just enough time to take a quick shower, and in less than ten minutes was dressed and ready for this leg of the assignment. Like it or not he was Elsie's tail—and he liked it. Who wouldn't?

Sergei answered his cell on the first ring. "Da?"

"Where are you right now?"

"Home. Rosslyn."

"Get out," she commanded. "Surveillance twenty-four seven. That's what we do. Don't let her out of your sight. Understood?"

"So . . . I am going to West Virginia? Oh man!" he fake moaned.

"Yes. West Virginia and wherever else she goes. What's your problem? Only three, four hours away."

"Don't you think I should check her house first? We don't know if she took out any documents."

"No, no. I'll take care of that. I want you where she is, round the clock. Also, I asked HQ to send us muscles. Things will get complicated, probably nasty. We need Simon. We need those documents and others."

"Okay. I'm leaving now."

"Make sure you have an extra gun."

He kept his primary weapon strapped to his ankle. The second he packed inside his duffel bag and threw in extra ammunition, then put his laptop and cell charger on top, though he knew there would be no reception.

* * * *

Greg waited in his golden beige Lexus, less than a block from Elsie's townhouse. He'd been here almost thirty minutes. His open laptop served both as prop and transmission reception for her landline activities.

He had monitored the frantic call telling her about the explosion. He had heard her agonized narration to the FBI guy, apparently her lover, Ryan Marcello. *Typical FBI hothead.*

He had listened to her calls in search of a woman named Lucy. He'd already gathered a few things on this woman: her job with an organization that dealt with genocide and child trafficking—in Cambodia. That karma angle again. Cambodia? A missing American reporter? Sami warning Elsie off Keller? What were the odds?

Greg noticed the silver gray Toyota Corolla as it approached the cul-de-sac, slowed down, and pulled into a tight parking spot between a truck and an old Chevrolet. He kept his eye on the car through his mirror. A few minutes passed, but there was no sign of the driver exiting. He could make out the gender: male, light blond, height five seven. He was wearing visors similar to his. Okay, who the hell was he? From where Greg was positioned he couldn't make out the license plate. He was debating whether to get out of the car to check out the plate when Elsie's red Saab approached the intersection.

He waited until she made a left turn and passed. Then he waited a little longer to see what the suspicious car would do. Confirmed: the car pulled out and followed Elsie. He waited another ten seconds, and then paced his speed and distance, following the gray Toyota that was following Elsie with only one car between.

They continued on Route 1 past the Pentagon and remained in the left lane toward Rosslyn-Key Bridge. They took the left ramp and crossed onto Wilson Boulevard, and headed north toward Ballston.

Greg slowed as he saw the gray car come to a stop, back up and pull into a parking spot. He increased speed and passed the gray car, now parked three slots behind Elsie. He turned left at the first intersection and parked his car in the first available spot, the one marked for handicaps—why he always carried a handicap sticker for all his cars in the States.

Greg got out and proceeded on foot. Rounding the corner, he spotted Elsie entering a small Hispanic bakery. Behind her was the gray Toyota, the driver still inside. Greg took out his cell and pretended to make a call as he approached the door of the store. His eyes followed Elsie, who went through to the far end and then disappeared.

He checked out the tall office building. The bakery was one of several shops on the mezzanine level. He walked past it and entered the building's main lobby. He crossed to the Entry–Exit glass doors on the other side and exited. This was where the delivery and maintenance entries were located. He opened the first back door and went through the musty corridor until he reached the half-open door to the bakery and small office. Here, in the annex, were six desktop computers, one main printer and two ancient copiers. Elsie was behind computer station number four. Her back was to him but he could see from the screen that she was writing e-mails. He quietly turned and left.

Out front, Greg talked into his cell while he waited for Elsie. He was talking to Iceland: a small but urgent task. Find out who she was communicating with and the nature of the business that required such secrecy.

* * * *

Elsie left the bakery with a dozen empanadas. Ryan had mentioned groceries; she could easily live off of these heavenly baked goods for two or three days.

She returned home after a quick stop to pick up flashlights, batteries, bananas and bottled water. She was planning to take a few bottles of wine as well. Why not? She would be stuck in the boonies with no Internet, phone or TV. Empanadas, wine, a good book or two; and before she knew it Ryan would be there. Then what? She wasn't going to think about that now.

She had called her neighbor three houses down who loved and offered to take care of Simba for the next few days. With Simba safe, she began to pack her duffel bag: underwear and toiletries, an extra pair of jeans, two sweaters, one sweatshirt, and her flannel PJs.

As she packed, she replayed her conversation with the NGO in New York. She had been able to locate and contact the organization where Lucy worked. She hadn't shown up for work that day, and according to her office, she hadn't called in, which was unusual. That was as much as Elsie could get; they wouldn't give her the home or cell number.

She hadn't been able to get anything out of the FBI's Patterson office either. Was she next of kin? No. She had no business, then, inquiring about an open investigation. Sami's body had gone to the medical examiner for an autopsy, and the car—what was left of it— was being checked out by the FBI forensic team. Elsie wondered if they'd checked Sami's phone. If they had, then they'd know that she,

Elsie, was perhaps the last person Sami had called before the deadly explosion. If true, wouldn't they want to talk to her? To find out what the call was about?

She also tried Sema's husband at his office. She didn't want to raise further alarms by calling Sema directly. She had warned Ziad, the husband, about possible snooping and intrusion by the bureau. He'd asked why. Her answers were cryptic. How could she explain? She'd said only that she wanted to make sure Sema knew that she hadn't shared a word about their meetings or the documents. Further, she warned that the bureau might try one of their favorite tactics: bluffing. She wanted to be sure that Sema didn't fall for their bluff. Ziad seemed to understand.

She grabbed her duffel bag and headed to the bedroom when her eyes caught the sketch. It somehow had fallen from the nightstand to the floor. She picked it up, carefully folded it on the crease, and placed it in the outside pocket of the duffel.

Next she took her portable mini–boom box and half a dozen CDs. Music made life more bearable. She put those inside her bag. *Anything else? No. All set.* Time to hit the road.

She was about to set her burglar alarm when she remembered. *No . . . everything not all set.* Ryan made her promise to take Ben's gun. She'd almost forgotten about it—most likely because she hated guns. Why had she given in? She sighed and went back upstairs. Retrieving the key from one of the drawers, she unlocked the bottom cabinet. There was the gun, still in its case, right where Ben always kept it. With care she removed it, along with the cardboard box filled with cartridges. Then she closed the cabinet and went downstairs.

She tossed the duffel bag into the backseat and carefully placed the gun case and cartridge box in the trunk. She went back inside and took an extra coat, just in case. She set the alarm and got into her car. It was 1:30 P.M. *Halloween. And so far this day has been haunted.* She would make it there before dark—god willing—even with a short stop for gas and another for her double espresso. *There was that feeling again.* She hooked her cell phone to the charger. Ryan would soon be calling about his status and arrival time.

She buckled her seat belt, started the engine, and adjusted her rearview mirror. She turned on the radio, switched it to CD and pressed number 4: Leonard Cohen. She selected track 2, "The Future," and eased out of her spot in reverse.

* * * *

Sergei watched Elsie's car back out and head in his direction. He had not noticed two other cars with drivers doing precisely that. Unlike Tatiana, he was not expecting any earth-shattering Simon operation; but hey, he didn't question his orders.

He dialed Tatiana's extension. She picked up on the third ring.

"Yes. What's up?" Today she was using English. Sergei didn't like that.

"She's on her way," he told her in Russian. "And we know where she's headed."

"Fine, but make sure you keep her in sight *at all times.* Are you right behind her?"

"Yah, yah. When will Marcello be back?"

"Not until tomorrow evening. That is, if he hits no delays."

"Did he contact you? Did he share the latest with you?"

"Not a peep. He is keeping his word to his damsel; tough cowboy."

"I used to think highly of your seducing skills. What happened, Tati? Age catching up with you?"

Tatiana kept her cool. "I don't care about Marcello. Our target is Simon. She is the prize."

Sergei started the engine. "I'll call you before entering the no-reception zone; after that, you won't be hearing from me . . . until we get back . . . to civilization. *Do svidaniya*."

* * * *

Greg was determined to wait out the tail. He now had a name: Sergei Bulinov. Russian, twenty-nine years old, on a student visa, enrolled at George Mason University for a graduate program on civil engineering. He lived alone in an apartment in Rosslyn, Virginia. So far that was all he had. Why would a Russian graduate student be following Elsie Simon around? He knew it wasn't a case of stalking; this wasn't a love-struck puppy. The most significant clue was his nationality. Was he a spy? Was he with the ever-expanding Russian mafia inside the States? Was he an FBI target? He'd find out. Soon.

Greg now had to practice his patience. What was taking Sergei so long? He was talking to someone on his cell; his boss? Was he reporting back to his handlers?

Now there was the *other* car to think about. The new player who'd shown up on the block, thirty minutes before Elsie left her house: tall, muscular, in a dark blue Dodge RAM 3500 with New Jersey plates. The car, the driver, and the timing fit the agency's MO perfectly.

Greg was expecting this. He knew what must have taken place within the first few hours after Keller's harried call to Shelby: Shelby would contact the unit head for the CIA's Russia-Caucasus–Central Asia operations and pass on Keller's report. That person then would contact a high-level company director within the agency and brief him. The director then would consult with higher-ups—and this is where things get nasty. The unit head would be given *the go*. Since dirty ops within U.S. borders are considered ultradirty, the agency unit head surely passed the hit back to Josh's boss, Marty Watterson. If Greg figured right, Watterson by now had gotten in touch with the special hit man unit: men inside the borders who once worked for the agency but had to be let go, and then were *unofficially contracted* for hit operations inside the United States as needed. These were trained thugs, ex-CIA, used for inside-the-border dirty ops without any official ties linking them back to the agency.

Greg knew that the driver of the Dodge was assigned to Elsie Simon by Marty Watterson. Highly likely he had followed and finished the punk's girlfriend, Lucy, as well as Sami Kruger, the FBI agent, due to her sheer bad luck. *Just like Mai.* Blue Dodge man's orders no doubt included a torture session to get further information from Elsie Simon—before taking her out for good.

Greg didn't like mess. He especially didn't like agency goons shitting all over his plans. He started the engine and began to drive. Following Sergei would lead him straight to where he needed to be.

* * * *

Elsie took the first exit for Front Royal. Taking this exit instead of the one coming up would add another ten minutes to her drive, but she wanted the scenic route. After all, what was ten more minutes?

She noticed a cardboard sign pointing to a dirt road: Pumpkins, 25 cents per pound (less than half a mile). *Why not?* she thought. *It's Halloween.* Checking for cars, she noticed a dusty blue Dodge truck right behind her and pulled off to the side to let it pass, then made a turn onto the dirt road. The pumpkin—a big one—was going right in front of the cabin.

Twenty minutes later, pumpkin on board, she was back on the country road. Spotting the Starbucks, she pulled into the lot and drove over to the gas pumping area. After filling it up, she parked and went inside for her tall-size "Trenta" with added espresso shots. As she was paying the cashier for the coffee and an expensive box of gum her cell phone rang: it was Ryan. "Hi . . ." she signed the credit card slip and walked outside. "Where are you?"

"Where are YOU?" he said severely. "I thought by now you'd be out of the reception zone!"

"Calm down, Ryan, I'm on my way . . . I just stopped for gas and coffee . . . I'm at Front Royal . . . and gum."

"Late start. Well good, you're on your way." He sounded somewhat relieved. "Must be . . . three o'clock your time."

"Yep. Three-fifteen. I barely escaped rush hour. From here on should be fast with no traffic." She got in the car, started the engine for heat, and took her first sip of hot coffee.

"Any news on Sami?"

Elsie felt that dagger again. Hearing Sami's name ripped her up. "Not really. I contacted the field office there, they wouldn't give me anything." She took another sip and added, "I finally found Lucy's NGO. She didn't show up at work today. No call, no e-mail . . . they wouldn't give me her home or cell. All that jazz about privacy. I take it she's missing or dead."

"Don't jump to conclusions, not yet. We don't know if any of that is connected. As you like to say: *first* you gather all the info, check and double check, and *then* you start to theorize. Correct?"

Elsie sighed.

"You still there?"

"Yes."

"They'll be boarding in thirty minutes or less. I'll be in Tokyo in eight hours. Then, a three-hour layover, and after that another fourteen hours or so to Dulles Airport . . . I should be out of Dulles around four, and with you by eight o'clock tomorrow night."

Elsie almost moaned. "That's too long."

"I'll be there in no time. Fix yourself a nice meal, have a glass of wine . . . sleep late. Oh, and don't go out running in the woods tomorrow morning, okay? You have the gun, right?"

"Yes, I have *a* gun. It's not loaded, but I've got ammo. I'm not into this kind of thing, Ryan. Does ammo have an expiration date? Do people tune up or service guns regularly? I don't know a thing about guns. Ben took me to the range oh, what, seven or eight years ago, and had me load and shoot. I sucked at it. I hated it . . ."

Ryan could tell from the speed and tone of her voice that she was nervous. "Sweet, don't worry. It's for peace of mind, mine included. Knowing that you have it will be comforting."

Though she hated the reasons, she liked that he was worried. Maybe *liked* isn't the right word; more that she was drawn so much closer by passion than concern; she could argue and defy him, but his intensity bound her to him in a way she couldn't explain. He got her doing things no other person could—including Ben. Is that horrible? It's true.

Even from as far as Jakarta, Ryan could sense her momentarily relax. "Now . . . drink your coffee . . . and drive carefully . . . until you reach *our* cabin, the one I'll see you in tomorrow."

Elsie missed him. His body, his scent. "Do you know what day it is?"

"October thirty-first?"

"Halloween. Of all nights. And I'll be alone in a cabin in the woods, completely cut off from all communications, out in the middle of nowhere on a freezing night with nothing but two bottles of Pinot Noir and a loaded gun for comfort. And *you* put me there—for protection! Don't you love the irony?"

Ryan had to give her that. The place certainly could be eerie. "Did you bring your costume with you? A sexy Lady Dracula?"

"You wish. No. But guess what? I stopped at this little country stand and bought their biggest pumpkin! It will be sitting here in front waiting for you, Ryan Marcello. When you get here I expect you to carve it, chop it, puree it, do whatever it is you have to do, to create gourmet pumpkin ravioli. Your chance to prove your Italian heritage!"

"Deal. I'll stop and get flour, nutmeg, cinnamon, butter, cream, sage and . . . what else . . . oh! kiss me good-bye."

And she did. Afterward, she sat for another three or four minutes holding the phone near her lips. It was almost 3:30. Taking several *grande* sips from the Caffeine Express, she started the engine, pulled out of the lot and headed further west toward I-81.

* * * *

Greg watched her leave the station. He went inside the minimart to purchase bottled water and a five-gallon gasoline cannister. Certain things might have to be burned. He came prepared. Ready gasoline was one item. Other items included extra guns, ammunition, commando knife, electrocution wire, nuts and dried fruits, water, poison, binoculars, sanitization solution for removal of trace evidence, flashlights, night-vision goggles, recorder, cash, various IDs, fingerprint device, as well as several others. He always made sure he had what was needed; the rest he would improvise.

The blue Dodge was registered to one Arnold Prick. *Prick.* Really? The agency had dozens like him around the country. People believed . . . well, the *ignorant masses* believed in fairy tales. Like reformed and restricted intelligence agencies. The supposed restrictions, FISA laws . . . these are dog and pony shows. Illusions are created to shield the system. Otherwise things could get sticky.

The CIA never for an instant ceased or restricted their operations within the United States. All they did was to implement new measures and procedures to decrease their chances of being exposed. Greg was well aware that despite the official policy that twisted and abused the public trust, the agency had operatives at the topmost level of decision making within news agencies and media organizations, including print, digital, TV and radio. These folks made sure that the elected players were under their control: Donald Keller, the perfect example, a powerful figure who reported directly to the Marty Wattersons and Joshes of this world. For such people, degeneracy is a fungible commodity. The public, meanwhile, must go on believing—not only because pride and a shared sense of values is at stake, but more perversely, that they've become *addicted to the illusion*—and, hence, inured to every kind of lie. Blind faith is demanded, false tenets are adhered to, corrupt ideologies are installed and perpetuated; no matter who is currently in power. Controlling entities well understand the value of public trust. People like Elsie Simon are a threat to that trust, and the unlucky ones, Greg knew, are those who get blown to bits in cars, stabbed to death and shot in bars, and sometimes found strangled in a cabin in the woods. All right here, in the U.S. of A.

He knew he was going to kill Blue Dodge Man. He had to make that Russian guy talk, and then eliminate him as well. With Elsie Simon . . . well, that was another story; one he hadn't finished writing yet. What would he do with her? His final answer partly depended on Elsie herself. How would she respond and react to him? What would she say? He had yet to make up his mind, which was new: the more he found out, the more he got to know this woman, the more complicated she became in his plans. Her position in his original scheme of operations had shifted. Her secret, for instance; those mysterious e-mails—how would they impact him? Greg needed to know. He had to find out first, before anything happened to her.

He got in his car and continued after Elsie. The blue Dodge was still one car behind her, but he had not seen the Russian guy in the gray Corolla. He was either taking a food and gas break or had decided to turn around and not pursue her further. He doubted the latter, though he'd find out soon.

Elsie took Exit 48 off I-81. Blue Dodge Man followed. Greg, leaving two other cars in between, followed the Dodge. A few minutes later, he spotted the Russian in the rearview mirror. The union was intact. He slowed down and turned left, after first letting the Russian pass. He waited a few minutes before swinging around and retaking Exit 48.

* * * *

Sergei at last understood there was a method to Tatiana's madness when it came to Elsie Simon. He was now fully aware of the third actor who had entered the play. The blue Dodge had been on her tail, on and off, since he'd caught up with her in Front Royal. The vehicle had New Jersey plates and its driver was big with dark hair. That was all he had for now.

He checked his marked map on the front passenger seat. They were less than ten miles from her final destination. The area was nothing but woods.

He decided to give his cell a try. He dialed Tatiana's number. Nothing. He tossed the phone on the passenger seat. The Dodge had slowed down, so he did as well. Elsie was the only one who'd accelerated. Without traffic as cover, a fair distance between them was the only way to remain unnoticed—by Elsie, that is; by now the blue Dodge surely had made him, just as he'd made the blue Dodge.

He checked his odometer. Less than four miles.

* * * *

Elsie cut her speed. It was almost 6 P.M. and the sky was now dark and she knew she was somewhere near the driveway. *There! The rusty iron gate.* She came to an almost full stop before turning left, onto the one-lane dirt-gravel path. She checked the road behind her: deserted; no cars in sight. For the last mile or so she hadn't seen a single house. It was just her, alone, in the woods.

She got out and opened the gate, made from a chain-link fence.

It snapped all the way open without having to force it. She drove through, stopped, and reattached the gate.

The gravel drive was almost a quarter mile long with trees and brush on both sides. She continued on until finally she saw its outline, against a starless sky: the weathered log cabin, a two-storey A-frame with fieldstone chimney, backed by a pond at the end of the path. Under ordinary circumstances, it might have even looked romantic. Not tonight.

She pulled all the way up and to the right at the entrance. She put the gearshift on P, turned off the motor, and sat for a minute without unbuckling her belt. Was this really wise? Maybe she shouldn't have listened. Her townhouse, in the middle of the city, armed with an alarm and surrounded by neighbors felt so much safer . . . at least in retrospect. Out here was spooky. And now it was night. Was it too late to back out and head back to Alexandria? She shook off these last-minute fears and doubts and unbuckled her seatbelt. She was being ridiculous . . . wasn't she?

She climbed the four steps leading to the cabin's porch and proceeded to the door. She ran her fingers over the top of the dusty windowsill until they came into contact with a set of keys. Then she opened the door without stepping inside and felt around for the light switch. She found the panel and flipped both switches. The lights on the front porch, entry and central living room flickered on at once.

She poked her head inside. Open plan kitchen, living and dining room: kitchen–dining area on the left (with walnut table for four), living room–fireplace on the right (with mismatched yet harmonious furniture).

She turned around and went back to unload the car. She started with the backseat, grabbing her duffel bag. Next, she opened the driver's side door and reached for her extra coat and cell phone. She took them inside, leaving them on the floor in the entry. Now she opened the trunk. She eyed the gun case but reached for the pumpkin instead, half lifting, half rolling the cumbersome object and setting it on the ground, careful not to crack it. Then she banged the trunk shut. Elsie rolled the pumpkin over to the front porch steps and with no small effort managed to carry it up a stair at a time and set it down in a prime viewing spot. Tomorrow she would clean it up; right now it was covered with crusty dry mud. Perfect for Halloween.

From the porch she pointed her key at the car and locked the vehicle remotely. Then she took in the forested surroundings. The temperature was dropping without any wind, and everything stood still. All so quiet. And peaceful. And yet . . .

She turned around, went inside, and closed the door behind her. Where would she start? *Heat.* Get a fire going; then find the electric heater per instruction. The place seemed tidy but needed dusting. After that, she'd warm up a couple of empanadas, slice some cheese and pair it with some prewashed grapes, open the wine to let it breathe . . . and try to enjoy this eerie night. Maybe a bit of reading in bed for distraction. As for tomorrow? She'd think about that later. Soon Ryan would be coming through that door; she smiled at the thought . . . and everything it conjured.

CHAPTER 11

Friday Evening, October 31, 2003
Near Elkins, West Virginia

The firewood was crackling. Elsie was pleased. She'd found the master bedroom and already had her duffel bag in there. Now it was time to check out the room: the four-poster bed was fitted with pillows, sheets, two layers of blankets and the bedspread. *Good.* She found the small electric heater, set it on low and put it next to the bed. She grabbed a fleece throw from the foot of the bed and headed back to the cozy living room. Dulce Pontes' fados softly filled the room.

She draped the throw over the two-seat sofa and went to the kitchen for another glass of wine. Her tension was beginning to melt. She was beginning to like the cabin. Especially now, warmed by wine and a fire.

It was almost eight. She would read for a couple of hours, finish her second glass, and then go to bed. Tonight she was skipping the bath.

* * * *

Greg stood stock-still, watching and listening from his well-chosen hide. He had parked his vehicle a quarter of a mile from the chain-link gate. By now he had changed into everything black, armed with everything he needed.

Twenty minutes earlier, Blue Dodge Man had driven onto the property, pulled the car off and away from the path, and killed the engine. Greg could see fairly well without resorting to goggles—the guy was eating potato chips. *Garbage*, Greg thought, *for garbage*.

The Russian arrived a few minutes after Dodge Man positioned himself. He came on foot, dressed in army surplus camouflage fatigues. Currently, he was crouched fifty feet or so away from the Dodge, solely intent on that car. He'd be easy as well: petite novice, a one-task man.

Greg could see everything inside the cabin. She had all the lights on, including the front porch. Right now she was on display, lying on the couch with a book. If the Dodge man wanted her dead, he could take aim and do it with a single shot from where he was parked; but that was not what the Dodge man had planned. First he'd subdue and interrogate her. Probably record the session for his bosses. Next he'd drag her someplace else where he'd finish her off and eliminate the body. The cabin belonged to an FBI man or his family; he wouldn't want to leave a treasure trove of evidence for the feds.

Blue Dodge threw the empty chips bag in the back before he guzzled from a large plastic bottle. Another plus for Greg. Muscle man was going to be a piece of cake.

The Dodge door opened. It was action time. He cock walked down the gravel path as if daring to be spotted. He was at least six three and moved more like a mafia hit man than an agency operative with some elite unit. He changed direction about 35 feet from the cabin. He planned to enter from the back. Most likely he was armed with a glass cutter. He would try his luck first with an unlocked window or cut a pane and undo the latch. Either way, Greg had several minutes; enough time to take care of Russia.

Greg quickly but quietly moved toward his target, who was watching the cabin and waiting. Greg would circle around and take him down from the back. Eight feet now behind his man, he was close enough to smell the cologne. With his gun butt-forward he coldcocked the Russian and brought him down clean. He did not plan to kill him, not yet. Instead, he gave him just enough sedative to knock him out for thirty minutes. Then he dragged away the unconscious heap to a hidden spot in the woods. He cuffed the man's hands behind him and removed his knife and each of his guns.

Now Greg checked the house. As expected, Dodge was on top of Elsie, doing something to her arms. Time for his next move. Retracing the intruder's steps, Greg proceeded to the back, where he spotted the window. No cut glass. Good. Less mess. Less evidence to destroy when he was finished.

* * * *

Elsie froze. She was tongue-tied. She hadn't put up any struggle. Everything happened so fast. One minute she was semidozing, and the next this bulky man was atop her, twisting her arms and flipping her on her back, explaining that they were going to talk. Talk? About what? Who was he? Someone the FBI had sent to scare her off? This wasn't their style. Was it someone Sullivan hired, because he was pissed off with her for going to Congress? Maybe. Was he some crazy killer rapist? Not likely; how many of them were interested in talking?

The man left her tied on the sofa, and went over to the dining table. He brought back a chair, set it down next to her, and pulled out a microdigital recorder, placing the device on the coffee table. He pressed Record. "Ms. Simon, I am going to ask you a few questions. You are going to answer them right away and truthfully. I suggest we do this in a civilized fashion. Then . . . well, then we'll be done. You understand?"

Elsie didn't respond right away. She tried to recall all the things she'd learned in her undergraduate psychology studies. Criminal psychology was her area of focus. How should she handle this situation? Complete cooperation? Make a personal connection? Try to buy herself time by dragging things? Why, though, would she try to buy time? Ryan wouldn't be here till the following evening. No one was coming to her rescue.

"Ah, I'm waiting, and I don't like to wait. Did you understand what I just said?"

Elsie nodded.

"Good. Now where are the documents? Where did you put the documents?"

Elsie tried a fake look of confusion. "What documents?" Her voice sounded small.

"Nah. Don't try it. That won't work. Where are the FBI documents you sang about to Congress?"

Not a killer rapist, she thought. That left Sullivan and, of course, the agency . . . with far too much at stake.

"I don't have those with me."

"Come on. Delaying won't get you anywhere. I would hate to use my skills on you. Pretty face, tiny body . . . you won't last more than half a minute."

"Why don't you go ahead and search me?" Elsie sounded defiant. "Search the house. My bag. I don't have the documents."

"*Where?*" He was growing impatient.

"I don't have them with me. There are several copies. FBI's got a few. Two copies were given to Congress. And . . . my trusted FBI friends—"

The man held his hands up. "Whoa! Let's not play the generality game. Specifics. Starting with Congress. Who in Congress, exactly?"

Elsie was regaining her quick-thinking skills. "Donald Keller's office."

"Useless. We have Keller covered. Who else?"

Elsie detected a slight movement in the corner, accompanied by a shadow. Someone else was here. Did this man have an accomplice? Was it someone on the side of good? *Was* there a side of good? Did Ryan ask someone to check on her? *Ryan*, Elsie thought. *Where are you?*

She decided to buy herself and the shadow more time. "Office of Congresswoman Sharon Woods. You know her? The Democratic Congresswoman from—"

"Go on. Who else?"

Elsie saw him—in her peripheral vision—at all costs maintaining eye contact with her assailant. He was tall, athletic, midforties, Russian- or Eastern European–looking . . . and with a gun aimed straight at the intruder.

She answered evenly, looking him in the eye. "I also sent a copy to the Senate. Senator—" Reflexively, she threw herself away and to the side of the report. Instantly, the man fell forward, the force of the shot propelling his bulk like toppled bags of sand. Elsie didn't scream. In fact, she didn't make a sound. She remained stomach down, hands tied behind her, without moving so much as a twitch.

She could see and hear the shooter approach. He heaved the dead man off the sofa, then carried him like a sack and unceremoniously dumped him on the floor next to the wall in the living room. She saw his feet return and shut her eyes. She could feel and smell the warm blood on her neck dripping down into her shirt. *Dead man's blood.* Yet she remained quiet and motionless.

The man began to speak. His voice, tone, and manner of speech were not at all what she'd expected. He had a deep and—dare she think it—almost soothing voice; comfort-inducing, even. "Ms. Simon. You may sit up now. My apologies for the mess. It couldn't be avoided, no matter how I aimed."

She opened her eyes. She tried to summon her strength to sit up. It was hard, especially with her hands so tied. Would he untie her? She decided not to wait and tried again. This time she succeeded.

She looked up. He was striking. Not handsome or beautiful but strong, confident, maybe even charismatic. His features stood out, particularly the eyes: gray-blue, piercing, forceful. Deep. He looked familiar. She had seen him before. But where? She knew it was recently but couldn't recall.

"And we finally meet."

"Who are you? Who are you with?" She was thinking about her tied hands.

The man's lips formed a quarter smile. "You may call me Greg. Greg McPhearson. Who am I with? I am with myself. With *me*. And you?"

Elsie narrowed her eyes. "I am sure you already know the answer. You've been following me?"

"Clearly. From what I've seen so far, you're popular. I'm not the only one; there are others."

Elsie, trying to avoid the bloody sight, gestured at the propped-up heap. "Who is he?"

Greg looked at the dead gray man. "Care to guess?"

"CIA. Was he CIA?"

Greg nodded. Everything about him was distinguished—so why didn't he untie her? This interview was humiliating enough; where were this person's manners? Despite the shock of what just happened, her natural defiance returned.

"CIA wants me killed. Is that it?" she asked sharply.

Greg appeared amused. "Don't tell me you're surprised. Not after all you've come to learn."

"You said *others*, plural. What did you mean by that?"

Greg allowed a half smile. "Very observant. Even in these circumstances. An important quality to have for reliable analysis." He paused. "You're right. Let's find out who the other one is." He started toward the door.

Elsie tried unsuccessfully to stand up. "Wait a minute! You haven't told me anything! Are you with Sullivan? Ryan? Where are you going? I need—"

"I'll be right back. Please remain seated, Ms. Simon." He carefully closed the door behind him and proceeded into the woods.

Elsie was confused. Who was this guy, and why had he rescued her? She tried to read the microwave clock but couldn't make out the numbers. Last time she had checked it was 8:30. She needed to use the bathroom. Why the hell was she still tied up?

She plummeted back down on the sofa. The fire was almost out. She was cold. Her eyes fixed on the darkening blood on the floor, the spatter all over the couch, which was soaked. She tried hard to look the other way, but she couldn't rid the air of that age-old scent, the smell of a fresh new kill.

* * * *

Greg found Sergei just where he'd left him. Grabbing under the arms, he lifted the weight to a standing position then shoulder-carried him back to the cabin. As he walked, his thoughts turned to Elsie. To her credit she was strong. No screaming, no demands. This was not typical. In fact she was anything but. The next two hours would determine her future—whether or not she had one. A phrase went through his mind like a koan: *Life asserts itself.* Against all odds; even in the face of death. Would Elsie Simon choose life? He wondered.

Greg opened the unlocked door with one hand as he carried Sergei inside. He flipped him into the chair next to the sofa. He would be returning to life any time now.

Elsie was riveted. "So who *is* he?"

Greg scanned her face. "Maybe, I don't know, I was hoping

you'd tell me. I haven't exactly been able to establish his link to you or your case."

Elsie studied the unconscious man. "Tell me what you know."

"Russian. Twenty-nine. Came here to the States in 2001 on a student visa, graduate studies at George Mason University, civil engineering. Lives in Rosslyn, Virginia, drives a silver-gray Toyota Corolla . . . does any of this ring a bell?"

Elsie shook her head. "I don't understand this. Unless . . ." She thought of Sullivan, and mostly, Tatiana.

"Unless . . ." Greg waited for more but Elsie was silent. Obviously, she was thinking.

She looked defiantly at Greg. "Well? Are you going to untie me?"

"No. Not yet. I apologize for the discomfort, but I have to keep you this way until . . ." He stopped himself right there.

"Until? What?"

"Let's put *Until* next to your *Unless* and take it from there."

Sergei began twitching. He was regaining consciousness but groggy. Greg and Elsie watched and waited. No one spoke.

Sergei finally was able to focus. To his right, on a blood-splattered sofa, was Elsie Simon. Across from him, seemingly nine feet tall, was a very strong man in his forties. He looked Russian. Could that be? What in the world was he doing here?

He checked his surround and tried to remember. That was one mother of a head bang. He was inside a cabin . . . That's right. He was following this woman. His eyes spied the dead man on the floor. Blue Dodge. Tailing Elsie and . . . what happened here? He was trying to protect her—as instructed. Then . . . then . . . nothing.

He looked up at Greg. Tatiana had talked about reinforcement. *Fortification* was the word. Was he that someone?

"Who are you?"

Greg held his gaze. "You first. Is it . . . Mister Bulinov?"

So he was *not* from his side of the fence. "My name is Sergei Bulinov." Elsie noticed the pronounced Russian accent.

"We established that," Greg said calmly. "But *who* are you? Why have you been following Ms. Simon here?"

Sergei turned to Elsie with her hands and ankles tied. It didn't make sense. If Dodge was a hit man removed by this giant, why then was the woman restrained? "You are okay?"

"I don't know." She looked at Greg. "I'm not sure. But I too want to know. Who are you? Why have you been following me? Are you with this guy?" She motioned her head toward the heap.

"N-no, no . . ." Sergei stammered, "I am not. I am on your side. I was about to come stop him when . . . when someone knocked me in the head . . ." he looked at Greg. "It was you?"

Greg ignored the question. "Who do you work for, Bulinov?"

Sergei chewed his upper lip and turned back to Elsie.

"Are you with the Sullivan team?" she asked. "Tatiana?"

"Now that is interesting!" Greg cut in. "Finally, someone I don't know. Who is Sullivan? I can't wait to hear about Tatiana. *Tatiana?* I don't like the sound of that."

Sergei made a quick decision. Elsie had given him a way out. "Y-Yes. Tatiana. I work under Tatiana." In a way it was true. He did indeed. But no, he had nothing to do with Sullivan.

Elsie twisted in rage. "He promised; he gave me *his word* he would stop. Fucking surveillance!"

Greg got in the middle, authoritative. "One of you had better provide me with details. *Sullivan* and *Tatiana*." He first looked to Elsie, who flat out didn't care. She was steaming. "All right then. You. Bulinov."

Sergei gave him the overview: Edward Sullivan the billionaire, his son's assassination in Cyprus, his quest for answers and vengeance, his own elite team—including Tatiana, Ryan, other former insiders, as well as techies and researchers.

Greg had heard of Edward Sullivan but nothing about the murder of his son. Another unexpected development: a glitch. It was not only Elsie Simon and her lover; others were lurking around his operation grounds. These were people with vested interests who would interfere with his plan. He didn't like it. "How many others does this team include?"

Sergei honestly didn't know. How could he? That was Tatiana's area.

Greg looked to Elsie, who stared right back, uncomfortable and defiant. "So he keeps it compartmentalized. What's it to you? You haven't even told me who you are. Who are you, and why are you here?"

Greg let the questions go. Instead, he was focused on inconsistencies. Holes. There were holes in Sergei's account. "You have been receiving quarterly money transfers from a bank in St. Petersburg—in *Russia*. Sullivan is American. His headquarters are here in the States. I can't see why he would pay you from a Russian bank, in Russia. Try again, *Sergei*."

Sergei already knew this guy was a pro. He thought about his options. Not many. "I'm with the Russians in this; FSB," he pointed his chin to Elsie. "We have a stake in all this."

Elsie began to process this bit. The transcripts: Azerbaijan, Georgia, Kyrgyzstan . . . joint operations with the new branch of Islamic Mujahideen, and the common target—Russia. Sullivan's son: what he must have found, the connection with Russia and other former Soviet states. Sema's smoking gun transcripts: all with Central Asia and Caucasus themes. Yousef Mahmoud's state-backed travels overseas: same Russian connections. Nazim and NATO-CIA had to be connected to Russia as well. Why else would there be such close ties and partnership between a heroin-smuggling operative and money launderer and NATO-U.S. Intel?

"Tatiana?" she questioned.

Sergei responded flatly. "Da. She is above me. I report to and take my orders from her. Sullivan Junior's killing had nothing to do with us . . . truly . . ." he looked up at his two inquisitors. "We believe it was part of the network working against our security and interests."

Elsie had to ask, "Does he know?"

"Of course not . . . but hey," he sounded almost mocking, "we have a common interest, same objective. As true with your case," he looked directly at Elsie. "Yours became far more important, top priority, than Sullivan's."

Elsie was flabbergasted. She and Ryan not only were being used as mercenaries by Sullivan; they were being utilized by Russian Intelligence as well—as pawns.

Greg pointed to Sergei. "All right, Bulinov, time for a walk in the woods. It will do us both good. Let's go."

With only his hands cuffed behind him, Sergei stood up and started toward the door. Greg let him pass and followed.

This was not a walk in the woods, Elsie knew. This was an execution. She cried out after Greg, "Don't do it! Please don't! You can use him—whatever it is you are after, you can use him . . ."

Greg was already out the door, making sure to close it behind him. He was not inconsiderate when it came to such matters. With Dodge Man he'd had no choice. He would not put Elsie through that again if he could help it.

* * * *

Elsie felt dizzy and sick. She was coming out of semishock and now began to fully feel the danger she was in. She was next in line. He was going to take her out. Once he was done. Once he'd gotten what he wanted. Yet what was that? She still didn't know. And she needed to go to the bathroom—badly. With her hands tied behind her she couldn't even pull her sweats down to go without doing it inside her pants.

The door opened and in walked Greg—minus Sergei, of course. Elsie couldn't stand meeting his eye.

"Why? Why take him out? You didn't have to. Why?"

Greg considered. There was no short answer, at least none that would satisfy a woman of her analytical capacity. "To be answered later . . . maybe."

"I need to use the bathroom. Really bad. If you are going to kill me, then please do it and get it over with now. Otherwise, please don't degrade me by making me urinate here . . . all over myself."

"I have no intention of humiliating you like that, Ms. Simon. Let me remove those from your ankles." He took out his commando knife and approached her.

The sight of the knife made her knees go weak. She'd rather die from a hollow-point bullet than being sliced and diced.

Greg dropped down next to her. She shut her eyes and waited. Instead of a stabbing wound, she heard the muffled snap of a tight rope cut. Then he sliced the rope in the middle, freeing her hands. They were numb but they were free. Elsie opened her eyes.

Greg stepped aside and pointed to the hallway. "Please. Go use the bathroom. And don't even think about running. You won't get far, and there's no place to go. So please. I'll wait right here."

Elsie took steps on shaky feet to the bathroom as Greg stood aside. Here was a peculiar man: bordering on insanity, with many layers of oddness and eccentricities; and yet, he was articulate and sounded calm at all times, even lucid, under these extreme conditions. Obviously, he was trained. What was his plan? Moreover, why was he here? She had specialized in criminal psychology. She had to think of how to deal with him. He was educated and highly intelligent but a murderer, a hit man, probably ex-CIA, and someone who felt things deeply. He seemed to have a capacity for empathy, so that ruled out sociopath. Labels at this point were useless. She had to find a way to reach him, to discover what might save her life.

After she relieved herself, Elsie went to the mirror and looked. Red crusted blood covered one whole side of her neck and continued down her light gray sweatshirt, leaving a patch design. She ripped it off and threw it in the bathtub, then examined the dried streaks on her chest and stomach. She felt the bile rising. In seconds she was gripping the toilet for balance while she heaved the entire contents of her stomach. Cold sweat ran down her back.

She opened the cabinet under the sink and found a stash of washcloths. She grabbed two, pumped some hand soap and soaked them with hot water, and began scrubbing herself hard until she freed her skin of all traces of blood and turned it raw and red. Next, she washed and dried her face; then brushed her teeth with the minty toothpaste using her index finger.

She walked out of the bathroom naked above the waist and went into the bedroom where she'd left her duffel bag. She stripped off her sweatpants, took out her jeans, clean underwear and a cream sweater from the bag and put them on. She brushed her hair with harsh strokes. She slapped on some clear lip balm, and sprayed herself with perfume. This had nothing to do with wanting to look good. It was about gaining her strength and confidence. She needed to pull herself out of fear and confusion. Every second of life depended on it.

She found Greg at the dining room table steeped in thought. She pulled up a chair.

"I'm ready. Time to talk."

He studied her face and new clothes with some amusement. She was good at playing strong. "Ms. Simon. I'm listening."

"No," she said, adamant. "I'm not playing that. It's your turn to talk. And while you're at it, quit calling me *Ms. Simon*. We are well past the *Ms.* and *Mr.* stage. I had to beg you to pee, for Christ's sake! That changes the dynamic. Elsie will do."

Greg was now truly amused. He preferred and respected direct-ness. So he began. "The people who ordered the hit on your friend in New Jersey, those who are set to take you out, are the same people who got my woman killed. The agency."

So he knew all about Sami, Elsie noted. What was the deal with "his" woman? "*Your* woman? You mean wife? Lover? Mistress? Kept?"

"Semantics. *My woman.* Granted, wrong place, wrong time; nonetheless, she was *killed.*"

"But why? You still haven't told me who you are. That would be a good starting point."

Greg gave her a concise thumbnail sketch: the punk, Cambodia, Josh and Maurice, Keller and, of course, Mai's shooting; precise in detail but lacking in explanation.

Elsie took in every word. "Lucy was the reporter's girlfriend." It was a statement, not a question. She remembered her lunch with Sami, the same day Lucy had gotten in touch; she'd insisted, Sami said, on a face-to-face meeting. *Oh, Sami, you chased the wrong case!* Elsie grieved.

Greg followed the subtle changes in her face, as though he could sense the direction of her thoughts.

"Now . . . tell me about you. Were you with the CIA?"

"Not exactly."

"And what is that supposed to mean? You either worked for the agency or you didn't. Simple. Now, did you or didn't you?"

Greg didn't answer right away. To do so would mean to explain . . . nearly everything. That could be fatal. Where then would be a good starting point, truly? For some reason, his own question triggered an answer.

"I began with the army; Special Forces, and after that, DIA. I have a solid education and a good set of language skills, like you. That moved me to another unit: Joint CIA-Pentagon Operations. A year later, I became one of the chosen ones for the company. That's where I spent the last twenty years."

"The company? But that's the agency—the CIA."

"Well, yes and no. The company is a special operations unit made up of several units: the Pentagon, on the top; NATO, CIA, and MI6. There are less than two hundred operatives in the company. All divided into their own small units. Separate pockets. Rigidly compartmentalized. The top tier, OGs one to ten, oversees the entire operation without ever coming into direct contact with the bottom units."

Elsie tilted her head to the left and began stroking the nape her neck. "OGs?"

Don't, Greg thought. He looked into her eyes. "Operation Gladio. Are you familiar?"

Elsie leaned back. "Sure. That was a Cold War unit. NATO's left-behind paramilitary and intelligence units . . . the so-called stay-behind secret armies."

Greg nodded, though he could see she had some difficulty following.

"But . . . the entire purpose of this was to act as a first resort fallback option in case of a Soviet invasion of Western Europe. It was all about the Cold War. That has been over for more than a decade."

"Has it really? You tell me. You're the expert. The Soviet Union fell, and now all its former states are sitting on the world's largest energy resources. Azerbaijan, Kazakhstan, Turkmenistan and Uzbekistan with large oil and gas reserves . . . Kyrgyzstan and Tajikistan with vast hydropower resources. With the Soviet Union gone—we're talking 1991—who was prepared to take control over this region? Russia? China? Or us?"

Elsie knew exactly but pretended otherwise for the sake of argument. "Put them up for bidding and have the highest bidders get the most?"

Greg offered one of his half smiles. "Elsie, you know better than that. Tell me, what kind of operations did Gladio engage in during the Cold War?"

She didn't have to think. "The strategy of tension and internal subversion operations." She had studied the subject during college. Internal subversion and *false flag* operations were explicitly considered and implemented by the CIA and stay-behind paramilitaries. On many occasions, stay-behind units became directly involved in right-wing terrorism, crime—including extortion, kidnapping, narcotics and murder—and, of course, coups d'états, their *coups de grâce*—the be-all and end-all of "regime change."

"Right you are. False flag terror operations were and *continue to be* a hallmark of Gladio Operations." Greg let this sink in. "Now, with the Soviet Union gone, we had to compete with and beat the Russians, and to a certain extent, China, for control over the new orphan states with their vast energy resources. How do you suppose they went about accomplishing this?"

Elsie already knew. "By using religion, language and heritage to bring them closer to the West . . . The Greater Turkic Republic is what they called it in Turkey. Turkey, a close U.S. ally and member of NATO, was the natural vehicle, of course."

He agreed but held up a hand. "*At first.* That was how we went about it. *At the beginning.* But it didn't work. Not good enough. So a switch was made to a new kind of strategy, and *Operation B* was implemented; it was modeled on our Afghan strategy of the nineteen eighties, only bigger. Much bigger: religious extremism under the guise of Islam, mosques and madrassas, using Mujahideen and our Arab operatives, creating Chechen commandos and several *unique* Islamic movements within that region—our very own terror cells."

Elsie held her breath. He was now getting into what had placed her in this situation: Sema and the transcripts, Yousef Mahmoud, her briefing session in Keller's office.

Greg, once more sensing her innermost thoughts, continued to piece things together. "Then you came in and stepped on some toes. Very wrong toes, as you must know by now. You and your discovery have upset a lot of people and, not so incidentally, my own plans for *my own* skin. You—an analyst—and your FBI lover chasing one of our men, Mahmoud, have set in play a wheel whose turn has brought me here, tonight. So, you see, honestly, if it hadn't been for you . . ."

Elsie desperately needed Greg to change tack. He was an animal in motion, intent on prey, if this thought was followed to conclusion. Her only hope right now was to intercede with a question. "We were directly responsible for *all* those terror attacks in the region?"

This brought him around. He stopped to think. "Many of them. At least . . . the significant ones." He looked to be running operations in his head.

"This explains Nazim's arrival on a NATO-agency plane," she followed up quickly. "And why he was shielded as well."

"Nazim?" Greg looked blank.

"It's his alias, he has several," Elsie went on. "He conducts heroin operations and exports to the States; his tentacles reach into every major hub in a massive money laundering network. Based on Sema's transcript, he may be a high-level Turkish military offic—"

Greg completed her thought. "Lieutenant General Mehmet Turkel."

Elsie looked wide-eyed. "You know him as well?"

"I do, or did. He was part of the Old Gladio, and seems to have become a liability. A few weeks ago I finished him off. He's dead."

"You took him out? Per the company's instruction?"

"No. That was part of my own operation."

Things were veering back to scary. Elsie pursued the personal. "What? Retired? Resigned from the company?"

Greg smiled again. "No one resigns. They don't accept resignations. I may be the first to get out. They are not keen on such moves, as you may already have guessed."

Nervous, Elsie asked point-blank, "2001?"

"What about it?"

"Was that the company? Your work?"

Greg let the question hang for a minute. The answer was an issue for him as well, his relation to the company, even before Mai's murder. Elsie could see that it bothered him. "I . . . *believe* so. Was I part of it? No. The company operates from a range of pockets; however, we are not going to discuss this now." He turned the question back. "Tell me about the transcripts. Not concrete enough for you?"

Elsie explained about Sema, where the copy was hidden, and what had taken place in the archives room while she was looking through those transcripts: the revocation of her clearance and subsequent dismissal.

Greg stated simply, "I may need those documents. If or when I do, I will get them."

Elsie found his conversation bizarre, and his operation a mystery; she had no other choice but to determine his status. "So tell me, you're on the run? They're after you, right?"

"Not yet. They don't know. That's why my time frame is limited. I took care of the first-stage missions, those were easy: Josh, Maurice, Rodman, Turkel and others in Belgium. I expected this stage to be predictable as well—until you and your hothead boyfriend, along with Sullivan, intervened. Of course, that's why I had to follow and take care of you. I have to do the same thing with your boyfriend, Sullivan and his team." He sounded perfectly calm.

The rational plan of a psychopath, thought Elsie. "So . . . are we back to the same place? Why are we talking, then? Why don't you go ahead and shoot me? Is this your sadistic side, enjoying yourself like a cat does with a mouse before devouring it?"

Greg actually looked hurt. "I mustn't leave you. They will get to you in no time. They *will* take you out. Probably, after they make you sing a tune or three. Think about it, Elsie. Your situation is similar to any fugitive's. You can't go back to your house; you can't use your cell phone or e-mail; you can't take out money from the bank or use your credit cards. You can't take your passport and leave by hopping on a plane! What are you going to do? Where are you going to go?"

He paused for effect then continued. "And that leaves me two options. I either finish you off, or, I protect you by staying with you; a miserable choice. Frankly, Elsie, I am the only person on this earth right now capable of keeping you alive. Do you see that?"

"I don't need your protection. I'm willing to take my own chances."

"Yes you do. You can deny it, sit here, pray for Jesus or the Rabbit to come be your savior, and take those—forgive me—extremely dubious odds; or you can be rational and accept that I am the only person now who can save you. Which will it be, Elsie? Me or the Rabbit?"

Elsie understood the point. She agreed with the facts of her fugitive status. But still. What could be in it for him, keeping her alive? Knowing what she did about survival and the psyche, she decided to ask him straight out. "Why, Greg, would you even consider not killing me? As you say, a *miserable* choice. It would be that much easier . . . and . . . without the *misery*." She harped on that word. His word. His choice.

Greg had been asking himself that question all day. The thought of ending Elsie's life felt miserable. He'd done the work, examined who she was, even located the fact of her secret. He'd interrogated her and explained things rationally; or at least as best he could. She seemed to understand. And now she was asking. What would he tell her? The woman deserved an answer.

So Greg decided as he always did when his brain was at war with his body: he went with his gut. It never lied. That feeling was always reliable. His was neither passion-driven nor rage-induced nor sentimental; it was cool.

"Once in a while, very rarely, I do refrain from the simpler option. You can call that 'saving' if you like, but I prefer to think that they *owe me one*. There are certain people, and I won't mention names, who each, for different reasons, owe me one. The reasons may not be valorous or noble—in fact, some of them are downright criminal—but sometimes, when and if the situation arises, I go and collect what they owe me: their debt. In your case, though it may seem counterintuitive, and as an analyst you might appreciate this, the more burdensome, complicated option is simpler. I like the idea of having you owe me one. You never know. One day I may be coming to collect. And when I do, I know you will pay."

Elsie didn't know what to do with this. Clearly, he was insane. At the same time, he operated according to a rigid set of principles— and she had to know his plan. Otherwise, she would be his slave for life. She would owe him forever, and who knows what that might entail? Blackmail, extortion; any kind of hateful act. If those were her choices, she'd rather have it out now. Get this over with.

"Who says I like the idea of owing you one? This takes two. What if my choice is the former—of *not* being saved? What if I'd rather go with Option A?"

This woman was not like anyone he'd ever dealt with. Talk about complicated! Maybe she was crazy? He hadn't fully considered it. "Are you telling me you've had enough of life and want me to turn off the switch? What about your father?"

"What *about* my father?" Elsie turned white hot. "What do you know? Why do you bring him up?"

Greg gave a careless shrug. "Not much. I know about the case."

"His case has nothing to do with this or you," she spat. "I don't need to be saved by a terrorist. I don't want to owe someone like you. Isn't that good enough? It's good enough for me."

"You would rather I'd let that man torture and kill you? There are killings, and there are killings. Not all are equal. Some are justified. Some have a purpose. I believe you believe that as well."

"All murderers see their acts as justified," she raged. "With you it goes even further. Your purposes involve *mass* murders. Isn't that what they do? The agency, the company? You?"

Greg felt provoked. "You too, Elsie, justify your murders. How many have you sent to their deaths? Three, five, ten?"

Elsie looked stunned. "What?"

"You have been sending them names: of covert operatives. You've been providing the people who've been searching for your father with the names of CIA operatives—agents in the field, under wraps, sent to Turkey and Iraq. You're outing them, Elsie! Aren't you? Don't tell me you don't know what they're doing with those names. How many are now *dead* because of you? How many *abducted* and *tortured*, thanks to you? Do you even keep count?"

"Those operatives are established murderers. Established and known human rights abusers. People like you. *They* are the ones who practice murder and torture. Like you! Helping with their elimination is helping humanity—it is an act of saving humanity! Have you seen Kurdish children blown to bits and pieces? Have you ever treated victims of torture . . . those who've been electrocuted, sodomized . . . You . . . one of the executioners . . . inflicting those things on innocent . . ." here she broke down. She was actually crying.

"So *those* are justified murders. I'm not at all sure the spouses and mothers of those names—to say nothing of their children—would agree. But that won't change your operation, will it? The end always justifies the means. Correct?"

Elsie was seeing black. "All he wanted was to cure and save people. He trusted your front men . . . they turned around and signed his death warrant. As they do every day. They participate in mass torture and killings. What kind of end is that? Where is the justifiable purpose?"

She was sure by now she had made the decision for him. Now the only option left was to kill her. He wouldn't entertain any thoughts of saving her. Not after this exchange. Not after spelling out how utterly she loathed him; how much she hated his guts.

Greg wasn't so easily moved. He expected her to hate him; how could she not? His presence on a mission presaged death.

"What if I were to slightly modify my second option?"

Elsie look confused. "You mean letting me live? Becoming my Jesus Rabbit?"

Greg moved toward her. They were inches apart. "I keep you safe, keep my eyes on you awhile. You help me with a few operations. When that's finished, I get you safely out of this country and provide you with a new place and identity. Then we'll call it even. You won't owe me one and will never hear back from me."

Elsie was baffled. If this were anyone else, she'd be dead by now. Since he appreciated honesty, she told him what she thought of his plan. "The idea of me spending time with you, being with you, *under your eyes*, even if only for days or a week, is nothing short of unbearable."

Here was another irrational side, he thought. Elsie Simon was arguing *against her own life*. He had never experienced that before. "This is because you assume it would be miserable, that time spent with me would be hell. Not so. It won't be like tonight. Nor will it be happy or intimate, but I assure you, we will be too focused and busy with the mission, and time will go fast. That's a promise. Everything will be done in less than three weeks. Then you'll be on a plane to your safe new home. And I'll be on my way to wherever I choose; preferably, away from bullets."

"What is this *mission* you're talking about?"

"They took Mai. Needlessly. Pointlessly. Not even to send a message. She happened to be there, yet she was targeted as though she were some kind of threat. I am going to avenge my woman's death. That's one. Number two, I will stop their current operation: Operation B. Not interfere or slightly damage it, but make it public and bring it to an end . . . at least for a while."

Elsie needed more. "You know about Dad. What made you join them and kill for them in the first place?"

"Simple. Russia. I hate the Russians. Always have, and one hundred percent sure always will."

This was surreal. Outrageous. Elsie was speechless.

"I can tell from your face you're impressed."

After a stunned silence, she found her voice. "What . . . Whatever did they do to you? How could every Russian be your enemy? It makes no sense!"

"My mother was Russian. And I am not going to stand here and analyze the root of my hatred for you, Elsie. You asked me a question, and I answered you frankly."

Elsie would let this go. *For now.* She knew where not to push. He was capable of sadistic violence, and his tone frightened her on this subject. Still, she needed more. "Can you at least provide me with some outline of your mission?"

Greg considered this, and decided to make it as short and as general as he could. "We are going to expose Keller. I have the audiovisual. That's one. I will be taking out Josh's boss, the man who ordered the hit. That's two. I am going to publicize Operation Gladio B and its role in the 2001 attack. That's three. There is to be another terror attack—a setup. Not big, but big enough. The purpose: expanding Georgia and extending further into Russian territory, through Dagestan and Chechnya. I still don't know the how and the when. The general time frame indicates less than three weeks from today. I will obtain specifics, and when I do I will utilize that intel for further sabotage of Operation B."

Elsie was amazed. Everything sounded completely far-fetched yet all of it in fact was true. That this man could plan and execute it all single-handed was perhaps strangest of all. The part about another "setup" terror attack received the bulk of her attention. "Do you know who and where they are targeting?"

"General. Washington, D.C., area. The executioners—the foot soldiers—must be from the region. They have to be, in order for the scheme to work."

Elsie accepted the explanation. "If I'm to be around you, under your watchful eyes, if I'm to aid and abet this mission, then I have one or two conditions of my own."

Greg was astonished. "What makes you think you are in any position at all to set conditions?"

Elsie ignored his arrogant stand. Her feelings were too strong and she would not be dissuaded. "You are not to touch Ryan Marcello. You are not to kill Sullivan or those on his team. Apart from the company-agency targets, you are not to kill innocent people. Those are my conditions. Accept them or shoot me."

"I'm disappointed, Elsie. A lesser man—and by that I mean a hotter head with much thinner skin—would take you up on that. Be careful what you say. Your belief that without a purpose or reason I would ever touch a life is disturbing and mistaken. The further accusation that I enjoy that kind of work is badly misguided, and I'd just as soon drop the subject. I do accept your conditions, though your man, if he has any hope of surviving, must cease his amateur operation. Sullivan and his people must not be allowed to interfere with our plans. That's right, *our* plans. If you want them to live, then you can be instrumental. One exception to the rule is Tatiana. She works for FSB. She is a Russian spy. She has to go—and I don't mean back to Moscow."

Despite her ill feelings for Tatiana, Elsie couldn't be a party to her execution. At the risk of further inflaming him, she had to say something now. "This is not rational, your taking her out. Tatiana, the FSB, and yes, *the Russians*, well, they are on the opposite side: they have been the target of the company. Why not utilize her for our mission?"

"Simply, that I would never work with them. Nor would I ever be of benefit or help to them. Accept this, Elsie, as a stone cold fact."

At the words *stone cold* his eyes went dead and his look and tone turned black. Elsie was shaken. That mother of his. What could she possibly have done to him?

"As to the rest of our agreement," Greg continued almost jovially, "you know this means no contact between you and Ryan. Not unless executed cautiously, under my supervision . . . for the mission."

Elsie felt her heart being squeezed. "For how long?"

"For as long as it takes." He was matter-of-fact. "Until long after I get you out."

Elsie let reality sink in. Then she asked, "Where will I be going?"

"I have yet to decide. Right now, focus on one day at a time."

"All right then. What do I do next?"

Greg sprung into action. "You have to get out of here. Take everything you brought, and put everything back in its place, exactly as you found it. Then, get on the road. You will be driving for four or five hours, taking the route I give you. You will arrive in Dutch Country, Pennsylvania, and will check into a motel. Once you get there, you sleep, rest, eat and clean up. Stay put until I arrive to pick you up. I will get rid of your car and phone. You will have no phone, and you will use no phone, computer, e-mail or letters . . . you will not communicate with anyone—and I mean *anyone*." He then added, "You won't be using credit cards or ATM machines. I will provide you with cash. You will use cash only."

"For how long? When will you join me there?"

"In less than forty-eight hours. I have cleanup here: I need to get rid of the bodies and cars, remove all blood and other traces from the cabin and leave everything as it was before your arrival. I will use Dodge's phone and computer to send the agency a *mission accomplished* message. That'll keep them oblivious for a while. I'll put together a kit for you then drive up there to pick you up."

"Kit?"

"New hair, makeup, clothes . . . in a different style. We don't want you to look like Elsie. Not talking major alterations, but enough."

Elsie understood. "My car?"

"You'll be driving the Russian guy's car. It'll be yours for the next forty-eight hours. While you are gathering your things I'll go switch plates. I'll check it out for tracers and replace his license plate with Dodge Man's." He remembered one more thing. "You promised Ryan you would bring Ben's gun. Where is it?"

This infuriated her, on a number of levels. "Monitoring my calls. Obviously stalking me. You tell me!"

Greg shrugged. "From where I was parked, I couldn't see."

Elsie frowned. "Inside the trunk."

Greg looked at her as a parent would a hapless child. "You come here armed and leave your gun in the car?" *Analyst*, he reminded himself. "What kind? Is it loaded?"

Considering what had happened that night, Elsie admitted it was dumb. She replied halfheartedly, "Thirty-eight revolver. No. Not loaded, but the ammo is next to it, inside a case . . ." Now she sounded even dumber.

"You would have made a great agent—for the *FBI*." He went over to the door and opened it. "I'll be checking the cars and the body. Time to start your tasks. I want you on your way no later than one."

She downed what was left of the coffee she'd made. She was going to need lots more of it. It was past 11 P.M. now; she probably wouldn't crash until 7 A.M. "All right," she told herself, "let's go. I can't get out of here soon enough." Some Halloween. It marked the end of Elsie's life as she'd known it for the last decade and a half.

* * * *

Saturday, Early Morning, November 1, 2003
Washington, D.C.

Another twenty miles and Greg would be back in his apartment for a shower, quick meal and short nap. He had not eaten in twenty-four hours.

Cleaning it all up took time. He had spotted the perfect derelict barn on an abandoned farm four miles from the cabin. The bodies of Sergei and the hit man were placed inside the Dodge, then driven to the rundown farm and parked inside the barn. Greg ran the four miles back to the cabin, then drove Elsie's car to the barn and parked inside, next to the Dodge. It would be days if not weeks or months before anyone found them.

Now he had to run the four miles back, to clean all traces of blood from the cabin. He scrubbed the floors and removed the ashes from the fireplace and cleaned all the dishes and cutlery. Everything returned to the cupboard. He triple-checked every room, even the refrigerator, before locking up. He knew Ryan was on his way. The man was law enforcement, and Greg wasn't taking any chances.

As he always did on such missions, Greg put himself in Ryan's place. Bewildered, then frantic, what would be the man's next move? He couldn't contact his friends at the bureau; considering what Elsie had been up to and the top-tier having become involved, that would be the last place he'd go. Nor would he contact local law enforcement. What would he tell them? That his girlfriend was to meet him here but somehow never arrived? No. That would entirely expose them. That left Marcello's boss, Sullivan, and his team. *Right.* And what a team it was! Tatiana, the Russian spy: wondering why she hadn't heard back from that bungler Sergei by now. The beauty of it, for him, was that she wouldn't be able to do a thing, not without Sullivan instantly suspecting; her cover would be blown. And Sullivan? He could summon private investigators from his roster and set them on a Find Elsie mission. Well, *good luck with that.*

He switched his thoughts back to Elsie Simon. He knew she had connected certain key facts. Still, she didn't have the entire picture. Neither did he, nor could he ever. What he'd told her about the company operation was true: highly compartmentalized, distinct pockets, separated from one another by design. It was brilliant, and the key to their enduring success. No matter how savvy or skilled, no one Gladio could ever unearth Gladio as a whole. It would be impossible.

Greg had Elsie in mind for two possible plans, but for those he had to think, and to think he had to eat. That was an unbreakable rule. No exceptions. The time to assess and analyze would be later, after dinner and before his artichoke tea.

He took the Rosslyn-Key Bridge exit, turned right on M Street after the bridge and continued toward the Rock Creek and Potomac Parkway. He was almost home—amid his targets and enemies—still the hunter, in the bosom of the prey.

* * * *

Saturday, Early Evening, November 1, 2003
Virginia

Ryan took the airport elevator to Parking and briskly walked the long corridor leading to the garage, hauling his carry-on behind him. Despite a sleepless, cramped forty-eight hours and frustrating layovers, he was energized now. *Three plus hours to Elsie.*

After a quick stop to fill up his tank he drove straight to the cabin, pulled up in front and got out to open the chain-link gate, thinking, *Good girl, Elsie; for a big city girl you pass the test on this one.*

He fairly barreled down the gravel path, surprised to see no lights on as he approached, and even more surprised when he didn't see her car. He stopped right in front of the cabin.

Popping the glove compartment, he retrieved his gun and jumped out, careful to avoid any traps. After securing the area, he ran up the steps and knocked. No answer. He knocked again. Nothing. Had she gone to the nearest town for supplies? One way to find out. He ran his fingers along the outside window frame. The keys on the rusty metal loop fell down and landed next to his foot.

He opened and entered. The dark living room and kitchen looked undisturbed and lonely. He flicked on the lights and headed for the bedrooms. He checked every single room. No sign of Elsie, her clothes or any other belongings. Next, he checked the bathroom: no toothbrush, unwrapped soap or dirty towels.

Don't panic, he ordered himself. *Calm down and think straight.* Had she decided last minute not to come? But then she would have called; he'd checked his voicemail more than once. No messages from Elsie. He'd called her cell too on the way over to be sure she was out of range; well now he was here. Then where the hell was she?

He switched off the lights and relocked the cabin. He was heading for his car when something made him stop and turn. There it was: the pumpkin. He remembered her words: *It will be sitting here in front waiting for you, Ryan Marcello. When you get here I expect you to carve it, chop it, puree it, do whatever it is you have to do . . .*

She'd been here. She'd made it. She'd unloaded her car—at least the pumpkin. Then where was she now? Why weren't there any other signs of her being here?

He headed back in. This time, utilizing every ounce of his training, he scanned the area as he would a crime scene. Everything appeared orderly and clean—maybe a bit too clean. Dust-free. He examined the bedrooms again. In each guest room the wood floors were coated thinly with dust, with some dust bunnies here and there. Yet the main bedroom—the one Elsie surely would have used—was immaculate. Not a speck on the floor. It almost looked polished. He returned to the living room. Same thing: vacuumed inside and out. No cobwebs, no spiders, not even one dead fly. What the hell?

He tried the fridge. An open box of baking soda near the back;

otherwise, empty. He stared at the coffee machine. If anything in this cabin was touched by Elsie Simon this was it. He lifted the lid and found droplets of water: it recently had been used.

He was going out of his mind. His next thought was to drive to Elkins, 15 or so miles away. There, with good reception, he would make a few calls: to Elsie's cell, to her house; she had mentioned Ben's son . . . what was his name? Who else? Who, apart from people at the bureau, could he call? It only just occurred to him that Elsie didn't have anyone. No parents or siblings here in the States; no close friends, or at least none that he knew of; likewise no close neighbors or acquaintances. With Ben and Sami gone, Elsie was alone. Well, except for him, of course. So why wasn't he with her now?

Jakarta. He started to fume. He wanted to throttle Sullivan. Why hadn't he resisted more? Okay, so he'd gotten some crumbs, a few extra details from that Turkish reporter's brother. Nothing earth-shattering; possibly significant. Nuray—the reporter—had mentioned certain bank accounts being connected to accounts in Romania that were tied to NATO military people. In particular, one account holder at a very high level within the Turkish military with ties to well-known mafia players in the heroin and gambling business. Internal bank transactions could back that up. What the NATO military people were doing with that laundered drug money was anybody's guess; Sullivan's son must have found out—and he wasn't around to tell anyone. So wasn't Sullivan, by sending him on those same leads, putting him directly into his son's own shoes? It would stand to reason; and Sullivan, too, went out of his way to get Elsie involved . . . and Elsie is *gone.* Ryan's rage turned to bile, and his blood went cold.

He pulled into Elkins and stopped at the first minimart. Immediately, he dialed Elsie's cell. Nothing. He dialed her home number and got her machine. He left a message anyway, to the effect that he was losing his mind.

So the bureau was out. Missing persons was out. Even speaking with the local sheriff would be ludicrous, of course. *Sir, my girlfriend didn't hook up with me in the cabin as promised . . .* What the hell could he report?

Another possibility occurred to him. Maybe she decided to contact Sullivan for help? The sense of her wishing to keep everything from Sullivan and his team was only now beginning to dawn on him, yet perhaps she figured out a way to use that connection to her advantage? There was one way to find out.

He called Tatiana's personal number, her cell phone. It was Saturday and almost 10 P.M. How else was he going to reach her?

Tatiana picked up on the third ring. "Ryan? You're back!"

Ryan didn't waste a moment. "Yeah—have you heard from Elsie? Do you know where she is?"

There followed a long, grim silence. "What do you mean *Elsie*? Why would I hear from Elsie after such an episode? Ryan, what's going on?"

Ryan gave her the condensed version, ending with *She is in danger.*

"Okay, let's calm down," she tried to reassure him. "Where are you now?"

"Fifteen miles from the cabin; Elkins, West Virginia. No cell reception there."

"Here is what I suggest you do: drive back to D.C. Right away. I'll call Sullivan and set up an emergency meeting first thing tomorrow morning. Let's say seven."

Ryan grunted. "We don't even have minutes, never mind tomorrow. That's nine hours from now. I can't just sit around waiting!"

"Yes, but you may be in danger as well. Think about it, if they are after her for sticking her nose where it doesn't belong, then they are certainly after *you*."

In fact Ryan had thought about it. Even more, that Sullivan himself, directly or indirectly, may have put them in harm's way. "Well then they better make their move," he barked, "because I'm ready for the bastards!" He instantly tried to quell his rage by closing his eyes and quieting, then added, much more calmly, "I'm armed. I'm trained. Let's not worry about me. Right now, we need to focus solely on her."

"Ryan . . . I understand. Did she take any documents with her? To the cabin?"

"Documents? Which ones?"

"I don't know. Maybe those related to the bureau's cover-up—"

"I don't know about any documents," he cut in. "She's not the kind who'd sneak out anything classified." This talk was going nowhere.

"Come to D.C., we'll have our meeting, put together resources, and go about finding her."

It all sounded pat. Ryan was quickly souring on this plan. "Fine," he said doubtfully. "See if you can set it up for earlier than seven." He hung up and forced himself to think even harder. The more he did, the less he could come up with.

* * * *

Tatiana began pacing. This was bad. She had not heard back from Sergei since the previous afternoon, when he took off after Elsie. This was an unexpected development. Wherever Elsie was, Sergei was either with her or right behind, watching over her. Unless they both were dead. Always a possibility.

She had to report this to her superiors right away. She didn't want to take chances. Any fuckup from here on in would be blamed on her. She dialed on her restricted cell. It was picked up on the first ring. She stated her code name and number and was put on hold, then transferred to her unit handler. She briefed him and asked for instructions. She was told to wait until after the meeting with Sullivan and Marcello. Maybe by then she'd hear back from Sergei, he told her.

After her briefing to FSB, Tatiana dialed Sullivan's personal secretary to arrange the 7 A.M. meeting. When that was done, she poured herself a double shot of high-end Russian vodka, knocked it back, and repeated. Her thoughts only swirled that much faster.

Something went wrong, she knew it.

* * * *

Sunday, November 2, 2003
Northern Virginia

At 6:15 A.M., Ryan left the twenty-four-hour diner. He had spent the last two hours here. He had gotten to D.C. around 3 A.M. He hadn't slept at all. He'd gone back to the cabin one more time and come up empty-handed. The woods felt haunted. He imagined Elsie alone there, how she must have felt when . . . when what? His imagination took off in a hundred scary directions at once. Any of them was a possibility. The more he thought, the more frightened he became. Out there alone in nowhereland, trying to evade professional killers whose only purpose is to find and erase you. And some of them had sick imaginations as well. Ryan wondered if his present torment might also be part of their psycho-sadist plan—whoever *they* may be; he needed sleep. The gallon of diner coffee had him wired, and right now he was being his own Torquemada.

The meeting was only eight blocks from the diner. He would be early.

Ryan didn't have to wait more than fifteen minutes. Tatiana was next to arrive. She looked frazzled. Without much makeup, her light skin and platinum dye, combined with too much vodka and an apparent lack of sleep, made her look beyond the grave. The lipstick was ghastly.

They talked in staccato sentences as they walked to the elevator.

"You look awful," Tatiana began. "Any news?"

"No, nothing. You?"

"Sullivan will be here by seven, latest. Did you check her house?"

"Yeah. Nothing."

"Maybe the FBI?" she suggested. "Considering the way they kicked her out."

"Not the way they operate. They don't abduct."

Tatiana slowed. "Maybe not abducting then."

Ryan looked at her askance.

"I mean detaining her for further questioning."

"She'd call her attorney and be out in less than an hour."

They rode the elevator up. Neither spoke.

Inside the conference room Ryan checked his watch. Ten to seven.

Sullivan soon arrived. He greeted the two and got right to business. They began with Tatiana's report.

She went over the string of events from the point of Elsie's dismissal. This included her friend Sami's coincidental death and her subsequent conversation with Ryan.

In his report, Ryan omitted the part with Keller's office when he'd talked with Tatiana the previous evening. He'd done so for several reasons: Sullivan had predicted Elsie going to Congress for disclosure, and Ryan didn't want to give him the satisfaction, not here, not now. Also, his gut feeling was to keep Keller and Sami's warning to himself. For now.

Sullivan glared at Ryan. "Why didn't you ask her to contact me?"

Ryan slammed his pen down on the table. "Who said I didn't? I did exactly that. You know how stubborn Elsie can be. She didn't want to hear it."

Sullivan still wasn't having any. "*You* could have let me know: as soon as you spoke with her. You didn't. I could have had her followed, for her own protection. That is, until you arrived."

Ryan kicked himself for not doing it. They wouldn't be sitting here now. "She held me to a promise; specifically, that you were not to know about the bureau's threats and retaliation."

Sullivan answered this sternly. "As an experienced agent, Marcello, you should know better. *Promise?* On account of pure stubbornness or some sentimental ploy, you went along with that?"

Ryan, clenching and unclenching his jaw muscles, replied through his teeth, "With all due respect, I don't need you to tell me what I should have done or why. I realize that now, and let's not waste time talking about *what ifs*. Instead, I would very much like us to concentrate on finding her." He was exhausted. His head was pounding. He was anxious—and he was angry: with himself, with Elsie, and with Sullivan for sending him on a fraught fool's errand to the other side of the world.

Sullivan turned to Tatiana. "Maybe I'll have a cup of tea. Cream, no sugar." Then back to Ryan. "Fair enough. And agreed."

Ryan continued. "The FBI option is out. They are involved. Or at least some high-level people are. The state police option is out. We don't have enough. They'll ask to wait forty-eight hours. We need to do this ourselves."

Sullivan brought his hands together, to signal he had come to a decision. "A team of PIs with solid connections and networks, round the clock. You understand that they'll need everything, every detail. That includes everything we do here. As a team."

"Good. I don't care if they find out more than what's needed." Ryan tapped his fingers nervously. "Right now I don't care about any of that."

"But I do." Tatiana brought Sullivan his teacup and placed it on the table before him. "Thank you Tati. How about you? Do you have any other suggestions? Thoughts?"

Tatiana looked at Ryan before she replied. "Not really. We know she got to Ryan's cabin. That rules out the FBI. Why would they wait for her to arrive? If others, however, know what she got, then . . . well . . . we may be looking at a hit operation." She tried to force Ryan's hand once again. "She may have taken out some documents, Ryan; documents that would be detrimental to certain powerful people or . . . *groups*. Did she take any documents?"

"I told you before, that's not Elsie. She wouldn't do that. I know her."

"What was the last thing she was researching, specifically?" Sullivan pointedly asked.

Ryan paused. "Yousef Mahmoud; Nazim, of course; and the missing FBI files—those pertaining to specific targets before 2001. She mentioned meetings and operations in Azerbaijan, Georgia, Turkey and Kyrgyzstan. She thought the answer could be buried within those files, during a certain period."

"And that's when things got ugly at the bureau," Tatiana concluded. "Right? They got ticked off. They thought they purged those files, and Elsie must have gotten hold of what they purged. Maybe we *are* looking at the bureau."

Ryan reflected. "Not necessarily. In Nazim's case, someone tipped off the State Department and the threats and pressure came from *them*—at which point we were called off by our own HQ. Considering what we found out about Nazim's agency plane *and* his diplomatic ties, it could well be the State Department together with CIA. It certainly wouldn't be the first time."

Tatiana had him where she wanted. Without Elsie, he was their best bet to get more.

Sullivan switched the topic abruptly. "What did you find in Jakarta?"

Ryan felt his rage boil over. Here he was being asked stupid questions again. "Listen," he began, as evenly as he could, "before

I answer any more of these questions, what about those promised PIs? When do you plan to call them? If it's true what she says"—he looked straight at Tatiana—"that somebody wants information, then we're talking about worse than a hit. Whoever it is could be pulling out her toenails one at a time this minute! Who knows, maybe even her eyes, and fingernails too. Crushing bones is always an option, to say nothing of water and electrocution. People are good at this. They enjoy it"—Ryan was getting worked up—"assuming she's even alive. Who knows what they're doing!"

Sullivan plainly could see his distress and made a calming motion, picking up the phone. A call was placed. That seemed to settle him down. "And now?" Sullivan asked Ryan.

Ryan delivered his Jakarta report, briefing them on Nuray's brother's leads involving Jason, and Nazim's suspected connection with his murder. "If what the brother says is correct, then it all boils down to your son," he concluded. "Did Jason share any of Nuray's information with anyone else?"

Tatiana jumped in. "I am sure we have pretty much exhausted all Russian angles. Definitely not a government operation; and based on what I have gotten, solid information, there are only two branches of the same mafia network in Cyprus: *both of them on the Greek side.* There have been no hit operations by them, on the northern side, since 1999."

Sullivan appeared satisfied. "I know the dismissiveness and cover-up all has come from our side, our own State Department. We keep coming back to this: Turkish government–connected players with ties to NATO and the CIA. Guys like Nazim. It's time to eliminate Russia completely. Time to look inward, into our own backyard."

Tatiana nodded. Apart from a hangover, she had another headache: whoever had Elsie had Sergei as well—that is, if either were still alive. Her bosses sent the requested fortification. They were on their way.

They better find Sergei, one way or the other, before the feds or others do, thought Tatiana. The last thing they needed was a publicized Russian operative fiasco in the middle of all this mayhem.

* * * *

Elsie felt tired but she couldn't sleep. Her body had been stuck in this odd sleeping pattern. She'd checked in to the motel the previous morning at almost eight o'clock. No sooner had she entered her room than she collapsed on the bed and passed out. She slept for eleven hours straight.

She had woken around seven to find both the room and outside her window pitch dark. After a quick shower and change she'd gone out in search of something to put into her body, appetite or no. Per reception's recommendation she'd driven less than two miles to eat at Yolanda's Dutch Cooking. After passing several tables occupied by families and couples, she was seated next to the window at a table for six, as if to magnify her lonely dining. The Hot Turkey Dinner included turkey breast, cornbread stuffing, potato pie, cranberry relish, Brussels sprouts cooked in bacon dripping, and an apple tart served with homemade whipped cream. Definitely not her usual kind of food; but this was Amish country.

As she cut her turkey into bite-size pieces she thought about Ben and the last Thanksgiving they shared; just the two of them, and Simba. Then she remembered the semiserious pledge that she and Sami recently made: spending Thanksgiving with pizza, good cheap wine and watching back-to-back episodes of a TV cop series. They would take turns picking the show. Now she was crying, over her plate, in the middle of a nearly full restaurant. She didn't look up but she knew there were many pairs of eyes on her. Elsie hoped for the restaurant's sake this wouldn't reflect poorly on the Hot Turkey Dinner. She quickly paid her bill and left without bothering to order dessert.

She returned to her claustrophobic room. No radio or TV in the Amish motel, so she read in bed—until six in the morning. Having spent the entire day in hibernationlike sleep, her body refused to go back to it. Now, just as the sun came up, she was feeling tired and sleepy. Where was Greg?

As if on a cue, she heard the knock. "Yes? Who is it?"

"Your companion for the next three weeks, madam."

She felt a shiver. *Three weeks.* She unlocked and unchained the door.

"May I come in?"

Funny, she thought, *his asking my permission.* She stepped aside and held the door wide, bidding him enter. He had with him a small Coach carry-on. Placing the bag on the bed, he unzipped and flipped the top.

"Time to change and put on some makeup. We need to be out of here in thirty minutes."

Elsie peeked into the contents of the bag: neatly folded clothes still in wrapping paper, a shoebox with the brand Jimmy Choo in red script, and a smaller paper bag filled with brand-name makeup products.

"I got a quality hairpiece as well. Wear it temporarily, until the new cut and color. Also, a chic pair of glasses. They go a long way in changing your face."

Elsie did not respond. She closed the bag and carried it to the bathroom. She shut the door and began to undress.

Greg walked over and called through the door, "Did you get enough sleep?"

"Yes."

Good, he thought. "Have you eaten today?"

Elsie stepped into a tight gray pencil skirt with a slit running to her upper thighs. "No."

"We'll stop on the way and have you eat. Of course, we will get you coffee. Espresso. Many shots of espresso. We don't want you going through withdrawal. Too risky."

Elsie buttoned her silk white blouse. Was the psycho making fun of her? He made love of coffee sound like a heroin addiction. "Right."

She stepped into the black four-inch stiletto heels. *Whore or femme fatale?* She shrugged. Time for hair and makeup. She began by brushing her teeth and washing her face. She finished with several pumps of perfume included in the kit. This man didn't miss a thing.

She checked herself in the mirror, under too-bright fluorescent light. *Pretty good, indeed.* Using the black liner, she had turned her eyes into cat eyes. Her wig was indeed top quality: a light honey brown long bob with lighter honey streaks that framed her chin with an angled curve. Her trendy frames were burgundy lacquered wood that matched her dark burgundy lipstick. Elsie Simon almost never wore dark lipstick. Another point for the man.

She stepped out of the bathroom and walked past Greg, who was standing in the middle of the room. She could feel his eyes on her. When she turned around to face him she saw something bordering approval. They locked eyes. She was unsure of the color of his: they went from milky light to steely gray blue, depending on his state of mind. They were a clue to his nature. His eyes. Cold, with something else behind them. Hatred? No . . . an insane drive? Perhaps.

They drove to Baltimore in complete silence.

After the exit, Greg took the ramp and headed toward Baltimore's Inner Harbor.

"We are going to have lunch. You need to eat and get caffeinated. I got you the best espresso machine on the market, grinder, whole beans. It's already in the kitchen."

Elsie rolled her eyes. *A big part of the pleasure comes from the coffeehouse itself, the baristas, and the scent of freshly roasted and ground coffee beans. The atmosphere. He wouldn't know. For the one-track mission-oriented types, atmosphere never counts. They are way too busy—*

Before she was able to complete that thought, he pulled into the Ritz Carlton driveway.

"They have a pretty decent restaurant and menu. Relatively healthy . . . nice ambiance and good service."

Ambiance? Well, what do you know.

They stopped in front of the entrance and two bellhops approached each side of the car in a synchronized move.

They were seated immediately, at a corner table next to the window, per Greg's request. Not a word passed between them and when the food arrived, they ate in silence. He paid the bill and left a generous tip. Out front, the car was already waiting.

Back on the road, another hour passed without conversation. They crossed Key Bridge and headed toward K Street. A few minutes later, Greg pulled into the Watergate complex. Elsie looked up in shock.

"Are you completely insane? Is this supposed to be symbolic or something?"

"The best apartment unit I could find for my operation; the best strategic location by far. Safe. And the penthouse is fairly large with decent views . . . by D.C. standards, that is."

Everything in the apartment was white and steel: shiny white marble and granite floors with light gray veining, white leather furniture, stainless steel counters, and curtainless windows letting in bright unfiltered light. All utterly cold and sterile.

Elsie had one word for it. "Soulless." Then added, "A perfect place for you."

CHAPTER 12

Tuesday Morning, November 4, 2003
Washington, D.C.

Elsie had been awake since 5 A.M. She tried to go back to sleep but gave up. It was now 5:45; might as well start the day.

She tiptoed out of her bedroom toward the kitchen downstairs. She noticed movement inside the exercise room and stopped. The door was ajar. Greg was on the floor, moving his entire body up and down smoothly and rhythmically. He was doing pushups; and he was completely naked.

Elsie froze. She couldn't take her eyes away. Ordinarily, the scene would have been gross and repulsive; yet this man was anything but ordinary. She was mesmerized. No huffing, no puffing, no grunts. She could barely hear him breathe. His body shimmered in the cold morning light, yet with no trace of sweat. It was strange and somewhat erotic.

She shook it off and continued on toward the kitchen. *Nineteen nights to go—or less.* Yes, she was counting. While not as miserable as she might have expected, she was sharing her life with a murderer. They were under one roof, and he had put her in the middle of his black operations: *necessary murders*, he called them.

She poured the freshly brewed coffee into a tall mug, added a shot of espresso and some sugar, and took it into the makeshift workspace, the dining room where Greg had three laptops set up. They were connected to the Internet in a way that couldn't be traced: something about bouncing from server to server to yet another place. She was not technology savvy that way; but she was glad to have her Internet back and be able to conduct her own research. She also helped Greg with his surveillance ops, monitoring certain lines when needed—not so much by force as by polite demand. Thus employing her skills made her feel less like a hostage; yet the man was hell-bent, and helping him at all upset her. Still, a deal was a deal. If not for her bargaining tactics, Ryan and many others by now would be dead. That was something to be grateful for.

She brought up her Word document on the dots: those various facts and points from her work at the bureau that connected to Gladio Operation B. She checked and double-checked those dots; then put them next to her search results on significant events from that part of the world and tried to establish connections. Or possible connections. Last night, for example, before going to bed she had put together the dates and places for Meltem Drake's trips—those she knew of—and then searched for significant developments and news in those areas. In October, a major terrorist attack took place in Georgia that targeted a police station in a city near the border: seven deaths resulted, five of them police officers. The attack, of course, was blamed on one of the historically moderate Chechen groups in Grozny known for its cooperation with the Russian government.

She hadn't noticed Greg enter the room. He'd been watching her stare at her screen.

"Morning. It's a bit early today." She jumped at his voice. "I'm sorry. Didn't mean to startle you."

She turned back to her monitor. "The conversation we had yesterday, about Gladio having two or three foot soldiers in the FBI? I believe I have one possible suspect. I'm not a hundred percent certain, but everything about her seems to add up."

"*Her.* Female," he called from the kitchen.

Greg returned with his steamy mug of malted milk. "Who is she?"

Elsie gave him a thumbnail sketch, complete with physical description.

"Anything else?"

Elsie returned to her monitor. "I've been trying to match her trips with significant events in areas that fit the general timeline. I have one in Georgia, October this year; a possible one in Baku, September; and others. I can't go beyond late 2001, since she wasn't with the bureau back then. If I had access to the DIA roster, I'd be checking her log against summer 2001."

"Why summer?"

"That massive terror attack in Moscow. The government day care center. I checked archived news: the Chechen woman suicide bomber made a couple of trips to Azerbaijan, Baku—*our* territory, even back then, correct? Meltem may have had her hand in that one as well. My hunch."

"No," he stated flatly. "That was mine."

Elsie almost jumped out of her chair. "The *day care suicide bombing?* With over sixty children, babies dead? What do you mean that one was yours?"

"That was my operation. I executed it."

Elsie's heart went cold. She felt her whole upper body being squeezed—by a monster's hand. She tried to speak but nothing came out.

"The company calls it *collateral damage,*" he calmly tried to explain.

Elsie gave him a look of horror and ran from the room, slamming her bedroom door.

Greg called to her through the barricade. "There's a range of meaning . . . and application . . . it isn't cut and dried."

Silence ensued. No sounds from her side of the door.

Greg didn't walk away. He remained in thought, considering exactly what he needed to say. She was in shock, and there was the matter of timing. Their operation had begun; he had a schedule to keep. Nothing could be accomplished this way.

"Earlier, Elsie, we spoke of purpose, of touching and taking life. You accused me of murder, specifically, of innocents. I objected then as I object to it now. It isn't right, this attitude of good versus bad; of white hats and black hats, of governments and victims. Are you religious, Elsie? Do you believe in a living, loving God? Because if you do, then you must know by now that all this pain and suffering and death is part of life, that a loving God created, the ultimate purpose of which is unknowable—and therefore cannot be judged. A plan must serve some purpose, correct? That in spite of what can never be known we have to maintain faith in that plan, not only as a group but as individuals striving, each in her and his own ways? Don't myriad religions and collective wisdom teach us that faith means courage? Do you believe that, Elsie?"

Elsie couldn't contain herself. She shouted through the door, "You are despicable! And twisted! You compare yourself with *God*? What kind of sick person are you?"

"No, Elsie, that's *not at all* what I'm saying . . ." He paused, weighing his next words carefully lest reality diverge and set him on a different course. "As I've tried and apparently failed to make clear, I did not select that target. I had nothing to do with the selection process. I implemented a plan that would have been executed no matter what. My belief and actions are incidental. I chose to be used, I own that; now I choose life, however it may or may not be possible. We may not survive. You must understand. Death goes on."

Elsie was shaking, vehement. "You are a criminal. You think your beliefs exonerate you? You choose life, so others have to die!"

Greg thought. This was pointless. It was turning in circles. He had no wish to argue further. "I have a meeting to attend," he told her through the door, "the one you helped me set up . . ." he listened for any kind of sound; there was nothing. "I . . . I'll see you later."

Elsie sat on the lounge chair next to the window, staring hollowly out at the river. She thought of her father and of what he had shown her at the field hospital, when she was still only a girl: the melted faces and sheared torsos, charred bits and blackened parts; *collateral damage*, he called it . . .

* * * *

Ryan paced as though he were caged. Where was Sullivan? Why was he so cryptic in his message? He had been asked—no, *ordered*—to the conference room at 9:30 A.M. sharp regarding Elsie. That was it; nothing more. Had he gotten some news? Was she still alive? If so, how could he know? Ryan himself was in charge of the PI team, and so far they had zilch.

Tatiana was not here either. Where the hell was she? This wasn't her style. He had called her twice and left messages both times. Why hadn't he yet heard back?

He slowed down his pacing just long enough to go get coffee. As he was heading back in, he ran into Sullivan.

"Ryan! Where is Tati?"

"Who knows? What's this about? Where's Elsie?"

Sullivan pulled a chair but didn't sit. "Elsie called me yesterday. Around five-thirty."

Ryan was dumbfounded. "Called *you*?" He was confused; why would she call him first, the man she so despised? "Where is she? She's all right? What did she say? I need—"

Sullivan put up his hand. "Ryan, take a seat. One question at a time."

Reluctantly, he sat. "All right. Tell me."

"She sounded all right. She didn't tell me where she was."

"Why not? Did you trace the call?"

"That was the first thing I did. The call came from a phone in Copenhagen."

"Copenhagen? As in Denmark?"

"Yes, indeed. She didn't say much. Only that she wanted to arrange a meeting between us and a man who would be representing her. Today. This morning. Less than thirty minutes from now."

"What? . . . Who?"

"She didn't give specifics. Just a first name: Gregory."

Ryan tried to process this but none of it made sense. "Are you sure it was Elsie?"

"Yes. I asked her for her team code and she aced it."

As a safeguard, every member of Sullivan's team had been assigned a four-digit number, a code. Since Elsie had refused to commit full time, they had given her the code name *Asterisk* as a kind of joke.

"Someone could have made her give up the code, easily."

"If that were true, she could have sent us a message somehow; a red flag. This was definitely Elsie, I could tell from her tone; an imposter wouldn't think to feign loathing."

Ryan smiled. It was true. "But why Denmark?"

"I'm sure we'll find out. Very soon. Which reminds me, a request she made . . ." Sullivan paused. "You're not going to like it."

Ryan narrowed his eyes.

"She asked me to have you hand me your gun. A precaution, I'm guessing, having witnessed your temper."

"You want us to meet with some prick named Gregory—no doubt a hit man—and do so unarmed? Have you lost your mind?"

"No. I haven't. Her instructions were explicit: he is to be trusted and given information and our cooperation. I'm going to take her word for it, Ryan. Now hand me your gun, or I'll have to exclude you from the meeting."

Ryan was tempted, but this well could be their only chance. *Bottle it*, he told himself. This Gregory was their only lead. Begrudgingly, he took his gun from its ankle holster, slid it across the table then sat back and crossed his arms.

The man who called himself Gregory entered the office precisely at ten. He was dressed in utility coveralls and was armed, Ryan could tell. He was tall, muscular, slim; very fit. He looked Russian or maybe Eastern European. He knocked on the open conference door twice, entered then closed the door. "Good morning, gentlemen."

He walked up to the table. "Shall we begin our brief meeting?"

Sullivan asked, "And you are?"

"Gregory."

"Gregory. No surname?"

"Not for our purpose here."

"*Gregory*," Sullivan continued, "we have one more we're waiting for; she should be here any minute."

"Ah. That must be Ms. Tatiana Schuliskova. She won't be joining us today. Or any other."

"What the fuck is that supposed to mean?"

"You must be Ryan." Greg looked him in the eye. "She decided to practice diving inside her tub. She never came back up."

Ryan moved forward but Sullivan stopped him.

"Please, Agent Marcello," Greg spoke coolly. "Before you place me under arrest, her name was not Tatiana Schuliskova. Her real name was Nadia Bychkov. She was an active agent with FSB—the Federal Security Service of the Russian Federation. You two were her mission—"

"Bullshit," Ryan interjected. "Expect us to believe—"

"Quiet, Ryan," Sullivan cut him short. "Gregory, I assume you will provide us with evidence. Correct?"

"Of course, that won't be a problem. Her handler, the man to whom she reported, is Luka Belinsky, in New York City. He operates behind a front financial company called LBC International." He turned to Ryan. "Elsie is safe. I am the only one who can keep her safe. She is very well aware of this."

"I don't believe you. Where is she?" Ryan wished he'd kept his gun; this guy was big, but he knew a thing or two about disarming fierce opponents.

Greg turned back to Sullivan. "I am here to ask you to stop, to cease, this operation of yours. You won't get anywhere with it, as evident by the noticeable lack of results."

Ryan was about to respond when Sullivan jumped in. "So—you want me to stop investigating the murder of my son?"

"Yes. I want you to stop right away. You are way over your head with this."

"And what makes you the expert?" Ryan sneered.

Greg kept his eyes on Sullivan. "I'm here to offer you a deal. You shut down this operation, and I will get you the responsible party or parties within thirty days. You give me thirty days, and I'll give you what and who you want."

"What sort of guarantee or referrals can you offer, that is, apart from your word?"

"What sort of guarantees have you had thus far? You've been duped by a Russian spy. You've hired a hotheaded FBI maverick with no apparent skills but steam; and you're nowhere near the answer you've been seeking, am I right? Throwing money around; gambling with make-believe ops. Do you really want to stick with this?"

"And you, one man, can find and deliver the answers?"

"I can do you one better. I will find the answers, apprehend the culprits and serve them on a platter. I'll give you a menu of options: electrocute and burn them slowly while they beg for your pardon? Water-board them while they beg for your mercy? Execute them as they did your son, down to the smallest detail? I can give you that and more. In thirty days or less."

Sullivan had been holding his breath. The imagery. The idea. Picturing his son's murderers being tortured and begging for his mercy. All that had given him energy, a yearning, even a slight erection. Yes. He wanted them to pay. For his son and only grandchild.

Ryan could see Sullivan falling for the bait. He had to do something. He had to intervene. "Mister Sullivan, we don't even know who this asshole really is. Don't listen to him; he's kidnapped Elsie."

Sullivan seemed as if in a trance. "This has nothing to do with you, Ryan. This is between me and him. We're only talking about thirty days. Let's consider this a pause. We can always start from where we left off. Isn't that right, Gregory?"

Greg assured him it was. "In the meantime, you back off, and keep Marcello out of my way."

Sullivan closed his eyes and pictured his son, their last gathering . . . he gave the go-ahead to Greg. "Tell me what it is you want. Don't leave anything out."

Greg sat. "Cease all your activities and operations as of now. Make sure you have this boy on a leash for the next thirty days. One more thing . . ."

Sullivan was waiting. "A last-minute condition! Very shrewd. What is it?"

"Shut down your plant in Russia and move your companies out. You leave your Russian employees with nothing. Nothing at all."

Dismayed, Sullivan reflected on this request. "Why would I do that?"

"Because I'm telling you to. Because I hate Russians—and one of my mottos has always been *fuck them every chance you get.*"

"Sullivan!" Ryan squawked. "This man is insane! A psychopath! Don't you see?"

Sullivan ignored him. "We all have our motives. Mister Gregory,

I accept your demand."

Ryan sprang to his feet and ran out. He had her. The psycho had Elsie.

Gregory shook the old man's hand. This was indeed a deal. "I gather you took away his gun?"

"Give him time. He'll calm down. You *will* take good care of Elsie, I assume? And when our business is done—"

"I promise she'll be safe. She's not happy, but she's doing fine." Sullivan seemed satisfied with that answer.

* * * *

Greg knew he was being tailed by Ryan. The hothead FBI was a novice. Having anticipated this move, he would have a little fun.

He pulled out Tatiana's cell and pressed four, which autodialed Ryan's number.

Ryan, two cars behind, picked up, distracted and astonished at once. "Tati?"

"Ever seen *The Godfather*?" a voice crackled through the phone. "Just a *heads up*, so you know I'm not *horsing around*." Then the line went dead.

Ryan immediately thought of Elsie. Slowing his car, he pulled off at the very next exit. He would have to find another way. Pursuing Greg was no longer an option.

* * * *

Elsie was waiting on the L-shaped white suede sofa when finally he arrived. She had gotten his package—the one waiting for her on the floor in front of her bedroom door. The DVD with a handwritten note attached: *What would you consider justice in this case?* She had watched, with horror, the entire episode of Keller, the pimp, the little girls—and last but not least, the CIA. What kind of world was this? What kind of people were these? Considering the entities involved, how could one hope to pursue or find justice? Where would one start—with the CIA? What laws do they follow or pretend to abide by? How about the sick elected politicians, or the aiding and abetting upper-level FBI? She once believed in the power of reform—changing the system from within—until now. Today had been a watershed. Almost all her beliefs had been smashed. Almost.

Greg turned on the light and lowered the dimmer. She hadn't realized she'd been sitting in the dark.

"Will you be joining me for dinner?"

Elsie met his strange eyes. "I'm not a squirrel. I don't eat nuts for my regular meals."

"Elsie. Right now you are part of the plan. *Our* plan. As in *together.* So as part of our plan, I suggest that together we dine. Your choice. Tonight, the city is your oyster."

"I don't eat oyster." Elsie thought hard. One way or another, she had to make her peace. Arguing only made things worse. Her temper in this case was a liability: she knew that emotional balance was the key. When she lost it, she lost his respect—and without his respect, she didn't stand a chance. Besides, she could do with a decent meal. "How about this? We go Japanese. You'll get to eat your half-cooked fish."

"I'll wait here and check my lines while you get ready."

"No real activity on any line." She paused and thought *Not now.* She got off the sofa and headed into the bedroom. "I'll be ready in fifteen minutes. We need a reservation. The place is called Chef Makoto."

They didn't speak much during the drive; Elsie was burning to know about Ryan but decided instead to soft-pedal it. When finally she made an oblique inquiry, Greg answered it abruptly.

"Hotheaded and irrational."

That put an end to that.

As per usual, they had gone through the entire dinner without a word. She was getting used to this; it made being with him that much more bearable. She could pretend he wasn't there, yet she didn't. She watched him consume his lightly seared yellowtail, steamed edamame without any salt, and, of course, the ubiquitous mineral water.

Waiting for dessert, Elsie broke the silence. "Have you gotten more on the *planned attack*?" The last two words were barely breathed.

"Not much. After the Watterson-Rodman project, I will be focusing on that."

Elsie shuddered. The way he used *project*. She shoved it from her mind. "You know when it's supposed to take place?"

"Not for another two weeks. In less than three." He changed the subject. "Are you ready for your small operation?"

Elsie put down her sake. "What operation?"

"You are going into your old office to take out those documents. The transcripts."

Elsie was shocked. "*You* were the one who said it was doable!" Several diners looked over. Elsie immediately lowered her tone. "That *you* were going to do it. I have a pretty good memory, Greg."

"I could. But with everything else on my plate right now, I want you to execute that one."

"Like how? They took away my access."

"I'll get you an access card. All you have to do is walk in there, take the papers, put them in your nice designer handbag and walk out. The building operates twenty-four seven. After six, most people will be gone. Even those who work longer shifts take their dinner break around that time. On top of that, you look different."

He sounded damn well serious. She too believed the documents were important: to make copies of and send to several papers—and if the lapdogs didn't have the balls to print, she would post them on the Internet and let everyone know what they needed to know. It used to be called the public's *right* to know—before whistleblowers were sent to jail. The prospect of executing this right excited her. "When?"

"Tomorrow evening, around six-thirty."

Elsie's voice went up a notch. "That's not enough time!"—the diners' heads turned—"It's less than twenty-four hours from now," she whispered.

"What more planning do you need? Unless you're afraid . . ."

That's it; he was playing the *daring* card. "A getaway car? Just in case."

"You won't need it. Act the way you're supposed to act. No one will notice. This isn't the CIA."

Elsie took the dig. Besides, she had no more allegiance to the bureau. "All right, I'll do it. Just so you know, I plan to keep copies for myself. I have my own uses."

"Fine, as long as you're well out of this country. You will not interfere with anything I do. Understood?"

"Understood."

* * * *

Ryan couldn't get horse heads out of his mind. Yet he couldn't just sit on his hands. Right now he was sitting inside his car, in front of Tatiana's townhouse. The entire area was cordoned off by yellow tape. There was no activity in and around the house. He guessed they were all finished by now, the detectives, pathologist, and forensics.

He needed to think, to come up with a plan. He wasn't even sure why he was here. To look for some clue as to Elsie's whereabouts? The psycho had her; and the psycho had been here. He wasn't buying Denmark. So what was he going to do?

They had his badge. He was no longer an agent. There were no more operations as a team. Sullivan had called him twice to let him know that he had a job: as chief of security for his Fairfax HQ, and that he didn't need to worry about salary or benefits. His family would be well provided for. How reassuring! It felt like a cosmic joke.

Then he had a thought. She called *Sullivan*, not him; his feelings were too hurt to have thought that through: there must've been a reason, something she had planned. Then this Gregory shows up, and calls them off. What was she up to? Already, she had managed to signal she was safe—assuming that the psycho could be taken at his word. For some reason, Ryan believed him. Elsie had, after all, placed the call; and according to Sullivan, she sounded okay. Not desperate or frightened, as if some ransom had to be paid. There *was no ransom*. So where does that leave them? And what's with the thirty days?

He focused on Gregory. Clearly, a hit man; but he wasn't with a mob. No way could he be with the Russians. Was he some sort of mercenary, and if so, who would hire him, and for what? He could be CIA; or, Special Forces—black ops. What then would they want with Elsie? Did she threaten them somehow? He knew how they dealt with threats: elimination. That would have happened by now. So what was she doing with Gregory? None of it made sense.

He had to try harder. He forced himself to recall every detail about Elsie's last weeks with the bureau; her research and anything related to that. There was the business with the transcripts. The translator, Sema, had been threatened, intimidated and ultimately fired. What was her last name? He'd check. What importance did those documents have? What area of the world and what period did they cover? Elsie had mentioned pre-2001, and some connections to, and joint operations with, top al-Hazar figures in Central Asia and the Caucasus. That is highly significant. How could the same killers who attacked this country be involved with the Pentagon and CIA in joint *ongoing* operations? It didn't figure. Yet, didn't this fit with everything they knew about Yousef Mahmoud? Why would the

U.S. government release this top terrorist from life without parole at a maximum-security prison to have him *run operations* for them? The two cases were connected: the business with the transcripts and Yousef Mahmoud—the former having very much to do with the latter.

He had to find Sema, to get her to talk. Okay. That was one course of action so far.

The next angle he had to focus on was Sami and Keller. Sami had gone to meet a Cambodian woman whose boyfriend was missing; missing where, in Southeast Asia? He needed to find out. Now for Donald Keller: the missing boyfriend had collected some dirt; and Elsie, as luck would have it, had picked Keller's office, of all places, to go and blow the whistle on the bureau and the transcripts. How did these two cases connect?

Let's say Keller was being blackmailed. The missing boyfriend had the goods. Assuming he is the blackmailer, how then does he connect to Sami—and from that connection, to Elsie? Again, it didn't make sense.

What would he do with the Keller angle? He could go to the man's office and pose as an investigator; but what would he find out that hadn't already been disclosed to him by Elsie? He had another thought: What if Keller had reported Elsie to the FBI, CIA or Pentagon? That happened all the time. The faithful government employee brings evidence of wrongdoing or neglect and incompetence to the responsible authorities, only to be intimidated, harassed and retaliated against. Elsie was already fired and her clearance revoked; even if this were CIA, what would be gained by abducting her? He felt like a dog chasing its tail.

There had to be more to the Keller angle; and he needed to find a way to talk with Sema without interested parties finding out.

* * * *

Wednesday, November 5, 2003
Washington, D.C.

In less than two hours, she had to be out of the apartment and on her way to the Washington Field Office. It was 3:30 P.M. now. Greg still hadn't given her the access card. His comings and goings were unannounced, and Elsie knew better than to ask where he'd be; the civilized part of her didn't want to know, and his forthright replies left her brutalized. He'd tell her, all right; after all, they were a team. She felt sure she was a criminal by now.

She checked the laptops: not much activity. Emboldened by her newfound sense of shame, she decided to go check out Greg's office. She would snoop. He hadn't warned her off anything, and kept all the doors and cabinets open. It was practically an invitation.

On his office desk were three other laptops, only one of them running. She moved the mouse and clicked for documents. Three files appeared: TXS-IS, LP-Cars and BNK-Malta. She clicked on the first. The entire document, nine pages total, was encrypted with some kind of code. Not her field. She clicked on the second: license plate numbers. She knew that he kept six cars. Four were downstairs in the parking garage, and two in undisclosed locations. He would switch out the cars every three or four days, along with the license plates. Not a secret. He'd told her all about it. The third file was encrypted as well.

She scanned the steel desk. A cell phone caught her eye. She picked it up and pressed the Contacts button. It was Tatiana's cell. She dropped it as though it contained a virus. *Just like a serial killer,* she thought. *This guy collects trophies; who's next?* She touched her wedding ring; she still hadn't taken it off.

Then she spied the drawers. Opening the first, she counted four digital tape recorders. She picked one up, turned it over and hit Play. Tatiana's voice filled the room.

"Who are you? Get out of here! I'm calling the police . . ."

Then Greg's voice, smooth and chilling. *"Good evening, Tatiana Schuliskova—or is it? Let's start over: Good evening, Nadia Bychkov, FSB 7844. That's better, no?"*

"What the fuck do you want?"

The answer came in Russian. Elsie didn't speak it. She fast-forwarded then clicked Stop and then Play: more Russian, this time, Nadia screaming in between Russian words.

Elsie couldn't stand it, the horrific sound of muffled screams and pitiful, painful begging, of Greg's calm cold voice interrupting her screams with questions, her cries and more terrifying screams . . . then water, filling up a sink or a tub . . .

She hit Stop and threw the recorder back in the drawer. She ran out of the office into her bedroom, holding her mouth. She barely made it to the toilet.

Yes, they had a deal—and yes, she had made a deal with a devil—one who wasn't holding her captive. She could walk out at any time. Then why didn't she? What was keeping her bound to this murderer? Her word? A sense of pride? What was it? She threw up more. Disgusted, she stripped and jumped in the shower. She had to try to rinse off the cries of the dead. She stood under the scalding hot water for a very long time, until her chest and arms were bright red. There was nothing left to do but to carry out her plan. The monster would be coming back soon.

She checked one more time in the mirror. She'd made an extra effort to not look like herself and she had succeeded: more than the wig and professional disguise, it was her expression. Her face had hardened. She didn't like it. Not a bit. The person looking back had different eyes. They were drinking her in and measuring the worth of everything she'd ever believed in. *Is this you now?* they seemed to be asking. They gave her no corner. The answer was yes—a yes with no compassion. She searched her face for any kindness toward herself and felt none, pierced instead by her own cruel eyes.

It was 5:45 P.M. Time to head out, to her old stomping ground. Had the devil returned? She needed the access card. She looked through the apartment and was about to check his bedroom when a small white square on the table caught her eye. Her name was written on the envelope. Attached was a blue Post-It note that read, *You will not only succeed but do good. You must. Failing is not an option. Greg.*

The note succeeded only in making her more nervous. Was he doing this on purpose? Ramping up her anxiety for kicks?

She grabbed the envelope, marched into her room for her camel coat, dropped the unopened envelope into her handbag and headed out of the unit.

Per Greg's earlier instruction she took the Mazda, a dark forest green sedan. She parked in the prepaid lot three blocks from the building; again, according to plan.

Despite uncomfortable stiletto heels, she managed the three blocks with short, quick steps, making sure to stop before turning the corner to retrieve the card from her bag and have it ready in her pocket.

It was 6:20 P.M., past the evening rush, but still a good deal of activity in the building. Blending fluidly, she climbed up the steps and went in without pause, slipping off her coat. She calmly proceeded to security, placing her coat and handbag on the conveyor belt and going through the body scan. The same uniformed guard who'd earlier marched her out was waiting on the other side. Instead of averting her face, Elsie looked the man in the eye and nodded. He returned it with his A-plus smile. She knew what brazen confidence could do and felt an adrenaline rush.

After collecting her belongings and slipping into her coat, she took the elevator up to four. Now corridor left, to the language division's secondary entryway. She stopped and took out her access card. It fell to the floor as she tried to swipe it through. Her hands were badly shaking. She bent over and picked it up quickly, this time with a death grip on it. She swiped. *Come on, come on . . .* The green light began blinking, giving her less than five seconds to open and enter.

She walked smoothly and directly to the archive storage room and entered after swiping her card a second time. One of the Pakistani translators was there, less than six feet from her target cabinet. She didn't remember his name but they certainly had interacted more than once. He turned and looked. She smiled, moving purposefully toward the cabinet.

She opened the cabinet and pulled out the drawer with authority. She immediately located her stack. By some miracle, no one had noticed it crammed haphazardly between two completely unrelated files. Lacking its folder, the stack was jammed in with the top portion sticking up at least two inches. Elsie naturally eased it out, as though it were exactly where it should be.

Then, to act the part, Elsie pretended to review it, examining the file as she would any transcript. Expertly, she pushed the drawer back in and quietly closed the cabinet before turning around; then she headed toward the door. This was it. She told herself to breathe, calmly and deeply. *Almost done.*

She pressed the Down arrow and checked out her surroundings. No one else was waiting. As soon as the doors opened and she saw she was alone, she pressed Close, waited for the doors to shut, and tucked the transcripts neatly inside her bag. She took another steadying breath.

Ground floor. She walked toward the exit in carefully measured steps, the clicking of her heels calling too much attention. As she went for the door handle, a man's voice called out "Ma'am? Ma'am!"

Elsie froze, and her heart began racing. She turned. It was the security guard. She gave him a confused and quizzical look.

The guard smiled sheepishly. "You have a great evening, ma'am."

He was flirting with her. Elsie forced a broad smile, dipped her head coyly and opened the door. She glided out and practically skipped down the steps, taking strides as she walked the first block. She turned left before stopping; she needed more air. Her chest still felt squeezed and she was shaking all over.

Elsie made it to her car, jumped in, turned it on, and cranked up the heat to 82. She quickly pulled out and began toward home—which it certainly wasn't, but would have to do for now. As of that moment, it was the only place she had.

Inside the elevator she reached in her coat and took out the card to examine it. She hadn't really looked at the face until now. When she saw it, her blood ran cold. The person looking back was Meltem Drake.

She dragged herself into the dark apartment. No sign of him. Good. She needed some time. Was it really her or . . . had he taken it by . . . which most likely meant . . . no—she couldn't go there. They had discussed her, she had told him about Meltem Drake; she had given him information, on the likelihood of her Gladio . . . *Oh my God, what have I done?* Had he acted? She looked at the card in her hand. *This is hers.* Elsie collapsed into a chair. Now, there could be no doubt. This card was no forgery; but was she . . .? She'd told him—emphasized the fact—that she could not be one hundred percent certain about Meltem. Did it matter? Did he need one hundred percent proof? What if she had signed Drake's death warrant by mentioning her to Greg?

She heard the key. He was home. She had forgotten about the lights. He switched them on.

"You did good. Very good."

Elsie couldn't meet his eye. Instead, she stared down at the table. "The security card was Meltem Drake's. Was it her actual card, or—"

Greg cut her off. "You were right on, Elsie, one hundred percent correct. She was Gladio; a very low-level one. She and I had already met, in June 2001, in Baku. I knew her as Maryam OG one thirty-six. She was part of the team in the Moscow day care bombing."

Elsie's voice was barely audible. "Quick? Or did you torture her like the others . . . on tape for posterity, for your trophy?"

"Ah, I see. You've gone through my treasures. There's a method to that madness, and for every tape, a purpose. Let me ask you something. How would you feel if I were to tell you that we now have the date and exact location of the planned home front attack? If knowing that information, and using it strategically, could *perhaps* prevent a set-up war—with potentially twenty-five thousand victims or more, certain death I'm talking, not casualties—and *perhaps* save over a thousand lives here, in the United States, *then* would you consider torture evil? Tell me, Elsie. How would you solve for that?"

Elsie looked up. He was standing with a bag filled with takeout containers. She noticed now the scent of cumin and garlic; Middle Eastern food.

This was not an ethics classroom. Meltem Drake was dead; tortured, by his hand. She would ignore his question. What would be the point of a debate? Right now, preventing the home front attack was the only thing that mattered. "Where . . . and when? Did she tell you?"

"See, this is what I mean. You are as interested as I in obtaining that answer." He paused, to let that reality sink in. Reality very much mattered to him, not ambiguous grays of a sliding morality. Greg continued, "Yes. I have the date and location. Less than two weeks, and here, within this region."

"You already knew that. Did she tell you more? Or not?"

"She did, and I am not prepared at this moment to share the details with you. I can't take the chance. Not with your passion-driven view of right and wrong."

Elsie glared. "So . . . you are going to let it happen, right? You will let the deaths rain down since it fits your warped sense of mission—your *insane cause*. I'm not a bit surprised."

"If this is your tactic to garner further clues, it won't work. I will let you know, I will tell you, when the time is right. Not now, not a minute too soon." He disappeared into the kitchen. "I stopped on the way and picked up some food. It's for you. Enjoy. I hope you like it."

In a different situation, the gesture would make her smile and feel giddy. Now, here, all she felt was spooked. This man could get into her head. He had memorized her habits, her likes and dislikes, as though he could somehow read her mind. *He:* a being programmed to accomplish murderous objectives but who acts as if he were guided along a spiritual plane.

She hesitated, considering her options. Currently she had none, other than biding time; at least for now—until she could figure out a way. Then she picked up one of two glasses on the tray and reached for the bottle of wine in Greg's hand.

CHAPTER 13

Thursday Morning, November 6, 2003
Arlington, Virginia

Watterson and Linda Rodman were unconscious. They had received the injections and would remain subdued for fifteen minutes or so. By the time they were transferred to the hospital and the morgue—respectively—the concoction would bear zero trace.

He sat on the leather side chair and began to envision his perfectly crafted scenario.

Linda had been sending teasing and semiblackmailing e-mails to Watterson, including a couple of short video clips of their kinky sessions, pressuring him for another promotion. The police would have a field day with those—as would the media, thanks to all the usual leaks.

He had e-mailed both using their own accounts. Watterson received one from Linda telling him their sex session was off and that instead, she wanted to talk. Linda received one from Watterson requesting that she cancel the male hooker because they needed to have a serious talk.

Watterson arrived on schedule: their regular Thursday 6:30 A.M. Then they began to argue . . .

Greg had chosen the best location for their fight: the living room.

The argument quickly escalated. Watterson slapped the woman. She began hitting back and scratching his face.

Greg would use her hands to scratch Watterson's face and neck. Good. Forensics loves skin under nails: evidence of defensive wounds. He had other goodies as well, such as a plastic baggie full of top-grade cocaine. The police would find it in Watterson's pocket, and his blood test would show midlevel traces.

The woman became hysterical; call it temporary insanity. She ran to her bedroom and grabbed her gun from the drawer in the nightstand.

Greg always did his homework. He had Linda Rodman's routines down pat.

She came back into the living room and pointed the gun at Watterson, now standing between the living room and the hallway leading to the bedroom. He went for his gun—shoulder holster—and was shot once, near the groin, the moment he moved.

Greg would use his silencer on each of the weapons, and then fire three rounds without the silencer later, a moment before leaving the apartment. While neighbors called the police, he'd be in his car and back in his apartment by the time the police arrived.

After the shot, Watterson doubled over, bleeding profusely from his balls; with what little strength he had left, he shakily aimed and fired twice. Then Rodman went down.

Greg closed his eyes and pictured the blood spatter patterns, calculating location, height, and his targets' distance from each other. Forensics would be recreating the scene based on all this evidence. He had to be precise, and execute perfectly.

Watterson was to live: a living hell, that is. He would be charged with first-degree murder. To sweeten the deal, his charges would include possession and consumption of an illegal substance. The Man Without Testicles would be a source of endless mirth and entertainment in the prison for years to come. Considering the guaranteed media circus, he would not enjoy any special privileges courtesy of the CIA—an outfit known to bury its own alive.

He stared at Rodman's lifeless hands dangling on either side. Long fingernails painted a tacky shimmery purple. They were perfect. Perfect for what they had to do next: scratch the helpless, unconscious and immobile Watterson's face and neck.

He checked his watch: 7:25 A.M. All according to plan and it would continue that way. He'd be back in his apartment by 8:05. He got up and walked over to Linda Rodman's corpse.

* * * *

Ryan hit the side of his truck in frustration. His meeting with Ziad Kaddisi was over: a dead end in less than two minutes. Sema was gone, out of the country. After Elsie's warning call of likely FBI harassment, Ziad persuaded her to take their daughter Zara, go to Lebanon, and live with his parents for a while. It did not take much convincing. They did not wish to put their lives or that of their daughter through that kind of hell again.

Ryan asked him for Sema's number in Lebanon.

Ziad was adamant. "No way. Please leave her alone. Look what you have caused us. You have made our lives miserable."

"I'm extremely sorry for what they put you through but that wasn't me. I'm out of the bureau. Elsie is somewhere in hiding, on the run. As long as they keep this information secret, none of us has a chance to live freely, without constantly looking over our shoulders—as you and I are now, and Sema and Elsie, to say nothing of your daughter."

It sounded good, but not good enough. Ziad politely asked him to leave—and to leave him, his wife and his daughter alone.

Ryan slammed his fist into the truck once more. The pressure had been building nonstop for days, and stress was becoming intolerable. He knew that the rational part of his brain couldn't function with this level of rage. No thought could get through—and he needed to think. He needed to begin phase two of his plan.

Keller.

It had to lead to something; if it didn't, well . . . then there *was no* other plan.

* * * *

Elsie was already awake when she heard him get up and begin to make sounds in the kitchen. It couldn't have been later than 5 A.M. She sprung out of bed, hastily pulled on her pajama bottoms and a tank top, and appeared like some wild Medusa in the hallway, her puffed-out hair a wiry tangle.

He asked her if she was feeling all right. She wanted to know what he had in mind next. He asked her to wait until his return for an answer, adding only the cryptic clue *Keller*. So where was he headed?

His unsettling response: "To go get a bit of justice for Mai and your friend."

This was a first. He hadn't used *my woman*. Were they becoming that familiar? *Oh Christ . . .*

* * * *

Almost 8 A.M. He wasn't back yet.

Elsie was working her tensions out in the apartment's gym room, which Greg had retrofitted with a new punching bag especially for her. As she pummeled away, a new kind of question occurred to her: What the hell was she going to do if he failed to return after one of his sprees? The man was not invincible; no one is. Assume, therefore, he isn't coming back. So what does she do? She can't just sit.

She was throwing back-to-back punches, ignoring the pain

shooting up and down her arms and shoulders. She focused on her status: no passport or ID, no credit cards or bank withdrawals. No one, apart from Ryan, whom she could count on—and as she was ever being reminded, any contact from her would endanger him: *consider his status as a father* was the threat; and with Greg, a threat is a promise. Thus a fugitive on the run, without a solid new identity or any sort of income, she knew she had no chance of survival.

Elsie heard the entry door close, so she stopped and listened, her muscles tensed. What if this wasn't Greg? She stepped into the hallway. It was. He was back. At once, her whole body was flooded with relief. Then she scolded herself for allowing it. She switched to aggression. "We need to talk. Can we? Now?"

"Why? Is it urgent?"

"It is. If something happened to you on a mission, say, and you didn't return . . . we need a contingency for that. Currently, there is none. We have to talk about this now."

Greg was dismissive. "Nothing is going to happen to me, not any time soon, and not during this operation."

"Is that your response? You're invincible?"

"Yes, I am. *Currently*, I'm invincible."

Elsie's eyes turned black and he knew it. She was gathering for a storm.

"You are two weeks away from a new identity, a new life, in a new country," he continued, in a softer tone. "I will definitely remain invincible during this time."

Elsie felt she was being mocked. How does one deal with this kind of stubborn insanity? Her plight was real. He needed to address it—and this man could not be told what to do. Fireworks were useless; likewise, tears. She knew she had to play the patience game. "Greg," she began, "you are an intelligent, thinking man, so please consider what I have to say."

Greg turned cold. "I have considered it and the answer is the same. You will be provided what you need when the time is right. There isn't any contingency plan. There is only Plan B, which we both agreed on. There's no going back. You know that by now. Everything has been planned, down to every last tape—which, by the way, you're free to listen to. Here's a new one." He tossed the cassette to Elsie, who had no other recourse but to catch it.

"No thank you!" she cried, getting rid of the thing as soon as it touched her hand. *He defaults to brutal*, she thought. *It's how he gets his way. Maybe some clue to his mother?* She filed this for future use; it seemed to her a key. *Now change the subject before he sees you, this devil of a mind reader.* "When will you begin the Keller action?"

Greg took off his jacket. "Tonight, at six P.M. Eastern Standard, we'll be finalizing Keller. You, Elsie, will be with me on this one."

She shook her head several times. "No way. I made it absolutely cle—"

"Elsie, get ready to be surprised." He grinned. She had never seen him smile. "We are going to New York City. You need to be dressed and ready. We leave for the train station at one P.M. We'll be taking the Amtrak Express. Dress beautifully but warmly, and do wear the mink coat."

Elsie felt thrown off balance. What were they up to? What were his plans? Would Keller be in New York tonight? She was entirely confused. "I-I don't wear real fur," she sputtered. It was all she could manage to say. He wouldn't give out more, she knew; a question would only provoke him. "I-I'm not into skinning rare animals," she continued in that vein.

"Remember, you are *not* dressing as Elsie Simon," he cautioned, as though she'd forgotten her part. "From here on, that person no longer exists; at least when we're out there, among civilians. Remember that. Now go dress and put on that coat." He didn't wait for an answer, just walked away toward his office; no doubt to finish executing God knows what.

* * * *

Thursday, Early Evening, November 6, 2003
New York City

It was already dark at 5:45 P.M. The limousine pulled over and let them out at the corner of Seventh Avenue and Forty-fourth Street in Times Square. As they crossed the busy intersection, Greg stopped in the median to scan the giant billboards and four-storey digital screens. Elsie turned to face him.

"Are we playing tourist or what? I've been to this city dozens of times. What are we doing here?"

His eyes still roaming the rotating billboards, he announced, "We're waiting for six o'clock. Remain patient. Aren't you glad you're wearing mink? It's pretty cold this evening."

"You're asking? No, you ordered me to wear it, this horrific thing. If your objective is to keep me warm, why not go for an eight hundred fill down jacket from Patagonia?"

Greg considered this. "Because it wouldn't suit the venue. At six-fifteen we are heading to one of the top restaurants in the city for our six-thirty dinner reservation. You are going to fit in perfectly with the rest of the women there."

Elsie was struck by a crazy image, right out of a *Godfather* movie: Keller dining in that restaurant, and Greg with a machine gun, mowing people down. Then he would sit and order up a meal.

"Will Keller be there?"

"Of course not. That would ruin your appetite, no? We are going to have a pleasant dinner then head back to Penn Station for our eight-thirty train to D.C."

Elsie shifted her weight from one foot to the other. What was going on? Why were they here? What did any of this have to do with Keller? She was beginning to get cold. The wind was picking up.

What were they doing in the median strip? Oh hell, was he trying to—

Before she could finish that thought, Greg gave her arm a gentle squeeze. She followed his gaze to the center screen, the one that advertised blockbuster features—the one you couldn't miss if you were twenty blocks away. Then she saw it. A giant image of Keller, with breaking news in a giant crawl: *Congressman Donald Keller in Pedophilic Sex Episode Gone Wrong . . . Starring Congressman Donald Keller (United States Congress) . . . Maurice Perdue (South Asia's Top Child Trafficker) . . . Josh Thompson (CIA Operative, Cambodia) . . . Sander Milton (CIA Technical Analyst) . . . Lou Brian (Reporter, Global Sun) . . . Thirteen-Year-Old Vietnamese Girl (Victim) . . . and Eleven-Year-Old Vietnamese Girl (Victim) . . . Congressman Donald Keller in Pedophilic Sex Episode Gone Wrong . . . Starring Congressman Donald Keller (United States Congress) . . .*

A better-edited version of the real film began to play, with subtitles at the bottom of the screen.

Elsie could feel the adrenaline surge. "My God . . . Greg . . . This is . . . it's brilliant . . ."

"Right now, this same film is playing on over sixty screens around the country: boxing screens in Vegas, horse racing screens in Baltimore and Phoenix, high-traffic billboards in Chicago . . . it is everywhere, Elsie. Everywhere."

"How? How did you pull this off?"

"A couple of expert sources; a few insiders. I also had it sent to major networks, cable channels and newspapers in the UK and here, and high-traffic bloggers around the world." He placed his hand behind her back. "Shall we? I suspect you'd rather not see the rest. By tomorrow morning, both houses in Congress will be in absolute turmoil. Chaos will ensue, and panic in the ranks of the CIA. The effects will go on for a couple of weeks . . ."

The paged limousine pulled up right alongside them. Greg

opened and held the door. "Unless, that is, we hit them with something even more majestic. Time to go to Karuma."

The driver didn't even need the address.

* * * *

Ryan brought his cheap Chinese takeout into the living room and plunked it down on the coffee table before the TV. He clicked past the sports channels one by one until he landed on the live news channel, NCN: and there was Keller's picture. He turned up the volume and dropped on the sofa, reading the ever-present NCN crawl: . . . *House Whip Donald Keller caught naked with two prepubescent Vietnamese girls . . .*

The station went to a commercial break. Ryan clicked on other news channels: all were covering the story with the same piece of footage, running in a continuous loop. Some came with a parental warning for violence and nudity, though most did not.

He sat back and stared at the TV screen, watching the endless violent images over and over until his food got cold. What was he supposed to do now? Keller was his only hope, his last link to finding Elsie. He'd been planning to pay Keller a visit tomorrow and now look what was happening! Somebody somewhere was preempting his plans. He'd had two; now he had none.

Who else to pursue? What angle was left to explore? He thought of Sullivan. Could he persuade that man to lend a hand, in the form of resources? Not likely; the psycho had him all tied up.

He flashed on the meeting. The creep had dropped a name—supposedly Tatiana's FSB handler here in the States. What was the name? Luke . . . Lucas . . . no, *Luka* Belinsky. The handler's front was something international in New York. Clearly, the Russians had a stake in all this. Especially now, with their operative killed. Psycho had said he hated the Russians; he wondered how far to take him at his word. Did Russia have a hand? If yes, then could he possibly use them to find Elsie?

He snapped off the set and tried to think. His brain was no longer cooperating. He couldn't see himself going to Russian spies. Yet, he was desperate, in desperate straits—and despair was fast becoming his default. Not a useful place to be. He needed to be useful and for that he needed rest. He would think on this and forge a plan—no, make that a *possibility for hope*, for him, for Elsie—tomorrow.

CHAPTER 14

Thirteen seconds. Good."

Elsie looked pleased. She had done this six times, but Greg still wasn't satisfied.

"Now, go change into the clothes you'll be wearing. Everything, including the headscarf."

"What difference does that make? It's a loose tunic over a long loose skirt and flat shoes . . . oh, and a headscarf."

"It's about state of mind," he patiently explained. "Believe it or not, what you are wearing can influence how you perform. The differences may seem negligible, but even slight variations between a practice run and actual conditions can have a profound effect."

Elsie went to her bedroom to put on the clothes. During the last two days, since the trip to New York, she had been far less contrarian and obstinate—partly because she resigned to the fact that it was her only chance for survival. Also, strange as it sounded to her ears, he could be taken at his word; and that matters, when life is at stake.

Last night, around eleven o'clock, she had come knocking on

his bedroom door. She had questions she needed answers to. None of it could wait. If she were to do what he was asking of her now—this new operation, with hidden recorders—certain factors in his agenda had to be clear.

True to form, Greg didn't disappoint. He had promised her information when the timing was right, and that time had arrived. She was ready. What had changed? *He answered all my questions.* Elsie reflected on their talk.

She'd begun by explaining that she couldn't get to sleep with all that was swirling in her head. Amenable to listening, Greg kept her at the door and they remained this way, with a barrier between them. *As open as he's ever going to be,* Elsie thought, *naked, behind a closed door.*

Seizing the moment, she'd asked her first question. "How deep does it go, the 2001 attack? Exactly how deep? Do you know?"

He had hesitated before answering with a question. "Not sure what you mean . . . remember what I told you about pockets?"

"Yes, about compartmentalization; but I know you know more. You said Gladio, for example, has two or three operatives inside the bureau, never the director himself. We identified two: Assistant Deputy Marshall and Drake; yet what about *inside the agency?* How many, and how far up?"

She could hear him thinking; did he know? "I would guess . . . at least a dozen. A minimum of twelve OG operatives within the agency. Unlike the FBI, the CIA director is directly involved. I would say somewhere between OG ten and fifteen."

"How about the president? Does it go up that high?"

She'd heard something like a laugh. "No, it doesn't. Presidents don't *want* to know. They have a general idea but that's it. No details."

"The president doesn't know about 2001? That's impossible."

"I didn't say that, did I? Look . . . they do the same as they do with people like Keller. You can't be president without certain *qual-*

ifications: criminal background, sex maniac, mafia connections, you name it. Those ingredients are necessary for any viable presidential candidate. Without them, they haven't a chance in hell . . .”

“So we're talking CIA and the Pentagon; then why did you rank the CIA director in the OG teens?”

“You're making a false assumption: that the absolute top must exist inside the government. Not so. There are others *outside* the government, and *they* are the ones on top. They are the true power that controls the second tier: the government front system—because government is a front. The CIA too sets up front companies; it's strikingly similar. The real power—the Deep State, let's call it—is out and above the actual visible government.”

She'd heard of the shadow government, but never from a source like this. “Major companies? The military-industrial complex? Oil companies? Is that what you are talking about?”

“Some of those; but maybe some others, who serve those companies under what they call their *vision*. They see themselves as visionaries and consider themselves gods. They analyze and set the agendas. They have one foot in and one foot out, and appear to have every leader's ear. You know them. I believe they would be within the first ten OG ranking.”

She had been quiet, thinking *permanent war* and *infinite death*.

“You get the gist. This is what I meant by Gladio Gods, and what they consider collateral damage: a small price paid for their vision . . .”

She didn't need to ask any more questions.

She was ready.

* * * *

Greg's operation was far from complete.

Thanks to Meltem Drake, he had gotten what he needed to

locate Yousef Mahmoud. He would soon be on his way to Houston, Texas, where the company's main mullah training center was based. Yousef would be attending the conference this year, as both a participant and trainer-speaker.

The company had set up a massive nonprofit in Houston under the name of The Islamic-Western Tolerance & Outreach Program. It was a well-designed front organization. On the surface, the organization assembled programs, seminars, speeches and literature to bridge the gap and decrease tensions between the U.S. Muslim community and the rest of the population, including state and federal government. The organization consisted of a massive office complex in downtown Houston that included conference centers, a printing facility, and a charity division for fundraising. They also had a fairly large mosque outside of town in a mixed residential-commercial area, with a school offering courses to children and adults.

The true purpose of this company-owned center was to groom and train selected candidates as mullahs, Muslim preachers, who then were assigned to specific regions and nations such as Azerbaijan, Kyrgyzstan, Tajikistan and Xinjiang. Here they would recruit, indoctrinate, brainwash and train fanatic Islamists to be used in myriad terror operations designed and executed by the company whenever needed. Their failure rate was less than point two percent.

The organization had been established and was led by a high-profile Islamic figure from Turkey: Imam Fatih Gumus. Despite his age—he was now seventy-six—he had been one of the best-performing assets for the company. Greg guessed the Imam's ranking to be in the upper twenties OG. The Imam had a knack for assessing and selecting the best mullah candidates. He excelled in training and preparing these mullahs fully for their assignments.

Greg thought of Imam Farajullah in Baku: educated in England, selected by Gumus for graduate studies (at the center, of course), and on to a stellar career producing well-trained suicide bombers. Greg had firsthand knowledge of his work. No mishaps. The bombs all went off. Farajullah would be attending the conference as well.

Kickoff was two days from now, on Monday, November 10. The location: the school behind the mosque. This venue was much less conspicuous, considering the profiles of the attendees.

Yousef Mahmoud was Greg's primary target. His four-step plan was to first take out CIA Agent Harold "Harry" Johnson and then kidnap, interrogate, and kill Mahmoud. Yousef had many valuable beans to spill, and his recorded "enhanced" interrogation would finalize Greg's masterpiece. A select clip then will be watched by hundreds of millions of people worldwide. Like Keller, on a much grander scale: Greg's plan, his carefully culled compilation, would stop the company dead in its tracks; that is, at least until they built new ones. It was the best he could do to buy the world—and himself—a bit of peace, if only for a little while.

Elsie's role was minor. She was to pose as a server for one of the center's contract catering companies. Her mission was to install hidden recorders on strategically selected objects in the room, then after the conference, to collect all devices and vanish from the stage.

Today they practiced installing a microdevice on a platter of roast chicken and citrus fruits while looking elsewhere and talking. Next, she practiced entering a room without calling attention to herself; then placing a recording stick inside a planter in a way that would not be noticed. She had done fairly well. Greg was exacting. Her performance had to be perfect.

They were leaving for Houston tomorrow. He was taking the early morning flight out of Reagan National; Elsie, the afternoon flight. He had to be there ahead of time to notify the catering company about a server's illness and her trustworthy cousin's opportune availability. Then he had to make sure the server was down.

He had timed every move and detail. Barring any unexpected surprise or glitch, they would be finished and back by noon on Tuesday—four days before the company's home front attack. In less than ten days, they would be out of the country.

Elsie entered, clad in a modest yet moderate Muslim outfit: loose and flowing black skirt extending to her feet and covering her ankles; a burgundy-colored long-sleeve tunic buttoned all the way up; and a thick, burgundy-black striped silk headscarf that covered every single strand of her hair. She wore no makeup except for a quarter-size birthmark painted on her lower cheek; and no jewelry other than her silver watch.

"I'm ready. Let's go."

If only he had more time. He might have been able to teach this woman patience.

* * * *

Monday Morning, November 10, 2003
Houston, Texas

At 7:15 A.M. Elsie was helping unload one of two midsize vans. She carried warmers, trays on wheels, pastry boxes, containers full of plates . . . the Turkish caterer overlooking everything with an eagle eye.

She had shown up at Ottoman Kosher Catering Services at 6:30 A.M. sharp. The supervisor, a meaty middle-aged man, already knew about her replacing Aysha. Without wasting any time he had given her an overview of their work for the day, in Turkish: unload, set up, prepare and set the station for the ten o'clock break, clean up, set up lunch for the twelve o'clock break, clean up, take out trash, load everything into the van . . . and that was it. She would be paid in cash, $75.

After unloading, she helped three others, two Turkish women and an Egyptian man, with the cookie and pastry plates—all while scanning the food, beverage and serving trays for optimum placement for recording devices. Her instructions were to place two in the separate break area where buffet-style food would be served; and two in the target conference room where the meeting and discussions would take place.

According to Greg's meeting list, fifteen figures: Imam Gumus and his right-hand man, eight other Imams including Farajullah, Yousef Mahmoud, Turkey's Chicago and Houston consul generals, the assistant deputy director for the CIA's Central Asian-Caucasus division Harold Johnson, and Colonel George Sherman from NATO HQ. Greg had shown Elsie pictures of each attendee. He'd produced three unique renderings of Yousef's appearance: he was expected to have altered it since 2001.

One server brewed a large pot of coffee. It smelled delicious—but she had to resist. She'd already had one cup, and Greg was adamant about no more until the end of her shift. Instead, she focused on the task at hand. She wanted to check out the conference room, the most important area.

She approached one of the Turkish women and asked in her native tongue, "How far do we have to carry the trays?"

The server responded, "Not too far. And we don't have a large group today, only fifteen. We usually deal with hundreds, so this will be a piece of cake."

Well that didn't tell me much, Elsie thought. "I'll go take a look . . ."

"Sure!" said the woman, trying to be kind. "I've been here several times. Let me show you around."

Damn, she thought, *a guided tour. That means no opportunity to install anything.*

She followed the woman into a wide corridor with three classrooms on each side. School was not in session this week and those doors were locked. They reached an atriumlike area. At one end was the main entrance to the complex. At the opposite end, a set of doors led to a covered walking path to the mosque. Directly across was a large wooden double door wide open with a sign in front: CONFERENCE, FALL 2003. She'd found the conference area.

They proceeded into a large area to be used for the buffet and breaks. Here, another wide double door led to the conference room. The server began pointing. "The beverage table will be set up here: coffee, tea, soft drinks, and water." Then she pointed to the opposite wall. "We'll have the buffet table set up there. We'll use it for pastries: cookies for the break; then take those out and place the meals for lunch. Next to it, we'll place a stand for the napkins and plates and cutlery."

"Got it." Then she pointed to the other room. "How about the conference room?"

The woman seemed doubtful. "Some take their plates and beverages in there during the break, but most will be here in this room while they talk and eat. We always leave a couple of water pitchers and glasses on the side table there. We'll periodically check the conference room to take out dirty plates, cups, glasses, and trash."

Elsie walked quickly into the room. "Let me see. Oh, it's a big conference table. How many people, you said?" She was buying time to scan the field of operations. No planters or vases. A large plasma screen, a table, heavy chairs for twenty-four, and three telephone units with speakers on the table, for conference calls, she guessed. So where would she place her devices?

She committed the layout and every single object to memory before exiting that room. She had to think.

Elsie and the server returned to the kitchen area where she considered possibilities as she worked. At 8:15 A.M. she and the male server went back to the conference area to deliver the water pitchers and coffee and hot water urns. The attendees would be arriving at any time. Fiddling with one of the cords, she excused herself to go get another then returned to the conference room alone. She walked around the enormous table and stared at the large-screen TV. Could she place one there, near the panel? Not the button-shaped device; no way to attach it securely. What about one of the ballpoint pen recorders? Too risky; side placement in the narrow slits might adversely affect sound quality. A poor or compromised result would be useless.

Elsie was fast getting frustrated. She didn't have much time. With no planters, easy grooves, and no food service inside the chamber she wasn't left with much . . . except her brain and imagination.

Her eyes moved around, and this time they settled on three phone units: placed in a line in the middle of the table about two and a half feet apart. Would they be used during the meeting? She had no idea; but she had to take a chance. Dipping into her tunic pocket, she quickly retrieved the pen recorder and slid it under the center phone. It was out in plain sight—the perfect hiding place. What could be more natural than a pen next to a phone?

She heard someone enter—the Egyptian server—and without missing a beat she remained near the phone and said, "This thing keeps beeping . . . do you think they're trying to call us from the kitchen?" It was a dumb thing to say, but who said she had to act smart?

"No," he said dismissively. "They never do that. They have our cell numbers, and that's how they communicate whenever they need to reach us. I keep mine on at all times."

Elsie immediately changed focus, moving away from the phones. "Oh, okay. I placed the water pitchers there. Is that good?"

The man peeked inside. "Good. Done. Let's go back. I forgot the condiments: creamer, sugar, honey, diet su—"

Elsie broke in, "I go bring them," and left before the man had a chance to respond. This was another golden opportunity. She went to fetch the condiment tray and on her way back, pretended to reach for something across the tray and knocked over the woven basket.

Instantly, she sank to her knees and began collecting the scattered honey packets, at the same time planting the small button-shaped device in the basket where the honey was arranged. That took care of the break area. The cookie plate was next.

When she arrived in the break area she found not only the server to whom she wanted to pass the tray but one of the attendees. His back was to her, and he was pouring himself a coffee. She was about to hand over the condiment tray when a thick and slightly accented voice stopped her.

"Oh good. I always use milk and sugar."

Elsie looked up at the tall man's face. Dark olive complexion, head completely shaved, broad shoulders, impeccable suit. His gaze held hers and he was smiling. Elsie knew him at once from his black onyx eyes. She was staring at Yousef Mahmoud.

"*Shukran.*" He spoke to her in Arabic, meaning *thanks*.

Elsie quickly looked down, as good Muslim women are supposed to: never look a stranger in the eye, especially not a *he*; avert eyes downward. "I do not speak Arabic."

"And where are you from?"

With eyes still averted Elsie replied, "Turkey. I speak Turkish. And, little English."

"Well, hello," he said in Turkish. "Ms. . . .? Ms. Turkish?"

The Egyptian server could see Mahmoud's come on. "That's good. You have to go back to the kitchen."

Elsie did as she was told, her knees shaking badly. She had stood less than six inches from Yousef—a man pursued to the ends of the earth for calculated untold heinous crimes—yet protected, she now knew, by those she had formerly worked for. Here stood one of the architects of the 2001 attack. She hadn't suspected the depth of her feeling, the extent of her true apprehension, until he'd pierced her and fixed her gaze to the ground with his own two death-black eyes.

* * * *

Greg had the white van parked at the corner of the block where the center stood. He'd recently purchased and modified the van to match Ottoman's Halal Catering. Its license plate was a perfect copy of one of the catering company's vehicles. He also had been tailing "Harry" Johnson through Houston to his ritzy downtown hotel. Greg knew Johnson from their company days; the two were selected around the same time. Johnson now was working on Egypt operations—and still hadn't given up chain-smoking, Greg noticed. That was one bad mark for the company: addicts simply could never be trusted.

He'd been waiting for Harry patiently. Since 8:45 A.M., in fact; that's a long time to go between cigarettes. Well, he had been out twice, but each time accompanied by attendees. *Smoking mullahs, what a joke.* No matter, he could wait.

His surveillance served another purpose as well. Greg was keeping an eye on Elsie, in a way, watching out for her. He had given her a special mini–cell phone that doubled as a real-time transmitter. He had her keep the unit on in a special belt inside her loose skirt. So far things seemed to be going fairly smoothly; but all that was about to change.

The crucial conference intel had come with only a four-day notice. Ordinarily, Greg liked to plan well in advance; some things, though, couldn't be controlled. This was one of them. It didn't mean compromising standards. He already had a Plan B and even C.

Only light security measures had been taken with this conference. Two security men stood inside, and the center's three twenty-four-hour cameras were for recording only, not monitoring live. Greg made certain to position his van on an angle where it would be captured by two cameras.

The light security detail made sense. It was a low-key affair, not a publicized event. It was here in the States; and they had never, to date, experienced any threats or incidents. Not yet.

Greg checked his watch: 12:27. The lunch break had started at noon. Johnson would be jonesing for his after-meal puff. This time he was not to be denied the opportunity, no matter who smoked next to him.

As if on cue, Johnson strolled out, turned right, and stood alone in the shade. On closer look, from inside the van, Greg spied a concrete ashtray and a bench. He'd found the Smokers' Corner.

Greg counted to ten, took two deep breaths, then began his auto-imprinted routine: reach for loaded rifle, snap on silencer, adjust scope, lower window, target, aim, click off safety, double-check his target and aim again, shoot, shoot, then shoot one more time, click safety back on, lower rifle, place on van floor, shift on D, pull out slowly, drive four blocks (observing speed limit), enter prepaid lot, park next to other car, change license plates back to original, get into other car, remove props, start engine, pull out, and proceed to exit.

He left the gun in the van. It belonged to Blue Dodge Man, so he was kind enough to return their property. He didn't have to wipe anything clean: he'd left a special set of fingerprints. Once inside his car, he carefully removed his long curly auburn beard. He removed the black yarmulke and the reddish-brown wig and placed it inside an opaque bag together with the beard. He was leaving a riddle, a puzzle for the agency: their own hit man's gun, the fingerprints of a Mossad agent posing as a rabbi they'd identified two years ago, and the security cameras' footage showing an Orthodox Jew who might or might not be that rabbi. It would be bewildering fun: chasing the Israeli op angle; and wondering about the missing Blue Dodge Man's connection to the Mossad. *Good*, Greg thought, *let them stew in it*.

As to the van, Greg had paid one month in advance for the space and registered its original plates and model with the attendant. He had implemented every step thoroughly and successfully. This particular leg of the mission was accomplished. Harry Johnson was dead.

* * * *

Elsie went back to the kitchen area to bring another bowl of salad to replace the one in the break room. She was pleased. She had noticed Agent Johnson and Mahmoud in deep discussion in the corner while holding their plates. They spoke in low tones at the furthest point from the device in that room. In one swift motion, she moved to the buffet table, lifted the dessert plate—the one with her device—and brought it over to the men.

"Very good cookies. Baked this morning." She placed the tray on the stand right next to them, and then returned to the buffet to artfully reposition the bread. Before she left the area, she checked them one more time. They remained engrossed in low conversation, next to her plate of cookies.

Elsie was handed the fresh salad bowl by one of the two Turkish women. She left the kitchen and walked the same route toward the lunch area. How many times she had done this today, going back and forth? Ten rounds? Fifteen?

Just as she reached the atrium area, hell broke loose. The security men were screaming in Arabic while Imam Gumus' assistant tried to yell over their voices; and the NATO colonel was being spirited away, out the back door by his driver.

Moments later, the guards, who had run outside, returned dragging Johnson's bloody body. Elsie watched, almost frozen. Gumus' assistant was next to the body wildly talking into his phone. Elsie strained to make out the words.

"We cannot call the police! This will ruin us . . . it will bring all sorts of unwanted attention . . . You come clean this up . . . No, you come take the body . . . Right. No more shots . . ."

She stared at the mangled body on the floor. Most of his head and face was gone. Then she looked away, to the lunch area. Most of the attendees were moved from the window. She felt someone's eyes. They were Yousef's. They held each others' gaze for what felt a good long while . . . until she was startled by her boss's commands.

"Let's get out of here! Now, right now! We have to move. We have to get out of here now! The vans are in the back, let's get moving."

When she finally found her voice, Elsie asked, "But what about finishing packing . . . taking the trash out . . .?"

"Didn't you hear me? NOW! Forget the goddamn plates, just get out. The police will be here any minute . . . the last thing I need is to get busted for some dumb workers . . ."

Okay, now she understood. These were illegal workers, without residency or permits. He figured Homeland Security for sure, and that meant trouble.

She had been faking bad English till now, but she didn't care—she needed those devices. "*I'm* not illegal," she protested. "I was filling in for Aysha. You go ahead. I'll take care of myself." Seeing him hesitate, she quickly added, "I'll let them know you'll be back to collect your things. *You* go ahead," as though her urgency was to protect his business.

He seemed to get it. He ran back into the kitchen and began shoving workers to the exit. Now the problem was to get back in, before everything was locked.

She saw her chance and took it, plunging into the forward-moving stream against the tide. No one would notice her moving backward in the rush to exit. Finally, she arrived in the now empty kitchen. Everyone was gone. She had it to herself. Her eyes scanned for trays. She went to one of the two on wheels, grabbed the handle, and began steering it into the corridor and from there, to the atrium. The body was gone, no longer on the floor. Someone had already taken it somewhere. No doubt whisked off to the CIA.

As she crossed to the conference room wing, she began to slip and before she knew it was falling down. She found herself kneeling in blood. It was everywhere. Her hands, her skirt and part of her tunic were sticky with patches of Johnson's blood. *Don't lose it*, she commanded, *I haven't come this far for* . . . Shakily, Elsie rose to her feet.

She trolleyed the cart into the almost empty break room where one of the guards remained stationed. Gumus' assistant and six other attendees were still inside. She parked her tray in a corner and began to randomly collect plates and platters. *There they are.* She found two. *Now the pen.*

How to do it, though? As Elsie pondered her options, Gumus' assistant walked in.

"What are you doing here? Where is your bo—" He stopped when he noticed the blood. "You are bleeding!"

Faking a stutter, she told him in Turkish, "Th-the big boss h-had to drive some people away . . . p-paper, permit issues . . . asked me to begin to clean up 'til he got here." Then quickly she added, "No. I am not bleeding. Some of the blood out there . . . in the atrium g-got on me . . ."

The assistant seemed to buy it. He was about to go back into the conference room when Elsie called out, "Oh! and one more thing. He asked me to give you a different cell number to reach him, just in case. I'll give it to you before I leave."

He nodded and went back in.

Elsie picked up a few more items and went back to the kitchen with her tray. Both devices were now securely zipped in her tunic but her hands were still shaking. They had to stop. She had to will them into steadiness.

She grabbed a piece of paper from the counter and wrote down a made-up number. She slightly smudged two digits, making them hard to read. Next, she filled two pitchers with fresh ice water and placed them on a tray with six clean glasses and hurried back to the conference room.

She knocked once gently and entered with the tray. The men, including Gumus' assistant, looked incredibly upset. And why not?

Here they had thought they were safe; instead, they found themselves in the unsecured annex of a company mosque, mourning the assassination of one of their own—in broad daylight. Right now, they seemed in a state of shock.

She parked the tray next to the table. "I brought you fresh cold water." She placed a pitcher and three glasses on her side of the table, then spoke directly to Gumus' assistant. "I brought his cell number." She unfolded the paper. "Oh! I have written messy during all the rush . . . this should be seven and . . ." She pretended to see the pen at this moment. "I write this down correctly . . ." and then she snatched it up. Moving now away from the table, Elsie scribbled down the digits, carefully folded the square of paper and placed it before the assistant. Without saying a word, she headed out with the cart toward the second door. Then she heard him call her.

"One more thing!"

Elsie felt cold panic set in. She stopped where she was.

"Yes sir?"

"Thank you for the fresh water. That was thoughtful of you."

"You're welcome." She didn't pause until she reached the kitchen area, the pen still tight in her grip. She went straight out the back service door and didn't stop moving until she was two blocks away.

* * * *

Greg saw her exit through the gate. Elsie was a sight: a Muslim woman, likely deranged, with bloody hands and blood-smeared face walking fast down the street. He knew she was in some kind of shock. He started the engine and followed her slowly.

Elsie didn't even notice the car. Greg lowered the passenger window.

"Elsie. Elsie, get in the car."

She turned to him with glassy eyes, her face a mask of white.

"You have blood on you. You're dressed like a Muslim woman. You'll be stopped and detained in no time. Get into the car, Elsie, now!"

Whatever he said must have registered. Robotically, she opened the door and got in.

As he sped up, Greg told her, "Put your seat belt on."

Something in her snapped. Loudly, she barked, "Shut up! Don't tell me! You have no right to tell me what to do!"

"Please put your seat belt on, for your safety."

"For my safety? My fucking *safety*? Are you fucking kidding? You *asshole!*"

She was shaking. Her entire body was quaking. This was a full-blown breakdown, Greg saw clearly. This time, he repeated calmly and slowly, "I know it was hard, very hard. I know it was tough, but you made it. You did good. Very good. I'm proud of you, Elsie."

Whatever he thought he was trying to do, it didn't work. His speech was pouring gas on a fire. "Why are you speaking as though I'm an idiot? You think I care if you're proud? I don't give a *flying fuck*. We are opposites. I'm not part of your world. Don't you get it?"

He had to try again. He wasn't any good at this. He had no talent for it. He recalled Mai's breakdown after seeing that disk; somehow, he had managed to calm her. What had he done? He'd urged her to try and get some sleep.

"Elsie, I'm taking you home . . . a *temporary* home. It will be safe. You can take a nice hot bath and clean off all this mess. I'll get you something nice to eat and then, I hope, you'll try to get sleep. That will help."

Elsie hated him now more than ever. She couldn't sustain such a level of rage and at once she felt drained, as though all her energy were leaving her body. She could barely talk; even worse, she realized she was crying.

Barely audible, she whimpered in between sniffs, "You did it on purpose . . . you sent me into that awful place on purpose . . . *sadist* . . ."

"Not really, Elsie. That decision I made yesterday afternoon. I knew you would think quickly and improvise. I was right. You performed extremely well. I was around, close to the center, just in case. I would not let you get into any big trouble. That wasn't part of our deal."

"Some deal!" She wiped her face with the sleeve of her tunic. "I got all three devices back . . . I couldn't place a second, a backup, inside the conference. Your training sucked. The room was impossible; nowhere to plant the devices safely."

Greg took the exit. "Not impossible. Very possible. That was part of your training. The best kind: real life training."

She unzipped her tunic and retrieved the devices, carelessly tossing them into the backseat. "Happy? I collected all three. I'm done. No more operations for you. I'm not your partner!" She looked out her side window. "Where the hell are we going? I want to go back to my hotel."

"I checked you out. I have your suitcase in the trunk. We are going to a house, an executive rental I arranged for us. Very chichi, the kind only oil executives can afford. We'll be there for nineteen hours."

Elsie changed the topic. "I saw Yousef. I even spoke with him. He is now bald. A shiny shaved head."

Greg slowed the car, using the remote to open the gate, and brought them to a stop in front of the mansion's four-vehicle garage. "Yes. I will be seeing him this evening. We're here!"

Elsie checked out the stucco McMansion. "So Texas. What they lack in taste they make up for in size."

"Nevertheless, a safehouse for the next several hours, where you'll take one or two hot baths, preferably eat and rest, while I finish my social rounds." He pulled into the garage where he'd earlier parked another just-in-case car.

They entered through an elaborate series of entryways that led them down a long marble hallway and finally deposited them in a three-storey-high chandeliered living room.

"Welcome home."

* * * *

Monday Evening, November 10, 2003
Houston, Texas

Elsie opened her eyes and peered at her surroundings. Olive-green thick velvet curtains with tassels, intricately carved glossy white crown moldings, rococo urns filled with handmade silk flowers . . . where was she? She was groggy and disoriented. She sat up in bed. Her eyes fell on the pile of sticky clothes on the richly carpeted bedroom floor. Then she remembered everything.

What time was it? She checked the ornate desk clock across from her Cal King bed: 10:36 P.M. She had been asleep for . . . for over seven hours. She had stripped, taken a long hot bath, and then collapsed naked into bed.

She wandered into the walk-in closet and spotted two fluffy white bathrobes. Reaching for the smaller, she wrapped herself up, secured the belt, and headed downstairs in bare feet.

On the kitchen counter was a note from Greg: *Check the fridge and get yourself something to eat.* She opened it and looked in. Every shelf was filled. There was a whole roast chicken in its fridge-to-oven container, a matching container packed with green beans, four different cheeses, grapes, hard salami, eggs, milk, orange juice, and even two bottles of wine, a Pinot Grigio and sparkling something.

She wasn't hungry. Instead, she decided to explore. First, she needed to check the garage. Both cars were there. No guarantee of anything, of course; the man was obsessive-compulsive about his vehicles, there could be half a dozen at any given time. She went back upstairs and checked every room, including the one with Greg's small carry-on propped in the corner. *Nope. Not here.*

Downstairs. In the middle of that cavernous living room she stared emptily into the baroque fireplace. *One evening 'round the fire must consume half a forest* was the thought; then she heard something. A sound, coming from below. She could sense the vibrations through her feet.

Out in the hallway she found another door. This one led to the basement. She could hear Greg's voice, and grunts . . . more like moans. She took six steps down and stopped at the scream. It was muffled, as though from a covered mouth. Taped over? Elsie went rigid. She knew what that was: the live sound of someone being tortured, and of one who liked to talk while doing it.

She collapsed into a sitting position on the stair. She could not go one step further. Greg was in the midst of his torture mission and she knew who the subject was: Mahmoud. It was Yousef. She could hear it all, every word.

"Joseph, don't you think you have had enough? Isn't it preferable to have this chat as two civilized people instead of this? I don't like the smell of burnt meat."

Oh God. He was burning him. A human being. She thought she could smell the flesh. Even sitting, she held fast to the stair.

"Joseph. We two go back, don't we, Joseph? You became one of the chosen: promoted, included in the bigger operation. I was demoted and pushed aside. So I set up a shop of my very own. Cooperate and I'll include you in my team. Would you like that? Joseph, what do you say?"

He must have given his consent; a nod? She could hear something being torn. Was it tape?

"That's much better. So, the price of admission to the team is a song. Let's have you sing. Tell me about the coming home front operation. I already know the general scheme. From you I want details."

Why was he calling him *Joseph?* Was Yousef Mahmoud a cover, given to him by the agency? The man asked for water, and she heard Greg's steps. Was he coming up? No. He must have water handy. An experienced sadist would have water at the ready, if only to further torment his victim. Then she heard the victim speak; she certainly recognized that voice.

"November fifteenth. MCI Center."

"I know. I want details. Who? How? Who are the organizers?"

"Two men. One Dagestani, the other one Chechen. Both live in the D.C. area. We set them up good. It is going to be clean. . . . We went through preselection as usual: expired visas, the father of one, wanted in Georgia. The guys were pretty much clean, but that doesn't mean anything to us . . . does it, Gregory?"

"No, it doesn't. Tell me how you set them up."

"We sent one of our sheep-dipped guys to establish contact and relationship with the men. Our guy is on the FBI's Wanted List—a terrorist from Yemen. You know how it goes."

"I do. Go on."

He was recording this whole session, Elsie knew. This one was to include video as well. Greg most likely would use this for insurance, as solid blackmail material.

"We recorded two weeks' worth of e-mail and phone chats between our sheep and the subjects; nothing illegal, just established connections. All we needed. Then our guys, posing as Homeland Security in uniforms, rounded up both candidates. We took them into an empty room in DHS's Arlington office. We hit them with transcripts of communications between them and our sheep, and showed them our sheep's FBI status: Wanted! One of them wet his pants."

The talk made Elsie shudder. This was how her government went about setting up innocent people as criminals. They manufacture both the terrorists and the terror, setting up attacks that target its civilians!

"So they realized they were in very deep shit. With their illegal status, no visa, and on-the-record association with a Ten Most Wanted international terrorist, they were fucked. So then we talked about possibly giving them a deal."

"What sort of a deal? I need details, Joseph."

Elsie wanted to get up and go upstairs, yet the story coming out had her in its spell. Slowly, then at once, she understood the genius. It was simple, as genius often tends to be: if you attempt to even begin to describe this to people who, at bottom, don't ever want to know, not only will you not be believed but they may wish that you be permanently locked away, against the precepts of their own rule of law. It's how nationalism works, and the perpetrators know it—no matter who or what gets destroyed.

"We said, 'okay, there may be a way for you to skip Guantanamo, water-boarding, and being sodomized'—you know, letting them know what we do once they're holed up in no-man's-land. They were more than willing to cooperate. We told them we were setting up a drill, that we wanted them to play mock suicide bombers. They would get apprehended at the end of the drill, but later, they'd be rewarded with new identities and federal witness protection status . . . all that bullshit jazz."

"What precisely do these roles entail?"

"Nothing big. They'll practice making bombs with our recipes. This week, on Saturday, they have instructions to go to the MCI Center for the big weekend game. They will already have tickets with our seat assignments. They will place their homemade bombs under certain seats, and wrap other explosives around their waists. Then they are to sit and wait. They will be expecting their DHS handlers to arrive, to apprehend them as promised, of course. The bombs are set to go off thirty minutes into the game. We'll be waiting outside for the fireworks. We have the transcripts of what will be given to the media. FBI will obtain the security tapes showing our men placing the bombs, and they will search the men's houses and find caches of goodies: e-mails, bomb-making powder and materials, phone records . . . you know the drill."

"And the end game this time? Georgia? Russia? Both?"

"Start a small Georgian-Russian war and then turn it big, really big. We'll get a nice chunk of the Caucasus. Hey, the Russians couldn't contain their own goddamn terrorists! So those bad people are now here, in our own backyard, killing thousands of our people—while relaxing at a game! The UN, EU, everyone is going to be on our side on this. They wouldn't want to be next, right? Isn't that how it works?"

Elsie shut her eyes. The pain was unbearable. She could see the corpses of thousands after the 2001 attacks. She could almost smell the guts when they showed it on TV—televised, yes, that was the point. It doesn't work if no one sees it. The people were nothing. She was nothing—nothing but an item checked off a list. Someone's list. Greg called it *collateral damage.*

"Now, let's revisit 2001. I was out of commission by then, sort of; since the Russian day care operation."

"I don't have all the details. I never did. They divided us into six separate units. I handled Egyptian and Yemeni operatives. I think I know who had the Saudi operatives . . ."

"Unusual operation; atypical. How did you make the suicide mission work, considering the profiles of those lovely people?"

"Suicide mission? Who said it was a suicide mission? They were not committing suicide, Greg. They were playing their role in a massive Red Team Operation and Drill."

Elsie straightened up. *Red Team Operation and Drill?* What was he talking about?

"We told them this was set up by Air Defense and FAA as one of the biggest drills in the history of air defense. They thought they were going to get medals for their participation in the grandest, most realistic drill ever. That's what. You didn't know that?"

Elsie heard the lengthy pause. Here was something Greg didn't know!

"Very smart. You guys even fooled me, and I am—was—one of you. Which agencies were directly involved?"

"Pentagon's OG division, CIA. We played the rest, and had them play their role."

"How about the FBI?"

Elsie knew why Greg was asking about the FBI. It was for her; maybe, even if indirectly, for Ryan's sake as well.

"We played them big time. The agency fed the feds real leads on the operatives, the attack, and who was up to what. They didn't know they were being played—at all. The agency then would step in and take over, claiming jurisdiction and shoving the bureau aside—that it was their op, and they were on top. Later, of course, the agency made sure all records of these communications were destroyed. That left the bureau in this fucked-up situation . . . no backup . . ."

"Why don't we start from the beginning? I want you to go over your biography, from Square One. How you were recruited by the agency after becoming a U.S. Army man, and how you came to be chosen for Operation Gladio."

"That was not our deal! You know that story. You are going to take me out, aren't you? It is not about recruiting me for some operation . . . I . . ."

Elsie couldn't take any more. She picked herself up off the stairs and got out. She was not going to be a witness.

CHAPTER 15

Thursday, November 13, 2003
Arlington, Virginia

Ryan parked his car in the underground lot of his apartment and took the elevator to the lobby. He stopped to check his mail. All junk.

He threw the pile on the kitchen counter and flipped on the lights. Then cracked open a beer. He had to eat something. So far today, it had only been half a bagel with cream cheese.

He opened the fridge again: nothing. Not even an egg. An old jar of pickles, well past expired, half a stick of butter, and something moldy. Oh, and beer. He opened the freezer: two empty ice cube trays, frozen peas, something solid, and a half-full bottle of Stoli.

He figured on Chinese food. He dialed the number and was placed on hold. As he waited, he shuffled through the stack of mail: *junk, junk, crap, bill, crap, crap, handwritten envelope without a stamp*— he dropped the receiver. He recognized the handwriting. It was Elsie's. He opened it carefully. One sheet of lined paper read *Friday, Noon, Pentagon, Ritz, 502. Your Sweet Asterisk*

It was her handwriting. He was sure. She had given him two words to confirm: *Sweet* and *Asterisk*.

His heart was pounding. Friday was less than eighteen hours. She'd selected the hotel smartly. If he was being followed, which likely he was, he could easily lose the tail in the busy shopping mall and enter the hotel from there.

This was the only break he'd had in a long, persistent line of failures. He'd spent two days in New York chasing a ghost. Luka Belinsky had vanished. The trail, what little of it there was, had gone cold. Ryan had questioned everyone he could. No one knew a thing. He'd staked out the midtown apartment and found nothing, no activity at all. He'd had to give up and return to D.C.

Then he decided to see Sullivan. The man wouldn't budge. Gregory seemed to be dangling the keys to heaven before Sullivan's desperate eyes. He kept repeating as a mantra, *"In less than three weeks we'll know . . . just three weeks, Ryan . . . in less than three weeks . . . if by the end of this thirty-day period, then . . ."* Never mind what happens to the members of his "team." Sullivan cared for one thing only: to make someone pay for what he could never get back. Well, Elsie was alive, and Ryan might not get her back; in fact he might not ever see her again. Didn't that count for more than five minutes of Sullivan's precious time?

In his frustration, he also had called the Russian embassy. Yes, he did, despite himself. He called to check if they had any inquiries into the death of Tatiana Schuliskova; and if yes, who might be in charge of that inquiry. It was his only way of getting a lead on the FSB-connected agents involved. He'd been placed on hold then told to expect a call in the next two days. This meant they would check him out further. Was he still connected to the FBI? Was he baiting them for information? Since his call, most likely they'd been tailing him.

Oh well. None of that mattered. He was seeing her Friday—and this time, he wouldn't ever let her go.

* * * *

Friday, November 14, 2003
Arlington, Virginia

Elsie paced.

It had been more than two weeks. And what two weeks! More than anything she could ever explain. This would be the last time she could see him, at least for a very long time. Still, she was thankful for the chance, this opportunity. It came as an unexpected gift.

Two days ago, Greg had told her about Ryan contacting the Russian embassy; words to the effect of, "Your boyfriend is out of control: I will not let him bring the Russians into this."

She knew what he meant, and after an hour of heated and painful discussion, she'd managed to wrangle this one last date. It was a concession on Greg's part, and Elsie knew that she had to live up to her end or it would mean the end to them both.

She heard the light knock and fell toward it. Would her knees buckle under? She opened the door and each stood frozen in the moment, gazing at the other. He'd lost weight, and his beard had grown thicker. He looked as though he'd lived a decade of anxiety, especially around the eyes.

She moved to the side without breaking contact. He came in, and closed the door behind him. *Please take me into your arms*—and he did, as if he heard the voice inside her.

He held her tight and devoured her scent. She buried herself in the embrace, and then tears began to pour. She had cried in the last two weeks more than when she was a little girl even, the shock of war having chased tears away. She remembers *wanting* to cry but she couldn't, and now . . . the dam burst. She melted and her knees gave away. He wouldn't let her fall; not today. Not ever.

He held her trembling face in his hands and lifted it to his. She could see the pain mixed with joy. His eyes responded with their own well of tears. He brought her into him and began kissing her lips. He touched her tears with the tip of his tongue. She closed her eyes. *Every precious second . . .* Her floodtide was rising for the soon-to-come drought.

He picked her up and carried her to the bedroom. Cradling her now, Ryan gently lowered her into the bed and stretched his body over hers, holding her arms above her head and kissing her all over. Their caresses gave way to a passionate urgency and they began peeling clothes off in a hurry. The layers, the distance, the separation out of the way, Ryan covered her body with his and entered her. She was his, and he wasn't going to let her be taken away from him again. They stayed that way for a good long time before ever so gently he started, letting the feel of her stiffen him so he could tease and time their deep-together thrusts. They made love to each other until they were spent—still not long enough to make up for what was lost, what was taken from them so viciously.

She couldn't undo time. They could never go back. All she could do was live the moment, savor each second, and remember how they were now. Precious.

She woke up and looked out. It was almost dark. Ryan was asleep. She checked the clock-radio: 5:10 P.M. Time was running too fast. She slipped out of bed and noiselessly made her way to the bathroom. Once more this person stood before the mirror, peering at herself. She too had lost weight. Ryan hadn't said a word about her new appearance; in fact neither had spoken hardly any words. She examined her postlovemaking nibbles and bites all over her neck, chest, and . . . everywhere. Why couldn't this last? She well knew why, but . . . *oh well.*

After a quick shower she put on her robe, combed and twisted her hair in a bun, and stepped out of the bathroom. He was sleeping soundly. She put her clothes back on, including her silk stockings and high-heel shoes.

She went into the alcove, a kind of sitting area, and opened her laptop then inserted a disk. She would show this to Ryan: segments from Greg's interrogation of Yousef. This was part of her plan. She was going to let Ryan watch it. He'd been after Yousef, burning with a need for revenge for his nephew and the 2001 attack. What he wanted had been done. Yousef had confessed, on record; and right or wrong, he'd been taken out. She would tell him about Nazim as well: same deal. Ryan's issues had been put to bed. The culprits had been dealt with—albeit by someone else—but that didn't change the results. He no longer had them to pursue.

She went over to the minibar area and fixed herself hotel coffee. This one wasn't too bad. She stirred the concoction, put the spoon on the napkin, and almost bumped into Ryan, who'd been standing right behind her. He startled her.

"Sorry, sweet, I didn't mean . . . well, sorry."

She smiled. "These days anything startles me."

"Why?"

"I . . . I haven't been okay . . . I've been surviving, kind of."

Ryan was about to speak but didn't. She knew what he wanted to ask: whether she'd be on the run forever, a permanent fugitive. She knew too that just like her, he was afraid of ruining what little time they had left with ugly facts and questions.

"Ryan. I can't stay here for long. In fact, I can't stay in the country for long."

His jaws clenched tight. "When? When are you leaving? Jesus . . . where will you go?"

"Soon." Elsie sighed. "Less than a week. I still don't know where. I guess he'll tell me at the very last minute. That's him. It's how he operates."

"*Him.* You mean that psycho creep."

"Creep or not, he's the only one who can keep me alive—and safe—and then get me out of here."

Ryan hated it. "Keller exposé . . . was that . . .?"

Elsie nodded. "One of his missions."

"How about the suicide? Was it staged?"

Keller hanged himself right after the scandal, from the hand-hewn beams of a cabin he owned. Greg, of course, had expected this. "No. That part wasn't Greg. He took his own miserable life."

"And what about you? Are you one of his missions?"

Elsie looked away. "I popped up in the middle of his operation. It was kill me or save me. For whatever reason, he decided on *save*."

Using every ounce of self-control, Ryan let this one go—for now. "Who is he with? Who does he work for?"

"He is with himself, with *Greg*. He isn't working for anyone. In fact, he's been working against the greatest powers."

"The agency."

"That's one. It is far more than that. Far bigger."

"What? I don't follow."

Elsie didn't know where to begin. She didn't know how to explain. "Select Pentagon, NATO, MI6, Special Forces . . . playing God, planting rulers, blowing people up, including here, in the United States . . ."

This sounded like someone else. "Has the killer-abductor added brainwashing to his list? This isn't Elsie talking . . . and by the way, why did you change your hair? And that makeup."

Elsie was expecting this. His criticism. His reservation. His rejection of what she needed to do now; and frankly, she might never be able to change his mind. She was running out of time. "No, Ryan. Have you heard about NATO's stay-behind army called *Gladio*? We are talking post–World War Two."

"No I haven't."

"Well, read about it later. Go to the library or check online. Supposedly Gladio suspended operation after the fall of the Soviet Union. They didn't. They changed to a different mode, a new and improved, souped-up version, and they've been at it, in spades, since

1996. One of their hallmarks, their biggest MO, is false flag operations: all over the globe. Since the midnineties, their operatives of choice—the ones they create from scratch, train, arm, and direct—have been the Jihadis; the Mujahideen, the so-called Islamists, such as al-Hazar." She stopped herself to check his reaction.

Ryan was quick but unwilling to see the obvious. "You're saying they recruited al-Hazar?"

"Not recruit; they *made* them. From the ground up. From bits and pieces, like Lego. Only these aren't children who are playing." She took a breath. "I need to show you something." She went to the desk and motioned him over.

She hit Play. "Please sit. You need to watch this."

With Ryan in the chair, Elsie went back to the sofa and watched him. His initial shock at Yousef's appearance gave way to abhorrence at the evidence of torture, which quickly turned to disgust. She wasn't sure if Ryan could process what Yousef had to say.

He stopped the player two thirds in and turned to face her. "Were *you* there?" He demanded her response—by way of accounting. There was accusation in his tone. This wasn't gently asked.

"I-I was . . . Yes. Kind of."

"What has he done to you?" he cried. "My God! What has he done to you?"

Now it was her turn to be shocked. "Didn't you hear him? That was Yousef himself, confessing!"

Ryan almost hissed, "He was being *tortured*, for Christ's sake! That is not a confession. Everyone knows that! People say and do anything under torture. The information is useless. It can never be relied on. So you, Elsie, participated in torture? You? My God, what's happened?"

Now she was really getting mad. She was fuming. "Excuse me? You're accusing me now and calling me a torturer? *He is your man*: Yousef Mahmoud—one of the top worst men in the world, directly responsible for murdering your nephew and five thousand other dead victims!"

Ryan stood up, done with the evidence. "And you, and this guy, go out hunting them down, to torture and kill these people, right?"

"You're a hypocrite, Ryan. A terrible hypocrite. Tell me, why were *you* chasing Yousef Mahmoud? What were *you* planning to do with him? Obviously, you couldn't have just handed him over because guess what? That was done already, and the bureau let him out, to be sent on more missions, to go kill again. So who were you planning to hand him to, assuming you ever even caught him? CIA? Well hallelujah! He is—make that *was*—CIA. To Congress? That's a joke: they take orders direct from the agency, exactly like Keller. Let's see . . . would you turn him over to the courts? He was already there—behind closed doors. In camera. These were the government lawyers and judges responsible for covering this up, and ensuring that it stayed that way." Elsie had to stop for breath. "Who's left? Tell me. With the Pentagon, CIA, Congress and the courts out of service, and with you now realizing the FBI's compromised position, to whom, precisely, would you turn your prize catch over for justice? Tell me, Ryan, I'm dying to hear!" She had to stop. She was shaking.

Ryan stared. "So that's how you justified torture and murder. Killing him is the answer. I see. Did he hypnotize you? Is he feeding you something? You talk as if he's now your partner. He's a hit man, a professional torturer-murderer; if you're his partner, then what does that make you?"

She felt smacked, as though he had slapped her, hard. He'd hurt her deeper than she thought he ever could. Was this how he viewed her now?

Elsie raised her chin, and in a calm, controlled voice, told him evenly, "Answering a question with a question is immature. You failed to give me an honest answer. What sort of justice did you have in mind for Yousef, assuming you caught him?"

Ryan refused to answer. He held her stare, silent.

"That's what I thought. You would have either taken him out or done nothing. Well, Ryan, he took *your* man out. By the way, Nazim has been taken out as well. That leaves you without any targets. No one left to investigate and chase. Now you can go work the desk for your boss, *Mister* Sullivan." She stood up and went into the bedroom.

Ryan followed her in. She was packing. "He took out Tatiana, Yousef, Nazim . . . who else? How many others has he killed so far? What makes you think you'll be safe? Because, Elsie, he sounds like a serial killer. He goes beyond professional hit man."

"It's not even that you don't understand; it's denial. When you're shown evidence, real evidence, against what you believe, you double down: you dig in your heels."

"What happened to you? Do you hear what you're saying?"

"I *do* know. Do you? Those victims, your nephew, are *collateral damage*. That's something you can't or don't want to hear."

Elsie began packing her laptop.

"Where are you going?"

"I told you, I don't know. I wanted to meet and tell you to stop looking for me. Maybe it was a mistake."

There was a catch in her voice and it brought him up short. He didn't know which part of that applied; a mistake to want to meet, or her wish that he stop his search for her? She looked so alone, with that ridiculous hair and her one little bag. The prospect of his world without her broke his heart. He could think of only one thing to say.

"If your wish is for me to ever stop looking, then you're nuts, insane. I love you Elsie Simon."

Now her heart was breaking. *How would he think if he knew about my father and my arrangement with those who are searching for him?* Tears began rolling down her face, she couldn't help it.

"Will I hear from you? Ever?"

Elsie commandeered her emotions. "Not for . . . not for at least a year. Until I'm at my final point and settled. Until the dust has settled . . . until I am me, or whoever this person is."

It was a chance. Ryan grabbed it. "Then let's say a year. Will you contact me? Will you let me know how you are—and how someday I might find you?"

Elsie couldn't give him an answer, not now. "I don't know . . . I guess so, but who knows how or who we'll be? It's hard enough now, this knowing, not knowing . . . how we think we feel, who we are. I can't promise, I *won't* promise, what I'm not able to deliver. None of us can. Now . . . I've got to go."

"Really?"

He said it like a little boy. He was pathetic, and she hated that she loved him. Elsie felt a knot forming; she didn't want to cry and break down again.

"I have to." She closed the lid to her carry-on and began pulling it toward the door.

She felt his eyes watching her go.

Turning the knob, she hesitated. *No.* She opened the door, quickly walked out, and let the door close by itself.

CHAPTER 16

Saturday, November 15, 2003
Washington, D.C.

Elsie fixed her eyes on the building across the street from her mile-high cocktail table. It was 6:50 P.M. and the MCI Center looked busy, as it always did before the game.

"Not to your liking? Can I change it for you?"

"Oh!" Elsie looked at her Classic Margarita on the rocks, which hadn't been touched. "No, that's okay. Maybe if you could top it off with ice?"

The waitress disappeared with the drink. Elsie turned back to the building. Then she saw them: two black FBI SUVs flashing red lights, pulling in front of the main entry. Behind them, four D.C. police cars converging all at once.

Doors flew open and five FBI agents, two of them with crackling transmitter radios, rushed in, followed by three D.C. police.

Elsie checked her watch: 6:57. She tapped her foot nervously, rattling the ice in her freshened-up drink. She noticed two more police cars arrive, followed by several ATF SUVs.

The game was scheduled for 7 P.M. but it wasn't going to happen.

The long white truck from Homeland Security's bomb squad unit pulled up in the middle of the street. She could see that evac already had begun. She asked for the bill and by the time she had her coat on, two officers arrived and were ordering everyone to evacuate immediately.

She exited the restaurant, crossed the street and then stopped. Dozens of others had done exactly the same. People were on their cell phones, pointing and wondering loudly: just what was going on?

The police had cordoned off the building, all four streets surrounding the center and the two cross streets. The number of people exiting the center were starting to thin out. The evac was going quickly and so far without incidents. The area was swarming with FBI, DHS, ATF and D.C. cars. Even a few media trucks had arrived.

Elsie, along with other bystanders, learned a few things by word of mouth from those who had just come from inside the center. The authorities found bombs—that is, more than one, in two separate locations in the stadium . . . they had the suspects subdued . . . they were Middle Eastern . . . five men . . . no, dozens of men . . . no, that wasn't right, there were only three . . .

Elsie didn't need the distraction. All she cared about right this moment was to see everyone safely out of the building, the bombs deactivated, and the suspects in custody.

She saw one reporter mouth something into a microphone and point animatedly to the entrance door. Elsie elbowed a couple of heavyset women for a clearer view when she saw them: five agents dragging out a young dark-haired man in handcuffs. She craned her neck to the side. *Where was the other one? Yousef mentioned two—* Then she saw him, the second patsy, well in hand, accompanied by three FBI agents.

She felt relieved. The building was evacuated. The bomb squad technicians were busy inside. The dupes were apprehended. It was time to go back. She rolled up her coat sleeve to check the hour:

7:21 P.M. The explosives were set to go off thirty minutes into the game. That meant the squad had less than ten minutes if they hadn't already neutralized the bombs.

She heard a shot, then a pause, then two more shots. Some of the bystanders had already thrown themselves to the ground, covering their heads with their hands. Elsie stayed where she was. She looked to where the shots were coming from but it was chaos, people running and diving; she turned the other way, toward the building's main entrance, and saw agents picking someone off the ground.

She pushed her way forward and got as close as she could to see the wounded man being placed on a gurney. She saw the cuffed hands and instantly knew he'd been shot, perhaps more than once. He had been the first one out.

She looked around for the second suspect. Had they already taken him away? She scanned the crowd: agents, dozens of government cars parked in the middle of both streets. She couldn't find him. She saw the bomb squad technicians carrying three metal containers out of the building—so that was good. At least the explosives were under control.

She headed back to her car. On the drive to the apartment she fiddled with the stations to try and find out more about the shooting, but details were sketchy. One suspect indeed was shot twice, his condition not known; the other was taken to FBI headquarters . . .

Elsie knew how it would all play out. With Gladio's home front operation thwarted, the planners and spinners would turn the whole thing around: instead of a pretext for their further encroachment into Russian territory—as a false flag attack would so richly provide—they would trumpet it a success, a great victory for our side. *And thus a public validation for their ever-expanding illegal ops—a victory no matter what,* Elsie thought.

How about suspect number two, the second set-up patsy? What would they do with him? They had so many options: they could

threaten him and force a false confession; use one of many unconventional means to force him into a scripted confession; or simply
take him out. Until a month ago Elsie would have considered this
line of thinking completely insane. Not now. Her own fugitive status
was proof. What had she done, that she couldn't go home? Use a
passport? Withdraw her own money from her own bank account? Or
simply phone a friend? She felt as if her whole existence was illegal;
and now she needed Greg. That's right. She needed him.

As she drove into the garage, she dreaded the idea of seeing him.
He would know who had tipped off the authorities—especially the
FBI. He knew her too well. For him, having the evidence was all that
mattered. He couldn't care less about casualties. *Collateral damage* is
how he thought of it; to him, an operation like this was mother's milk
... *but what in God's name kind of mother?* she wondered.

She found Greg in the living room actually watching the news.
This was the first time she'd seen him even look at TV. She went
over to the sofa and joined him. He nodded to her wordlessly.

The anchorwoman was interrupted by a news update: *"Just in—
the terror suspect who was earlier shot while in custody just outside the
MCI Center was declared dead on arrival at George Washington University Hospital this evening . . ."*

Without missing a beat Elsie simply said, "They killed him.
The agency."

Greg nodded, eyes on the screen.

Elsie looked straight ahead. "What will they do with the other
one?"

He thought about it. "He may have a preexisting heart condition that may have caused his heart to stop during long interrogation. He may have hanged himself before the closed-door trial . . . or
something similar."

Elsie sighed. *Just as expected.*

Another late-breaking banner of news began its crawl across the screen before the anchor was interrupted again: *"According to FBI sources, the bureau received tips from two separate individuals, one male and one female, via telephone this evening . . ."*

Two? How, who . . .? Male? She turned and stared.

Greg kept on watching as the anchor continued, *"The FBI is now asking the two individuals to come forward since even the smallest details they may have . . ."*

* * * *

Tuesday Morning, November 18, 2003
Washington, D.C.

Greg listened carefully, and jotted down the letters and numbers as his source read him the code: *G895DCD2003DI.* Greg repeated the code back twice. All set. He hung up and checked his watch: 9:35 A.M. All on schedule.

This was the final step of the operation. Tomorrow she would leave for Florida, and from there leave the country with the help of his source, a man who *owed him one.* He was proved right by following his gut in the case of Elsie Simon. Once again he had listened, and once again that feeling had proven to be reliable.

Elsie was preparing for her final operation. She was in the bedroom getting ready per Greg's instructions: a jet-black wig that curled toward her chin in a chic Asian fashion, strongly arched eyebrows, almond-shaped eyes lifted upward with the help of black eyeliner and framed by long faux lashes, enhanced cheekbones in light matt brown, and red lips lined in the shape of a heart with a round black mole in the corner of the upper left lip. A full-length ivory cashmere coat would go over her white silk blouse and long tight black pencil skirt. Stilettos, for sure: snakeskin in black and ivory.

She sashayed into the room and struck a pose. Elsie looked

perfect: precisely executed, to the letter. She was a disaster when it came to arms and physical operations. Yet, the woman had noteworthy strengths: a respectable brain and processing capability, paired with unusual and highly attractive physical attributes.

"Good enough?" she honestly asked.

"Better than good."

She seemed pleased. Elsie had no reservations on this last operation. First, for the obvious reason: that it didn't involve guns, explosives, extortion, blackmail, kidnapping, torture, or murder. Second, it required a quick mind, good memory, some acting, and attractive physical features; she knew she had them all and felt confident. Third, she liked and believed in what she was about to do. Finally, knowing this would be her last day and last operation with Greg, Elsie was overjoyed and relieved. She couldn't wait to be rid of him for good.

They had gone over the big picture, little picture, and all the details in between. He had explained the way in which the company operated the major media outlets when needed. They had the top ten global news outlets enrolled; each of them discreetly, that is. The company had one or two of their top-level people placed in each outlet as contacts.

The rule was simple and straightforward: whenever required, the company would send a messenger to their contact in each news organization. The messenger was always an attractive, well-dressed woman with a black mole above her upper left lip. She would be asked a series of questions by the executive for identification as a security measure. Once she passed, she would deliver the packet of information: written or recorded audio and/or video and give the delivery schedule. The executive then made certain the transcript, audio and/or video would be broadcast or printed verbatim. No questions asked. No other permission required. It was treated as an absolute order issued by an absolute power. No other agency or official of any kind could ever override such an order; no one. Not even the president of the United States. The arrangement had been working perfectly for at least four decades. They had never had a single glitch, complication or subordination from their media arms. Not once.

Greg knew it would work perfectly this time as well. Elsie was going to two top TV news outlets: one cable, one network; and two major newspapers. The TV news outlets were going to air Greg's special video during prime time tonight, at 8. The two major newspapers were devoting their entire front page—and several following pages—to the transcript written and prepared by Greg.

"Okay. I have the code for this month. We have to go through the steps one more time."

"I have it down pat. We've been through it nine times," Elsie vigorously assured him. "Name: *Lauren Ivy*. Status code: *Alice in Wonderland*. Funny, eh? *Elsie* in Wonderland? Okay, never mind. Project name: *The New Century Mockingbird* . . . I got it, Greg. Now, what's the project code for this month?"

They went over the steps two more times. She was ready, physically, mentally, and emotionally. He checked the time: 9:55 A.M.

Quickly, they reviewed the schedule. The town car would be here in five minutes. She would be dropped off at Reagan National Airport for her shuttle flight at 11:50 A.M. There, in New York, she'd be picked up by a town car and taken first to the cable news network's headquarters on the West Side. Next stop: the network news headquarters four blocks away, before 2 P.M. Her last stop in the city would be the paper's headquarters in midtown Manhattan just before 3. She'd be back here by 6 P.M. and go directly to the paper's headquarters in Northwest D.C. The entire mission would be over and done with by 7:30 P.M.

"I better get going." Elsie went to fetch her leather briefcase, handbag, and coat.

On her way out, she turned to face him. "I was thinking . . . What do you say to one final dinner? A sort of nonintimate celebration?"

"Do you have a place in mind?"

Elsie smiled. "I do. Let it be a surprise. I'll drive."

Greg scanned her face. She was planning something mischievous; a zinger of some sort? It was a dare, so he took it. "All right. We're on."

Elsie smiled again. "Good. See you around seven-thirty."

* * * *

Tuesday Evening, November 18, 2003
Washington, D.C.

It was 8:05 P.M. Nicole Ratner was in the main newsroom watching the segment air with the rest of her crew. In fact, they all were watching it with the rest of the *world*—tens of millions, at least. They all looked shell-shocked, with good reason.

The broadcast showed how Yousef Mahmoud, the terrorist mastermind of the 2001 attack, widely known to be rotting in a prison cell in Illinois, in fact had been out, operating and traveling freely and—undisputedly—performing further terror operations for his bosses, who happened to be top officials in the CIA, Pentagon, NATO, and MI6. He was telling the world a story that wildly contradicted everything they'd been told about what actually had occurred that day: leaving nothing out, the top operative explained in convincing detail exactly how it occurred and why.

The telecast included CIA Agent Harold Johnson getting shot in real time in front of the nation's largest Islamic center in Texas. Graphic footage showed the body being moved by the center's security guards, including audio, in which a discussion can be heard on letting the CIA recover the body and cover it up to prevent public scrutiny into the Islamic center's joint operations with the CIA.

The images and audio and all they contained went beyond shocking: it was the biggest, most game-changing event in the history of this country. After this, there could be no more standard operating procedure; every part of the system would have to change.

Or would it?

What would happen if there was no reaction? If people thought this was some kind of test? What if they pretended that it never happened, or treated these revelations as a joke? Even more shocking, from Nicole's point of view, was why the powers would hand over this material and have them air it in the first place: to what purpose? Were they planning something? Then what? She couldn't figure it out. What was the objective here? Were they changing course, and this was a way to obfuscate their tracks? Still a journalist at heart, Nicole couldn't stop asking journalistic questions. Maybe the objective was to shake up the order, to eliminate certain players within the ranks . . . *and feed them to the lions?* She had scratched her head on this all day long; from the instant she viewed the documents. She still didn't have a logical answer—but it didn't matter. It wasn't her job. Her role was straightforward: she was given the material and told to air it. No questions asked, no explanation provided.

Her train of thought was interrupted by "Nicole, phone for you: It's the CIA, John Wolfe."

Wolfe was the deputy director. One of very few calls she could never ignore. "I'll take it from my office. Thanks, Jeremy."

She picked up before she sat down. "Hello, John. I assume you've been watching the insane segment—"

"Just what the fuck do you think you're doing?" Wolfe howled at her. "Cut. Cut. Cut now. We have to figure out a way to explain it. But go and cut it out now!"

Nicole steadied herself. "I can't do that John. I'm under orders."

"*This* is an order. We'll fuck you four ways to Sunday . . . you cunt. This is an absolute order. Cut it now!"

Nicole remained calm. "Sir, as you know, their order overrides yours. I'm sorry."

"Who the fuck is *they*, Nicole? You want me to get the director himself and have *him* give you the order?"

"N-No, sir. I mean no disrespect but . . . he cannot override them. Not even the president—"

"Are you telling me this came from the company?"

"Yes! Of course it did. And I checked everything; every step was implemented for authentication."

"I . . . have to call you back. I don't understand," Wolfe sounded confused. ". . . Let me call you back."

Nicole hung up. Too late, she thought. The segment was almost over.

* * * *

Tuesday Evening, November 18, 2003
Langley, Virginia

At 8:25 P.M., General Richard Schumacher turned off the lights and collapsed in his chair with his head between his hands, supported by his elbows on the desk. He needed a few minutes to collect himself. His thoughts were going in too many directions at once.

In the entire fifty-nine years of his fucked-up life he had never seen crazy like this past month. The inexplicable chain of events at first appeared random; yet now, in some god-awful way, they seemed part of a message—a single message—specifically addressed to them. But *who*, and more important, *why*?

The mess had begun with that lowlife operative Josh Thompson in Cambodia, a bloody double murder. Then they had gotten their man, case closed. At the time it had made perfect sense: one of their many unhinged agents going bonkers and out for revenge.

Then, the unexplained explosion of one of their vessels in the Black Sea, loaded with tens of millions' worth of cargo. That was no accident. Forensics closed that case as well; maybe too quickly. It reeked with their man Turkel's MO. The disgruntled, unhappy lieutenant general was proving his skills and worth to the Russians. Again, it made sense—especially when he later went underground, then disappeared altogether. Rumor had him in St. Petersburg, but they had gone to their reliable grapevine in Russia and gotten a solid negative. So who had blown up the ship? Where was Turkel? Was Turkey fucking with them—the newly elected administration flexing nonexistent muscles?

Next, only days after the explosion, they had the triple OG murders in their very own artery, NATO HQ in Brussels. The camera footage and fingerprint records yielded zero. They surmised that the assassin had impersonated their OG colonel, Winston Tanner, then made Tanner disappear. *Just like Turkel.* To cover it up, in a sorry-ass op, they had to kill a poor bastard—a NATO employee—and present his head on a fucking platter as the deranged assassin who then, without warning or reason, took his own life. What a goddamn fucking mess!

Add to that the Keller fiasco. It had exposed their entire Congress blackmail operation in less than twenty minutes, to everyone in the country at once. *Fucking brilliant . . .* They were left to clean shit as far as was humanly possible—which wasn't too far; things weren't going too well. Whoever had done it also took out Rodman's whore and Watterson's balls. *Shit fuck and damn.*

Then Harry Johnson, assassination-style, in daylight, in front of their very own Islamic Center. The culprit? A rabbi, or someone posing as one; and now tonight . . . Mahmoud, 2001, and, of course, the entire Operation Gladio B.

Someone was knocking urgently.

"What?"

It was his deputy, Wolfe. "It's urgent, Rich."

What next? What could possibly happen next? "Come in. It's open."

"The segment is over," Wolfe told him, "on both channels . . . I did everything I could to stop it. Nicole wouldn't budge. I finally found out why. You are not going to like this, Rich."

The general looked him in the eye. Wolfe's director days were over. His head had to roll for them to save face and make it look as if all the shitty things were straightened out. "He's one of us."

"Excuse me? Who?"

"Whoever's been doing all this. He's one of us. He's Gladio."

Wolfe understood. "That's what Nicole said. I thought she'd gotten it wrong; maybe duped. But it makes sense. She said the woman passed all credentials questions, and that neither you nor the president could override."

Schumacher nodded as he crumbled in his chair. "Yeah, it's a Gladio. He clearly has a partner, an assistant—the woman who acted as his courier."

"We have to find out his identity. We have to establish that right away."

Schumacher laughed, and then looked at him blackly. "It won't matter. It's already too late. Operation B is going to be folded: as of *tonight*. And we will have to step aside. Our role has officially ended. It is now up to the *ten* to plan and phase in the next operation. New faces, new tactics, new operatives . . . excepting, of course, the *top ten* themselves."

Another knock.

"Yes?"

It was his secretary. "Sir, I have the president on the special line."

"All right. Put him through."

He pointed to the side chair. "Sit. I have to answer to the bozo." He picked up the receiver. "Yes, Mister President . . ."

Wolfe could hear tinny plumes of rage crackling from the receiver. In a way, it was amusing, hearing the president this way; he eavesdropped on the general's half of a rankling conversation.

". . . Mister President. We have seven active investigations. We are seeking answers full force . . ." *crackle crackle* "No, sir. It is *not* the Russians. Neither the Russians nor any nation's military or intelligence is capable of pulling all this off . . ." *crackle crackle* "No, Mister President, not al-Hazar . . ."

Wolfe thought he could make out the words *obviously you know* and he looked at the general, who for some unknown reason was smiling.

Schumacher was thinking, *Why not?* This operation had come to an end. He himself was a goner. So . . . "Mister President, it is Gladio. To be precise, it's the work of a *lone Gladio*. Sir."

Wolfe could now hear much more furious crackling, with a lot of rising exclamations.

Holding out the receiver, Schumacher turned it to Wolfe with a knowing look and a shrug. Here he was, for the first time ever in his long career, being honest and truthful with the president of the United States. Go figure.

* * * *

Tuesday Evening, November 18, 2003
Washington, D.C.

Greg watched as she picked up her long-stem crystal flute and took a well-earned sip of champagne: *Sovetskoye Shampanskoye*, the most common brand of Russian sparkling.

He knew what she had in mind as soon as they'd stopped in front of the trendy new restaurant, The Minsk. *This is why she'd insisted on driving.* She'd wanted, no doubt, to get a rise out of him; to provoke some reaction that might crack what she considered his mask of indifference. Right there, she was wrong. There was no mask. He was merely indifferent to many things in life. She was going to be very disappointed.

She tried to be cute, but Psychology 101 wasn't working.

She scanned the fancily printed menu with ornate and elaborate curlicue fonts, in script. "I was thinking of ordering Sevruga with bellini pancakes and maybe some borscht. Oh look, they have sturgeon! You can have it done rare. Just the way you like it."

Elsie felt aglow. It came from inside her, knowing all this was over. She kept her end of the bargain, and now she would be gone in less than twenty-four hours. Finally, she would be rid of him.

He picked up the menu and pretended to read it. "I thought you were mindful of endangered species? I guess tonight you're making an exception, devouring the endangered eggs of their young?"

She made an effort to maintain her smile. No. He was not going to turn this around. "I thought nowadays they were farmed."

Greg shrugged. "Sure. Same as they did for the wolves—who remain endangered, last I checked. Eat up! You deserve it. As far as I'm concerned, Russian fish and their spawn deserve it as well."

The headwaiter took their order. The man addressed him in Russian. Almost all Russians did, going by his looks. He'd answered him in English, making clear his desire which language to speak. Elsie keenly observed their exchange, watching for the slightest crack.

A three-piece band played old Russian songs: sentimental, lugubrious nonsense. Contrary to what she may be thinking, none of the symbolic stuff got under his skin, not in the least. His hatred was not about Russian songs, language, food or décor.

"Where am I going after Florida?" she cut in to his evident ruminations. This was the first time she'd asked about a final destination; make that a *temporary* final destination.

"You'll find out tomorrow. Hank, the driver, has everything you need: passports, tickets, hotel itinerary . . . all planned and under control."

She didn't press further. Instead, Elsie asked, "How about you?"

Greg looked noncommittal. "I'll be leaving a day after you arrive at your second transit destination." He didn't mention his plan, his final trump, to be used as further insurance: sending the agency the never-aired, never-exposed footage of their botched MCI Center operation. He would send them an unambiguous message: *You cease chasing me or more will be public. You wouldn't want to give out that much to the Russians, would you?*

He continued, "After leaving here, I have one more operation to finish . . . before I call the mission complete."

Elsie thought about this. "Sullivan's son."

"Yes. I told him thirty days or less, and I'm going to deliver on time."

"Cyprus?"

"And wherever else need be."

"Was it connected to Gladio?"

"Yes it was. The bank has been one of the company's facilitators. The kid likely raised flags asking inconvenient questions, going to the wrong connected people."

"Well, Greg. You did it. You exposed and ended the operation. Here's to that." She raised her glass and took another sip. "And I believe that's it for me. I no longer owe you. I fulfilled my obligation and kept my end of our deal." Elsie lifted her glass high and drained it. "Even Steven."

Greg narrowed his eyes. "That was Operation *B*. You are right: it ended. But Operation *C* has already kicked in and is hard at work . . . as we speak. We might have cut two tiny heads off the beast, but the hydra's got hundreds more, you can bet your life on it."

Two Russian waitresses appeared with the trays, laden with way too much food. Elsie had ordered with hungry eyes when she was fired up with enthusiasm. Now, deflated by Greg's grim speech, she was neither hungry nor fired up for anything.

* * * *

Wednesday Afternoon, November 19, 2003
Pine Island, Florida

She observed the man's profile as he paid the toll on the approach to the Caloosahatchee River Bridge. He looked like Buddha: an African American in his early fifties, Hank looked like a caricature. He was short, with a beach ball belly, completely shaved head, and a round happy face.

He'd been waiting at the gate for arrivals at Southwest Florida International Airport in Fort Myers in his rusty white pickup. Greg clearly must have sent him a picture because he pulled up right in front, rolled down the window and hollered in some sort of southern drawl, "Maggie! Hop in, girl. We gotta go."

They hadn't spoken much since. He'd asked her if she'd like to stop for some sweetened iced tea; she'd said no. Oh, and he had made a semicute remark about Greg knowing how to pick *good-lookin' gals.* Other than that, he came across as someone who mostly kept to himself in a laid-back, contented sort of way.

She thought about this morning at the apartment. Greg had taken her to the airport only after spending more than an hour teaching her one of his invaluable skills: fingerprint creation, to avoid a trace. He had her practice in front of him four times, making sure not to miss a step: *wash the sink and hands thoroughly, dry hands, fill up the sink with water and drop in the tablet, insert hands in the gelatinous liquid and keep them submerged for exactly two minutes; always use the timer . . .*

He had carried her small carry-on case all the way to the security checkpoint. Another one of his lessons: *Always travel light, first class, and refrain from checking in bags.*

They had stopped at the security checkpoint entrance. It was time to say good-bye. She felt relieved, happy, sad, lost, excited, lonely, scared, filled with doubt and confidence at once; peculiar, ambivalent . . . She looked at him. She was finally free. He had been the source of her original fear, disgust, frustration, horror, and loathing. At the same time, he was a source of awe, a perverse kind of respect, trust, and yes, even dependency. Hadn't he said that? That he was going to be her savior and only source of survival? Well, a big part of that was true; he certainly prevented her from being murdered, most likely more than once, and on that, she shuddered to think any further. She had placed her survival in his hands, for which he'd exacted the price of her complicity. And indeed she had not only survived but was about to assume a new life, in a brand-new place.

Her voice trembled when she'd told him, "I guess that's it. You won't have to babysit or put up with me now, Gregory McPhearson."

Greg had looked at her for what seemed a long time. "Make sure you follow all my instructions. You're going to like your new country. The food will certainly be to your liking."

"I hope you won't find any more causes to tor—" She stopped herself. Why ruin the moment? Did she really think he'd listen? "Good-bye, Greg."

She then proceeded quickly through security. As she gathered her handbag and carry-on at the other end of the conveyor belt, she'd caught a glimpse of him still standing there, he hadn't moved one inch. The further away she walked, the more he seemed an aberration. Someone deadly dangerous whose many contradictions made war a permanent feature of his life, of his world, and everyone who came in contact with it. Someone who had lost his way, and if you were hapless enough to have stumbled across it then you were probably dead by now. All along, she'd had an unfailing, uncanny sense that she'd been the exceptional exception to the rule. Yes. She survived; and survived his world. Now she would embark in a new one.

* * * *

They turned onto Pine Island Road and passed through a quaint fishing-art village named Matlacha, crossing the drawbridge over Matlacha Pass. At last, the sign came into view: WELCOME TO PINE ISLAND FLORIDA!

After a few more miles and many turns, Hank stopped the truck at a weathered wooden shack. "Welcome to my home sweet home, Maggie. I have a pitcher of proper southern sweetened iced tea in the fridge. You'll drink some, pee, and do whatever else you need, because in less than an hour we'll be leaving."

They climbed three steps to the screened-in porch and entered the sparsely furnished shack. While Elsie looked around, Hank brought them two tall glasses of lemon iced tea.

"D.C. must have been cold and windy when you left, am I right? I never did care for that damn sin city; neither for the nasty weather nor the nasty pieces of work who work there."

"Believe it or not, I've never heard of Pine Island before. Sanibel, Marco Island? Sure."

"And we like to keep it that way. It's paradise. Even with these mosquitoes I wouldn't change it for anyplace else. Hold on, let me bring you the packet." He disappeared into another room.

Elsie checked the time: 2:40 P.M. Anxiety pulled at her, playing games with her heart. Where would she be going? Would she even be able to speak the language? Would Greg play that kind of a trick, just for kicks? Sending her to Norway, for instance, where she would have nothing but bland boiled fish every day? He wouldn't do that to her, would he?

Hank came back with a large yellow envelope. "Here it is. I'm to go over this with you. Are you ready, hon?"

She was.

"All right. Maggie Linden, I'll be taking you to Havana, Cuba. You'll stay for three days, and then you'll take CubaJet to Paris. That's only transit. You'll take Air France to Saigon, Vietnam. That's another transit. Your last flight is to Laos on Vietnam Airlines. Luang Prabang, Laos, is your final destination."

Her excitement picked up. "Laos? Does it say for how long?"

Hank shook his head no. "Until further instructions via human messenger you are to stay put in Luang Prabang." He added, "I'm sure Greg went through all this with you, but no e-mail or phone contact with anyone, period."

She signaled that she understood.

"Well, sure am glad I didn't have to come to that awful D.C. to get you. You made it here yourself."

She was puzzled. "I don't get it. Why would you do that?"

"Greg gave me a couple of possible scenarios. This was the preferred best one. But he had an alternative all set to go. If something were to happen to him before you got here, then I'd pick you up there and bring you back here, give you this folder, and take you to Havana."

She looked stunned. "When, precisely, did he give you this folder and instructions?"

Hank tried to pinpoint the timeframe. "Hmmm . . . I'd say a little over two weeks ago."

She felt a pang. She recalled their conversation, when she'd confronted him about contingency plans, that night when he'd sounded so arrogant. Yet here was Plan B, it had been here all along. She was touched.

She returned to the present. Who was Hank? Why was he doing all this for Greg? She deeply wanted to know, if for no other reason than that they touched each other's lives in that fateful moment. So she asked.

"I owe him one—a *big* one. He saved my life. I was with the agency, and they were somehow misinformed. They had received a false report that I was a double. They were going to take me out. He stepped in. Requested a twenty-four-hour hold. And he found the evidence to exonerate me. He didn't have to; it's not like we were pals or anything. Being pals was impossible anyway, you kidding? He is a collusion of devil and angel. That's right. Both devil and angel in one. That's my Big Bang theory about Greg."

Again, she smiled. She knew. "So, are you an agency man?"

"Nah, not anymore. No longer. Used to be. I got out eight years ago. Set up my own business, I operate solo. Once in a while I have to throw crumbs to the vultures, but other than that, they leave me alone."

"You and your plane: I don't see how. You must have some waiver, no?"

Hank laughed heartily. "You sure are sharp. The way I work it, I'm *my own* courier. I bring in loads from Colombia, Cuba, and sometimes Belize. The thing of it is, everyone thinks I'm an asset with a waiver; sort of untouchable."

He poured himself more tea and continued. "The coast guard once was told by the agency that I was their man. Long time ago, when I truly was. So, when DEA came looking, coast guard says *don't go touching this guy, he's with the CIA.* And after that, when the FBI got on my case, DEA waved them off with the *asset* flag, so the FBI thinks I'm a DEA asset. Fast-forward to post–2001: I get on Homeland Security's radar, and they're coming after me, but the FBI steps in and tells them I have asset status. The DHS guys go away thinking I'm an FBI asset . . . so you see, each one thinks I'm the other one's asset."

Hank paused and took a big gulp of tea. "And I tell you what, I ain't no asset anymore. I had my share of that filth. It wasn't me. Never was. My current occupation is far more clean. And *honest.* I guess you know what I mean."

She did. It was a story simply told but far from simple. He was right. When it came to self-respect in this work, how could one cede the moral high ground to big criminal fish eating littler ones? That so many are elected and appointed with medals and honors only makes it worse.

Hank clapped his hands. "If you need to use the bathroom do it now 'cause we're leaving." She took this sage advice.

They drove less than a mile to a marshland that seemed to be an extension of the bay. Hank stopped the car. She craned her neck and spotted the small twin-engine plane. That was it, her getaway vehicle.

He carried her carry-on and together they quickly walked to the plane. Five minutes later they were buckled in, and in less than ten they were in the air.

She felt that familiar knot. This country had been her home for over fifteen years. Now she was leaving, probably for good. A thick and heavy sadness filled her. The plane began to climb. They now were in the clouds over ocean, on the way to Havana . . . and from there to Paris, and after that, Saigon, and finally to Luang Prabang. Somewhere back there they were scouring the ground for a dot called Elsie Simon. Up here, Maggie Linden, thirty-four and half Dutch, was beginning the first leg of her journey to Laos, to work with a small NGO helping orphanages run by monks. There was no more Elsie, for now; or at least for some unknown, indeterminate while.

EPILOGUE

Sunday, July 18, 2004
Luang Prabang, Laos

Maggie filled the bowl with two cups of rice and water. Then she began gently massaging the rice with her fingertips. She carefully emptied the starchy water, filled the bowl with clear water, and repeated the process several times. This had become part of her daily ritual, modeled on that of Laotian women: rinse the rice until the water stays clear, soak the grains overnight in cold water, drain, and cook on low heat with water, coconut milk, and salt.

Tonight they were going to celebrate Helen's fiftieth birthday in town, only a few kilometers away yet vastly different from her quiet home village in Ban Nong Xai. Her two regular modes of transport here were feet and bike. This evening would be bike. Helen's older brother and his wife were here to visit and celebrate as well. The tough, gruff, witty Australian Helen had become her good friend and, in certain ways, the mother she never had.

She thought she heard a faint sound. Was the baby awake? She dried her hands and went into the only bedroom in the wood and bamboo-paneled house. In the last couple of months it had begun to feel like home, even the way it slightly shook as she walked barefoot from one end to the other.

She could see her stirring. Eyes wide open. In the last few days she had been trying to roll over, all by herself. So far, without success; but she was a toughie. Sanya, at two months, with silky black hair and the blackest eyes she'd ever seen in the tiniest little face accentuated with beautiful cherry pink lips, had been living with her now for over a month.

The mother's congenital heart defect had caused complications during delivery. She was still in the hospital under intensive care. With no space available at the orphanage, and no immediate family willing to take the baby girl, Sanya had come to live with her. After the first two weeks and with help from one of the village women, Maggie had become the girl's sole caregiver.

She bent over the bamboo bed and looked into her eyes with a smile. The baby began kicking her legs, making razzing sounds, and blowing tiny raspberries. "Are you happy to see me, baby? 'Cause I certainly am happy to see you."

She noticed right away the wet ring on the towel. Maggie had gone Laotian all the way: diaper free! She wiped her, changed the cotton wrap and towel underneath, and then reached for the rectangular fabric baby carrier. She tied the straps around her waist. Next, she picked up Sanya and held her while placing the body of the fabric over her and tying the straps. This was how she was able to carry her everywhere and work—essentially, like a mama kangaroo. Both were equally satisfied.

With Sanya snuggled on her chest, as she gently swayed from side to side waiting for water to boil for the baby's formula meal, something on the front porch caught her eye. She saw movement: a furry white animal, crossing from one side of her porch to the other. *That's strange.* While the streets here were filled with stray cats and dogs, she'd never before seen a white one. An albino?

Perhaps. Curious, she walked to the bamboo door with her arms around Sanya, snugly attached. As soon as she opened it, the white long-haired cat scooted between her legs, almost causing her to trip. Then the cat began rubbing itself against her right leg.

She looked down: a healthy, white Chinchilla Persian, here, in her shack, in a village outside Luang Prabang. In Laos. Was she hallucinating? She noticed an ID collar with a tag around the animal's neck: both identical in shape and color to Simba's.

She lowered herself and gently, cautiously, petted the cat, inducing a purr. She looked at the tag: SIMBA, 7036281188. *But how?*

They locked eyes. Neither one blinked for almost a minute. This was her Simba. She felt tears welling up. "Simba, my darling, Simba, I missed you so much . . ."

Right away, she straightened up, walked out, and scanned the street up and down. Other than two half-naked toddlers playing in the mud, the coast was clear. Then she heard a small creak. Then she saw him.

There, on the left side of her porch, was Greg McPhearson. He looked as he had during their three weeks from hell: same posture, same poise, same mien and aspect, almost smug, overconfident, shaved and clean, dressed in crisp khakis and a light gray-green polo shirt.

They stared at each other, her look of surprise met with the usual flat poker face. She imagined what he saw: a woman so different from the one he knew, different in nearly every way. She was in peasant garb, practically speaking: loose, gauzy drawstring-waist pants with matching long-sleeved shirt and no shoes; her unpainted toes shortly clipped and semiblack. Her hair had gone long and wavy, kept in a single braid, and she wore no makeup; not a trace. Her chapped hands, with naked short nails, were bronzed like the rest of her body. Oh, and she wore a baby.

She broke the silence. "Well, Greg McPhearson. You had to go out of your way and beyond to fetch and smuggle in my cat. All that so I end up owing you one! How typical."

Greg didn't try to hide his crooked half smile. "I must admit you are faster than I thought. Less than eight months and a baby already; it fits with that highly impatient personality."

She suppressed the urge to laugh. She hadn't done so yet and she wasn't about to start. Any form of joining would give him the edge.

"May I come in? I'm being targeted by Laotian mosquitoes, every one of them out for blood. There's no negotiating, none of them owe me . . ."

Now she had to turn around to try and hide her smile, calling over her shoulder casually, "Sure. Why not. Do come in. I have to feed Sanya before she runs out of that rare thing, patience. You know . . . where in the world will she ever get it?"

Now she was back in the kitchen to finish what she had started. Turn on the electric kettle, measure three full spoons of formula, rinse the bottle with boiled water . . .

Greg stood at the entrance and watched. She felt self-conscious with those eyes on her, having this side of her on display: Mama Elsie—*no, make that Mama Maggie!* She still was getting used to it.

She took a small earth bowl from the cupboard and filled it halfway with water; then she placed it on the kitchen floor. "We have to figure out a modified meal plan for you, Simba. Fancy Cat doesn't export to Laos, as far as I know."

She went to the small but comfortable sitting area with the warm formula bottle and sat on the wide wicker chair. She gently undid the straps around her shoulder, lifted out the baby, and positioned her against the crook of her arm. Sanya snatched the nipple with her mouth and began sucking heartily.

Elsie looked over at Greg and pointed to a typical Laotian low stool. "You can sit there. Not comfortable for people your height, but better than hovering like the angel of dea— . . . like an ang— . . . oh never mind."

Greg considered it. He calculated the degree and angle, and then lowered himself cautiously, minding his elbows and feet.

"So. You still haven't answered my question. You went to all this trouble, and I'm certainly thankful, truly . . . but I'm also dying to know . . . so? Is someone trying to kill me? An end we overlooked? Something loose and dangling that requires some immediate specifically unmentionable attention?"

Greg shook his head. "No, nothing like that . . ." This wasn't superman Greg. This was just a man who looked a little weary, slightly worn out, possibly even friendly, and now seated before her in a ridiculous position.

She regarded him now bemused and more than a little impressed. "Okay then, if it isn't my life, what is it?"

Greg paused. He was fumbling with something in his pocket. He had to stand in order to retrieve it. With great care, he produced an antique silver pocket watch and placed it gently in her lap.

She looked down at the watch. On its silver back were monogrammed three dates: 1913, 1958, and 2004. All at once, the color drained from her face. An agonized muffled sound escaped her lips.

"Is he . . . is . . . He is dead, isn't he?"

"No. He is very much alive. He's okay. He wants you to know that."

She felt that flood of relief and let out her breath, placing Sanya over her shoulder, patting the tiny baby's back. "Where is he?"

"He doesn't want you to know. He figures you are as crazy as he is."

"I have to know! I have the right to know!"

Greg realized he was facing a madwoman and a baby. He had to give her something real, and fast. "He is somewhere in the Iran-Turkey border area . . . his health is fairly good . . . he's recovering from mild nerve damage in his right arm caused by shrapnel, a wound from a few months back . . . other than that, he's fine."

Elsie switched the baby to her other shoulder. "Why? Why would you seek him out?"

A shadow crossed his face. "I was in the area. I thought I'd do you a favor. Of course, this one I won't write off. Elsie."

She flashed a tired smile. "He's the only family I've got. I don't have anyone else. I want to be with him. I have to. I . . ." She swallowed the knot in her throat. "You have no idea. I miss him so much. I need him."

"Perhaps when the time is right. Now it is not."

"But why? Why does he want to stay there? I don't understand. It's one thing to escape Turkey and the death warrant issued; but he can get out. He can leave the region, and go . . . I don't know . . . he could go anywhere. Maybe even Laos . . ."

"He too is driven by a sense of mission; his purpose. He says he isn't done. You have to respect and accept th—"

"Couldn't *you* do something about that?" she broke in. "Couldn't you help him out . . . somehow? You could, I know . . ."

"He doesn't want my help—or yours. At least not now." He studied her face, calculating. "Don't even think of it. Not some crazy thing on your own. We have a deal. You are to stay put here for at least another year."

Elsie was now rocking Sanya in her arms. The baby was drifting off. She brushed her tiny cheeks gently with a finger, and in a low voice told him, "I understand. Her mother has been in the hospital, you know. They're saying she won't make it. Like me, Sanya doesn't have anyone either. I was thinking of maybe adopting her. She needs me. And I need her."

Greg was quiet. He sensed there was more.

She looked at him. "Considering who you are and what you do . . . you won't understand. Do you even like children? No. I don't think so. I can't see someone like you even considering the idea."

"Mai did. During her last six months she went visiting to a neighbor's house daily. It was solely to hold and touch their new baby: a not very welcome fourth. I suspect she wanted one; maybe two. She never said anything about it but, well . . . you know." He looked out the window. "Mai knew, deep inside, she would never have children with me. This may come as a surprise, but I can be somewhat considerate. Could you imagine the addition to this world of others carrying my genes? You, Elsie Simon, pride yourself as someone devoted to the practice of fairness and kindness, especially to those unable to protect themselves in an otherwise hostile universe. Would it be fair and kind to people that universe with more who are just like me? I know where half of my print comes from and that's frightening enough; who knows what the other half may bring? So yes, I can be fair. At times. I've given the world a present by making sure there are no more like me."

This bordered insanity, she thought. He viewed himself as a genetic anomaly, his hatred went that far. The way he spoke, he was killing his children from the point even before conception, as some kind of insurance. He was taking out his own genes.

Attempting to change the charged topic, she marveled, "You know, today is the *first time in nearly eight months* that anyone has called me Elsie. I almost forgot what it felt like . . . to be Elsie Simon. I've been playing Maggie and think I've done a decent job . . . I like the orphanage work, it feels right . . ." She stopped to reflect. "I even have a friend, Helen, from the Land Down Under. You know, she reminds me of Sami. Tough, rough, but with a big soft heart."

In a voice gentler than his usual curt, Greg told her, "That's good, but don't get too attached. You know it's not permanent. None of this is. It's a stop along your way. So long as you keep that in mind."

She held Sanya tighter. "I can't think of anywhere else to go—even after your imposed extra year. Where to? I'd rather not learn to play someone else. I consider myself adapted! No thanks, I'd much rather stay."

Greg stood at the door, awash in brilliant red-orange light. "Maybe you will. A year can be a long time." Then he added, "I better get going."

As he turned to go, Elsie called out, "You'll be back to collect my debt!" It sounded strange even to her own ears, as if she *wanted* him to come back. It was more a request than a statement of fact; and she knew he had heard it that way.

Away, down the path, Greg said back, "No doubt . . . you can count on it, Elsie."

She watched him go until his familiar form blended inconspicuously with the trees. *He's a chameleon*, she thought, *moving through the world disguised as a cipher, so that no one can see . . . the unspeakable, unmentionab—* at once she thought of her father. Then she heard Hank's voice: *Both devil and angel.* He was. And she owed him one.

ACKNOWLEDGMENTS

Michael Wilde, my editor—you are the best editor a person could have. As before, you took this challenging task with passion and as a kindred soul, and did so during an incredibly difficult period. Thank you for all your work and support.

Christine Van Bree—you are a dream designer. The jacket captures so much of the book's spirit. Many thanks for all your hard work, persistence, and endless energy.

Lorie Pagnozzi and Cecilia Molinari—you transformed this project from a manuscript into a real book. Thank you for your wonderful collaboration giving this book its format and final polish.

Matthew—this book would not have been a reality without your encouragement, patience, and endless support. Thank you.

Ela, my daughter and light of my life—your existence alone makes everything good possible for me. I am grateful for you and all that you bring into my world.

My partners and vigilant supporters at Boiling Frogs Post—you keep my hope alive in the struggle for truth, peace and justice. Your endless support and belief in me has kept me going. I thank you all from the bottom of my heart.

CPSIA information can be obtained
at www.ICGtesting.com
Printed in the USA
LVOW04s0133041016
507169LV00002B/71/P